MAKING UP THE GODS

Marion Agnew

Library and Archives Canada Cataloguing in Publication

Title: Making up the gods / Marion Agnew.
Names: Agnew, Marion, 1960- author.
Identifiers: Canadiana (print) 20230472532 | Canadiana (ebook) 20230472540 | ISBN 9781988989686
  (softcover) | ISBN 9781988989693 (EPUB)
Subjects: LCGFT: Novels.
Classification: LCC PS8601.G66 M35 2023 | DDC C813/.6—dc23

Printed and Bound in Canada on 100% Recycled Paper
Cover Artwork: Erin Stewart
Author Photo: Alan Dickson

Published by:
Latitude 46 Publishing
info@latitude46publishing.com
Latitude46publishing.com

We acknowledge the generous support of the Ontario Arts Council.

ONTARIO ARTS COUNCIL
CONSEIL DES ARTS DE L'ONTARIO
an Ontario government agency
un organisme du gouvernement de l'Ontario

For my family
by birth, by law, and by love,
especially Jacob Edwards, Isaac Edwards, and Daniel Goertz

Praise for Making Up the Gods

How do we learn to trust in the wake of sudden tragedy? In *Making Up the Gods*, three grieving strangers—an elderly widow, a young boy, and a middle-aged alcoholic in tenuous recovery—meet on the cusp of spring at a lakeside camp to face down their ghosts, their fears, and a pair of hungry bears. In the process, they forge connection, friendship, even something like family. This wise, funny, and generous-hearted novel shows us how shared labour and shared love for a distinctive landscape can become a vehicle for healing, mutual understanding, and growth.
—Susan Olding, author of *Big Reader*

Full of humour and heart, both a love letter to northern Ontario, and a moving meditation on grief, community, and family—the one we are born with, and the one we choose. No matter where you are in the world, reading *Making Up the Gods* will make you feel like you are standing on the shores of Lake Superior, and, like the memory of skipping rocks across the water or spotting the silhouette of a bear on the horizon, this story and these characters will stay with you for a long time.
—Amy Jones, author of *We're All in This Together* and *Pebble & Dove*

Marion Agnew gathers together a cast of unlikely characters and sets them on the shore of Lake Superior with their ghosts. While each of them holds on to the past, like a collection of rocks plucked from the shore, it's their connection to each other that helps them find the strength to surrender their loss like stones returned to the sea. A heartwarming story of grief, love and hope, the healing power of community and the creation of family through shared experiences, friendship and trust. You'll be charmed by Chen, cherish Simone and cheer for Martin as their lives intersect in *Making Up the Gods*. A welcome addition to stories set in Northwestern Ontario where characters draw strength and inspiration from the inland sea that is Lake Superior.
—Jean E. Pendziwol, bestselling author of *The Lightkeeper's Daughters*

Marion Agnew's novel, *Making Up the Gods*, explores the effects of loss and grief on individuals and communities and our intrinsic need for connection. When three strangers' lives intersect in a Northern Ontario town in the wake of a tragedy, unlikely friendships are formed and the path to healing begins. With vivid prose and humorous insight, Agnew's haunting novel will stay with the reader long after the last page.
—Liisa Kovala, author of *Sisu's Winter War*

MAKING UP THE GODS

MARION AGNEW

"Mrs. Miniver looked towards the window. The dark sky had already paled a little in its frame of cherry-pink chintz. Eternity framed in domesticity. Never mind. One had to frame it in something, to see it at all."

- Jan Strother, Mrs. Miniver

"The lake giveth, and the lake taketh away."

- Susan LeCaine, punning on Job 1:21

HOW IT STARTED

SIMONE

Late one April afternoon, I headed into the kitchen to bake, as I had every week for the past three months. I pulled out flour and sugar and flipped through my recipe box. Pumpkin muffins? Blueberry squares? Something with bananas?

The phone rang—the house phone, not the cell in my pocket. I paused at my banana bread recipe.

"Phone." Carmen smirked at me from her favourite chair at the kitchen table.

After four rings, the answering machine clicked, but before William's voice began its "so sorry to miss your call" spiel, the caller hung up.

I blinked to prevent the tears from starting. Almost five years on, I no longer played the message for the painful pleasure of hearing his voice. But I couldn't help feeling disappointed to miss it.

Carmen drummed her fingernails, red-lacquered and shiny as her lipstick, on the arms of her chair. Click-click-click-click. "It was probably David." Click-click-click-click.

"I know." I returned my attention to the banana bread.

Then I remembered Rev. Phil's face as he relieved me of last week's heavy, foil-wrapped cranberry-nut loaf. He'd smiled, but with only one corner of his mouth. His voice, rich with extra heartiness, boomed through the church hallway. "Thank you—I'll just share this with the choir."

Was that pity in his eyes?

The choir, he'd said. Not the bereaved families.

Then I'd wanted to fall through the floor, because sure, I remembered. Our committee had decided that the families of people killed in the January accident didn't need baking anymore. We'd had a long, thorough discussion about other ways to support them—to which I'd even contributed an idea or two.

There in the privacy of my own kitchen, my face burned. How embarrassing to have forgotten, however briefly. Now for the second time.

Apprehensive, I glanced at Carmen, but she didn't seem to notice. Instead, she gazed out across the lake, hands still, face smooth. Today she wore a kimono-style robe—red, naturally—and a floral head wrap over the curlers in her artificially vivid auburn hair.

I looked out the window, too, trying to collect myself. Maybe I didn't forget, exactly. Maybe I just didn't want to remember. I'd looked forward to baking every week, which had surprised the hell out of me. I'd never really enjoyed cooking, even for William, who was happy enough to eat anything I felt like making. But cooking wore on me. Every day, more meals. Three! Relentless!

This baking, for the families, had been a whole different experience. Producing loaves and muffins and cookies had enlivened those draggy winter days. The kitchen had warmed with good smells—cinnamon and nutmeg, vanilla, and almond. Apple. Pumpkin. Berries.

I'd also felt a whisper of camaraderie with other "ladies of the church." The ten years' age difference between me and a few of the older stalwarts had dissipated as we shared recipes. They'd made my special cornbread-cranberry muffins. Two or three women around my age had become almost friends—not quite hugging-type friends, but maybe close. The banana loaf I'd wanted to make was Carole's recipe.

Most of all, I'd enjoyed having a way to help people whose lives held serious hurt. Even if the help was "just baking." But apparently the season for baked goods had passed.

The phone rang again: once.

Carmen said, "Phone."

"Yes."

Another ring.

Click-click-click-click. Again: "Probably David." A cackling laugh. "David, your stepson. Step. Son. Stepson! Ha. Imagine *you* having one of *those*."

Annoyed, I yelled, "Could be anyone," but the third ring drowned me out.

She sat with her elbows on the table and chin in her hands, batting her eyelashes at me while we both waited for another ring. As the silence lengthened, she smiled without humour. "It's not David after all. It's the twentieth century calling—it wants its antique phones back. All the ones without caller ID."

"Ha."

"No wait, that's not the twentieth century—in fact, it *is* David calling to see if you're still breathing, and oh by the way do you want to sell the house yet? It's been five years, you know."

"That was an off-hand comment in the middle of a stressful moment. I just needed to buy myself some time." I inhaled deeply, the way those meditation folks suggested, and tried to exhale my annoyance with both her and David.

Without much success, though I managed to calm my voice. "Really. Could be anyone." At her rolled eyes, I added, "Fine. Say

5

it's David. What does he really want? Other than to kick me out of here."

Her smile grew catlike. "Maybe he just wants to talk with you. You know, to touch base. Catch up. Like a regular person. Family." With exaggerated enunciation: "A loved one."

I snorted. "You don't really know, do you."

Carmen raised an eyebrow and looked out at the lake again.

Hands on my hips, I sighed. I put away the flour and sugar before pouring myself a mug of coffee and settling into the chair opposite Carmen in the kitchen.

The phone rang again. If it wasn't David, it could be Donnie, the handyman who'd helped with chores at our summer place for a couple of decades.

I didn't move. If it was Donnie, he might be threatening to retire again. He and I were about the same age, but I liked to think he complained more about bodily aches and unwelcome ailments. Worse than his talk of arthritis and digestion was his determination to help me. For several years, I'd been fending off his earnest and helpful suggestions, either for selling or for doing what he called "serious renovations," which amounted to remodeling. As he'd explained, it wasn't worth re-roofing the summer camp because the next owners would want to tear it down anyway. Meanwhile, I still didn't like how the roof leaked during the storms that came when summer turned to autumn.

Carmen said, "Any buyer would probably be from southern Ontario, and they'd build a *cottage*, like on one of those TV shows, not a regular, humble *camp*." Her voice dripped with disgust.

"Camps can be pretty fancy around here, too," I pointed out, though I agreed with her. "Not ours, of course. Which is how I like it, same as you."

"Good thing. But it needs a new roof."

"Thanks, I know that."

"And Donnie's not wrong: you're not getting younger."

6

Which was roughly what David would say, if he and I were on speaking terms.

The phone stopped ringing, timed to avoid the answering machine.

Carmen turned to look at me. "You can't keep up with the camp and this house both, not really. Not the way it deserves. And it will never get easier, on your own."

I kept my voice calm. "Yep. That's what Donnie would say, all right. I wonder what great idea he has now."

"You'll have to answer the phone to find out. But you won't."

"No, I won't." I paused. "You taught me that. When in doubt, say no."

"Don't blame me." Carmen disappeared in a cloud of citrus scent, heavy on lime.

The kitchen sat empty of life except for me and a cactus on the windowsill. Carmen always got the last word.

From the bowl in the middle of the table, I picked up a rock— pinkish granite, speckled with bits of quartz and mica, the size and shape of a hen's egg—and ran my fingers and thumb over it. I looked out over Lake Superior.

Without the distraction of baking banana bread, I needed something different to dwell on. The rock helped me set aside both Donnie and David. Instead, I thought of the accident, the whole reason for baking in the first place. The three months since it happened felt sometimes like three hours but sometimes like three years. Other people seemed to be moving past it. But the weight of the accident rested heavily on my shoulders, like a midwinter coat I couldn't shrug off.

It happened in late January. By then, most of us remembered our winter driving skills: slow down, stay back, stay home if you're unsure. But skill can't remove all the danger. That Saturday night, the temperature dropped and the wind rose. Black ice grew on dark asphalt. Blinded by a snow squall, a transport driver lost control. His rig jackknifed into oncoming traffic. Gas tanks exploded. Eleven people died in the pileup and fire, with a dozen others injured. The driver died in hospital before any of his family could arrive. I don't know how many times I heard or thought or said aloud, "It could have been any of us." And it was an accident—nobody's fault. No one to blame.

Many people in town knew someone who'd been hurt or killed. I didn't, but the accident still haunted me. Of course I hurt for the families. And especially that driver—all alone, no one with him at the end.

At least we "ladies of the church" had concrete things to do. We baked squares and made coffee for funerals—I attended several funerals myself, sitting in the back and slipping out early to work in the kitchen for the reception afterward. We wrote and mailed cards. We dropped by homes, bearing casseroles in no-return-necessary pans.

After a few weeks, the injured began to mend. We kept baking—some families found it helpful to have muffins and whatnot. But gradually, there was less for strangers to do, as families drew more help from those close to them. We were reduced to those tired "thoughts and prayers."

There at the kitchen table, I set down my mug.

"What are you gloomy about now? Still that accident?" Carmen, again across from me, adjusted the belt on her red kimono. "It's the driver, dying alone, isn't it?"

"Yes. It's just—sad. Unexpected."

"Well, something's on its way for you, too."

"Something like what? Something good? Or something like that January ice storm?"

Carmen laughed. "You keep hoping for something good, your heart will break."

"It already has." But she was gone again.

Abandoning my first rock, I dug a dun-coloured chunk of

smooth sandstone from the bowl. It was about the size of a holiday postage stamp, as thick as a pad of paper.

I weighed the rock in my hand. The phone rang again. I wondered: what if "something good" announces itself by phone?

Then reason returned. It was most likely a telemarketer. The best reason to ignore it.

Again, three rings and silence.

There. No more decisions to be made.

Cradling the rock in my palm, I watched the day settle toward evening.

I was less tired than "sick and tired," Carmen's phrase for her malaise when something or anything didn't suit her. I'd never learned why she thought the solution lay at the bottom of a bottle of gin.

Sick and tired. Nothing serious, like loneliness. Like wishing for a purpose, with my seventieth birthday coming this summer. Or a family. Nope.

I frowned at the stained porcelain in the bottom of my mug. I used to blame the brownish rings on William's tea habit—he'd brew a mug, ignore it, warm it up in the microwave, ignore it, et cetera until he poured it into the sink in the evening. But nowadays I was the only one staining mugs around here.

What was it William said to tease me from a funk? Back of his hand to forehead, voice rich like someone reciting Shakespeare? Right: "Why was man born to suffer and die?" I smiled, just a bit.

Behind me, the living room window framed the sunset in a blaze of gold, orange, and red that filtered through the line of pines sheltering our house from the main road. To the east through my kitchen window, the light receded up the cliffs of the Sibley peninsula, across the wide bay of Lake Superior, turning its rock face fuchsia. Lavenders and blues washed up from the horizon to chase shades of pink high above my head.

William and I weren't traditionally religious, in spite of my church affiliation. He'd always attributed sunrises and sunsets to The Sky-Painter. Just one of many soft and sentimental spots he kept well-hidden from everyone else.

In the twilight I caught a clean scent, fresh-mown grass: William. *Hello, love. Hello.*

A trace of summer's warmth on my neck drifted slowly through my body, golden and comfortable and familiar. A gift from my husband's ghost.

He'd stopped in tonight, all on his own, to give me a lighter heart. I accepted it, with gratitude. I raised my shoulder to my ear, to catch his touch and keep it, just for a moment. But it wisped away.

I put the rock back into the bowl and stood up.

Dead or alive, William couldn't work miracles. He couldn't bring me full-blown hope, but he could remind me to stop and look for it.

I felt a bit like a bear in her den, stretching and sniffing the air, testing for spring but deciding "not yet" before rolling over again.

MARTIN

Martin had thought about buying a hat. There at the Value Village, a soft old fedora sat on the shelf near the baseball caps. It looked to him like something a genuine adult would wear, a prime minister or president, Sinatra maybe—someone who'd wind up in a history book or on TV. He wasn't sure he could pull off a hat.

A few years back, when Martin went to AA meetings more for the coffee and occasional pastry than sobriety, he'd lucked into a great sponsor, a guy named Harry. Harry sometimes played piano in a jazz band. At gigs, he'd wear a black hat with a little turned-up brim, a bowler, like Laurel and Hardy used to wear, only it looked cool on Harry. One Saturday, they'd gone to a hat store and Harry had taught Martin about hats, showing him the pinch at the front of the crown of the fedora that distinguished it from a homburg.

Harry had dropped a fedora on Martin's head. "See? It's classic. Homburgs look stuffy. But you can wear a fedora anywhere and not look out of place."

"Well, *you* can," Martin had said. He knew he was boring,

nothing like Harry, not that creative or sophisticated. The only thing they'd had in common was the booze.

Harry had laughed but said, "Hats give you something to aspire to. Something to be worthy of."

Martin had never believed him. Which was why he left the fedora at Value Village for someone more like a prime minister. Or Harry.

Harry had also lectured Martin about *acting responsible, like a grown-up, for Chrissakes.* Martin assumed, when he got this new job from that old buddy of Harry's at the food truck, that *being a grown-up* included wearing a suit at least, and maybe even a hat to meetings like this one. A meeting where he'd get—he loved how this sounded—his *assignment.* And maybe a chance to get back to a life he'd hoped for.

He waited in the back booth of the donut shop, eerily like the one near his sub-sub-sublet room close to the construction jobsite. Weird that in Toronto you could get on a bus for forty minutes and arrive at more or less the same place. The other guys there, in their coveralls and filthy scuffed boots, all waited to get hired for an under-the-table grunt job in construction, the kind Martin hoped to put behind him with this *assignment,* once he finished it successfully. There'd be more work for him, better work.

Lots of these guys looked like Martin used to feel—sort of grey around the ears, like they'd heard the same old stories from the same old friends day after day after day. Like they didn't have a lead on a better life, the way Martin did. That better life would be free of debts, both financial and those pesky intangible ones, favours that you started out appreciating but later resented.

Maybe that better life was still a ways off. But this new job would get him there. And even if it didn't, it was an assignment. A clean one. Either way, Martin felt good about it.

A guy came in and looked around. He had to be the guy Martin was meeting—he was wearing a suit and had shaved that morning. Martin resisted waving. Guys wearing suits, as he was and his new boss was, didn't wave. Instead, he caught the guy's eye and lifted his chin, a move he'd seen on cop shows. Then he hoped he'd guessed right. The slim, zippered portfolio the guy carried looked promising.

The guy came over, ignoring the convention of buying coffee. Martin stood up and held out his hand. "Mr. Smith?"

His new boss curled his upper lip a little and nodded, touching Martin's hand for as brief a time as possible. He slid into the seat across from Martin, though he didn't sit so much as alight momentarily, like a hummingbird. The table jiggled, and his knee kept the jiggle going.

"So." Martin looked him over. *Mr. Smith*, Harry's buddy had called him. Martin was pretty sure that wasn't anybody's real name, least of all a guy like this, whose suit hadn't been bought at Value Village. His hairline suggested he was over 40, but he was still younger than Martin, likely with a smoother path behind him. He'd probably come to live in the big city on purpose. He probably felt like a success.

Mr. Smith set the zippered portfolio on the table. When Martin made a move to reach for it, Mr. Smith drew it more closely to him and spoke, his voice low and rapid in the bustle of the coffee shop. "Here's the deal. You're going to buy a property. From a woman. Everything you need to know is in here. You get some cash for expenses up front and a cut of the sale price." He looked out the window, then back at Martin. "And another thing. You're her cousin. All you need to know about that is in there too." The table jiggled more furiously.

"Wait, what?" Martin wasn't sure he'd heard correctly. "I'm her cousin?" At Mr. Smith's pained expression, he thought, *This is going off the rails.* Deliberately, he sat back in the booth, relaxing his shoulders and arms. *Calm, stay calm.* Then he looked Mr. Smith in the eye and repeated, slowly, in a voice that held only curiosity and interest, "Her cousin. Okay. That's interesting."

Mr. Smith shifted in his chair and the table stopped jiggling. "Yes. Her cousin. She has a soft spot for family."

"I see. And I'm buying what, a house? That she wants to sell?"

"She *will* want to sell to *her cousin*, once you convince her of it."

Martin considered. "Okay, but—I mean, I thought this was a sales job, like I'd be the one selling *her* something."

Mr. Smith cocked his head and, to Martin's surprise, seemed to listen. "Something like what?"

Put on the spot, Martin thought *financial guy* and said something at random. "A racehorse?" Mr. Smith raised his eyebrows, so Martin thought quickly. "But no, you're in real estate, right? So maybe a condo? A place she could live if she sold her house?"

"But why would I want to sell her a condo?"

Martin backpedaled. "I don't know. But here's the thing: it's easier to sell a person something, a thing they can see, than to talk someone into selling something they don't want to sell." He swallowed and added, "In my experience, at least."

"Well, she does want to sell, even if she doesn't know it. And you are selling something. You're selling yourself. You're her cousin. You're family. You're someone who would love to have her place."

Martin considered. If he took this assignment, he'd be lying. In fact, he'd be a walking, talking lie. It was the kind of lie that could get Martin in trouble, that could make him have to tell more lies, and that, in the past, had usually led him back to booze or gambling. Sometimes both.

But. A percentage of the sale price of an expensive property. That would be helpful, to say the least. Successfully completing an assignment for someone who might have other work for him, or who might put in a good word for him with another employer, would be extra helpful. Maybe, just maybe, one assignment at a time, he could become a new version of himself. Or maybe the same self, but better.

At last, Martin said, "Okay. So I'm her cousin and I'm just in the area to meet her and oh by the way, I want to buy her house? Wouldn't I just call her from here?"

"She never answers her phone." Mr. Smith sighed. "She'd ignore mail, too."

"Well, that would be a problem." Martin paused. "What if she starts asking questions?"

Mr. Smith frowned at him. "The man who recommended you said you were intelligent. He said you used to sell furniture and were quick on your feet. I assume he was correct."

Martin flashed his "trust-me" smile. "Yes, he was, about all of it. I've had a few good jobs in my day. Lately, more in landscaping and construction than furniture, but I know Modern from Classic and I can talk a lady into a leather recliner by showing her that durability doesn't rule out texture and softness."

"Good God, I don't need details. Just present yourself plausibly." Mr. Smith met Martin's eyes and patted the portfolio. "You'll find a *very fair* price to offer here. Comps, too."

"All right. Got it."

Mr. Smith looked down at the portfolio. "There's a contract for her to sign. And a prepaid card. The balance should get you there and support you for a week or two."

"Weeks? What do I do the rest of the time?"

"Yes, a week or two, though I guess that depends on how good a salesman you are, doesn't it?" At Martin's frown, Mr. Smith elaborated. "She might need time to warm up to you. She might need to go to the bank or talk to a lawyer. You just stay out of trouble."

"Trouble like what?"

"I don't know what trouble you specialize in. I don't know anything about you and I don't want to. Keep a low profile. Don't call attention to yourself in any way at any place. Do not make friends. Did you get the burner?"

Martin blinked. "Sorry?"

Mr. Smith's face darkened, but his voice was calm. "The cell phone? Untraceable?"

"Oh. Yeah. I don't know why I need it, though. I have a cell phone, a regular one. It's not fancy, but I can search for things. It's even got maps." Martin was proud of his phone, which had been a treat two months ago, when he'd paid the last of his least-pleasant debt.

"All our business will happen on the burner." Mr. Smith's voice was firm. "I don't want any record of me on your regular phone. I don't want any record of this trip on your regular phone. It all goes on the burner. I will tell you when to get rid of it."

"Sure." The conversation was changing tone again, and Martin didn't enjoy it. Nevertheless, he felt in the breast pocket of his suit jacket for a card where he'd written the number. He extended it, gripped between his calloused index and middle finger, toward Mr. Smith. But when Mr. Smith reached for it, he crooked his fingers to pull it back, keeping his smile friendly. "You have a number to give me? You know, in case."

Mr. Smith's eyes narrowed and he shook his head. "I'll call you. Don't call me first, not ever. All the other instructions are in here." He tapped the portfolio.

Martin nodded and re-extended the card, simultaneously pulling the portfolio toward him. He started to ask another question, but Mr. Smith had the look his father used to get when a twelve-year-old Martin entered the mechanic's garage. He'd look up from under a hood and yell, "Get the hell out of my hair" and sometimes throw something, like a wrench.

Mr. Smith said, "You'll get your cut when the sale closes." He looked Martin up and down. "And Jesus, try to blend in. You're supposed to be an upper-middle-class son grieving your late father and looking for family, not, I don't know. Sam Whoever. Spade. Try to look like you've just finished a round of golf with your broker. Casual."

He slid out of the booth and held up Martin's card. "I'll be in touch." Martin felt the unsaid "Don't screw up." Then Mr. Smith walked out of the donut shop and became a blue-suited guy in the crowd heading toward a job in an office, maybe even in a bank somewhere a taxi ride away.

And that was that. Martin didn't have the chance to say anything. Nothing about being grateful and reliable, even about repeat business. He waited one more moment before unzipping the portfolio, hoping his dismay would fade and his courage would burn a little brighter.

First things first. He found a manila envelope with some cash and the prepaid card. Enough to pay that guy at that evening meeting the fifty bucks he owed him and catch up on his room rent. That would be that, his last debt paid. Harry would be proud.

In the first folder, he found the page of instructions on top, which he skimmed. He flipped through several real estate brochures. More papers in the second folder. The third folder held a black-and-white photocopy of a studio portrait showing a woman and a man together, maybe in their forties. Neat block letters under the woman spelled out SIMONE. Then another page had copies of a black-and-white snapshot in a weird size—tiny, two inches by three, a young sailor in uniform and a boy. There was also a small envelope marked ORIGINAL: DO NOT LOSE.

Martin could feel the instructions swirling around inside him, like strangers on the street, walking by and waving but not stopping. He closed the folder with the photos and sat back. The case held even more folders that he couldn't stand to look in, not yet. He rested his hands on the stack and felt the paper warm under his hands. His fingers tingled. All the instructions in those papers whispered, trying to tell him about cunning and guile.

He wasn't sure he could do it. He was almost sure he couldn't. But he'd try anything if it meant getting to a better life. He'd just prepare well and do his best. He hoped.

CHEN

Notebook
Samown. Simone LeMay
Cruz and Revrend
Raisins
Brave

Mum told me I had to come in here and write down what was bothering me, to talk to Dr. Samuelson about. She said, "Chenoweth, I really need you to be a good sport about this."

So the problem. Mum's going on the cruise all by herself. It was bad enough when I had to stay with Grandmother and Gumpy. Grandmother always asks how old I am. I always have to say nine going on ten, because if I just say nine, she always says, "You're nine going on ten!"

And I have to laugh like it's funny.

That's better than Gumpy. Sometimes he still calls me Junior because he thinks I should be Andrew like Daddy instead of having the last name of Gramm, Mum's Mum, for my name. And both Grandmother and Gumpy yell at me for weird things.

When I was little, I told Mum and Daddy one time they were grounchy, and that made Daddy laugh. Mum told me it was really grouchy (no n), but we all call it grounchy now. Or we did. I guess just Mum and me say grounchy now.

Anyway, now Gumpy's sick and Mum wants to leave me with that weird lady from church. Simone. Mum just spelled it for me. That Reverend guy said that lady would be good for me to stay with.

Mum's trying to talk herself into calling. It's nighttime though, so she probably won't. She's talked on the phone a lot today and texted too, about Gumpy. She keeps hoping Gumpy will be okay and she won't have to call that weird lady.

Earlier, Mum said, "It's not nice to call her weird. She lives in the country. Not like Grandmother and Gumpy, when they used to live on the farm. She's out by the lake."

I don't know why that was supposed to make it easier. She's still a stranger if she lives at a lake. But I don't want to stay with Grandmother and Gumpy, either. So I didn't ask.

Mum said, "She's the one who said you can call her Simka instead of Ms. Lemay."

I said, "I know. Why?"

"Why what?"

"Why am I supposed to call her that? It's not her name."

Mum said, "I don't know, Chen. You could ask her. When you're there. It will give you something to talk about."

She sighed and I thought about how when she sighs big and heavy like that Daddy says, "Woo-Woo! Tornado coming through!"

Or he used to.

She said, "It's okay, right? That you're not coming with me?"

"Yeah." I knew Mum wasn't really asking. She was telling. I said it was okay because it would make Mum feel better about going without me. But I don't know why I can't go with her. Not really.

She told me. She said, "It's not like a Disneyland Cruise. It's to Alaska. For grownups."

But I'm good at going places with grownups. Plus, I'll be staying with a grownup who's a stranger. And a kid at church said he heard this lady was crazy. He made a face. He rolled up his eyes and stretched out his mouth with his fingers and stuck out his tongue. Which was stupid. And gross. And Mum says crazy is a bad word for someone who's really sick so don't say it. But that Simka lady never looked sick, back when we went to church. I hope she's not grounchy.

When Mum first said I couldn't go I wanted to know why. Mum said, "Reasons."

At first I thought she said raisins, and I told her, "I like raisins so why can't I go?" Haha that's a joke I knew she said reasons. But I still don't know what reasons means?

I hoped she would laugh at me being silly. But she didn't.

Mum said, "Chenoweth, I do not need this right now."

Maybe this is what Dr. Samuelson said one time. Sometimes Mum can't talk about things and one thing is reasons. Dr. Samuelson said sometimes we have to be brave with each other, me and Mum. And I have to think about what would help Mum and I have to do that, even if it's hard. Not all the time. Dr. Samuelson said it's okay for me to be sad sometimes and mad about Daddy dying sometimes, but sometimes Mum just needs me to cooperate.

Some things hurt and then hurt more before they get better. Like a splinter. It hurts. And getting it taken out hurts more. But then it's over.

I still wanted to know things from Dr. Samuelson like did it hurt Ry and Daddy when they died? But it seemed like she wants to talk more about me being brave than them hurting. I guess the hurt is over for Daddy and Ry now, and that's good. If they have to be dead.

Okay. I will be brave and stay with this lady I don't know hardly. At least I'm not dead. I hope Mum doesn't die, either. I never used to have to think about it. But now I hope it every day.

HOW IT WENT

WEDNESDAY

SIMONE

The phone rang again, late in the morning on an almost-May Wednesday, and I was home and indoors, and I answered it. A miraculous confluence of events. But I thought it was Carole, needing to change the time of our lunch date, or I wouldn't have picked up.

"Um, hello, Simone?"

Not Carole. I used the brusque "Yes?" I kept for telemarketers.

"This is Jessica Robertson. I'm, uh, Chen's mother?"

Chen. Holy cats, what a name. I pulled myself together before Jessica had to remind me—the young mother and widow I'd met at Northside United Church.

Usually I could talk to widows, being one myself, but this time I just babbled. "And how are you? You know I really mean that. So many people say that but don't. As you probably know. But I do. Mean it."

"Thanks, I'm fine. I'm—well, you know how it goes. Holding on. Anyway, I'm actually calling because of that."

A buzz of puzzlement headed toward my stomach and turned to dread. At the end of the kitchen table, Carmen appeared, this time wearing a ruby-red satin cocktail dress, her hair piled high like Ethel Merman in *Gypsy*. She raised a champagne glass to toast me before draining it in a gulp. She held it up again and presto! It was full. Her version of heaven.

I closed my eyes so I could focus on Jessica in my ear.

"Um, I'm going on a trip. Andrew and I planned and paid for it at Christmas. And then, in January—you know, the accident?"

"Right." I spared her saying, "My husband and stepson were killed."

"I've been debating, but I really need to get away. And I can't take Chen. It's a cruise, an anniversary cruise to Alaska—it's just not a kid thing. Besides, I could really use a break. I've been home-schooling Chen since the accident. It was tough. We, both of us, weren't doing so well. I'm better, and Chen's fine. It's just been a lot of togetherness lately. He's kind of, um—energetic."

She paused to breathe, and I offered, mystified, "Well, he's young, right—so sure, energetic."

"I had it all worked out with the grandparents, but then Andrew's dad got sick and now he's in hospital. This is super-short notice, but I called Rev. Phil in a total panic, and he suggested you. It would be really hard to be here in town for our—what would be—our tenth—would have been. Even Mother's Day will be different, without both—with just Chen. Anyway, Sarah said she can take him maybe Monday, when she goes back on days, for sure on Tuesday, and she can come get him wherever is convenient for you."

Wait, what? But I didn't get a chance to say it.

"Sorry, I'm so spacey—can Chen stay with you while I'm gone? Just for the first weekend, this Friday through Monday."

I had been making notes all through this. I always did when someone called, so I didn't later think I dreamed the whole thing.

I looked down at the pad of paper by the phone: *Jessica R. Chen. Togetherness, cruise. ????!!!* Or, to put that last part into words, *Danger.*

Fear leaped out of my mouth. "Oh, no. No, Jessica, I can't keep Chen. It's just not possible. It can't be done. Sorry. I'm sure you'll find someone."

I hung up.

Carmen said, "That'll teach you to answer the phone. Though it did give you another chance to say 'no' without thinking."

I looked at my mother. "You're the one who taught me about camels and tents. Besides, let me get this straight—yesterday, I should have answered the phone, but today, I should have known better, is that how it goes?"

"You're lonely."

"That's a non sequitur." I turned off the answering machine in case Jessica called back to plead, widow to widow. I might not be able to keep saying no to that.

In the entry, where I pulled on my light coat and found my purse, I could still hear Carmen.

"You need a family."

I yelled, "That's your fault—you lied to me about Daddy!" It felt so good to slam the door on her. But it still didn't drown out the whisper in my ear: *widow to widow.*

At lunch, Carole did most of the talking. Her husband was scheduled for hip replacement surgery on Friday, and she was full of acronyms and logistics and details. I mostly nodded. Truthfully, I didn't understand most of what she was going through. My William had never had surgeries or illness beyond an annual cold—not even the flu. He was completely and fully alive. Then suddenly, he wasn't. No lingering, no time to prepare, no last words together.

Fortunately, Carole didn't need me to say anything. She needed to rehearse the next few weeks aloud, and she needed me to be interested and nod. Occasionally, I'd say, "I'm sure you two will figure all that out afterwards." Or "They replace hips all the time. It's routine for them, though I know it's not for you."

Besides listening, I wanted to show Carole that even her worst-case scenario, life as a widow, is possible. It wasn't something she needed to worry about, unless something went horribly awry with the hip replacement. But it sits in the future for all couples. One or the other will eventually be alone. And, eventually, you adjust. You may feel unbalanced for a while, but you find new balance, and you're alone only if you want to be. Which I knew first-hand, from William's ghostly presence in my evenings. To say nothing of my mother, probably still drinking champagne at my kitchen table. And my long-dead grandfather, whom I'd seen most recently down by the lake the previous Sunday, when I had checked for signs of spring.

Lost in thoughts of my ghosts, I wasn't prepared when the conversation turned my way. Carole's question was innocent enough.

"Any news from David? Still wheeling and dealing?"

I made my voice chipper. "Well, you know how he is. Always got some great opportunity on the go."

Carole had taught my stepson French in grades six, seven, and eight. Thunder Bay is a very small town masquerading as a city. She laughed. "Oh, I remember, all right."

I gathered some thoughts and plowed ahead. "This year, he's into commercial buildings and those hobby farms in the country." I hoped it sounded reasonable—I'd embroidered from the mass Christmas email David sent clients (and me) and a few of the home shows I watched on TV.

She seemed to buy it. "Back in the day, he used to sell pencils and calculators at school. He always was a go-getter."

"Yep. He still is. More so, even." I had occasionally wondered where David had put all the years of his six-figure income, plus bonuses, from the investment company he worked for. Some of his gambles wouldn't have paid off, not that he ever admitted to losing money. But still, he'd done all right. He certainly moved in a different financial world than I did.

Carole seemed to want me to know something else, but she had to work up to it. "I just wondered. My Kelsey's coming up to help after the surgery. She said David called her out of the blue a few weeks back. She used to have quite the crush on him in high school, you know. But that was a long time ago. Their thirtieth high school reunion is this summer."

"Wow, time flies. Did Kelsey say what David wanted?" I knew I'd come close when Carole laughed a little, embarrassed.

"She was pretty teed off, to be honest. It seemed like he wondered if she knew any rich people from high school who lived in Thunder Bay. Like he was trolling for clients. She, of course, hoped for something more personal."

I winced. "Sorry about that. And, I'm sorry to say, I'm not surprised. He's all business." I cleared my throat. "How long is Kelsey planning to stay?" And Carole cheerfully took over the conversation again.

To say David and I weren't close was an understatement. He'd been in his first year at the University of Toronto when his mother died, and almost finished when I met his father. He'd never come back to northwestern Ontario except for brief, obligatory visits when William was alive. I knew a few things: he was a manager at some investment company, he enjoyed smoking expensive cigars, and he was ecstatic to not live in Thunder Bay. In terms of distance, Toronto, which he loved, might as well be Taiwan instead of a one-hour flight away.

People like Carole believed that David and I would draw closer with William's death. You know, we're the only two left who loved him, that kind of thing. It happens in books and movies. Just not, somehow, with David and me. It might have been something in David's nature. Or maybe my own love of solitude was the problem.

If it was a problem. Regardless, the gulf between us remained. I tried to chalk it up more to distance than to active ill-will. Though I never enjoyed feeling condescended to, which is what David radiated.

As we slid on our coats before leaving, Carole brought up a church project. "How many plots do you want Graveside Gardens to tend this year? We need people to sign up and pay so we can buy supplies."

In the summer months, the church's avid gardeners tended flowers around headstones to raise funds. Most of their customers lived elsewhere and wanted their family plots cared for. I always signed up, too. I had enough lawn and planters at my house—no need to care for a garden in town.

"Oh, just the usual—my mother and her parents. I'll give you a cheque." I dug into my purse to avoid Carole's sideway glance.

She seemed surprised. "That's all? I thought you'd changed your mind about—"

I interrupted her. "Oh, bother, I can't find my chequebook. I'll drop it at the church office tonight. I'm driving in for the Social Justice Committee. Say, would you look at the time. I need to get going." I waved and escaped.

But I couldn't get away from the dead people. My route home passed the cemetery, formerly at the outskirts of town. Since the 1950s, the town had grown up around it, and now this pocket of quiet and gravestones sat in the big middle of everything. I was tempted to stop. I knew what I'd see if I drove its tidy, white-graveled paths. I'd park under the row of spruces at the near end, beside the odd-angled corner with the Featherhams' angel statue. Around the base on the angel's north side, snow from a late-April storm might linger where the sun hadn't found it, even as May approached.

Across from that statue sat two rough, rose-granite stones with matching polished faces, inscribed with my grandparents' names and dates. Near them, I'd placed a similar stone for my mother, though her ashes were scattered at our family camp on Lake Superior, just downhill from my home.

These places, this corner, these particular stones served as the addresses of my family, even though I knew, probably better than most, that they weren't actually there. I avoided even thinking about another stone, in the newer section, bearing the name of the person I loved more than breathing. I'd found a way to make my life better, and I wouldn't risk it by going back there to face the reality of that stone and what lay beneath. Instead, I went home.

Home. Sometimes I considered making the half-hour drive into town just for the pleasure of coming home again. Turning into my driveway that afternoon, I felt again the lift in my heart. Even with William no longer technically alive, and even though April never showed the place to its best advantage—nothing like the gleeful green warmth of July, the crisping orange of September, or even January's blue-white serenity—I loved the palette of early spring. Its brown and blue-gray and deep dusty charcoal-green gave life to the muddy rocks and the water and the trees. I could have cried, it was so beautiful.

I might have felt like crying for other reasons. On the way home, I finally admitted exactly how selfish I was. Sure, I liked my solitude, and obviously I didn't know anything about kids. But truthfully, I'd told Jessica no because I was afraid. What if Chen saw me talking to William's ghost? He'd tell someone. And that someone could tell someone, and the wrong people, meaning David, would have actual proof that his stepmother was unbalanced. One terrible night, I'd overheard him refer to me as "batshit crazy Simone." I didn't want to prove him right.

Even worse: what if having Chen around caused William's ghost to disappear, forever?

I'd die myself. Or want to.

CHEN

<u>Notebook</u>
Daddy's scores
Laser tag cars and tourney
Simone said no?
Cuzzins ~~I don't like~~
Yuck

Natatorium is the only game I've played since Daddy died. Some of the other games still have his score in the standings. I don't know for sure how to keep them for always, so I don't play them.

But he didn't play Natatorium. I played with Ryan sometimes. Till he said it was too baby. He said a Natatorium was really a swimming pool not a beach and the game was stupid, just an *environment*, not a real game. He threw down the control and it broke.

So I made him into a jellyfish and left him unprotected, and when the tide went out he burned up on the beach.

That was a while back, when I was seven. I feel kind of bad about that now. Only kind of, though.

With games, for a long time Ry just wanted to race cars, and then he'd smash into me on purpose. That made me mad. Mum too.

She'd say to Daddy, "Andrew! Do something."

He'd say, "No yelling and no tears, boys. Work it out."

Which meant I had to be a good sport. Till Ryan went back home to his Mum's, anyway. Then I hid those games. He'd find them the next week. Always.

Now they stay hidden. I don't feel bad about that.

It wasn't always yucky, though. This past Christmas, we both got these cool laser cars. You point with a laser and the cars go up the wall and on the ceiling. At first he was better than me but he showed me how to get better.

The best part was the tournament. He and Daddy set up brackets, double elimination and the best two out of three, so we could play lots of games. Even Mum played so we could play more games. The final was me vs Ryan, and it went to three races before he won. It was really fun. He wasn't mean about winning, either. Mum made medals of construction paper, gold for Ry and silver for me, and put them on ribbons. We wore them around our necks and Daddy took a picture. It's still on the fridge.

That was just in December, a month before the accident. Mum said one time wasn't it nice to have that good time with Ryan to think about. And yeah it is, but it kind of makes me sadder to know he didn't hate me all the time but he's still dead.

Mum's been on the phone with that lady. She hung up. I thought she'd make me stop playing but she didn't. She sat on the couch hard. Like she was falling into it. When Daddy used to do it, she'd say he was a lump on a log.

She blew her nose and didn't say anything.

When the moon came up in Natatorium, that was the end of the day. I stopped playing and went to sit by her. She put her arm around me and kissed the top of my head, and I let her.

She said, "We'll figure out something. Won't we?"

There was lots I was thinking about. Gumpy in the hospital and Grandmother being sad about that. The cousins I don't like, they're older than me and mean like Ry always was until lately. I'd probably have to stay with them, maybe with them babysitting me, and they'd be ten times meaner. I could feel the yuck building up.

But I said, "Sure."

She hugged me some more.

MARTIN

Martin tried not to think about pretending to be a stranger's cousin. Instead, he did another thing Harry always told him: Do the next thing that needs doing. Rent a car, check. Drive two days into nowhere and beyond, around gigantic bodies of water, check. Find a dumpy motel in his crappy price range (*say "economy," it's nicer,* Harry would say), check. Stay sober, stay out of casinos, yep. One day at a time.

He'd almost memorized the family stuff in Mr. Smith's folders. The kid, Jimmy. The guy in uniform, Charles. Charlie? The couple—who looked nice enough, like regular people—in that portrait. He should be able to find common ground with that woman. Simone.

But just in case, Martin had gone to the library and printed some pages about condos in Florida. One was on the third floor of some building, with a view of the Gulf. Not the ocean—that would be the other side of the state. He'd read about that difference online.

He wasn't really sure how "a view of the Gulf" would translate in an actual building, though. In southern Ontario, a "water view" meant "if you lean way out over your balcony and crane your neck just right, you can see a glimmer of water." And of course he had no idea if a view of the water, whatever it was or wasn't, would appeal to Simone.

He wondered, for the hundredth time, what she was like.

During the two days of driving, he had plenty of time to wonder about both Simone and the job itself.

Some of it was starting to make more sense, like the interrogation from Harry's buddy at the food truck, long before he'd met Mr. Smith. Questions, questions. Could he drive and did he have a license, could he get away completely for several days in a row, and was he comfortable going up north?

"How far north," Martin had asked, "like Sudbury?" He'd heard of Sudbury, though he'd never been. People in Toronto acted like it was a long way away and sort of made fun of it.

The guy laughed. When he looked Martin in the eye, Martin met his gaze. Not threatening, but not apologizing for anything, either. Steady. Frank, open, and honest, like Harry always talked about. Part of how you had to live, after you quit drinking.

It came in handy. And Martin knew he wasn't threatening—he looked sort of medium. Neither tall nor short. Not fat, but not an athlete. Even when he used to drink, nobody was afraid of him. He could walk through life without attracting attention. That part used to bug Martin, being overlooked, but later he saw the upside. He was more likely to be the one heading home at the end of the evening under his own power, unbeaten, without a new bullet hole.

The food truck guy had said, "Talk to me."

Martin said, "I can drive anywhere there are roads. Might need a map." The guy waited, so Martin recited a commercial for Ontario produce.

The guy nodded, muttering and looking at a list, "White, check. No accent, check."

Now that Martin knew he was pretending to be someone's

cousin, that part made sense too.

In the car, Martin practiced answers to questions Simone might ask that Mr. Smith hadn't covered. Like what he did for a living. Martin would answer, "Oh, I'm in construction. Been with the same crew for ten years now." Hopefully that was vague enough. No need for her to know he didn't have licenses and did mostly cleanup and errands.

In this imaginary conversation, his new cousin Simone would say, "How worthwhile. Do you enjoy it?"

Aloud in the car, Martin said, "It's like my old friend Harry always says, there's no feeling like it—you're hands-on building a home, a place where little kids will study and eat breakfast and play games and grow up." And after Harry said it, they'd both down their cold cans of ginger ale.

Martin had to take Harry's word for it. Eating breakfast at a table with a family, studying for school—Martin didn't have any first-hand experiences like that. Not in his father's mechanic shop, a dump with a kitchenette and a couple of rooms in the back. Martin's mother had died when he was born, so it had only ever been the two of them.

Sometimes, at work, Martin had pretended. He had to walk around the rooms to test the floor underlay for creaks and to sweep up nails and sawdust before the carpet crew came in. He'd think, this is the room the son will sleep in, and the daughter will get the room at the front. He'd look out the son's window, at the house next door going up with the reverse floor plan, and know the son's best friend would live there. They'd text each other or maybe use flashlights to communicate in Morse code when their parents took their phones away.

It always made Martin feel good to imagine a happy family living in a place where he worked. And Harry, his boss and sponsor, had given him all these words for it. Which he would share with Simone, who was a nice older lady who obviously didn't need a house anymore and would be happy to sell it to a family member. Him.

The information in Mr. Smith's portfolio had answered other questions. Martin was an independent salesperson for a numbered company. He'd looked at the contract and comparable properties Mr. Smith had mentioned, and the prices seemed on the up-and-up. And Mr. Smith said he'd be in touch when it came time to transfer money and deal with other logistics.

So mostly, Martin felt pretty good, though the burner phone, and Mr. Smith's evident desire to stay at a distance from the transaction, bothered him.

Sometimes he couldn't keep from imagining the worst. Like what if, after he helped Mr. Smith buy this house, something terrible happened to Simone? One of those TV shows with kidnappings and mysterious disappearances would get wind of it. She'd be the sweet-faced granny. He'd be the obvious suspect, the last person to see her alive. Nobody would believe him about being hired by Mr. Smith. Martin might end up in a prison somewhere, never getting out, for something he didn't do.

(Harry would say, *Cut out that TV, Martin.*)

Right, calm down. He had an assignment, and he'd do it well. He didn't need to know everything to buy a house from Simone. All he had to do was keep on keeping on.

Simone

I had a conscience. I knew what I should do. I stewed about it the rest of the day and into the evening's meeting at Northside United Church.

I liked Social Justice Committee meetings. It's nice to feel that you're righting wrongs and doing something good for someone else. But that week, the phrase "widow to widow" on repeat in my inner ear distracted me.

We talked about all the usual options, like partnering with non-profits that fight disease. We'd sponsor a group from the congregation for this walk, or that one. Fine but boring. Nothing as direct as the baking I'd so enjoyed.

I heard it again: *Widow to widow*. I thought about Chen. Nope, too hands-on for me. Baking. That's all I wanted.

In the meeting, I offered it at random. "Isn't there someone else, another group maybe, we could bake for?"

Pleasure lit Rev. Phil's face. "What did you have in mind?"

I was surprised I'd said that much and had no further ideas.

41

Next to me, Gerald said, "They just opened that Indigenous Youth Centre. Kids like banana bread and cookies."

Bettina's voice dripped acid. "Support for the Food Bank is a better choice. It serves *everybody* who's hungry." Other people chimed in to support the Food Bank.

I sighed. As usual, the conversation skirted the difficult issues, like poverty and racism, need and plenty. I quit listening and instead wondered if Chen liked banana bread. Scones, maybe. Muffins? Chocolate chip cookies, for sure—though they were a pain to drop onto cookie sheets. Not that it mattered. Because I wouldn't be baking for him.

At last, the meeting broke up. I slipped into the office to leave my Graveside Gardens cheque in the administrator's top desk drawer. Rev. Phil stuck his head around the door of his inner office.

"Simone! I hoped that was you. When is Jessica dropping off Chen?"

I gave him a look that would have turned the rest of his hair white, if I'd had my mother's talent. "Never. I told her no, absolutely not. I cannot do it. It does not work for me. I can't understand why you think I'd be interested."

He smiled in that exasperating way of essentially jovial people. "Come on, Simone—I've known you for a long time. You'd enjoy yourself. Chen's a great kid. You know him."

"Hardly. I've had maybe two conversations with him!"

"That puts you two conversations ahead of most other people here."

"Oh come on, why not Carole? She's the obvious choice."

He reddened, and I knew he'd thought about suggesting her to Jessica. "She's busy, remember? She really doesn't need anything extra at the moment."

"Right." Her husband's hip replacement.

Rev. Phil took advantage of my silence to say, "And anyway, Jessica has asked *you*. She's really stuck—she needs you."

She needs you. Sure. Just like my mother had. Everyone back home in Missouri had said so, and I'd sworn never again to be that responsible for someone else, up close and personal. I'd never admitted such a hateful thing aloud, not even to William, and certainly not to Rev. Phil.

I shook my head. "Can't. Won't happen."

The pink in his cheeks darkened to red, and I could see him choosing words. "Just last week, you said you'd do anything to help those families. That you were grateful to the church, and we—the church, our whole community—could depend on you. Here's your opportunity. For just a few days. You can even phone me, if you get into trouble. What could it hurt?"

I narrowed my eyes at him before leaving.

He called after me, "Think about it."

I grumbled the whole way home. Rev. Phil had found my soft spot—how kind the people at that church had been to me. Most recently at William's death, but really ever since the summer vacations of my childhood, when Carmen and I drove north for our respite from Missouri's heat at our summer camp.

Two hard days' drive each way, for ten days of vacation. And well worth it to both of us, for different reasons. My mother wanted to drink without worrying about work. And despite her love of kimonos and drama in the afterlife, when living she seemed to enjoy puttering around in the canoe and cooking over the woodstove, at least while I was young. When I was a teenager, she wanted to gloat about leaving a backward town—once Port Arthur, now amalgamated with Fort William to become Thunder Bay.

At some point during the two weeks, we'd go to church, sit through the service, drop a U.S. five-dollar bill into the offering plate, smile, drink coffee, and escape. The whole way back to camp, she'd complain—how ordinary those people were, just schoolteachers and store clerks and minor bureaucrats. She took great delight at leaving them all behind.

For me, whether child or teen or ostensible adult, those precious weeks at camp were different—magical, mystical, miraculous. From my earliest memories, I craved my yearly dose of the breeze off the lake. Trips to town were the price I had to pay to be there. The crushing drive back to Missouri felt like leaving home, not returning.

After Carmen's death, I moved here to stay. Those same church members welcomed me. With practiced tact, they expressed sadness at my mother's death. They even told me about my grandparents.

It was a thrill to open a church cookbook from the 1940s, compiled by the Ladies of Christ United Church (Northside United hadn't been created yet), and see a recipe by Mrs. H. C. Jackson. Inevitably, the recipe was for a gelatin salad—one of the savoury ones, with lime gelatin, sliced cucumbers, and cottage cheese—so I wasn't tempted to make it. And I wished my grandmother had been able to share her own name, Muriel, instead of hewing to tradition. But rewriting the past, with its culture and customs, isn't possible. Clinging to it, though—well, that's my specialty.

Grateful as I was for the church's gentle embrace, I didn't attend often until Rev. Phil did my William's funeral almost five years ago. After that, I'd wanted to give back. I even joined committees.

And, to my surprise, I enjoyed it. I'd never been a joiner before. When I was young, my life was too different from my classmates in Missouri. They had fathers at home and mothers who didn't need tending all the time. Then between leaving home and finding William, I focused on work and kept to myself so I could afford to move here someday. And once here, William was all I needed. But since he'd gone, I'd enjoyed, cautiously, being part of a group. Here and there. Even at the church, I might never feel a part of the inner circle—that darn Canadian politeness, so difficult to overcome—but I enjoyed the people. Most of them. Well, some of them. At times.

I even enjoyed Sunday mornings, when I honoured my

foremothers and my late husband in that great grey stone building, with its lovely, polished wooden pews. Sunshine through stained glass cast a blessing over all of us, in reds and blues and golds.

But. Church membership came with inconvenient expectations. And ever since Jessica had called, I'd walked around with a heart full of dark stones.

...

It was still early, just nine p.m., when I got home from the meeting. I found "Andrew Robertson" in the phone book. I wrote down the number and a couple of questions. I took a breath. *Oh God oh God oh God.* Maybe that counted as a prayer. I picked up the receiver, punched in the number, and pressed the green button marked Talk.

I hung up before the call went through, long before anyone could answer. Like a coward. Even though I knew calling was the right thing to do.

I sat again at the kitchen table and stared out across the lake. I couldn't bring myself to reach into the bowl for a rock to keep me company.

As night came on, I stood by the window with my arms crossed, hugging myself a little. On the lawn below, a dark shadow emerged from the stand of birch and fir at the edge of the grass. Low to the ground, it lumbered across the yard and disappeared into the alder before I really saw it. If I saw it at all.

I waited. The sky had turned full dark before I felt a thickening of the quiet nothing-noises of the night. A warmth slid over my arms and shoulders, soft as a clean cotton work shirt on a summer morning. A breath touched my cheek, a light flick where I might smile. Then nothing.

"William?" I had no time to say anything more.

Yes. Reminding me that he loved me still. And what else?

William would say, *You have something to offer this mother and son. Time outdoors. New experiences.*

But William wasn't always right. When he was alive, he'd been wrong about me often. He thought I was a better person than I could bring myself to be. To my shame.

I wanted to argue with him, but he hadn't stayed long enough. Convenient.

I nodded to the moon, which had climbed the sky when I hadn't noticed. Then I marched myself off to bed, probably the only widow anywhere still actively disagreeing with her husband.

THURSDAY

SIMONE

The morning after I didn't call Jessica back, but before I was done feeling bad about it, a knock made me look up from my book. At first I thought it was a bird, braining itself on the bay window on the road side of the house, a sound that had startled me from a nap a million times. But it came again. I put down my book and headed toward the front door.

"Door!" Carmen's voice carried from the kitchen table. I bit my lip to keep from shouting back, "I know!"

I opened the door a crack. Yep, someone was there. I stepped onto the front porch and pulled the door almost closed behind me. We needed a storm door. Also, a peephole. *We* meaning *me and my ghosts.*

"Cousin Simone?" This from a middling-looking man, not too tall, younger—maybe fifty. Beige-to-brown hair, thinning on top, some grey at the temples. He wore a light jacket, tan. His hands, in the pockets of his khaki slacks, didn't seem to be hiding a weapon. He was, in fact, distinctly un-threatening.

"What." It was not a question.

"Are you Simone LeMay? I'm your cousin, Martin."

"I don't have cousins." I pushed back against the door, one step away from safety.

"On your father's side."

I stopped. In theory, I could have some of those. "And?"

My voice held no more warmth than before, but I'd stopped, and he'd noticed.

"I tried to call, but I couldn't seem to reach you." He half-turned and waved at the road, behind the red pines. "I was just—"

"Do *not* say you were in the neighbourhood." I kept my voice uninviting.

He pulled the corners of his mouth back toward his ears, a smile of a man trying too hard. "Right. Sorry. I wanted to see *you*."

I debated. With my nearest neighbour a mile or more away, I had to be careful. Senior scams were a regular feature on the evening news. Carole's friend had paid a guy $300 to stain her deck. He took cash to buy stain and disappeared. You just never knew.

On the other hand, the guy in front of me wasn't dressed for work like that. And drama bored me. My rarely used cellphone sat in my pocket. I could always use it if I got worried.

Most of all, I was tired of being mean. I already felt like a jerk about Jessica. I might not be ready to keep her kid, but I didn't have to be rude to this stranger. So, I indulged my mild curiosity. "Look, come in for a cup of coffee."

In the entryway, he sat on the bench to slip off shoes—the semi-dressy lace-up kind, I noticed—and padded in dark socks down the hallway to the window over the kitchen table. I followed and was relieved that Carmen had disappeared.

He whistled. "Some view."

I glanced out too, though I'd looked at it every day for decades. In the distance, the lake winked at me, mostly ice-free. Some small floes lingered near the shore, waiting for one last windstorm to push them out into the big lake.

I moved the bowl of rocks from the table to the counter and set out a mug, milk, sugar, and a spoon. "Sorry I can't offer you a muffin or something. I can't keep them around. They seem to get stale too quickly." *Great, why don't you just tell him you live out here all alone?*

"Do you feed the birds?"

That question surprised me. I assumed, cousin or not, he was selling something, and birdseed wasn't on whatever scammer's script I thought he'd have. Although maybe he was selling a bird feeder and expensive specialty seed on a subscription plan that was impossible to get out of, like a gym membership.

"Sometimes. I don't put out feeders because I don't want to attract other wildlife. But when I see whiskey jacks around, I put out crumbs. They're quick eaters."

I pointed at the kitchen table, and he sat down. I filled our mugs and we sat, fiddling with milk and sugar. I came to the point. "Now. Martin, was it? Martin. Who are you really?"

"Your cousin! Really." He laughed and then hemmed and hawed around.

Eventually, his story was smooth enough. His father had died a few months back. The father's will mentioned his older brother, who had a daughter. Me.

Ah, the catch. "He died leaving debt, I presume, and you're looking to share responsibility?"

Martin's shock didn't look fake. "No, nothing like that. He'd consolidated his affairs a while back. There was a little cash and some real estate. You know, a condo in Florida, another in Ottawa. But the information about you—well, it was a surprise."

"Hmm." I let him drink coffee for a moment before pushing

ahead. "I'm sorry for your loss, by the way. Was it recent, his death?"

"Late last summer. August. And expected. He'd been sick. But still, paperwork takes time." He looked down at his coffee cup and back up at me, flashing a brief smile, a real-looking one. "When I couldn't get you by phone, this seemed like a good time of year for a road trip."

"You're lucky. We often get snowstorms in late April. Where are you from?"

"Oakland. In Southern Ontario, not California." His laugh was almost exactly a "ha-ha," which amused me. "And I have to say, spring was a lot farther along down there than it is up here. Lots of daffodils and crocus, even hyacinth blooming. Do you garden?"

"Just a planter or two, usually. I let Nature take care of the rest. I do mow. And rake leaves. And cut up trees that fall."

"You do? That's impressive."

He meant, "for my age," and although I was proud of my chainsaw prowess, I didn't bite. "So tell me about your family."

"My mother died when I was fourteen. I have a sister in London."

"Ontario?"

"England. I haven't seen her in a while. She and my father weren't close. I get along with her okay, but I imagine she'll never come back to Canada. Not to stay."

"Sometimes people find the right place for them and don't see the need to leave."

"That's how she is." A pause. "You don't have brothers or sisters, right?"

I shrugged, unwilling to confirm personal information to a stranger.

He waved a hand. "Sorry, uncomfortable question. I forget you didn't know about me until, like, five minutes ago."

I was doing so well—I understood what he was claiming and was pretty sure it wasn't true. Then Carmen sat down at the other end of the table. Instead of cocktail attire, today she wore work clothes, her other preferred fashion. Her baggy navy slacks had ragged hems. A grey Lakehead U sweatshirt, ripped at the elbow, sported splotches of primer on the shoulders. I caught a whiff of enamel paint. I tried not to stare, but I was interested in that primer—was it wet? What kind of hell-like heaven required priming before painting?

She spoke, doing her "I'm just a little-ole housewife from the Missouri hills" act, which she'd adopted to make fun of our neighbours. "Time's a-wastin'. Let's git his story and git him outta here."

I felt slightly dizzy, as I sometimes did when my mother appeared, and my face heated up. Martin didn't seem to notice either my flush or Carmen. I was a little surprised he hadn't disappeared into the vortex of her larger-than-life personality. She'd been charismatic, a born salesperson most of the day and a sharp-tongued, booze-loving bundle of bitterness at home. She always demanded I call her "Carmen," never "Mom" or "Mother," and I was supposed to care for her, without complaint, when the gin got the upper hand.

I looked out the window and thought about my father, and Martin. "So how are we related, really?"

Martin looked out the window, too. I cleared my throat in case I had forgotten to ask aloud. But before I repeated myself, he sighed and shifted his mug on the table. "I know I said his name in the will was a surprise, but I have to say, I was shocked. I don't know how I didn't know anything about him—or you, either."

"Yes, about that. Did he have my address? Maybe my father's? How did you find me?" I cast a sideways glance at him, and his eyes darted away from mine.

"Nope. Internet." He swallowed.

"Oh, of course."

He relaxed. Ergo, he thought I was technologically inept. But he was wrong. I knew the basics. I checked email on the computer in the den. I'd set up a Facebook account when the church sponsored one of those "Seniors and Gadgets" workshops, though I hadn't used it since. Okay, my cell was a "dumb" phone—it made calls, nothing else. Even that was more connection than I wanted, but Rev. Phil pointed out all the times I was alone, out mowing grass or even downhill at the summer camp, and might need help. Mostly, technology didn't interest me. Figuring out this world, the one with people, remained challenging enough. Especially with ghosts.

Still, I knew more than Martin thought, and I was pretty sure Martin couldn't have found me online—at least not much beyond the "survived by" line from William's obituary. Public records would give him more, maybe.

I regrouped, blinking against the smell of paint wafting from my mother. I tried a little charm on Martin. "Why don't you tell me about your father? What sort of man was he?"

Again, Martin took his own sweet time answering. Meanwhile, I worried I'd said something horribly wrong. Maybe he didn't like answering questions about parents—I sure didn't. Maybe his father had embarrassed him. *Way to be rude, Simone.*

Finally, he spoke, his voice casual. "There's not much to say. When I was a kid, he worked for a while for the government up near Ottawa, but I never knew what he did. He carried a briefcase. Wore a suit and tie. He worked long days, and I didn't see him much. When I was about ten, maybe, he started selling cars. He liked being his own boss and did well, becoming part-owner of the dealership. But I still never saw him. Then Mum died from cancer, and I started skipping school. You know." He flashed a sheepish smile that made him almost handsome.

"Sure. It would be a tough time."

"Really, it was just kid stuff. Anyway, because of it, my father sent me down to live with my aunt, my Mum's sister, near Brampton. I finished school there. Dad wanted me to come back and work as a mechanic for the dealership, but I liked southern Ontario."

Martin spoke easily and naturally, looking out the window when speaking of his mother. I believed him, mostly. For one thing, his father sounded a lot like my father, at least the briefcase and rarely home part. For the rest? Well, who could say. We all tell ourselves stories about our past. "And your sister?"

"Oh, well. We talk occasionally. You know, we email. She's a little older. After Mum died, she did one of those Eurail passes. Went all over Europe. Met a guy and never left England. She works in an office. Insurance." He cleared his throat. "But we're there for each other, you know? When the hard stuff happens. That's how family works, right?"

Martin pulled out his wallet and extracted a dog-eared photo. I expected it to be him and his sister, but it showed a slim young man in a white navy uniform laughing down at a freckled kid of 6 or so who saluted him. I'd never seen it. I knew my father had served in some branch of the military, in some capacity. Still. In this blurry black-and-white picture, the man in uniform could have been anyone's father. Same with the kid.

I stared at it, trying to get the man to speak to me, perhaps in some ghostly way. Nothing. I turned it over, both to examine the back and to give my mother the chance to see it. She didn't seem to care, which surprised me. Then again, I found her interests hard to predict.

"Huh. No writing on the back." I gave it back to Martin.

"The kid is my father. James, always called Jimmy. With your father. Charles, right?" It was Martin's turn to stare at the figures.

"Yes. Charles. Never Charlie. And—James? Jimmy. Do you have any other pictures of your father?"

Martin's eyes darted to the photo and back to my face. "Um."

I pressed harder. "That's okay, I don't generally carry around family photos, either. So, do you want to swab my cheek or something? Maybe we'd match up on some online DNA site."

Where I was not even remotely interested in registering, but he didn't know that—though, smart move, Simone, what if he took me up on it?

What if he really was my cousin?

And what if he wasn't?

Having lost patience with myself and the whole situation, I stood up. "Well, no matter. This is a lot to take in, you know. Leave me some information about your family. You're staying in town for a bit? Excellent. Write your phone number somewhere." Ha. As if I'd call.

Martin looked some combination of surprised and relieved. He slid the photo back into his wallet and pulled out a small piece of paper with "Martin LeMay" and a phone number written on it. And he talked all the way to the door.

"Thank you for the chat. You have a great place, nice view. I'd love to hear how you came to live here."

He sat to deal with his shoes. They were loose in the heel. His thin socks would have a hole soon.

More babbling. "Don't you get lonely out here, all by yourself? Safety, that's probably a concern." He tied a bow. "And lots of upkeep on a place like this. Especially in winter. I'd love a tour." He zipped his jacket against the breeze.

"Sure, okay." Real estate. I bet that was his interest in coming. Was everybody obsessed with owning property and making money?

Finally, he was on the porch. I smiled to keep my voice pleasant. Fruitlessly, as it turned out. "Look. You show up here out of the blue with a wild story, and I need a chance to think about it. Don't come back for, I don't know, a week. Enjoy the area—maybe drive out to Ouimet Canyon, hike at the park on the Sibley peninsula. There's a historic fort. Go look at the lake." I sighed. I knew I'd been rude. I said, "Just give me time, okay?" and closed the door.

My mother's voice carried all the way from the kitchen table. "No need to waste energy worrying about him. He's a fraud.

Harmless enough, though."

I stood at the bay window facing the road to wave goodbye. When William was alive, we'd always waved to visitors. I could do this polite thing, at least. It had the added benefit of letting me be sure he'd really gone.

To my surprise, Martin lifted his hand from the wheel and waved before he backed up.

Back in the kitchen, I said to Carmen, "So he's a fraud?"

She shrugged and raised an eyebrow.

I cleared my throat to ask directly. "Could I have a cousin on Daddy's side?"

"Depends on how lonely you are."

"I'm not lonely!" I sounded like a thirteen-year-old.

"You don't want it to be true. You want to say 'no' right away."

I muttered, "Sometimes it's easier that way."

Carmen disappeared.

I took this to mean I could have a cousin. I wondered if I owed Martin an apology. Maybe I'd misjudged him. Online, I searched for senior scams. "Grandchild in distress" cons were at the top, followed by real estate. I wondered where "long-lost cousins" came in.

But what if he really was my cousin?

I wondered if he'd stay away a full week. If I got as far as Monday without seeing him again, I'd consider that a win.

While I was at my computer, with a search engine open, I typed "'James LeMay' + 'Charles LeMay.'" My pinkie drew circles on the return key. I clicked out of the browser and left the den, turning out the light on my way.

MARTIN

Martin played it cool. He met Simone's glance and lifted his hand to wave, as if they'd had a normal discussion and she were a normal person. Which maybe she was, but also maybe wasn't. Like things had been going okay, until suddenly she'd stood up, and that was that. He'd hardly had time to ask anything about her or her house.

Still. He felt good. Like he'd got somewhere.

And he must have looked the part. He'd gone back to Value Village for polo shirts and khakis, and they'd worked on his behalf today. While he was shopping, though, he'd also bought the prime minister hat and he'd kept the suit, too. Just in case.

It felt good to have *left* southern Ontario—not *fled*. The way other people decide to go somewhere and just go there.

The steering wheel felt solid under his palms, the curves in the road gentle and intuitive. To his left, the lake whizzed past the windows.

Simone had seemed suspicious, but who could blame her? Anyone would be surprised by new relatives. She'd even brought up DNA. Lucky for Martin she hadn't pushed it. Did Mr. Smith have a plan about that? Lots of people were finding unknown family. It didn't sound like she was on one of those sites yet, but what if she wanted to be? If she really wanted family, she might be. Should he swab his cheek if she was serious about it?

A flash of fear shot through him. What was he even doing? Wasn't this pretty risky? What if she found out he wasn't her cousin and turned him in to the cops?

Whoa, Harry's voice said in his ear. *Calm yourself.*

Right. Martin could always just leave town if things got too bad.

Besides, Simone had invited him in. That meant something. She'd trusted him that much. He'd had coffee, made small talk. He didn't even have to pretend. He knew a thing or two about general decency.

But she sure acted like her mind was elsewhere. Or maybe like she was seeing something he wasn't. She blinked a lot. Nevertheless, he hadn't lost his way. He'd said a lot of what he meant to say. She hadn't banned him from coming back.

He'd count all that as a win, when Mr. Smith called.

People. Tough to gauge, sometimes. Working with patio stones and bushes, drywall and hammers was way easier. But this paid better. So far. He liked having a little money. Imagine what his life could be like after he got the rest of this fee.

I want to make this money work for me. The thought came out of the blue.

He knew the wrong way to do that. Harry had made him stay out of casinos, as a condition of being Martin's sponsor. Not that Harry had been perfect—picking up women between sets in jazz clubs, a ringer for Wynton Marsalis so good-looking he didn't have to buy groupies a drink to bring them home. (Harry: *Stop taking my inventory, Martin, just keep your eyes on your own life.*)

Fine. It was just a random thought. Which led to others. Like how much he owed Harry, starting from the early days of Martin's tenuous sobriety. Harry had asked Martin to do a few jobs, quick things. An evening here or there in the winter, watching who came and went from a corner apartment. He'd bundled up in several coats and walked briskly up and down, like he had a purpose, for that one. And then later, for a friend of a friend of Harry's, Martin had delivered an envelope a week to a guy at a dry cleaner's down on Queen, all through the winter. It was better for Martin to forget those names and stay incurious, so he had. But a while ago, Harry cleaned that out of his life. Still, when the guy at the food truck called him for this, Martin had been flattered. Harry had come through again.

At the hotel, he parked and walked through the lobby on his way to his room. That good-looking gal who'd checked him in, Barb, wasn't behind the desk. Too bad.

Yesterday, Barb had been friendly. Maybe just hospitality-industry friendly. But maybe more. She had smiled all the way up to her brown eyes as she gave him his key. "Here you go, Martin. Got any special plans while you're here?"

He'd mentioned visiting a cousin, taking a few days in the area. She'd offered brochures about other things to do.

"I really like your jacket," she'd said. "Looks like a nice weight for our variable spring weather."

Martin had managed not to mention where he'd bought it. "Yeah, it's great. Not too heavy, but warm enough when I zip it," he'd said. After her approval, he'd worn it today with more confidence.

They'd chatted for maybe five more minutes. Then they'd said goodbye and she'd sat back down behind the desk, earrings dangling.

He'd found his room, all the while marveling at the difference clean clothes, a debit card, and some official-looking papers made. People treated him like a regular person, a good guy.

On his way through the lobby, wishing Barb were there, he automatically looked behind the counter. Because yesterday, in spite of being a really good guy, he couldn't help noticing where Barb had left her purse. Not under her feet at the front desk or in the back office. Not sitting right out on the counter, either, but shoved into the corner under the shelf. A zip wallet with a long chain. She probably wore it across her body. Not so easy to get into when she was wearing it. But easy enough, when she was temporarily in the back, to unzip and grab a twenty, maybe her cards.

Good thing he wasn't that guy.

Nobody behind the desk at the moment. Maybe in an office somewhere. No purse in evidence.

After meeting Simone, he had more to chat about with Barb.

And some things to do in the area. Plus, maybe look into the value of houses out on Lakeshore Drive, just to double-check the comps Mr. Smith had put in his folder. But hadn't Mr. Smith said it was right on the lake? Simone's house was too high and far away. From what he had seen so far, anyway. Something to research.

He hoped Barb would be back on duty soon. He wouldn't mind another chance to make small talk with her. Like the honest, good guy he was.

SIMONE

I continued my interrupted day—a few chores from my list, an hour with a book, lunch at home—and wondered about my father, the photo, and Martin.

Maybe I was too hard on Martin for sharing only an outline of easily memorized facts. I didn't know much about my father. I'd been forbidden to ask about him, so I'd listened to what Carmen told other people, but even that varied.

He was anywhere from five to ten years older than Carmen. Sometimes she claimed that Daddy, whom she called "your father" or "Charles LeMay" or even "that asshole," but never "Charlie," had boarded with her parents during the war. He'd come to town to manage finances for the manufacturing plant that turned out planes. "Helldivers," she'd called them. Or maybe she meant Daddy, though it didn't seem to fit the vague, quiet man I semi-remembered.

Other times, she said Daddy had come to Port Arthur on a military exchange program to teach math. Most recruits didn't know enough basic arithmetic to aim the machinery of war where it would do the most damage. This version always ended in the same way, with Carmen's deadpan voice: "He taught them how to kill."

Another version made him her teacher, when she took an advanced certificate in business math after high school. That would have been something to see—Carmen at 17 or 18, making eyes at her teacher-in-uniform, maybe sneaking out behind the school to share a cigarette.

Unless he hadn't actually been in uniform. Or in the military. Or a teacher, hers or anyone else's. Or lived with her family.

Whatever the details, the result was the same: each found the other charming. They eloped a few months later, in June of 1945, perhaps for the romance of elopement but perhaps because Carmen's parents objected.

The young LeMays traded a life in the Lakehead, a bustling grain port on Lake Superior, for a peacetime assignment at a small-town Air Force base in Missouri. I came along a decent amount of time later. My birth certificate listed Daddy's profession as "engineer." Through the years, I deduced that my parents' marriage had in some way fractured Carmen's relationship with her parents. Then again, her personality alone might have been enough.

Of my father's history before Carmen, I knew nothing. I'd never heard about parents or family. Absence of information that was also information, in its way.

So sure, Charles LeMay could have had a brother named James, giving me an Uncle Jimmy and a cousin named Martin and some other cousin somewhere in England. But really?

Part of what made me suspicious was the surprise of it all. It was unnerving, suddenly having relatives. Even if I wanted to believe it.

And what had he said? "Family's always there for you." Everybody said that, but what did that even mean?

Carmen stood next to the kitchen table, still in jeans and sweatshirt. "Maybe they mean you pick up the phone when David calls." She tossed filthy garden gloves onto the kitchen table and adjusted a straw hat on her head.

I considered. "Maybe. Or maybe they mean, don't call your stepmother 'batshit crazy Simone.' Or maybe they mean, don't lie to your daughter about her father. How about those options?"

"Rude." She made as if to go but paused. "Why are you acting like such a teenager about having cousins you didn't know about?"

"Because, for one, maybe they aren't my cousins. And for another, you always kept me from finding friends when I was a kid and could have used them."

She rolled her eyes. "Come on, missy, that was your doing. How many girls did you invite over after school? None. How many guys asking for dates did you turn down, without even talking it over with me?"

"All of them. Because I knew you'd be drunk and embarrass me and my potential friends, and I'd wish for the ground to open up, right there."

"Friends? Hmph. You mean Janey? You're still on about her? How old were you, eight?"

"Ten. We were friends, like almost real friends, until her mother met you. Then suddenly she wasn't allowed to play with me, never mind sit with me at lunchtime."

"Janey," Carmen enunciated this carefully, "was very. Very. Ordinary."

"I know! How I wanted to be an ordinary kid in Missouri in the '60s. Instead, I was *your* daughter." I enunciated a bit myself: "Except for the drinking. I made sure I didn't take after you in *that* way."

Carmen, lower lip trembling, picked up her gloves and disappeared.

I blinked. Was she upset—even crying, maybe? I couldn't remember seeing her anything other than angry, and that showed mostly in her eyes and gritted teeth.

Upset or not, she wasn't wrong. Of course I'd said "no" to

almost everything, more often than I'd wanted. After high school graduation, I moved to Taos, just far enough from her but not too far, and kept books for small mom-and-pop businesses. But I smiled and avoided their invitations to dinner to meet their available brother, the holiday celebrations including wine and mistletoe. Instead, I hiked alone, ate alone, went to museums alone, and steered clear of the folks making Taos a "personal growth" destination.

Mostly I waited, enduring "personal growth" of my own, a chrysalis undergoing transformation invisible to the naked eye. I needed to prepare myself for a time when I was free of Carmen and ready to move across the northern border.

I smiled at the thought: Free of Carmen. Which I had been, through all the years William was alive. In fact, until William's ghost arrived, when she showed up, too. And Grandpa Jackson. I guess they were a package deal.

In any case, as usual, she hadn't shared useful information, though surely she knew the answers. And as usual, I was left to puzzle out life on my own.

Did I have cousins? Possibly. And I wasn't sure how I felt about that—hopeful? Afraid?

I put on a jacket and headed out to the garage to find my own work gloves, trying hard to think about something else.

CHEN

<u>Notebook</u>
Mayans
School

Today I was reading about Mayans.

Grandmother and Gumpy gave us their encyclopaedias when they moved into town from the farm. They can be hard to read but I like that.

Mum made me promise to stop reading about Mayan sacrifices if I got scared. I'm not, though. I like learning about Indigenous traditions from everywhere. It's fun to be able to read what I want instead of being at school and doing what they want.

The other kids were kinda boring. We'd all started school at the same time, but it seemed like they all knew each other already. Mostly they ignored me. Then last fall I was the one who was nice to Joseph, the new kid who was Indigenous, and they ignored both of us.

Then the accident. After, I had to go back to school. I tried for one full entire whole week.

The kid in my class everybody likes, Aaron, said, "Nobody else lost a brother. You're famous."

Some of the kids laughed. Except Joseph, because his cousin died. I think maybe a girl had an aunt who died. So I don't know why Aaron said that.

I said, "I wish I wasn't."

The teacher made Aaron be quiet.

How he said it made my stomach hurt. Like I'd done something bad and got away with it. Or I was supposed to be happy Daddy and Ry died.

Ryan didn't even go to my school. Nobody knew him, just that he was dead. That made me the weird kid with the dead brother.

I didn't want the other kids to know about stuff. Like seeing Dr. Samuelson and having bad dreams. My stomach hurt a lot that week.

It's better now. I like learning on my own. Mum says I'm motivated. She said that's why it works for me to learn at home. And she's home to supervise because of being on leave from the bank. Sometimes I do math worksheets. I get to read whatever I want.

Ry was not motivated. He didn't want to learn about anything I liked, like planets or spiders. Mostly just baseball. We all went to two Border Cats games last summer. Mum and I didn't like the games as much as he did, so we didn't go anymore. But Ryan went to a bunch, sometimes with Daddy and sometimes with his Mum. The players aren't famous or anything, just going to university I guess. But he got the players to sign a lot of baseballs, and then he gave Daddy one for his birthday in August, and I got one for my birthday in September. All three of us had these signed baseballs. It was kind of cool.

He did read a lot about baseball and memorized lots of jokes. He liked a guy named Yogi Berra. Daddy pretended he meant

Yogi Bear but Mum told me that's an old cartoon and the guy with jokes was Berra.

Ry talked a lot about that time he saw the bear and I didn't, when we were all in the car. We were going fishing at a river. The bear was on Ryan's side of the car, not mine, and I couldn't see, even when I tried to look in the mirrors or turn around. After that he started telling more Yogi Berra jokes.

I want to see a bear too. I want to do more things than he did.

MARTIN

Martin's room key—old-fashioned, an actual metal key on a ring with a plastic rounded-diamond fob—slid into the lock with a nice feel. His clothes, including the suit, hung from the metal bar and shelf that pretended to be a closet. His fedora looked great on the shelf, and his three pairs of shoes sat side-by-side on the tired, mud-brown carpet. Almost like he lived here, though he'd never kept any place he'd lived this tidy.

He took in his small room with its faux-wood paneling and heavy drapes on cords. When he'd first picked up work at job sites, he'd stayed in a bunch of motel rooms like this one. He'd even done demolition and then quick renos to motels like this—sink at the back of the room, tiny mini-fridge stuck beneath, and a toilet and shower behind the bathroom door. Recently, he'd worked more at new builds in the suburbs. Somehow the years had gone by. He bet some of the motel renos he'd done were themselves gone.

But that's how life worked, it seemed. Days add up to years, and pretty soon you're in debt and drunk a lot and staying in cheap apartments and then in even cheaper rooms until you're on someone's couch. Then you work your ass off to stay sober and get out of debt, and the days and years add up some more. And all you had to show for it was just some sobriety.

Which was not nothing. But it wasn't where he'd meant to be.

He'd meant to go places, somewhere beyond his father's despair and his dead mother. After he got his Grade 12, he'd left his father muttering about too-fancy imported cars in his rundown mechanics shop, which was full of grease and bad business deals with alleged gang members.

Martin wanted something that felt cleaner and at last found work in greenhouses and nurseries. Sometimes even day labour, picking fruit. After many winters, he found a job selling furniture, which he'd enjoyed. But then that industry had changed, with direct-to-consumer and discount chains, and Martin was supposed to sell financing, which was always a bad deal for his customers, and he had a hard time with it. Just to take the edge off, he'd started downing a shot or two before coming to work, and they'd fired him. He'd gone to a bar and hadn't left for a while. Years. Then construction labour.

Nothing but dead ends.

Until now.

What he'd told Simone wasn't so much his dream life as one of its possibilities, if he'd had a whole different family. His story about his father, Ottawa, and the car dealership matched what Mr. Smith wanted, someone who could buy Simone's place. The sister in London, on any continent, was as fictional as the briefcase-carrying father. Sadly, Martin's mother's death, though at his birth and not from cancer, had been real enough. His father had died too, sometime before Martin got sober.

But Martin liked having a pretend sister, someone who'd gone overseas and found a home for herself.

I really need to write this down, he thought. *I can't lose track of what I said.*

He'd stacked his folder and other papers neatly on the small desk. Beside them stood a card folded like a tent, advertising the casino just up the block from his hotel. There was always a casino.

Geez, he missed casinos—magical, marvelous places. Full of glamour and lights, hope and celebration. Also sadness and despair, sure, but hope. And fun. People. Possibilities.

Nope. No possibilities for him. He pulled open the nightstand drawer and tossed the tent card on top of the Bible and slammed the drawer closed.

Now came the hard part: putting in time while he waited till it was okay to see Simone again.

What could he do? Go to a meeting, of course. He felt a quick burble of rebellion. Surely being away from his old haunts would be enough to keep him on the straight and narrow? He didn't even know the names of any bars in this town. In his mind, every door on this street led to a diner or coffee shop. Okay, or a casino.

What if he called Harry? He didn't need to look in his wallet for the plastic card—just "Harry" and his phone number embossed onto it, like a credit card. Harry gave them to everybody he sponsored. Martin had memorized the number long ago. Called it from this pay phone and that one, and when those had been increasingly hard to find, from this friend's cell and that one. He'd had one or two other temporary, rudimentary cell phones and called it from them, too. When he got what he thought of as his "real" cell phone, Harry's was the first number he'd put into it. He hadn't saved it in the burner phone for Mr. Smith's assignment, though. Somehow, he wanted to keep Harry separate.

What would happen if he called the number now?

Better to find a meeting.

A quick search turned up one at seven that evening, at a church marked on the map in his room. Meanwhile, he'd take advantage of the weak sun and walk up to that grocery store. He could pick up supper and a notebook, so he could write down what he'd had to make up—including the condos in Ottawa and Florida. He could keep this notebook with his papers, all official.

Outdoors, he zipped up his jacket. The sinking sun brought on a cool breeze. The day could turn on you, take you right back to winter, make you sorry you'd trusted the calendar. He picked up his pace.

The street dead-ended at Harbour Foods. The store sat between two parking lots, its windows staring at Martin, its entrances like ears on either side.

As Martin got closer, six or so people clotting one entrance scattered into the parking lot, chased by a couple of yelling men. One of the chasers—an older balding guy wearing a black apron over his white shirt—got redder and redder in the face. The other chaser, a little younger, kept getting between the manager and the kids, trying to calm things down.

Kids. Were they out of high school? Probably. But maybe not as old as twenty, for sure not yet thirty.

All the yelling made Martin uneasy. He swung left to the other entrance, intent on his errand, minding his own business. (Harry: *Well done.*)

Once inside, he passed the Mother's Day cards and selected a small notebook. It might fit into his jacket pocket. He didn't want to check by slipping it in, in case someone saw and accused him of shoplifting. (Harry: *You can't be too careful about how things look.*) Especially given the parking lot kerfuffle.

At the deli, he went to look at the soup, peering over someone's shoulder. The sign next to it read Thai Chicken Curry.

Beside him, an older lady, maybe Simone's age, said, "Have you tried this? It smells so good, but the last soup I got here was too spicy."

Martin said, "No ma'am, I haven't, but it does say 'curry,' so

74

you might want to skip it." He didn't stay for her response, instead retreating to the pre-made sandwiches and chips to pick up supper before heading to the till. He'd eat back in the motel, or maybe he'd find a park before his meeting, if the wind had died down.

Martin waited at the Express till while a young guy with a red nose and sniffles rang through items for a slow moving old dude. Grapefruit. Another grapefruit. Frozen lasagne. Cough drops. A newspaper.

While Martin waited, the balding guy in the black apron stalked by, heading toward the office. The checker called to him, "Did you get it back?"

The balding guy didn't break stride. "No. I'm calling the cops."

The geezer collected his bag and shuffled off.

The cashier scanned Martin's items. "They can't do anything."

"Excuse me?" Martin handed over cash.

"Cops. They can't do anything to shoplifters. These ones like to take meat from the warmer." He nodded toward the deli, where whole roast chickens and pans of meatloaf sat under red-hot lights. "Outside, they tear the food apart. Drop it on the ground. They'll pick it up, brush it off, eat it. Even if we got it back, we couldn't sell it. And then they disappear fast, before a cop can get anywhere near."

"Huh." Martin took his change.

The checker eyed him. "You walking? Watch yourself. Last week they caught up to a lady with a stroller, had two kids in it. Grabbed her bags and took off in different directions. Her wallet was in with her groceries, too. Have a nice day."

Martin looked toward the door he'd come in, but the geezer was heading that direction at about one-quarter the speed of a tortoise. So Martin turned toward the other door, where the "excitement" had been. As the automatic door closed behind him, he saw, in the far corner of the parking lot, a skinny kid hunched into a black hoodie, staring in his direction. Three of the kid's buddies sat on the asphalt behind him, tearing into a roast chicken, waving drumsticks and wings in the air to cool them off. Martin slowed and tried not to look their way too obviously, but the kid noticed him looking and scowled, dark eyebrows pulled together like a slash across his face above a purplish bruise on his cheekbone. One of the buddies handed a piece of chicken up to the kid, who took a bite but didn't stop glaring at Martin.

Martin turned his head toward the "mind your own business" zone and inspected the kid from the corner of his eye. Dark eyes, dark and wispy facial hair. The kid chewed with urgency, like the food could be taken from him at any moment. The hunch, protection from a life that rained down on him. Martin felt a stab of recognition.

Keep surviving, kid.

Well. Life like that happened to a lot of people. There were other ways to live. Martin turned toward his hotel, toward safety. His future. Which would be different from his past. Maybe more like what he'd told Simone. He would make it so.

Starting with a meeting. Tonight, at seven, that's where he'd be.

SIMONE

All that wondering about Martin was unsettling. So that afternoon, before I could talk myself out of it, I dialed the phone. This time I let it ring. When she picked up, I started right in.

"Jessica. It's Simone. Simone LeMay? If you haven't made other arrangements, I'd be honoured to take Chen for—for a while, you know. The long weekend or whatever."

When she got over her surprise, I could hear she was pleased. "Oh, thank you! And Chen will be happy. He's, well." Her voice got wry. "Resilient. As they say. And he'll be okay with his cousins next week. Just this weekend was hard to work out."

I backtracked up the list I'd made to prevent myself from chickening out of the whole thing. "So you mentioned homeschool. Did you need me to do anything about that?" I tried to keep the alarm out of my voice.

"No, no need. It's just for a weekend. And anyway, we keep it low-key." She cleared her throat. "We've been doing weather, and he's interested in Indigenous cultures here and around the world.

But just having someone new to talk with, that's plenty."

I moved down my list. We talked about food—Chen had no allergies, only preferences. He didn't like hot dogs, but burgers were okay. Yes to pizza and chicken fingers.

Jessica would bring him out Friday, early in the afternoon. I'd be giving up the weekly coffee time with a few of the ladies from church, but no matter. As the seasons turned and the days warmed, I tended to skip those anyway in favour of being outdoors.

She said it more than once: "Are you sure this is okay?"

"Absolutely." I made myself sound more confident than I felt. *Take that, Rev. Phil.*

Just a weekend. More or less. Three full days and bits of two more, so call it four. That's 48 twice, so 96. Wow. Almost 100 hours. That's a lot of hours with a kid. If I were William's ghost, I'd probably disappear, too. What on earth had I set in motion?

I was still sure it was the right thing to do. It's the kind of thing family does, even when they're not your family, when your family's gone and you wish they weren't. That didn't keep me from feeling something like regret for my lost solitude.

The back of my neck prickled, and sunshine warmed the top of my head, like a blessing. William was proud of me. I tried to focus on that, instead of my feeling of impending doom.

CHEN

New notebook starting tomorrow
Pictchures, keepin them

When Mum got her suitcase out for the trip, I tried to give her this notebook. It's almost full. I'm starting my red one tomorrow. I wanted her to take the old one so she'd remember me. And maybe miss me a little.

It's weird to think of her going away on purpose. She says Daddy didn't want to leave, Ryan neither. But she wants to. Even if sometimes she cries about it and hugs on me, she's still going.

She got kinda mad about the notebook. She said, "Chenoweth, what are you thinking? It's less than two weeks! Do you think I'm leaving forever?"

She didn't say she wasn't, though. So on purpose I didn't think about that.

She showed me her phone. "Look. Here's these pictures of

you and Daddy. These ones we printed and put on the fridge, and there's this one of you and Daddy and Ry at Christmas a couple of years ago. I'll have all those with me. And furthermore, young man, I will call you regularly. And I'll come back, safe and sound."

"Okay," I said. I was glad to hear about the coming back. Lots of the yuck went away and I felt pretty okay. Plus, I like my new red notebook. I like all the empty pages and I like seeing my writing on them. What Daddy would call a win-win.

She said, "When you pack your duffel you can put in this picture off the fridge. When you get to Simka's you can put it near your bed and look at it."

The picture was the one held on with letter magnets spelled XMAS. It's of me and her and Daddy. She's not all the way in the picture because she's taking it, but half her face is smiling. Daddy and I are in our matching pajamas that we get every year and we always open on Christmas Eve and wear that night and the next morning. These ones have penguins on them.

I had them on the night I was sick and Mum answered the phone and it was the police and it was terrible. That night.

I don't wear mine now. It doesn't seem right to wear them if Daddy can't.

She gave me the other picture from the fridge, too, of me and Ryan in the medals from the laser car tournament. Just for a second, I kind of wished Ryan was still around so he could come with me to stay with this lady. It might be fun. Or at least we could share being brave.

I didn't say anything about it, though. Because both Mum and I know that what we really want is for there never to have been an accident. And she doesn't need me to say it.

Mum said, "There. You have lots of pictures of family with you. And so do I."

She hugged me some more and I hugged her back, hard.

SIMONE

I'd never been around kids much, even to babysit. My biggest experience with children was having been one, some sixty years in the past. Taking care of a child, solo, for a weekend seemed a little like leaping into the lake in June without wading first.

But since I was doing it, I wanted more than to get through each day, however mixed my feelings remained. I wanted to enjoy myself. Even more, I wanted him to enjoy himself, and me, and this place. He deserved to have some fun.

It all sounded so fine and noble, which was usually a bad sign. I needed a plan, so after I called Jessica, I settled in at the table with a pencil, paper, and calendar.

Friday, tomorrow, was May 1. Luckily, May was the perfect time of year to open the summer camp. That would give Chen and me something to do together.

Like "cottages" in southern Ontario and "cabins" in Manitoba, a "camp" could be anything from a year-round home to a primitive structure. My place, formerly Carmen's and her parents' before that, was definitely primitive. And I adored it.

Every year I made a list, because although every year was the same—leaves fell, grass grew—every year was different. Trees came down over paths, moose maple and alder grew too big to be ignored. Animals spun webs and dug burrows, often in inconvenient-to-me places.

I made a cross between a list and a mind map, like someone—Colton? Ethan? Nathan?—did when the Sunday School kids planned the Christmas skit.

Deadfall
Garden
Eaves
Shutters
Back paths
Rowboat

I had help. Somewhere between "Garden" and "Eaves," I smelled vanilla and evergreen. A smiling, square-faced man of about 60 sat at the table in the place to my right, where he could read over what I'd written. Grandpa Jackson, Carmen's father. Under his flat newsboy-style cap, his hair was white. He sometimes spoke—more than William, less than my mother. He usually showed up for conversations about upkeep of the camp, which he'd built by hand nearly a hundred years earlier.

This time, he hummed a marching song that made me think of a hymn, but I couldn't quite place it. When he finished reading the list, he beamed at me, a smile as sweet as ice cream.

"Well done."

"You approve, I take it?"

"Quite and very much so. Of course, it's just the beginning."

I sighed. "I know, Grandpa, I know—the foundation, the roof, the windows. I know!"

His smile grew wistful. "It might need more money and skill than you have, all alone."

My breath caught. Grandpa and I didn't always agree on what needed doing, but never before had he questioned my ability to do it.

He was right. Every year, I did the bare minimum to keep the camp structure upright and the trees off the path, and that was about my limit, even with the help of a handyman. Which reminded me of Donnie, who'd taken the place of Gordon, who'd replaced someone else who'd helped Grandpa back in the day, and Donnie's desire to retire. I'd have to find someone new to help with the water lines and larger chainsawing projects. I felt like groaning.

"I wish I could help." Grandpa's voice, high and thready with age, cracked.

I smiled at him. "Oh, Grandpa, you are helping. It's an honour to have it at all, and I love it. You were a genius. I just want to do right by you."

The vanilla scent grew stronger. With a wistful smile and tug at his cap, he said, "Carry on." When he disappeared, so did the vanilla.

I reviewed my list. Crusty snow lingered in spots deep in the bush, but sunny days would make quick work of those. We'd rake the dry and wet leaves and cut back the alder and moose maple. Cutting is always fun. Chen might enjoy using loppers. Clearing up afterwards—well, it had to be done. And we'd both rake.

Would any of this sound appealing? I'd met Chen at church once or twice, but that was all. He'd seemed smart but subdued. Understandable, given the accident.

I'd have loved it, but by his age, I was already swoony over our place.

And why not? Out the camp's front door lay Lake Superior, an inland sea, crisp and clear. Even on the warmest August days, the air felt clean, not thick with the heat of a Missouri afternoon.

The camp itself sat amid groups of tall evergreens and birches, with rocky outcrops sheltering moss.

I couldn't wait to tell Chen about it. Wherever I looked, I saw family. Grandpa had built the square shack in the mid-1920s, when Carmen was born. It never looked like much from the outside. The paint always peeled, even though most years we'd "scrape a little and slap on a coat," as Carmen said.

Inside, Grandpa's ingenuity shone. Some of the decades-old trees he'd felled to make room for the camp served as foundation, and he brought others indoors to support the roof. The outside walls came from a lumberyard, but for interior walls, he used paneling discarded from grain cars after they unloaded at the elevators in town. The multi-paned old windows, their glass rippling with age, came from another discard pile. To build the corner fireplace, Carmen and Grandma stacked rocks from the beach, and Grandpa held them in place with concrete he mixed using beach sand and water with the cement.

At an early age, I lost the distinction between doing chores and having fun. One of my jobs was to replenish tinder in the woodbox. I collected bark and twigs while wandering among trees, listening to woodpeckers drumming coded messages. Sweeping the sand out was still sweeping, a futile effort to distinguish indoors from outdoors, but it let me examine every corner of the marvelous structure—not only its floors but its rafters, where spiders created intricate cobwebs overnight for us to enjoy in the morning.

Inconveniences became adventures. A lack of running water meant bathing in the lake. That, in turn, meant lathering up after a swim, and who cared if the soap floated away in the freezing water or I could never get the sap off the bottom of my feet.

The chilly August mornings smelled of woodsmoke and oatmeal. Pulling long pants and a flannel shirt over my pajamas, I'd sit on the cold stone hearth and feed finger-thick sticks onto the flaming pile of birchbark and tiny twigs. When they caught, I'd give it a piece or two of extra-dry driftwood before trying a birch split that was too long for the cookstove. I learned not to skimp on the succession of small twigs a fire needs to catch properly. Carmen grumbled at me only occasionally.

As the August sun climbed the sky, so did the temperature. Out in the rowboat, I could shed layers, beaching it to refresh myself by wading and splashing in our shallow bay.

Carmen's voice interrupted my trip back in time. "Quit daydreaming. This kid isn't you."

I looked around but couldn't see her. "He might enjoy it, though."

Her laughter swelled and faded.

I whispered, "I want to do this better than you did. I want him to have a good time because he's enjoying the place, not a good time in spite of me."

Because why not? Though I didn't know Chen, not really, we had chatted briefly a time or two after church, and I knew he was curious.

And maybe, just maybe, Chen was the kind of kid who'd comb the beach for shells and interesting bits of driftwood and show them to me, his face lit with excitement. He could learn a lot here, like how the sandy lake bottom under your toes makes the cold water seem warmer, and how you can see familiar faces in the boulders along the shore.

What if Chen were the kind of kid who appreciated enchantment and magic?

"And ghosts?" Carmen said behind me. I jumped, and she laughed again.

Right. Ghosts. I'd have to be careful about that.

MARTIN

Martin had been to thousands of AA meetings in his seven years, four months, and twenty-three days of sobriety. Not one a day, but in extra-bad times, more than one a day, so easily 2500 now.

In his experience, they all looked pretty much the same. He'd been to a few at treatment centres, but most had been in church basements and community centres around southern and southeastern Ontario.

This evening, like the others, progressed in a familiar pattern. Outdoors, people in groups of two or three smoked near the side door. Martin said "hey" and kept moving. Indoors, he went down a half-flight of stairs and along a hallway lined with bulletin boards, where pushpins trapped flyers for rummage sales, bake sales, and potluck dinners. In the fluorescent-lit meeting room, he found a row of metal folding chairs, a table in the back holding a coffee urn and disposable cups, plus brochures for other meetings. This meeting didn't have Danish or day-old donuts with the coffee, like some did.

In the chairs, people. All different, but the same in at least one significant way: their relationship with alcohol. As usual, Martin saw a couple of tidy guys in dress shirts, unbuttoned at the collar, their ties in suit coat pockets. One or two retired-looking guys in sweater vests. And blue-collar guys, some young and some seasoned. They wore work boots and layers of jackets. About half the people in chairs were women, most in black gym type clothing or office wear, a few in scrubs.

Most looked like regulars, welcoming and friendly, but not too forward. A visitor, like he was tonight, might feel shy, but if they were regulars at a different meeting, they might blend in.

Newcomers usually stayed to the edges of the room, sometimes slipping in late. They were welcome, but they didn't quite believe it. Not yet.

Martin had been on the edges of meetings lots of times in lots of places. He'd gone to a meeting in St. Catharine's after a trip to Niagara Falls, and another way east in Belleville, when Harry had a gig somewhere in Prince Edward County and Martin had tagged along. But most of his meetings had been where the new subdivisions were going in near Toronto proper at the edges of established suburbs.

He picked a chair not at the back but not at the front, not far from a guy in a plaid flannel jacket.

He nodded at the guy. "I'm Martin."

"Alex." A pause. "You new?"

"In town visiting."

A brief nod, and that was that. Martin knew he'd been seen and welcomed. Then the meeting started.

...

After it was over, Martin walked out with Alex, who carried a cigarette and lighter down the hall and lit up the moment they stepped outside.

Alex blew out smoke, eyeing Martin. "So you're visiting someone?"

"My cousin. You from here?"

"Yeah. But didn't I see you up at Harbour Foods earlier? Near the soup, talking to a lady? Your cousin?"

Martin was surprised he'd been noticed. "I was there, but I didn't know her. I was picking up supper. Hey, can I ask you something about what you said at the meeting?"

Alex shrugged. "You can ask."

"About wanting to call your uncle. But he died in some accident. Everybody seemed to know what you meant. What happened?" Martin wanted to bring the question around to Harry but wasn't sure how. In a rush, he added, "If you don't mind."

"At the end of January, on the expressway, big rig couldn't stop, huge pileup and fire. A lot of people died. Still hard to believe sometimes. Maybe because it was in January. You think when the seasons change, the sun's back, spring's coming, things will be different. But Uncle Reg is still dead." He shook his head, tapped ash off.

"Oh. That sounds rough. Sorry." Martin abandoned his idea to talk about Harry and cast about for something else to say.

Alex took over. "So are you staying with your cousin? She live in the neighbourhood?"

"No, I'm at a hotel. We're, uh, not close. Distant cousins, you could say." Martin laughed at his own joke.

Alex smiled briefly. "When you were at Harbour Foods, did you see that gang in the parking lot?"

"Oh, the kids? Yeah I guess, but I didn't exactly know what was going on." Martin kept his answer vague.

"Did you get a good look at the leader? Skinny, dark hair?" At Martin's hesitation, Alex added, "Reason I ask, I know a guy, Ken, who's worried about that kid. He's Ken's nephew, a runaway, but Ken can't get off work to catch up to him. He thinks the kid spends time at the skate park at the waterfront, but he doesn't know for sure. I thought I'd see about it tomorrow, but I can't, I got called in to work at midnight, twelve hours plus OT. Do you want to do it?"

"Well, uh." Martin scrambled. "I'm not sure. I don't have any experience with anything like this." Which was not strictly true, given those odd jobs for Harry. But he wasn't sure how he felt about spying on that kid, who was probably just trying to keep his life together.

Alex turned his head to exhale smoke. "It's easy. Just, if you see him, call this guy, the uncle. Ken." Alex talked about the kid's mother, picked up for passing bad cheques, and then the kid was kicked out by the mother's boyfriend. Martin didn't try to keep all the details straight, but it sounded plausible. Like Ken just wanted to keep his nephew out of trouble.

There's always another way to spin it, Harry reminded him. But what would it hurt to keep an eye on the kid? Martin didn't have anything special to do for the next few days.

Alex tapped more ash off his cigarette. "And there's payment. A reward, I guess you'd say." He pulled out a phone. "Look. I got his number here, do you want it?"

Martin took out Mr. Smith's burner phone. "Sure, I guess." While he was adding the contact information, he asked, "How do you know Ken?"

Alex exhaled, and smoke drifted up into the cool night. "Worked with him at the City, in road maintenance. But then I got on at the mill. Better money. Okay, so I'll tell him a guy named Martin is on it."

And just like that, Martin had something to do the next day.

FRIDAY

SIMONE

After listing everything Chen and I could do, I worried about food. After William's death, I'd fallen out of the habit of cooking for other people, hence the pleasure of baking for the families bereaved in the accident. But baking was different from daily cooking. Back to planning, producing, and serving three meals a day, ugh. And this time for a stranger, a kid, even though his mother claimed he wasn't a picky eater. I wanted to lie down and pull the covers over my head.

My first grocery list: bread and brownie mix. You can't go wrong with brownie mix. I added what Carmen called "staples" and anything I could imagine a young boy might eat, like lunch meat, canned and fresh vegetables for soup, cookies, mandarin oranges, apples, chicken fingers, potato chips (*just one bag*, I told myself), and ice cream. Those last two were for me.

I cheered up when I remembered that I could also bake for Chen. And Martin might be around, too. Truth be told, I might not mind it too much. "Baking for my cousin, who's visiting" sounded kind of nice, in its way.

Friday morning at the grocery store, I sailed through the aisles with my list. At home, I rechecked my to-do list and wiped out my kitchen sink for the millionth time. At last, I heard car doors slam.

I stood on the porch, trying my darnedest to feel hearty and competent. "Hi there! Welcome! Come in! Chen, nice to see you again. Why don't you take your bag up the stairs to the room on the right." He lugged a duffel bag, so I didn't even offer to shake hands.

Jessica gave Chen a look and followed me into the living room, where we perched on opposite ends of the couch.

She handed me folded papers. "I wrote down his doctors and clipped his health card to it. Just in case. Though I'm sure you won't need it."

"Doctors? Plural?"

"Yeah, since the accident." I heard a muffled thump upstairs, and Jessica dropped her voice. "He's been seeing a counsellor. We both have."

I made sure my voice didn't betray surprise. "Of course. Perfectly understandable. Is there anything, uh—anything I need to know about?"

"Early on, he had nightmares about fires, but not lately. Dr. Samuelson, that's his psychiatrist, had him write in a notebook. Just a word or two, notes to remind him of what he wants to talk about. At first, they met a couple of times a week, and he started sleeping better. He still writes in the notebook and sees her every month. It would be nice if you could encourage him to keep writing." She paused. "What else. Oh, my cell number and Sarah's are there. And the phone numbers for Andrew's parents."

"I'm sorry, I should have asked. How's your father-in-law?"

Jessica worked at a smile. "Recuperating—he'll be fine, once he gets enough antibiotics in him. The accident, though, aged them both. It's been a really hard blow. Andrew's sister looks after them, mostly."

"That's good." I didn't really know what else to say, familiar though I was with difficult family relationships. She sat silent, too, and at last I thought to look through the papers she'd given me. "Ah, your itinerary. Looks like a nice trip."

"I hope so." She bit her lip. "Andrew—we picked it out together. Before Andrew, I travelled a lot, mostly Europe, some Central America. But we hadn't gone anywhere since Chen was born. When we were coming up on our ten-year anniversary, Andrew said he really wanted to see a glacier. We built the whole trip around it."

"I think it's really, uh, nice that you're going." I thought *brave* but managed not to volunteer it, or *weird* or *glutton for punishment*, two other options.

"Thanks. I'm out of practice going places alone." She hesitated. "I'm scattering Andrew's ashes—some of them—at the glacier."

"Oh. Well." I knew she honoured me by confessing. "What an interesting idea."

She flushed. "Strange, right?"

I collected myself. "No, not at all. I understand completely." I did. And I no longer thought her weird, though *brave* was still on the table, as well as perhaps *glutton for punishment*.

"It's not *closure*." She rolled her eyes at the word. "It'll be nice to take this trip, but I have to come back eventually."

I nodded like wheat on a stem. "It's good to have a break from millions of decisions, all competing for attention."

"Yes." Our eyes met. "I haven't told Chen about the ashes, but I think he knows. I thought you should, too."

"Thanks." I waited, but she didn't say anything or move. "So, is there anything else? Want to see Chen's room? You're welcome to stay."

She stood up before I could finish the sentence. "No, no need."

I stood, too. "Well, I hope you'll have a great time." Then I heard myself. "Sorry. I mean, you know."

Fortunately, she smiled. "I do know. Thank you, really. I so appreciate this." Her face sagged a bit, folding in on itself.

I didn't want her to cry, or Chen either. I called up the stairs. "Chen, your mother's leaving."

He thumped downstairs immediately and grabbed her in a hug. "Bye, Mum."

She hugged him back. Neither of them actually cried, though I think it was close.

And that was that. Chen and I stood in the window to wave.

CHEN

Notebook: Friday, May 1
No snooping, Aunt Simka
Daddy in a sandwhich bag
Memdicant
Penumbrell

I'm waiting for Mum to get done telling Aunt Simka about doctors and things. Aunt sent me up with my suitcase and Mum gave me that look that meant leave them alone.

I'm glad my old notebook was done. Being with Aunt Simka should have its own notebook. Also, in case she snoops—that means you, Aunt Simka. You don't need to know about things that happened before I came here.

Snooping is a good word. A favourite of mine. I learned all about it from Ry. He said it to me all the time. Only like, don't do it.

When he was at his Mum's I'd go in his room at my house. He slept in my room in the top bunk but he had his room too, the little bitty room, all to himself. No bed. He kept some clothes and papers in his dresser in there. I know because I snooped.

I knew Ry didn't want me in there. That's why I did it. I was not cooperating with Ry.

Now we keep the door to his room closed. I go in there, though. I know what's in all his drawers. One time I was supposed to wash my socks and the towels but I got clean socks from his dresser instead. Also, that picture of Daddy and Ry from the TV room, when Daddy coached Ry's t-ball team and they're wearing yellow shirts, I put it in the dresser and slammed the drawer shut.

But being in there isn't as fun now that Ry can't be mad.

I know Mum has some of Daddy with her. She's taking him to Alaska.

Grandmother and Gumpy made us bury a big jar full of Daddy, and a different one full of Ry, in the cemetery. But Mum took some of Daddy out before she gave them the jar. She has a box of him in the closet of her bedroom. Bigger than her phone and lots thicker, like a regular book. I know because I saw it. Mum had a bad day, one where she stayed in bed, and wanted me to bring her Daddy's bathrobe. The box was on the floor in the back. It was gray cardboard and it had "Andrew Robertson" written on it in black marker.

I wasn't snooping. I just saw it.

This morning I peeked in her room before I pushed the door open all the way. She sat on the floor with a plastic bag like sandwiches go in. She used the drinking cup from the bathroom to put some of Daddy into the plastic bag. She squeezed the strip to seal the bag.

I wanted to ask her about that bag. What's in it. I mean, what part of burned-up Daddy. Like is it his eyes or his fingernails or what.

I'm not supposed to think about that. Dr. S would get mad. If I told her.

Sometimes it feels like all my family is going away. Not just because Ry and Daddy died, and not just because Mum's going on this vacation with some of Daddy and without me. But also because Mum's different now. Like part of her went somewhere else.

I guess maybe part of me is gone, too, the part that was Daddy. I read about DNA a little bit, and I know that's not how the science goes. Bits of Mum and bits of Daddy are swimming all around in my body and in my teeth and hair and bones, too.

But it still feels like part of me is missing. When I look in the mirror I'm all there, though.

When we were driving, I almost asked Mum about why she's taking some of Daddy. But she put the radio on, plus she wanted me to call out address numbers on the driveway signs so we didn't miss Aunt Simka's house.

I still want to know things. Why and how much she took. And how much of Daddy is left. Maybe I wanted some for me to have in case I felt sad while she was gone.

But then I stopped to think. Dr. S says sometimes I should think. Not about what part of Daddy's in the bag. She means think about Mum before I say or ask something. Not all the time. Just sometimes. Like cooperating.

I thought asking Mum might make her sad, and it seems like she doesn't need any help.

When we were driving, they said some words on the CBC. Memdicant. Penumbrell. Memdicant, the announcer meant it like holy. Penumbrell reminds me of umbrella. It's about shadows, like standing under an umbrella? Or a tree?

I wonder if Aunt has a dictionary. I'll ask after Mum leaves. On the shelves in here, there aren't any books, just owls. Lots. Some are made out of china, and some are stuffies but they're old, not bright colours, like mine. And some carved out of wood.

Whoever sleeps in this room likes yellow and doesn't read much. I wonder whose room it is. It doesn't look like a kid room.

Simka's got a couple of pictures downstairs on the walls. One's a high school kid with grownups that aren't her. I didn't look at them good yet. I guess if it's her son he'd be old, like Mum, or older. He wouldn't live here anymore.

I like to pretend Ryan moved away. I don't think about it too much because then Daddy must have moved with him.

And thinking about that would make Mum sad. Me too.

MARTIN

Wandering along the Thunder Bay waterfront, Martin turned to look out at Lake Superior. Free of ice, it spread left and right like the stage of a huge amphitheatre, its backdrop that stone Sleeping Giant across 20 kilometres of water. Behind Martin, the buildings along the shore and rising into the hills served as the tiered seating for an audience waiting for the show.

New money spent on condo towers and a hotel didn't tidy up the old grain elevators. Martin could practically hear them whispering, "Nothing wrong with honest hard work." Snooty folks in the city, maybe even Simone, might call them eyesores. Well, they weren't wrong, exactly—the elevators were pretty filthy.

But then, that's what work is like. You get dirty working, no matter what kind of work it is. Martin had learned that when he'd escaped his father's greasy garage only to learn that vegetables grow in dirt. He was never sorry to have done outdoor work, though. That kind of dirt washed off.

This city liked parks. They'd put a couple of tidy ones right by the water with benches where parents could linger while little kids played on the grass. Plenty of geese and gulls already hung around waiting to be fed. Great places for kids to run around. Use up some energy.

Parents. Martin didn't have kids. He'd worked with fathers who boasted about being no-nonsense, tough guys. But every one of them pulled out a phone to make him look at a picture of a bunch of hockey gear with a stick clutched upright in a mitt, a kid maybe buried in the middle.

Martin drifted around the park and water, enjoying the sun, staying out of the mud. He followed paved trails near railroad tracks, but they all seemed to lead to abandoned industrial buildings, where it looked like nothing good had happened in a long time. Around noon, several cars came to the main park and settled into spaces overlooking the lake—refugees from office jobs, Martin guessed, looking for a lunchtime view.

The play areas stayed quiet, but the skatepark, farther back from the water, saw more action. Early afternoon, an ever-changing clot of kids showed up, with from four to a dozen there at any given time. Half of them tried complicated jumps on their manufactured playground while the rest stood to socialize.

Martin watched, impressed by their courage. There wasn't any reason for them to flip themselves up into the air off the moving boards or even glide back and forth over concrete. They weren't leaping to grab fruit from a tree, like he'd seen people do at that u-pick orchard near Milton (stupid, that—just use a fruit-picking pole). They weren't going back and forth to tamp down pea gravel before laying flagstones. They were just doing it. For fun. A semi-dangerous sort of fun Martin couldn't really understand. He felt old.

A black hoodie on the sidelines caught his eye. At last. Martin recognized the scowl and fading bruise—the kid from Harbour Foods, talking with a couple of his buddies. The kid laughed, then grimaced. Martin remembered the wince, the ache. He'd attracted a few shiners during his drinking days. Only a few, because he was mostly the one who grabbed an arm to lead a combatant away. Still, sometimes he got caught in the middle in spite of himself.

While Martin pretended not to watch, an older, burlier guy, balding, maybe 30, came up to the kid and laughed, then grabbed his shoulder. Martin half-stood but sat again and turned his head away to watch from the corner of his eye. The older guy released the kid's shoulder and poked him once or twice. The kid's friends hung back, taking swigs from a bottle in a paper bag. The guy kept talking to the kid, putting an arm around him, pulling him close and rubbing the top of his head. The kid smiled, even breaking into a laugh.

But the kid caught him looking and scowled. Loud and clear: *Mind your own business, creep.*

Martin couldn't blame him. He maybe did look like a creep. But he knew something. Friends who pretend to rough you up sometimes stop pretending and actually do it. Maybe the kid didn't really believe that yet, in spite of his fading black eye.

Regardless, it was time to head out. Martin wandered off to sit on a sunny bench near the water, far away from kids with skateboards. He pulled out his burner phone and called Ken's number. No one answered, so he left a message: the kid was at the skatepark, and some other, older guys were hanging around, but nothing bad seemed to be happening.

There. He'd done his duty by this unknown Ken guy—everything Alex had told him to do. He didn't even care about the "reward," so much, though every little bit of money helped. But doing this job had cost him nothing.

And mostly Martin couldn't help but feel sorry for the kid and his friends. He hoped Ken would keep that kid out of trouble.

Meanwhile, he'd just enjoy the warm day and mind his own business.

SIMONE

"Auntie Simka," Chen said, "Can I ask you something?"

"Yeah, sure."

We'd watched Jessica back out of the driveway, and then I led the way down the steep part of the house's back lawn, across the asphalt circle, and along the two-track path to the beach at my family's camp. Now we stood ankle-deep in the just-barely melted waters of Lake Superior, wishing for a little more warmth from the sun and a little less breeze. At least I did. Chen seemed impervious to cold and unaware of the water lapping perilously close to the rolled-up legs of his jeans.

I was hoping he'd finally ask about the camp. Up to this point, he'd shown no curiosity. But he had other things on his mind.

"You know how in some places, they have more than one god?"

"Yes, kiddo, I know that."

The bare branches of the birches behind me, beyond the rocks and sand of the beach, rustled softly on another early-May breath. I slipped my hands up the opposite sleeves of my fleece jacket and grasped my elbows.

"So, you know how when there's more than one god in a culture, there's usually one that's a trickster."

"Huh. Now that you mention it, yeah. Like the coyote."

"Yeah, or a raven." Then the real question: "How come?"

I waited. Maybe he'd answer it himself. Also, I had no idea.

He looked toward the cliffs to the left and then the islands in front of us, squinting into the sun. Then he turned toward me, hand to forehead, shading his eyes.

"I mean, Auntie, doesn't that kind of suck?"

"In what way?" I tried not to register either amusement or shock at the expression, no doubt learned from school or his brother.

He leaned back to look skyward. He hadn't fallen butt-first into the water. Yet. It was still his first day.

He talked to the sky. "If you're creating gods, wouldn't you want to believe in something really *really* powerful? Like *mega*-powerful, the most ultimate powerful thing *ever*? Because back then, people couldn't control *anything*." He returned to earth to look at me. "Not the weather, not a sabre-toothed tiger." He waved his arms for emphasis and then went absolutely still to re-balance himself on the slick rocks.

"Right. Not sickness and infections." I thought but didn't say, *Not accidents or fires, not fathers and stepbrothers who go out one evening and don't come home.*

"Or the size of a herd of something. Some animal."

It was interesting to watch him come up against the limits of what he knew. In another conversation we'd had on a Sunday in February, he'd mixed events in the Pleistocene with those from the Flintstones and from a Discovery Channel show in which a veterinarian travels back in time to bring dinosaurs to present-day Australia. Facts, stories, truth.

"If you can't control anything, and you tell stories about gods, on Olympus or somewhere, on some stone pyramid in Maya—."

I interrupted. "Mexico is the country." William had taught high school geography and insisted on accuracy.

"Mexico. Why not make up a god that's comforting? One you can count on?"

"Not capricious, you mean." I counted three colours in the blue jeans on his right leg—the denim, the lighter underside of the rolled-up leg, and a medium blue where the water soaked the roll. And then the shocking white meat of his lower leg. This was an indoors, city kid.

"I guess."

"Unpredictable. That's what 'capricious' means."

"Okay." He bent forward, watching his toes wiggle among the pebbles four inches below the surface.

I thought aloud. "What about seasons? Three months ago, where you're standing now, that was ice. Three months from now, it'll be warmer and little fish will nibble your toes. Seasons can make big changes. Would your god change, too?"

He bit his upper lip. "But every year, seasons are the same. Fall, winter, spring, summer. That's the same."

"True. So you'd look at the pattern. A whole year at a time. And that's how your god would be?"

"Yeah, I guess that's what I'd do. If I got to make up the gods."

Some people would object to gods being made up, but I let it go. Greater minds than his and mine had been debating the existence of God (or gods) for millennia and would continue long after both of us were gone.

All that was a quick thought when Chen said, eyes wide, "Aunt Simka!"

"Yes!" We were already looking at each other.

"Do we have one of those?"

"We? We who we?"

"Christians."

"Ah. Have a trickster?"

He nodded. "Not a god, I guess. But something? An angel? Or maybe the Devil?"

"Ask Job," yelled my mother from where she sat at the camp's kitchen table in her paint-stained sweatshirt, writing in pencil on a legal pad. "He'd have some insight." Speaking of capricious. What the hell would she be writing?

I swallowed to rid my mouth of a metallic taste. "Do you know about Job? Guy in the Old Testament?"

Chen nodded in a sort of shrug.

I hid a smile. "Me neither. We can look him up together."

I looked up at a few clouds scudding across the blue sky. "What a great day. Lots warmer than I was worried about."

My mother, still in the camp, snorted. "That just goes to show that you lack imagination."

She always did sell me short. I didn't bother to argue.

I must not, absolutely mustn't, talk to her in front of Chen. I didn't want him afraid to be around me. Before us lay three-and-a-bit days of togetherness. Just me to bear the responsibility. Me taking care of him, entertaining him. A flick of fear nudged my neck. What was I doing, agreeing to this? What was Rev. Phil thinking, encouraging me—guilting me—into doing it?

My nerves began to fizz, and I could feel regret building. Then my mother snickered, and I remembered. *Oh right. I took care of you my whole life long.* Chen's voice returned me to the present.

"It's so quiet." He stared off across the bay.

"It won't be, come July. The first warm day will bring out the jet skis. They stay pretty far out, though."

And, thankfully, never dropped in here for a visit. Others might enjoy entertaining hordes of visitors—what glossy magazines called "cottaging," at lavish summer homes. In contrast, I cherished my privacy.

I noticed Chen's silence. "You okay?"

"Yeah." He looked down at the water. "It's just." He sighed.

"Other people."

Of course he was lonely—no brother, no father. I gave myself a pep talk. We could invite one or two of his friends, maybe for Monday. But only two kids. With any more, I'd need another adult around. Even two, I wouldn't enjoy. I'd do it, though. Chen deserved to have a good time.

His voice was small. "Sometimes, I wish people weren't so, you know, everywhere."

Whoa. I liked the sound of that. "Like what?"

"Like all the rules. Sharing. Taking turns." His forehead wrinkled.

"With your friends?" I stopped myself on the edge of "brother."

"With everybody. Just one guy at school I really liked, Joseph. He was new after Halloween. His family came from up north so his brother could go to high school in town. Mrs. Murray assigned me to be his study buddy, and I showed him where to put things. He was real good at math, and we did homework together. The other kids, they—." He stopped.

I kept my voice nonchalant and my face turned to the clouds and sky. "Let me guess—they picked on you. For being smart?"

"Maybe. And my weird name. Him too, for being new. And Indigenous. The teasing was easier to take, with two of us. I hope he's okay now that I'm not at school."

"Sounds tough." I'd been there. Different reasons, but a similar place.

"At school, nobody really liked the same things I do. Like, I'm really good at Natatorium," he looked at me, "it's a game online. But everybody else is into hockey or soccer. Or those war games Mum won't let me play."

I searched for something to say. "Sorry you and—Joseph, was it?—had to deal with that. It's not always easy to find someone you like to do things with." He stared down at his feet in the water. "I hope the things we do are fun for you. They might not sound like it. But you can help me a lot. Together we can open up this place so it's ready when summer finally gets here."

At that moment, I could see a million things that needed work (sweeping, raking, lopping, to say nothing of painting or roofing) and tried not to dwell on them. *Tomorrow will be soon enough.* "Time to go back to the house."

He splashed out of the water and stood on the sandy beach, looking around.

I handed him a towel. "Sit on your bum on the dry sand, up here, then use the towel on your feet."

"Do I have to?"

I tamped down exasperation. "Think about it. Your feet are wet and sandy. You want to put your socks and shoes over top of that mess? And then walk uphill? Remember, it's a hike, all the way up to the house. What do you think will happen?"

His mouth got small, but he didn't otherwise move.

"Suit yourself." Let him learn all about chafing and blisters first-hand. I wandered down the beach a few feet and found a beautiful coral-coloured rock. I slipped it into my jeans pocket.

Chen crammed his wet dirty feet into his runners, sans socks, which he stuck into his back pockets.

I picked up the towel. We walked, and I searched for something to say. "Take this hill a few times every day and you'll play better baseball. Do you play baseball?"

"I don't mind throwing, I guess." A pause. "Ryan liked baseball." His matter-of-fact tone was a shut door. I left it closed.

The whole way up, Chen showed zero interest in our surroundings. A couple hundred yards of winding grass-and-rock driveway led from the camp to an asphalt circle that served as a turnaround spot at the end of the paved access road. The asphalt circle separated what had come to me through my mother from what had been William's.

We crossed the circle and attacked the steep, zigzagging section of the lawn. William had bought the house at the top of the hill with Joyce, his first wife, when David was a young teenager. About the time David picked a university, Joyce contracted cancer. Perhaps her death factored into David's reluctance to leave Toronto and confront her absence.

Then I showed up—though I'd been there all along, really. My grandfather had built the summer camp decades before a house on the hill was possible, before any road ran along the ridge. Grandpa had willed the camp to my mother, and I'd bought it from her when she got too sick to keep it.

When William and I were together, we blurred the "yours or mine?" lines between the two properties. If a tree came down over the driveway to the camp, we cut it up together. Its firewood might become a summer bonfire at "my" camp, but it might appear in 'his" house in the woodburning stove on a winter's night.

What was his and mine became ours, and when he died, I stayed in the house. Eventually it would go to David. My camp would, too, though I wasn't happy about it. David wouldn't want a house, much less a camp, in northwestern Ontario. Of course he'd sell. And my childhood heaven would go to someone who might not feel its magic.

At last, Chen and I conquered the steepest part of the path to the house, and he still hadn't asked any questions. I paused on the lawn's edge to catch my breath and look back at the lake, still winking in the sun, though white clouds to the north seemed to be growing and darkening.

We crossed the lawn, and Chen began to talk. "Aunt, one time Ryan saw a bear. We were all in the car going fishing, and he saw it and Daddy did too, and even Mum. But I didn't because it wasn't on my side of the car. Daddy asked if we smelled a skunk because I guess that's what bears smell like."

"They do, kind of."

"And then Ry almost saw one another time, with his other

grandmother. His Mum's mum, not Grandmother and Gumpy. They were outside after supper and Ry smelled something, his grandmother said like a bear. They kept walking around the lake. Then they heard scritching, like someone rubbing sticks together. His grandmother looked up and saw a baby in the tree. Its claws were scratching. Ry didn't see it. She made them hurry back to the house and stay inside."

"How exciting!"

"Yeah. I guess where there's a baby bear, there's a mama. She checked all around their camp. She shook her car keys real loud to warn the bear. Maybe scare it away."

I was impressed. "Smart, to use your keys like that." I'd served sandwiches and coffee after the joint funeral for Ryan and Andrew but hadn't met this grandmother.

"She didn't see the mama, ever. But Ry said it stank real bad all night, and the next morning the camp next door had their trash everywhere. Can I see a bear?"

"Maybe. You'll have to be very careful. Like Ryan's grandmother, making noise while we're walking."

"Okay. Hey, to make noise now I'll tell you about my game, Natatorium."

And then he was off. His chatter was a good sign and all, but making "I'm listening" noises wore me out. I'd need quiet time soon, and more than a little bit, but I might have to be okay with only a little bit.

My mother never understood that I needed a moment, just a moment, to savour being at home, separate from her moods. *How are you, my home? Did you miss me?* Nearing the house with Chen, I felt like a kid of twelve, a time when Carmen didn't have a steady job.

Back then, when I came in the door after school, I'd close the door gently so as not to set her off. Some days, she'd be "asleep," our euphemism for "passed out." Other days, she'd hold up a glass and demand I make her a gin and tonic. Then she'd start in with questions. "Why don't you bring friends home from school?" She meant, "You're a loser." Over time, I grew to prefer the "asleep" version.

Now on the porch, I pushed open the door and stood aside for him to go in. "Chen."

"And then I did the fourth level again, because there had to be more there, extras, like weapons or a bonus for creating the mightiest team, because you'd think that the team with the archers wouldn't be as good as a team that can fight hand-to-hand, they'd always have to run far enough back for arrows to land. That's how the levels always go."

I closed the door behind us. "Chen. *Chen.*" I grasped his shoulders and turned him to face me.

"What." He wriggled free. "I was telling a story, Simka."

I flushed. "Sorry, but I need you to be quiet."

"Oh-kaay." He dropped his head and sat down, *whump*, to take his shoes off.

Poof. Just like that, the stillness I so craved was full of guilt. And sand, when he took his shoes off. I decided not to say anything. Walking in sandy shoes would have been uncomfortable enough for him.

I hunted out an old *Discover* magazine. "Can you read for a while?"

He accepted it, head down. In the living room, he opened the recliner's leg rest in a way that made me wonder if he'd mess with it and I'd have to yell at him. But he sat quietly with the magazine and at least pretended to read, without much unnecessary rocking or bouncing.

After sweeping up sand, I glanced at the clock: 5:08. I flipped through the week's mail, stacked on the entryway buffet, and threw out the junk. I saw the card with Martin's phone number. I wondered if he'd show up soon. It would be inconvenient, with Chen here.

Thwunk and the leg rest closed. Sock feet on carpet. "Aunt." Chen's voice lingered between question and complaint. "Can I talk yet?"

I looked at him. "Depends. What is it you need to say?"

He half-smiled. "Dunno."

"How about not, then." I kept my tone light, but I was borderline desperate.

"Okay." He didn't seem to take offense. Standing at the kitchen counter, he picked up the metal-topped glass sugar container and tipped it, experimentally, not far enough to pour it out but almost, then in the other direction.

I watched the sugar fall, gather, fall again. Finally I caught myself. "You, young man, are in serious need of a project."

"You won't let me play my online game."

"How about your notebook? Have you written for today?"

He squinted up at me. "Yeah."

"Write some more."

"Ohhhh-kaaaaay." The *thud-thud-thud* of his feet on the stairs, then a series of *thunks* as he jumped back down. He sat at the kitchen table and turned to a fresh sheet, clicking his mechanical pencil.

He squinted at me, face solemn. "This is private. Between me and Dr. Samuelson. Not even Mum reads it."

"Okay. I won't watch." I transferred chicken breasts from the freezer to the fridge to thaw for the next day. I turned, though, at hollow thumps. Chen drummed the edge of the table with his palms.

"Seriously?"

He grinned and stopped.

I sighed. "See that clock? It's 5:29. Find something to do until six. It has to be quiet and mostly stationary. Not electronic. I could find you a book. What do you like to read?"

Shrug, without a look at me.

"I can't hear you when you don't use words."

He looked up, eyes wide. "You said I had to be quiet."

I successfully neither smiled nor gritted my teeth. "One point for you. Do you want a book?"

"I'll just write in my notebook." At last, with a minimum of clicking the pencil lead, he got down to business.

CHEN

Notebook: More Friday May 1
Motormouth
Eraser
~~Patiens~~ paitiense
Sirious lesson
Bears

I already wrote today but Aunt Simka told me to write more. I was being a motormouth. She got the look Mum has almost all the time since the accident. Not where Mum has to lie down in bed under the covers and close the bedroom door. Just the one where Mum is about to run out of patience.

I wish my pencil had a better eraser. This one is old and it makes dark marks on the page. So I just line through the words if they look funny. I had an eraser at school. It was pink. I hardly used it at school and didn't write in a notebook at home then.

But anyway Dr. S said sometimes when you rub out something

it's because you are afraid of what you wrote. Or you're mad. She said when you write it's honest. So just draw a line through things so she can still read them and we can talk about them.

She says it works too if you think something bad or scary, like if I see a picture in my head about Daddy or Ry burning up. I can pretend to draw a line through it. It won't go away but then I can think about something else.

Aunt Simka and I were talking about gods when we were at the water, which is interesting because of Indigenous traditions. And I got to wade and put my shoes on and walk up hill. My shoes felt pinchy and scratchy when I got back to the house, and my feet hurt, but I tried to walk normal.

I thought Aunt would make me have a Serious Lesson about shoes and socks and sand, but she didn't. Maybe she didn't notice? Or forgot?

Mum would have yelled at me, probably.

I was telling Aunt about the times Ryan saw a bear or almost. One time I wasn't there but the time I was there, I didn't see and everybody else did. It bugs me.

So far I still think staying here might be interesting. Aunt Simka is sure different from Grandmother and Gumpy. She might tell me not to talk but she doesn't seem grounchy about everything. That's good.

SIMONE

Supper was chicken fingers with sweet mustard and grape dipping sauces, which Chen loved, and green beans, which he ate to be polite.

Like our conversation. "Where did your name come from? Chenoweth isn't common."

"That's why Mum picked it, it's special. Her Mum, Gramm, used to have that for her last name. Daddy had to make Grandmother and Gumpy stop calling me Junior, after Daddy. I guess Ryan was supposed to be named for Daddy, too. Gumpy said they'd lost out that first time, you couldn't blame them for hoping. But Daddy said they'd decided on Chenoweth. Gumpy still kind of tries to call me Junior, though."

"Well, I like Chenoweth. I like Chen for short, too." I guess if your names were Jessica and Andrew, you might not appreciate the downsides of such a special name. Simone LeMay hadn't been especially easy to carry in Missouri—people thought I was French. Maybe I even was, who knows. I hadn't thought about it seriously until Martin showed up. Darn him.

Names and families—so fraught.

He said it with an air of remembering. "Oh. How come I call you Simka? And not Mrs. LeMay?"

"I'm not *Mrs.* LeMay because that was my last name growing up, not a married name. And Simka came from a kid at church a while back who couldn't say 'Simone.' You're the only person who's ever called me Aunt Simka, though."

"My parents make me call all grownups 'Aunt' and 'Uncle' and not just their first names. Hardly anybody else does. The kids at school think it's weird."

"It's nice." I stacked our plates. "Let's save dessert till later."

"When's later?"

"Are you hungry?" I kept my tone light, but I wondered what this was about.

He looked at the ceiling. "Sometimes I just like to know what's coming next."

Fair enough. "We'll have dessert at 7:45. Do you want to know what?"

He thought for a second. "Not really."

"Okay." I hoped he liked ice cream.

While he had screen time, I cleaned up the kitchen, drifting in my head from *Aunt Simka* to *family*. Except for David (and Martin notwithstanding), I'd lost all the relatives I'd known.

As my mother used to say when she pretended that life in Missouri had given her some homespun southern charm, you can't always pick your folks, but you can pick your folks. You can't pick the circumstances of your birth, but you can choose who you claim relation to.

Now with Martin's appearance, maybe I did have actual relatives. And although Chen seemed to have lots of grandparents already, maybe he'd want another old lady in his life.

What will be, you know. Can't foresee. Blood: it's thicker than. It'll out. All that.

CHEN

Notebook: Even More Friday
Hardly any screen time
Simone = stricked like Grandmother?
My room
Dessert
Mendicant = begger, their job?
Penumbral = part shade part light, eclipse

Aunt Simka just made a big deal about how screen time was special. I bet Mum told Aunt Simka to limit it. That sucks. I want to play lots of games and look up things. Maybe Simka is like Grandmother. Ry says Grandmother is strict. She liked to say "no" all the time but just to him and me. Not to her other grandkids, those cousins. I know Mum doesn't like Grandmother and Gumpy much. She's sad Gumpy's sick, though.

Grandmother cried a lot at the funerals. Even the one for Ry's Mum. And Grandmother used to talk bad about Ry's Mum,

119

like at holidays. At her house at Christmas two years ago, she said some mean things. Later I found Ry in a bedroom where he wasn't supposed to be. I thought he was snooping, but he was crying. At first he was mad that I saw, but I didn't make fun, so he pretend-punched me in the shoulder, like thanks.

I'm sad Ry's dead, and I'm real sad about Daddy. But I want to have fun out here anyway.

He's lucky to have another grandmother. My other grandmother, Gramm, is dead. Gramps, my grandfather, too. I don't remember them.

Simone's house is nice. It's got stuff in it. Like our house. Not like Daddy's rent houses. They're all empty except for trash in them left over from the people who lived there before. Broken crayons and dust bunnies and chewed gum sometimes. His main rent house always had broken things like sinks and toilets. When Ryan was with us on weekends we fixed things at that main rent house. Daddy let us help.

Always it turned out we had to go to Canadian Tire. When it was warm in the summer we got hot dogs there. Mum never let us eat hot dogs at home. She says they're bad for us and she always said, "Chen, you don't even like them." But I liked them with Daddy at Canadian Tire.

One time we all went to the rent house, Mum too. She was mad. Renters left it a big mess, and she had to wear gloves to spray bleach everywhere and shampoo the carpets. Daddy was fixing the faucet in the downstairs kitchen. He was using washers. I know two kinds of washers, one for clothes and one for dishes, but he meant little flat metal rings.

Mum yelled at Daddy, "The carpet is disgusting. This place is more than normal dirty, it's filthy. When are you painting?"

Daddy decided he needed different washers.

Mum put on her suspicious face. She said, "I'm not falling for that one, Buddy."

Daddy's name was Andrew. She mostly called him that or Andy, but it was Buddy when she was mad. Like when she calls me Chenoweth.

She said, "No way you're gone all day chasing down things you don't need while I'm stuck here cleaning. You'd better get the right size washers the first try. Why not get lots of different sizes while you're at it?"

Daddy and Ryan started to leave, and I begged Mum and she let me go too. I had to sit in the back and Ryan sat in the front with Daddy. Daddy says Ryan gets to always sit in front when he lives with us Wednesdays and weekends. It's not fair. But at least Ryan couldn't knuckle-punch my arm from the front seat.

At the store, Ryan said, "Daddy, remember to get different sizes of washers."

Daddy laughed. He said, "What a suck you are. I'll get just one size, thanks, and I might even get the wrong size on purpose, because nobody at Canadian Tire is yelling at me and making up jobs for me to do."

And then he winked at me and I felt good and Ryan felt bad. I knew he did because he cried, not just having some tears but real crying like Mum calls ugly crying. There was snot and everything.

I don't remember any more about that day. I was glad to go back home after we finished at the rent house. I'm always happy at home. We have good games. Daddy and I played games a lot when Ry wasn't there. And I have a bike and books.

My books are in my room. My desk too. I kept things off my desk because Ry messed them up. He was supposed to keep all his things in the bitty room but he didn't, there was always his stuff on my little desk and my dresser. Plus, he'd pick up something I had, a K-man or something little, even a pen with googly eyes on the end, and he'd tear it up.

It bugged me.

Now I don't have to keep my desk clear. But I like to.

It will be nice to go home again after being with Aunt. But being here is okay, I guess.

I like the story about the washers. It makes me feel good. But it's not true.

It was me Daddy called a suck. He said, "When did you get to be such a suck?"

Ryan said, "Mama's boy."

He was singing it over and over. And Daddy let him. He and Ryan laughed at me.

But I didn't cry. Mostly.

FINALLY Aunt Simka let me have screen time in the den. I don't know how to spell dessert, so I typed in "desert" and it said car racing, so I made it look up "dezert + food" and it said desert and dessert. And I meant dessert. Desert is the place with cactus.

I meant mendicant I think. A person who makes a living by begging. That's like their job, which would be hard. Penumbral, penumbra is related word. It means shadow but not like a real light or real dark. Not full shade or full light. Like in an eclipse. Or I guess maybe under an umbrella or the trees?

SIMONE

After supper and cleaning up, Chen was thrilled to get screen time.

Meanwhile, I poked around on shelves in the living room for a Bible. I had to hunt for Job, but eventually I found him in the Old Testament, right there before the Psalms. I parked myself in the big recliner and read the first paragraph.

"Aunt, it's 7:50," a high voice said behind me.

I jumped. "Geez, Chen."

He grinned. "Did I scare you?"

"No, not scared—startled." I might have been napping, but he didn't need to know that.

"You said 7:45 is dessert." He clutched his notebook in his left hand and flipped a pencil into the air with his right, catching it without looking.

"Yes. Vanilla ice cream?"

"The best."

As we ate, we watched the light change. This far west in the Eastern time zone, the sun wouldn't set till after 9:00, but the day was on its last legs. I suspected Chen was, too. Jessica claimed his bedtime was 8:00, but I figured that was more aspirational than fact.

So after he put his bowl into the dishwasher, I read aloud about Job, the man who had everything and lost it—or, more accurately, had it taken from him. After the setup, I stopped. "I'll save some for another night."

Chen's voice was flat. "It was a bet. Satan bet God that this important guy wouldn't believe in God anymore if he didn't have all the good stuff, right? And God took the bet. So does that make God the trickster for us? Or Satan?"

"I don't know. I don't even know how for sure the story turns out. Maybe it gets better for Job later." My inner schoolmarm chimed in. "Maybe we should keep an open mind."

"My mind's open." He didn't look happy about it. In fact, he looked like he might be near tears.

Maybe he missed his mother. I tried to think of something upbeat to forestall them and came up empty. "Time for bed. I'll show you where things are."

"Naah, I got it. Can you come turn out the light when I'm ready?"

When the thumping feet and running water stopped, I went upstairs. "I turned on a nightlight in the bathroom. I'll close my door once I'm in bed, but knock if you need something. Your door—open or closed?"

"Open." He yawned.

"Good night." I turned off the light. Downstairs, I sat in the blue chair where I could best hear him, should he need me. But all was quiet.

After another half-hour, I stood beside the kitchen table, looking at the evening, hugging myself. Soon enough, a warm breeze descended, carrying William's amusement and kindness and the warm green scent of cut grass on a June afternoon.

I whispered one of my common questions: "Is everything

going to be okay?" Sometimes I knew what "everything" meant, and sometimes I didn't. Tonight, it was hard to put into words, but something like, "Can I juggle this boy and cousins and the ghosts and wants and needs without everybody hating me when it's over?"

The answer: a distant-feeling *Yes, someday everything will be okay* in my ear, and a chuckle. A caress along the back of my neck, and I was alone again.

Someday. Someday, I'd feel better. Better able to manage life, people, ghosts. I could accept that.

I'd clung to *someday* from the first moment of my widowhood, when each day, already cruelly long in June, lasted a terrible forever.

The first hundred or so hours after William's death overflowed with logistics. David's flights. The details of a service—hymns, pallbearers, readings, a speech to somehow sum up a man in a few hundred words—when I wasn't especially comfortable at church yet. Then the late-morning funeral and a lunch spread of sandwiches and dainties in the church hall, for which I had zero appetite. The cemetery, a private family burial—Rev. Phil, David, and me, though I remembered very little. The first lawyer meeting that afternoon, set to accommodate David's flight at nine the next morning.

In that meeting, I said only "No." No changes. No *other* changes. Not until I understood this one, because I didn't. I simply could not understand that he was gone.

That night, I knew I'd slept only because I woke up at six. Through my window, open for the summer breezes, I heard creaks of the wooden deck below—David pacing while talking on his phone.

"It's a gold mine, three-plus-two plus an en-suite off the master, good shape, incredible view, three acres. This is the season to show, and it'll sell. Same with her camp, incredible lakefront. But she won't even think of selling either of them. Won't get an appraisal. Won't even discuss it. It's nuts, she's nuts, just batshit crazy—my stepmother, batshit crazy Simone."

I broke into a sweat, shame both from eavesdropping and from what I'd heard. Then a chill descended over me: rebellion. *Maybe I am crazy. Stubborn, too.* From my mother, I'd learned that when your world disintegrates, you pick a spot to stand while the pieces fall. When, at 17, I saw how her instability threatened our camp ownership, I'd organized my life to keep it. And at William's death, I picked the house and my camp, both together, as my place to stand.

After overhearing David, sleep was out of the question. Downstairs in the kitchen, I clattered around making coffee. He slipped his phone into his shirt pocket and squinted at the sun rising over the lake. When he came in, he looked like he wanted to say something.

Instead, I handed him a travel mug. "No. No business talk. Give me time. Like five years." I cleared my throat. "When do you need to leave for the airport?"

And that was that.

That summer, in the newly empty house, the clock ticked and tocked. The sun rose and set. In the grass, the dandelions sprung and shone their cheery faces and blew wishes on the wind. Lilacs came and went, and the roses appeared, the palest pinks and lavenders on the lake side of the house, always the last bush to blossom. The white bunchberry flowers became August's deep red berries.

I ate all the casseroles and wrote the thank-you notes. I saw a few people—from church, mostly. They phoned every week or so. Usually they wanted me to do something beyond my ability. They "just wanted to drop by," and they expected me to serve them tea and have a chat. Some days, that was too much.

People are idiots, that's all. It's not their fault. They're just doing what they know to do.

I went to about a million meetings that first year. Lawyers. Bankers. More lawyers. As the first anniversary of William's death approached, proud that I'd survived a whole year without him, I decided I'd stay in the house forever, or at least my forever.

Back then, that *someday* I'd hoped for—when "everything was okay" again—hadn't appeared. But I'd coped.

And although these few days with Chen would be challenging, they were nowhere near as horrible, or permanent, as becoming a widow. In fact, they could be fun, between the hard parts. So I'd cope with this long weekend with Chen, too.

I reviewed our time together so far. The dropoff and afternoon had gone okay. Only a few more days before he'd be leaving.

Perhaps sometimes I'd be able to stop asking—I'd just believe everything was already okay. Someday.

SATURDAY

MARTIN

Saturday morning was sunny but cool, like a respectable spring morning should be. Martin took a couple of brochures, one about a canyon and another from a provincial park, to the lobby to entertain him while he drank coffee and ate toast in the hotel's sparse "free breakfast" room. From what he could figure out looking at maps, the provincial park sat across a finger of water from Simone's house. It'd take maybe an hour to get there.

Back in his room, a question nagged at him. Mr. Smith said Simone's property was on the lake. But her house wasn't, from what he could see. And she'd talked about a backyard, not waterfront. He looked at the maps again and confused himself further.

He paced back and forth in his small room, perplexity knotting in his stomach. Harry would say, *Take it one step at a time, Martin.* Right. Like homework.

He sat properly at the desk in his motel room and opened the portfolio. He read Mr. Smith's notes again. Some of them, the first time, hadn't made sense, so he'd focused on the family connection, Jimmy, the little brother to Charlie. This time, he read more carefully.

You're buying her camp property, right on Lake Superior. Not her home on Lakeshore Drive.

It felt like Mr. Smith was talking directly to him. Even yelling at him a little bit.

Camp? That was confusing. A campground? With places for trailers? Surely not.

Again, Mr. Smith's note was helpful. *Some camps are like second homes, but hers is an ancient, rundown shack, maybe 100 years old. No hydro, no indoor plumbing. It's too hard for her to keep up by herself. She has several acres, and selling her property would be a smart financial move at her age, as you can see from the comparable properties listed below.*

Right. The smart financial move part, that was understandable.

On cue, his burner phone rang. Again, Mr. Smith dispensed with niceties, like "hello." "Have you bought it yet?"

"Um," Martin answered. "I haven't seen it yet. I'm just looking at the map."

Mr. Smith groaned. "What have you been doing?"

Martin tried to keep the defensiveness out of his voice. "I've been busy. I met her. I told her I was her cousin, and I think she believes me. But she told me to leave her alone for a week to think about it. That was Thursday morning. It's just Saturday."

"Well, get out there again. Don't wait for an invitation. Nobody gets them." He snorted. "And talk to her soon, like today. Tomorrow morning, she'll be at church. Try charming her. Bring a present. Why do I have to tell you this? You're supposed to be the sales guru."

Martin regrouped. "And I am. I got this, I swear. It's just, I don't exactly understand where this place I'm buying actually is."

"Come *on*. Look up the address. It's more or less downhill from her house. She's probably there right now. I'll get back to you in a couple of days. Be closer to buying it."

"Sure, okay," Martin said to dead air.

Well, Mr. Smith was certainly no salesman. Not at all encouraging or motivating. No attempts to build Martin's confidence.

Harry would tell him, *Don't mistake business partners for friends.* Good advice, because Mr. Smith was most definitely not his friend.

Furthermore, Mr. Smith hadn't talked with Simone, as Martin had. Martin had heard, loud and clear, that she needed a little time and space to think about having a cousin, let alone feeling friendly and selling a chunk of property. He wasn't going to mess with that, whatever Mr. Smith might say. She was facing a big decision, and in his experience, pushing big decisions just brought more trouble down the road. Second thoughts. Returns and refunds.

Martin scrutinized the maps on his phone. Simone's lakeside place was at the end of a paved cul-de-sac. Even better, it was barely out of his way to the provincial park.

But whatever Mr. Smith advised, he didn't want to see Simone yet. He'd trust his gut there. He'd go later in the day, after his hike. If this cottage, uh, camp didn't have electricity or indoor plumbing, she wouldn't be staying overnight yet. No risk of seeing her accidentally. She'd think he was stalking her.

Aren't you? Harry would have asked. Martin ignored him. Instead, he said, "smart move" aloud and immediately felt foolish, all alone in his room giving himself a pat on the back.

He went out to the hotel's "executive suite," which was a desktop and a printer in a former closet off the lobby. On the way, he looked in vain for Barb behind the counter. After printing the directions to Simone's camp, he headed off on the day's excursion.

SIMONE

At the breakfast table—our first morning—Chen eyed me.

I cleared my throat. "For breakfast, we have toast and we have oatmeal."

"Eww! I'll have toast."

"Will you?" I waited. He looked puzzled. "You'll have toast—please?"

He reddened and shrank. "Sorry. Can I have toast, please." He followed it with a small smile.

I felt like a giant jerk, so I didn't correct his "can" to "may." "Absolutely, you may have toast. But I'm going to make oatmeal anyway. I'll make enough for you to have some."

"I don't want any."

I measured and poured and stirred and readied raisins and maple syrup—the real kind, not that fake pancake stuff. "Have you ever even tried oatmeal?"

"Just in cookies. To eat by itself it's gross."

"You don't know that. You have to try it before you say it's gross."

"It looks gross."

"How can you say that, with the lovely brown sugar and these cute raisins? You like raisins, right?"

He nodded. I thought I might win this after all. Not that it mattered, really.

While it cooked, I made his toast and opened the new red jam. Everybody, even William, liked red jam the best. William, it must be said, also wouldn't eat oatmeal.

At last, I spooned oatmeal into my bowl, topped with raisins and a sprinkle of sugar, then went "once around" with the maple syrup.

Chen watched me, chewing toast.

"What?"

"Nothing." He looked at my pants and smirked.

Maybe I looked funny. Okay, probably I looked funny. My usual uniform for early May consisted of old jeans, a long-sleeved t-shirt, and a tattered navy-blue sweatshirt over top. As the weather warmed, I'd trade the long sleeves for short and the sweatshirt for a denim shirt, and I might wear jeans that didn't sag so much, or I might not. My shoe choice depended on the job: old runners for mowing, hiking boots for chainsaws, rubber boots for anything boat- or water-related. Leather gloves—lined for early spring and fall, lighter ones for midsummer. For Chen, I'd dug up an old pair of gloves, dirty and too big, but I thought he might get a kick out of wearing them.

"These are work clothes. If we're going to open up the camp, we've got work to do."

"Aww."

"Like I said yesterday. Raking leaves from around the foundations is first, and clearing the beach. Then lopping, and taking off the shutters, and sweeping indoors. If there's time, we can sweep the eaves and down the sides of the house."

"How long is this gonna take?"

"Got somewhere else to be?"

A shrug.

"I think it's really fun stuff. You get to be outside, for one thing. Lots of neat things to see out there."

He didn't seem convinced.

I relented. "A few days. If nothing major is wrong inside, and the weather stays clear and warm, maybe we can eat lunch on the beach before you go."

Chen had stuck a ball of chewed toast in his cheek, which had a red smear on it, as if the jelly were attempting to escape through his skin. "You don't look like other ladies." He took another bite.

I couldn't help myself. "You know, that wad of food in your cheek is gross. How about swallowing everything you've got in there before you take another bite or talk. I know what I put on your plate. I don't need to see it again."

He nodded. He chewed and swallowed while I ate. Then he showed me his empty mouth.

"Thanks." My bowl was empty, so I got up to fuss with dishes. "I love oatmeal, especially with maple syrup. This is your last chance to try some." I waved the serving spoon and saucepan.

He didn't say no. I sensed an opening. "How about a little bit, with raisins and maple syrup?"

"What if I don't want it? Like, more than a bite?"

"Look, I'll just put a little in the bowl. See? Here's the raisins. And syrup."

He scooped some into a spoon and blew on it. He touched his tongue to it before finally putting the whole spoon in his mouth. He swallowed. "Tastes like raisin. And sweet."

"Exactly. Isn't it great?"

He looked at me. "Great?"

"I think so. I could eat it every day." I loaded the dishwasher:

more plates and bowls than usual. I kind of liked it.

Chen watched. "You really don't act like other grown-ups. Especially not old ladies. Not like Grandmother."

"I should hope not. I'm unique, just like everybody else. And so are you." I ran water in the oatmeal saucepan while he puzzled on that.

"But doesn't 'unique' mean it's the only one of the thing it is?"

"Yes, precisely. Which is why I actually am like all those other ladies."

"But you aren't. You don't dress the same."

"I told you before: work clothes. Go put on some of your own." He was wearing what he slept in. "Your shirt's okay, unless you just want to change it, but you need jeans, and you'll need socks and real shoes. And a jacket."

He got up from the table, propelled by a long sigh.

I told his back, "You're welcome for breakfast."

He didn't slow down. "Thank you, geez." More softly: "Oatmeal is gross."

I raised both the volume and the pitch of my voice. "Boy, do I love oatmeal."

...

I don't know what Chen's family had done about chores, but Chen could barely distinguish the business end of the rake from the handle, and I don't think he was reverse Tom-Sawyering me. Still, nobody had helped me rake at the camp, not since I'd been old enough for Carmen to foist the job off on me. William preferred jobs that required power tools. So Chen was entering novel territory.

I stood right next to him and made a leaf pile, so he could see what the job looked like. Every year when I raked, I tried to get up each dead leaf before I remembered the futility and let my standards devolve. On purpose, I began closer to realism. Chen caught on quickly.

When I thought he might be tiring, I looked at my watch. Did Chen have the ability to stop time? We'd trailed down to the camp at about nine, and it was just ten. "Another half-hour and then let's go throw rocks in the water."

We knocked off a bit early to bring plastic chairs from the breezeway down to the beach. I'd had the foresight to bring a small box of apple juice for him and a thermal mug of coffee for me. In spite of the work surrounding us, I wanted to savour the sun.

May mornings stayed crisp—much like late September, except with a hint of excitement at the summer ahead instead of wistfulness at impending autumn. The lake lay mostly quiet, resting in this lull between winter's ice and full-on boating season. It hissed and swished along the beach's assorted rocks and pebbles—pink and gray granite, black basalt, shockingly white quartz, different kinds and colors of sandstone, and a host of other rocks whose names I'd never learned.

How beautiful. Even with mud on the path down and the icy crusts back deep under trees, even though green grass wouldn't appear for weeks. Then again, I always thought it was beautiful.

I inhaled deeply. "Smell that?"

Chen stopped chewing on the straw in his apple juice and sniffed. "What?"

"What do you smell?"

He tried again. "Air?" He dropped the leather gloves he'd been wearing and sniffed his hands. "They smell like... dog?" He sniffed again.

"Rinse your hands in the water and see if they smell different." Then I got to watch him dance back and forth while he bent over and tried to wet his hands in the near-quiet lapping lake while not getting his shoes wet.

Smart kid—he wet one hand and rubbed it against the other.

He sniffed and shrugged. "They just smell wet. And still kinda like a dog."

I changed the subject. "How many is your best skip so far?"

"Four." Yesterday, he'd told me about learning to skip rocks at the pond at his grandparents' farm.

"Not bad. Better than I can do regularly, till I get warmed up a bit. Today's a good day to practice. The lake's quiet, so there's no waves to mess up the skip. You're all warmed up from raking, but not too tired. The water's low, so you have lots of rocks to choose from."

He walked down the beach, kicking in the loose sand.

"Look for flat ones that fit into your hand."

"I *know*." He tried three or four that were too big for his strength, but eventually one skipped six times, and he seemed satisfied.

"If you do some every day, you'll notice an improvement pretty fast." *Shut up, Simone, not everything has to be a lesson.*

I stood at the water's edge to look at the rocks underwater—one of my favorite things to do. Black and red and white and golden and orange, almost every color I could think of, rounded and squared off and lumpy. I squatted and reached into the water to pick one up, a rounded opaque white quartz about the diameter of a nickel. While I was down there, I picked up a few palm-sized pieces of broken plastic. The quartz went into my pocket, and the plastic into a grocery bag I carried in my jacket pocket.

When I looked up Chen was looking at me. "What did you put in your pocket?"

I showed him the rock. "It's quartz, I think."

"Why?"

"Because it's white."

"I meant why'd you keep it."

"Because it's pretty."

"What do you do with it?"

I didn't know how to answer. "I look at it."

"Is it a collection? Do you figure out all their names from a book? And keep them in their own box or drawer, with labels? Or just in that bowl on the table?"

I laughed. "If I'm lucky, I remember to take them out of my pocket when I get back to the house." Besides the bowl on the table, I had bowls in the living room and on my bedroom dresser. A row of rocks lined the windowsill of the kitchen. Others probably lingered in places I'd ceased to see.

"What if you're not lucky?"

"I find them thunk-ka-thunking in the dryer after I wash my jeans."

He threw a rock, a three-skipper, then turned back. "That's not a real collection, if you don't learn what they are and label them and have a place for them."

"I still keep them, which I think makes them a collection even if they're not like in a museum. I'll show you when we get back. Oh look, it's almost lunchtime."

On the walk up to the house, we talked collections. Using "we" loosely.

"I used to collect Pokémon cards. And in my game, Natatorium, I have lots of bonus awards, one of every kind. But they aren't things." He listed all the kinds of awards and then skipped ahead. He did remember to stop at the asphalt turnaround to check for cars before crossing. He waited for me at the steeper section that was technically the house's backyard. "Ryan used to have things. Lots at his Mum's house, but some stuff at our house, too. Like a trophy from school."

"Where is it now?"

"Still in his room. He and his mum both died, when Daddy did."

"I know. I'm sorry."

"Mum said maybe someday she'll box it up for Grandmother

and Gumpy. Maybe they'd want it."

"Is that your father's parents?"

He nodded. "Ry always said he was their favourite grandson."

His tone didn't hold resentment, but I still wanted to argue on his behalf. "Seems to me, the person most worried about being the favourite, isn't. I bet your grandparents love you and Ryan both the same. But, you know, different. Because you're different people." *Ugh, Simone, stop talking.*

He looked slantwise up at me and his lips twitched. "Unique, like everybody else?"

Delight rose from somewhere inside my chest. "Exactly."

"I kind of wish his stuff wasn't around, but where else would it go. Mum says sometimes it's hard to get rid of things. Or clean things out."

"Huh. She might have a point." I still had some of William's shirts on the top shelf of my closet, along with the sheets that had been on the bed the day he died, all folded neatly but unwashed. The rest of the house was full, too. Large-framed pictures hung on the living room walls—David's high school graduation photo, one of William and Joyce with David, and a smaller one of William and me at our wedding. I didn't really see them anymore. They'd become wallpaper.

In the middle of making sandwiches, I remembered. "Oh, hey—see the bowl of rocks in the living room? They're part of my collection, too. And these here." I pointed at the window row.

He stood at the sink, picking up and putting down each rock. "Why do you keep them?"

"To look at. They're pretty."

"They're rocks." Pause.

"Yes. I enjoy looking at them."

"Are you gonna look at every rock everywhere?"

I answered at random. "Maybe."

"There's a lot of rocks in the world."

"Doesn't every rock deserve to be looked at?" *Does that ever sound stupid.*

I watched him thinking about the rocks the whole time he ate his sandwich and potato chips and pushed the raw carrots around on his plate. Meanwhile, I wondered how to make another round of leaf-raking sound appealing. If we had any hope of getting to the fun stuff, we had to keep working.

But sometimes I made things harder than they need to be.

"Ready for more? It's time to drive the wheelbarrow." And off we went.

I worked more than he did, but I liked the work. Raking leaves and filling the wheelbarrow felt satisfying, like bringing order from chaos. Between wheeling loads to the dump pile, Chen dug holes in the beach.

Working gave me mental space into which Martin surfaced. What was the likelihood that my father had a brother? None— well, slim at best. Maybe Martin was another thing I was making too hard.

...

About five on Saturday, Jessica called. Chen's part of the conversation was "fine," "yeah," "fine," "okay." He told her about his notebook and his screen time and Job.

I went into the living room so he could complain in private, if he wanted. He whispered a little and then came into the living room.

"Love you, Mum, see you soon, love you. Bye." He held the phone out to me and I saw a tear, but he turned his face away and wiped it with his sleeve before sitting again at his notebook.

"Hi, Simone, thanks again." Jessica had cleared any sadness from her voice.

"We're having a good time. At least I am."

"He seems to be, too. I think he was ready for something new."

"How has your trip been? Seen anything interesting so far?" I didn't want to pry, but maybe she needed someone to talk to.

Jessica laughed. "The flight was great. The ship sails tomorrow."

"Good. Well, I'm glad it's working out so well, for you and for us."

She effused about that a little too strongly, so grateful I'd do this for her and Chen, et and cetera, and then we hung up.

I didn't know her from a hole in the ground, but I knew widows. I recognized where she was: mostly going through the motions but surfacing periodically to take real interest in her surroundings. She was smart to take a trip, so near all those difficult occasions—anniversary, birthday, Mother's Day. Maybe she'd enjoy some of it.

"Aunt, why are you making those faces?"

"What faces?" I knew what he meant, though. "That was just me not saying things aloud."

"Does my face do that?" Concern creased his forehead.

"I haven't noticed it, but I'll let you know." He went back to his notebook, but I asked, "Did you like talking with your Mum?"

A shrug.

"It's okay to miss her."

He looked at me, blinking, his face full of patience. "I know that."

"Good." Over supper, I asked about what he'd done the previous summer, a time well before the accident. He talked about Ryan, and baseball, and how it was to live with a brother who was there only sometimes.

I found it mystifying. What would it be like to have a sibling—a sister, say? Like the women I knew at church, who went shopping and to movies with relatives. They hugged when they saw each other. Some took trips together, sisters and spouses, like double-dates. It seemed exotic, though these women were all ordinary women, capri pants in the summer, fleece jackets in spring and fall. Much like me.

Beyond having a sister, what would it be like to lose one? And were brothers different? I had no way to know.

Maybe even that much remembering was too much for Chen. After supper and screen time, I read more of Job aloud. Chen and I agreed that it wasn't fair for Job to lose everything, when he'd been doing everything right.

Chen seemed tired and went to bed without protest. For a while, all was quiet, but when I checked an hour later, I heard him sniffling.

At the end of the bed, I put my hand on the covers, over his foot. "Hey, bud. You okay?"

He rubbed at his eyes and sniffed, then nodded.

"Bad dream?" No reaction. "I have them sometimes. Usually I'm late to something."

Sniff. "Mine's about the accident."

I nodded. "It hurts to think about. Even for me. I keep thinking about that driver, all alone. And everybody else, like you, who misses family now."

I handed Chen a tissue, and he wiped his eyes and handed it back to me.

"Anything I can get you? A drink of water?"

A quick shake of his head.

"Okay then. You know where to find me. Good night."

A quiet "G'night" and another sniff.

On my way to bed later, I looked in again. He seemed to be asleep. Our first full day, done. Only two, or about a million, more to go.

SUNDAY

SIMONE

The next morning, Chen was cheerful. Which was good, because we were going to church. When I told him so, he sagged a bit, though after he ate toast and juice he put on long pants and a shirt with a collar, all without complaint.

In return, he got to have screen time before we left, and he voiced only a small "aw" when I told him it was time to get his shoes on. Apparently, he was saving up his objections to share in the car.

"Aunt Sim-m-m-mka."

After a pause: "Ye-e-e-ss?"

He finally got it out: "Why-y-y do we have to go to church?"

I glanced over. His sullen face matched his voice. I weighed my options. He might be staying with me, but that didn't mean I belonged to him 100 percent of the time. I had other things to tend to. Life things. Like time with adults or quiet time alone.

But. *He has a right to his feelings*, I reminded myself (I'd read it in a book somewhere), *and I don't have to agree with them to hear them.*

Something about the movement of the car helped me recognize his mood. When I was about ten, my mother would demand I go to the grocery store with her, promising "Just a head of lettuce and milk." After depriving me of my basic freedom for an excruciating hour, we'd have two weeks' worth of random food. I'd make some of it into meals for myself, but much of it rotted while she drank. I pointed out the waste of both food and time, but she ignored both. I felt powerless: literally, along for the ride.

My silence got Chen's attention. He stirred his arms around as if he might ask again.

Finally, I knew what I wanted to say. "I'm going to church because I want to. So technically, you're the only one who 'has to' go. It's maybe not fair, but you know what, lots of life isn't fair. As I'm sure you've noticed."

I didn't say that there was a little part of me, a teeny little part, who wanted Rev. Phil and Carole to see that Chen and I were doing very well together, thank you.

"Yeah. And I feel lots better." He sounded as annoyed as a TV teenager.

"You and your Mum used to come to church. I saw you there a couple of months ago."

He looked out the window. "We never went before, when Daddy—before. He always said religion was stupid. People make up stuff to feel better, is what he said. We quit coming because Mum said it might be good and everything, but doing it wore her out. I think Daddy's right. Religion's stupid."

I stayed silent in case he wasn't done thinking.

He sighed. "I guess everyplace does seem to have religion and gods. So maybe everybody is stupid." He kicked the underneath of the glovebox.

"Easy with that kicking, tiger." He stopped. "Why don't you ask me why I want to go to church?"

"Because I don't care."

"Oh. Okay." I certainly wasn't asking him any more about why he didn't want to go. It was a silent drive all the way to the four-way stop at Hodder and Arundel.

Even then, he was annoyed. "Okay. *Why* do you want to go to church?"

"Actually, I'm not sure, but I've enjoyed thinking about it."

"You're weird." Then he muttered something about rocks.

"Thanks for sharing." I never liked being called weird, but it was mild, nothing like your beloved husband's only son calling you "batshit crazy."

As we approached the intersection on the north side of town where five churches opened their doors to welcome the faithful, I gently reminded Chen about the service. We'd sit in the pews for the first part. He'd participate in the children's time appropriately, meaning he would not answer all the questions or drown out the other kids. He could choose to go down to Sunday School with the other kids or stay upstairs to listen to the sermon.

"Yeah, like I'd want to do *that*."

"Well, Rev. Phil's pretty smart and good with computers."

As the organist played the prelude, I took a silent moment while admiring the morning light through stained glass to congratulate myself for not throttling Chen. So far.

As I suspected, Rev. Phil's iPad caught Chen's attention, and the three or four other kids trooped downstairs without him. Rev. Phil had video clips about quantum physics. His point that morning was that science answers questions in one realm and religion addresses other human needs, and we shouldn't confuse the two.

At lunch later, I let Chen chatter to Rev. Phil about Indigenous traditions while I ate.

I heard Phil say my name. "I'll bet Simone has told you 'Life isn't fair.'"

I looked up, teeth gritted. "Maybe even this morning."

Phil threw me a smile. "Well, it's especially unfair that we can't know the reasons why things happen. But sometimes there aren't reasons, except physics. Like this."

He set the salt and pepper shakers in front of us.

"I can put them side-by-side. If I tried to stack them, I'd make a mess. They can't sit in the exact same spot on the table at the same time, at least in our world. That's how and why things happen. Maybe there isn't some religious reason. If Simone backed her car into someone else's, she might choose to see it as God telling her to be more careful, but that would be her choice. Maybe it happened because two things can't be in the same place at the same time."

Chen smirked at the example, and I defended myself. "I've never backed into anybody. So how come, if God doesn't make bad stuff happen, he gets credit for good stuff?"

Rev. Phil smiled. "These are the important questions."

I looked at Chen, who scowled at a few French fries left on his plate, and spoke for both of us. "I'm not hearing answers."

"Yeah," Chen added. "This is why Daddy said religion was a waste of time. It was a big fight with Grandmother and Gumpy, because they said they raised him better than that and he should make me go."

Rev. Phil tapped his empty coffee cup on the table. "I do like it when people come to church, but only if they want to. I see it as a place to investigate questions, not find answers."

I thought briefly of Job, and how that story didn't make me feel any better at all. Rev. Phil had recommended a book but also warned me that Job would be tricky going. I tried to keep the gloom out of my voice. "You ready to go, Chen? I don't know about you, but I've got all the questions I can handle."

As we left, Rev. Phil cheered up Chen with compliments

for the intriguing lunch discussion. We both felt better after our stop at the bookstore, where I got an easier-to-read book of Bible stories, along with that book Rev. Phil suggested, and Chen got a chocolate-chip cookie. Okay, so did I.

At home, we changed into work clothes and went down to the lake to throw rocks into the water and enjoy the warm afternoon sun. I brought up church again.

"Here's why I go to church, Chen. Because it's full of people, like Rev. Phil, who try to do what they think is right."

He threw a three-skip rock. "Does it make you happy? My grandparents go and they don't seem very happy."

"Everybody goes for different reasons, I guess."

"I still think God is stupid. And I only asked because you made me." He threw another rock, hard.

I worked hard to keep my voice mild. "I know you don't really care. But I do enjoy talking sometimes." I walked down the beach to throw more rocks at my annoyance. Maybe it would dissipate.

Instead, I heard my mother laughing. She sat under the big spruce at the edge of the sandy part of the beach. For years I'd tried to understand why she was so mean as to laugh at my frustrations. I had to give her points for consistency—equally annoying both in this world and the next.

Carmen said, "It's not his fault you're mad. Cut him a break." She looked from Chen to me. "He's just a kid. They don't notice or appreciate things. You never did."

Screw you, I wanted to say, but didn't. Chen might notice. And why give her the satisfaction? I had to admit, she was also right. *Dammit*.

"Aunt." Chen was quite a ways down the beach.

I swallowed my impatience. "Yes?"

"You're making those faces again."

"If you're done throwing rocks, we can go back to the house."

"Can I play my game?"

"For an hour. Then you should read something with pages. Like a book."

"I didn't bring any."

"I'll find one for you." Too bad I hadn't thought of it earlier, when we were in the bookstore. Maybe he'd like Calvin and Hobbes. I'd hunt one out from William's bookshelf in our bedroom.

On our way back to the house, he ran ahead and grabbed a stick, then bent over to poke something under a tree and walked on, face up to the sky.

I smiled in spite of my irritation. It was good to see him acting like a kid. I wish I didn't have to be the adult *all* the time.

For supper, I pulled a pizza from the freezer. Later, as I put our dishes in the dishwasher, I pointed at Chen. "Notebook time." He complied without a single complaint.

Yielding to an impulse, I found a notebook and pen in the den. Maybe it was time to think, in an organized way, about Martin and the possibility of having cousins. It was far easier to daydream about them—fun, even. I could pretend I wasn't so socially inept. Like I wouldn't be one of those ladies who lies dead for weeks before her body is found.

But I did have questions. Several. And I should face those before my cousin fantasies made me do something stupid, like trust someone untrustworthy.

Chen looked up when I settled across the table.

I said only, "Hey, it works for you, maybe it will for me, too." He seemed to like it.

And whatever tiff we'd had about church seemed to be over.

MARTIN

"Charm her," Mr. Smith had said on Saturday. Martin could think only of candy and flowers. Candy seemed pretty complicated. He understood from TV commercials that most women liked chocolate, but what kind? Bars, chips, fancy assortments in boxes or gold foil? He knew more about plants, from his time in landscaping. Flowers were easier and safer.

Or so he thought, until he stood overwhelmed even among the meagre choices in the floral department of Harbour Foods. The prices weren't bad. Mother's Day was a week away, so a dozen cut roses were on a special sale. But Simone wasn't his mother. It'd be weird to give her Mother's Day flowers. The other bouquets looked cheap, not just inexpensive. Garish and all the same, in their artificially bright colours and plastic wrap.

He turned to the small potted plants. Giving her a cactus seemed rude. And she had one already in the kitchen. Something else, then, maybe an ornamental pepper. Martin chose a bland cream-coloured pot holding a healthy-looking pepper plant that wouldn't need repotting too soon. Heading toward the Express till, Martin noticed a tall, impassive man in a black windbreaker and tuque leaning against the wall near the door.

Martin blinked a couple of times and turned down an aisle at random. He circled back toward the tills just in time to see a slender young guy come in. Martin was sure it was the kid—same hoodie, same skinny build.

The man at the door stood straighter. The kid looked over the sandwiches in the refrigerator case before finally turning to the hot soups and ladling some into a cup. As the kid came deeper into the store to pay, the man at the door casually shifted position so he could observe the kid from his post.

Martin, lurking near the frozen waffles, watched it all. Security. The store had hired security guards. Geez. Even if the store lost a roast chicken every day, the guard would cost more.

The kid paid at the express till and headed out the door with his cardboard container of warm soup. He looked right at the guard, rattling the change in his hand, cheeky. The guard nodded without smiling.

Then the guard looked at Martin. Martin looked back. Carrying his ornamental pepper, he strolled over to the deli and picked out a turkey-and-swiss sandwich. After paying, he passed the guard, meeting his eyes and lifting his chin.

Outdoors, the kid was sitting near the door, out of the wind.

"Here." Martin handed him the sandwich and, while the kid turned a sullen face toward him, checked the bruise on the kid's cheek. Still there, but fading. And nothing new. Good. He walked off quickly, the pepper plant tucked safely under his arm.

...

After that night's meeting, Martin helped fold chairs and thanked the night's leader before heading upstairs. Alex, from last week, wasn't around. Zipping his jacket, Martin said goodbye to the smokers and headed back to his motel. Within a block, he heard his name.

"Hey. Martin."

Martin looked. It was the security guard from Harbour Foods. "What."

"I'm Ken. So thanks for the info—."

Martin interrupted, "You said that kid was your nephew and you were looking out for him. You never said I'd be getting him in trouble."

"He's not in any more trouble than he was before. And besides, what do you care?" Ken held out an envelope.

Good question. Martin wasn't sure. "It's just—I thought you were going to help him. Maybe get him off the street and out of trouble. But a security guard? You're making it worse."

Ken shrugged. "He keeps bad company. Birds of a feather and all that." He tilted his head at Martin. "And none of this is your business." He waved the envelope close to Martin's face.

"Well, keep that envelope." Martin tried to brush past Ken, but Ken grabbed his arm.

In a kind voice that belied his tightening grip, Ken said, "No more sandwiches, okay? No more helping out a young criminal who's responsible for significant business losses."

He tucked the envelope in Martin's jacket pocket. After a final squeeze that Martin felt through his jacket sleeve, Ken let go. "See you around." He strolled off.

Martin headed downhill toward the motel, frowning over the conversation. He felt the envelope in his pocket. Why did he take it?

On the other hand, why did he even care about this kid? Martin had known plenty of people who'd made their lives harder than they had to be. His father, for one. Maybe even himself. This kid, he was young, though. And was driven to steal to eat. It didn't seem fair. Seemed like there'd be other ways for him to find food.

Soup kitchens. Community outreach.

But what did Martin know. Nothing about this city. Nothing about that kid. If he kept worrying about stuff that wasn't his problem, he'd drive himself right around the bend.

By the time he slid his key into the lock of his room, he felt better. One thing he knew for sure: he wasn't doing any more work for Ken. Martin's job now was to stay uninvolved. On the sidelines. Luckily, that was Martin's specialty.

CHEN

Notebook: Sunday nite
Bein on a team with Daddy
Church yuck (Ryan) (me to)
Revrend Phil + Indigenous traditions
Nightmare almost

While I was writing my list, Aunt Simka got a notebook. She's sitting across the table. If she tries to read upside down, I bet she makes those same faces like when she's not saying things.

Daddy's face moves like that. When he tells Mum a funny lie as a joke, he makes his nostrils big and his eyes open wider. Or he did. In the past.

Mum never noticed, though. I think. I wonder if Daddy knew he gave it all away.

When I was a little kid he made big faces behind her back to let me know me and him were on a team, even when Mum got mad.

Before the accident, Sunday nite was always my bestest time.

Especially after Ryan went home. Just the three of us—Mum, Daddy, and me—ate Sunday supper.

Daddy and I would be the team again, and sometimes we'd get to have special sandwiches, Sloppy Joes like Gramps taught Mum to make. Ryan didn't like them. Mum made them as a treat to welcome our normal lives back. And for a few days Ryan wasn't on our team any more. He had to be on his own team again. Or one with his Mum, maybe. I don't know.

I guess Sloppy Joes were Gramps's favourite Sunday night supper. Mum said his name was Joe. It was confusing when I was a kid because wasn't his name Gramps? And anyway, he was already dead. He died of sickness and being old. A picture of him and me when I was a baby is still stuck to the side of the fridge at home.

So maybe Ryan is on Gramps's team, now that they're both dead. Except Ry and Gramps weren't relatives. Not really.

Mum explained this. Me and Ry are relatives with Gumpy because Gumpy is Daddy's father and Gumpy's our grandfather. I'm relatives with Gramps because he's Mum's father, but Daddy isn't relatives with Gramps, and Ry isn't either.

Now Gumpy is sick but still alive, and Daddy's dead. So maybe Ry doesn't need Gramps for a team. Maybe just the two of them, Ry and Daddy, are a team forever.

I don't like that. I wish Daddy didn't die at all. And I don't like how Daddy died with Ryan. I would like to draw a line through it or even erase it, but that wouldn't make it go away.

Dr. S says Daddy didn't want to die. But she also said I can't help how I feel. So I can say it feels like Daddy picked Ryan to be on his team forever.

Not me. Ryan.

That's how it feels.

Sunday nights are different now. For a while after the accident, Mum and me, we had Sunday night dinner with Daddy's family. Sometimes out at the farm and sometimes in town at Grandmother and Gumpy's senior apartment. Auntie Sarah and those cousins I don't like were there. It seemed like they were extra-mean. Mum said that was because everybody was sad, and we all had to be understanding.

But on the way home in the car one time, Mum said, "Chenoweth, sometimes I just cannot deal with that family."

She said that a lot, actually. But that time she meant it. Later that week, she said on the phone to Grandmother, "We can't come, we are so busy, there's just been one thing and another."

I wondered what those things were but I didn't ask. We didn't have to eat with them anymore and that was the best thing of all. Not as good as before, with Sloppy Joes, but better.

...

Sometimes I talk to Ry like he's here with me. He doesn't get to talk. That's nice.

When he talked he complained a lot. Like if Ry was here he'd say it was stupid we had to go to church today. Daddy too.

Mum and me went to church after the funerals. The kids there were okay. I didn't know any from school, but they still knew about the accident and me and Mum. I guess they came to the funerals or the big service at the auditorium, the one for everybody who died. We had to leave that service early because my stomach hurt and Mum couldn't stop crying.

A couple of the kids at church were Grade 6. They whispered about me. And that one said something mean about Aunt Simka. After a while, we went to church sometimes and then mostly not and finally we just stopped. I was okay with that.

And today Ry was right, church was stupid. Like school.

Talking with Rev. Phil later was okay. We talked about Indigenous traditions some. It's interesting because I know a lot about traditions all over North and Central America and I guess Rev. Phil does too.

Sometimes I feel like everybody's talking about the accident even if they're not talking about it. Like the people at church, they all want to say something nice, but it's weird. It feels kind of like the kids at school, how they couldn't go back to normal and ignore me like usual. They ignored me different.

...

I started to have one of my nightmares last night, the one with Ry's fingers on fire, and I can't save Daddy.

Dr. Samuelson and I talked about that dream lots. I started to have them less. She said, "That's normal. You might have bad dreams from time to time. But hopefully less."

I didn't have it for a long time and last night I didn't have it all the way, just like I knew it was going to be next so I woke up.

I had tears but not a lot. And when I was awake I did what Dr. S. said about picturing Ry being safe and Daddy being safe and feeling safe myself.

For Ry I think about him at his Mum's house, and for me I think about Sunday night when Ry's gone home and Mum and Daddy and I eat Sloppy Joes. I went back to sleep.

Bad dreams from time to time is still a lot of bad dreams. I wish I would have that dream no times. Dr. S says she hopes that too. But the main thing is I am safe.

Simka came to see if I was OK when I had tears.

We've been doing lots of things. I was afraid she might be real religious like Grandmother because we talked about gods that first day, and we've been reading about Job. And we went to church. But she seems more like a regular person, mostly happy. Not like Grandmother.

Tomorrow or the next day Aunt says we're taking shudders

off the camp so we can go indoors down there. That will be interesting.

Maybe shudders are hard work and I'll be too tired to dream anymore.

MONDAY

MARTIN

When Martin rang Simone's doorbell on Monday, a boy answered.

"Good morning." In spite of his surprise, Martin looked him over so he could describe him later to Mr. Smith. Pale skin, blondish-brown hair. Age ten, though that was a guess.

"Hi." The boy, in turn, looked Martin up and down before running back toward the kitchen. "Aunt Simka, there's a man here. With a plant."

Martin stood on the porch, calculating. *Aunt?* No way Simone could have nieces or nephews. Mr. Smith's folders claimed Simone was an only child. So who the hell was this kid, and how could he be her nephew? And anyway, wasn't she too old?

Don't panic. The kid returned with Simone, who was drying her hands on a towel.

"Hello, Martin."

Not exactly welcoming. He held out the plant. "Good morning, Cousin! This is for you. The peppers are just ornamental, of course, but pretty colours. I saw them yesterday, and they were so cheerful I couldn't resist them, and then I was out for a drive and thought I'd just stop in. You know, for a visit."

She took the plant. "Yeah, okay. Come in. Coffee? You've missed the oatmeal, but we have scones today." She headed toward the kitchen.

Martin slipped off his shoes. Driving out, he'd decided to ask for a tour of the camp. That should be a natural lead-in to the question of buying her property or selling her a condo. He'd brought the information about condos he'd printed out before he left home, but he'd decided to leave it in the car. Less pushy.

And, a bonus: with that kid around, Simone probably hadn't thought about cheek swabs, which was good, because on Saturday Mr. Smith had hung up before Martin had asked about DNA tests.

Now in his sock feet, he looked up. The kid, who'd been standing in front of him, stuck out his hand. "I'm Chenoweth Robertson. You can call me Chen."

Chenoweth? Chen? Odd, but whatever. "I'm Martin. I'm Simone's, uh, cousin. On her father's side."

After they shook hands, Chen stood on one foot and then the other. "I'm her—she's my—aunt, but nothing, really. I'm staying with her for the weekend. Mum's gone to scatter Daddy's ashes in Alaska. Some of them. He died in that car wreck in January." He yelled toward the kitchen. "Hey Aunt, are we related?"

The answer floated back on a wave of good-smelling baking. "Sure. You're my Chen. Do you want some juice?"

"Yippee!" Chen ran-and-slid on the linoleum into the kitchen.

Martin followed. All over again, the view out over the lake took his breath away. "Wow. That's beautiful. Do you ever get used to it?"

Simone had set the ornamental pepper on the counter beside the sink. Now, a plate of scones in one hand and the coffeepot in the other, she also looked through the kitchen window. "I don't always remember to look, but when I do, it makes all the crap of life seem not too important." She set the plate on the table. "Sit. Help yourself."

Chen already perched in a chair on the table's long side. From the chair at the end, Martin could see not only the lake and peninsula across the bay but also a small deck and grassy yard that plateaued for a few metres before dropping steeply. Simone poured him coffee. He split a scone to sandwich some butter and looked at the sparkling lake while the butter melted.

"So, does the whole lake freeze?" He'd thought up this question earlier. If he was interested in her lake, maybe she'd be friendlier.

Simone, absorbed in her own scone and butter, answered absently. "Sometimes. Not usually. Superior's a big lake. This bay, you know, Thunder Bay the bay not the town, almost always does. Right across at the mouth, and all the way northeast up to Bay's End." She paused. "The water's shallow up there. Back in the day, my mother and I played in the waves there a few times. Giant rollers from town break on the sandbars. It's all private land now."

A smile! It's working. "So when does the ice leave?"

"Depends. The surface gets rotten in late March or early April, and the spring storms break it up and blow it out toward the big lake and then back in. One year along the south shore, that's Wisconsin and Michigan, they had ice chunks on the beach for their Memorial Day holiday, the weekend after the May Long. But this year, it's cleared out already, with May just getting started."

The Chen kid said, "There's still some crusty snow back under the trees. I poked it yesterday with my stick to make it melt faster. But we've been wading already!"

"Wasn't it cold?"

"Freezing. On a really sunny day and everything. Aunt Simka said I almost froze her feet right off!" He giggled until Simone narrowed her right eye at him.

Martin trudged along the line of questioning he'd rehearsed. "So you must like the winter, unless you go south for a bit. Seriously, you've never thought of snowbirding?"

Simone shook her head. "I like it here. All year." She smiled a little. "Though some years, late snow does lose its appeal. But don't we all, from time to time?"

Martin laughed a little, pretty sure she'd meant it as a joke. "So, I maybe mentioned it before. My father bought a condo in Florida years back. Left it to me." He watched her carefully. Did she believe Martin could have inherited that kind of money? Was he pulling it off?

"Just you? Not to your sister?"

"Oh, her too. But I'm buying her out. She'd rather get a place closer to London."

"I hear Portugal is popular with people in the UK."

Martin didn't know anything of the kind, though he was pretty sure Portugal was somewhere in Europe. At least she didn't ask questions about his own condo (*that you don't have,* Harry pointed out). It seemed a good time to change the subject. "Do people go ice fishing out here?"

Simone frowned. "Yep. Some idiots drive their cars right out there. Even in March, sometimes. They trust the ice more than I do. Though usually they use snow machines, not cars." She turned to Martin. "Have you gone ice fishing?"

Had he? In real life yes, but Martin wasn't sure what to say. "A little, here and there."

And then the question he dreaded. "Oh, so where, exactly?"

Martin stuck to the truth. Mostly. "A little lake up near Ottawa. With friends, and their friends. That type of thing."

"I see."

Uneasy, Martin sipped his coffee and added more sugar. Had Simone faded out again? She stared out the window, blinking. From the corner of his eye, Martin watched Chen. The kid swung his legs under the table while looking at Simone, then out over the water, then back to Simone, then at Martin, chewing the whole time.

At last, Martin opened his scone—warm and flaky, leaps and bounds better than the crappy toast at the hotel. After he finished it, he licked his lips and proceeded with his sorta-plan.

"So, Simone, I don't know what you hoped to do this morning, but I was wondering about getting a tour. Your house and yard, even your place down by the lake? You have two places, right?"

Simone got up and stacked plates. "Yes, two. I'm flush with real estate. And sure, we were headed down that way anyway, to do some work." She looked at his sock feet. "If you don't mind muddy shoes, we can walk."

Martin fetched a pair of tennis shoes from the car. Back in the house, Simone and Chen already sat side-by-side on the bench in the entry hall, tying their shoes.

Simone pointed to the living room. "You can use a chair in there."

Martin entered the dim room cautiously, looking around as he slipped off one pair of shoes and tied the laces on the other. The living room gave the impression of tidy, clean comfort. To Martin's eye, most of the furniture was from the early 90s, but he didn't have time to inspect it or inventory her possessions. Not that he had a real reason to, besides curiosity.

At Simone's "Ready?" Martin jumped up to follow. And looked at the wall.

And tried not to do a double-take.

Wow. Um. Wow. Martin for the first time realized how little he really knew about Simone. Or about his assignment, either.

Because he had no idea, zero, none, why a picture of Mr. Smith would be hanging on the wall of Simone's living room.

• • •

The three of them headed through the back yard toward the steeper section, where a wide path led through sparse stands of poplar and balsam fir.

Driving up from Toronto, Martin had noticed a change in the trees. Through the Toronto suburbs and north to Barrie, he saw a lot of white pines. Their branches, spread like arms, drew your eyes toward the sky and made you think of nice things.

But here, farther north and west, he'd seen more spruce trees. They looked patchy near the tops, their branches dark, maybe tired of holding up their loads of needles and cones. And those balsam firs were every-damn-where, with branches stuck straight out, no grace to them at all.

Not welcoming and cheerful, like the white pines.

Spring up here was later, too. The poplars and birches were still leafless. The stands on hillsides, grown up in the wake of road construction or logging, were all the same colour, grey. But there'd come a day when you'd look at them from far off and notice something different. Maybe a different colour, a lighter grey in the trunks. And then, when you looked at that same hill five hours or maybe a day later, whoa, the leaves would have popped out to turn the whole hillside light green, nearly neon. Blink and you'd miss it.

If Martin did well enough with this assignment, he might still be around to see it happen. But what if, after this assignment, nothing changed in his life? He felt a flick of fear. What if he had to go back to iffy temporary jobs? He had to keep his wits. Figure out what was what.

Starting with Mr. Smith, who must be related to Simone somehow—otherwise, why would she have his picture on her wall? And it was definitely Mr. Smith. Oh, the young man in the photo wore a cap with a tassel. His face in the picture was softer, and he was smiling, but Martin was sure. And the man, the father—he was in that other picture of Simone, in the folder on his desk back at the hotel. Which made Mr. Smith Simone's stepson.

This relationship changed things, though he wasn't quite sure how. Until he figured it out, today wasn't a good day to bring up buying her land or push her about buying his condo in Florida. (*Still don't have it,* Harry reminded him.) That would take the pressure off. He could walk around on a couple of nice pieces of land and just talk to this strange lady and this kid, and enjoy himself.

He thought again of the white pines, lifting their arms to the sky. Martin had lost track of them somewhere. He'd seen the last one maybe near Sudbury or the Soo. But really, how can you know for sure you've seen the last of something? Another one might appear. Things could still surprise you. In a good way.

SIMONE

I wasn't surprised when Martin showed up. In fact, I didn't mind his presence—that is, I wouldn't, if I didn't also have Chen to think about. I hadn't been brave enough to try searching again for his father, or mine, but I'd enjoyed thinking I might have relatives. In theory.

But relative or not, and I wasn't one hundred percent sure yet either way, I knew better than to leave him alone with Chen.

I also wasn't surprised at Martin's interest in this place. When you live in the country, especially beside a lake, people say, "You're so lucky." But that's their fantasy of country life talking.

Take water. To wash their faces at night, they run water in the sink until it's warm, letting all that perfectly good cold water go right down the drain. They wash load after load of clothes, or even half-loads, without worry. They never consider wells that run dry or cantankerous septic systems that can freeze in a bitter, snowless winter.

Speaking of winter, it gets long. When it snows, city folks

sprinkle a little salt or sand on their steps and driveways, skip around with a plastic shovel for ten minutes, and they're done. Whereas I had an hour-long date with a snowblower every single storm. Come March, I was sick of it, far more so than I'd let on to Martin. In the spring—by which I mean well into April, while I waited for spring to show up—condos in Florida could look appealing. Martin wasn't wrong to ask about being a snowbird.

Then again, I was the kind of person who stood at the front window in winter, smiling at bulky-coated deer picking their way along my newly cleared driveway, as if they appreciated my hard work. I watched as dusk gathered, in case the lynx padded past in pursuit of a snowshoe hare.

I didn't even mind the un-pretty parts of winter. Early on, before winter properly arrives in December, the formerly glorious gold and orange leaves of October lie browning and drab on the paths, and it's hard to remember it's still autumn. And months later, as the winter ostensibly wanes, the snow might drip a little and the light might linger a little later every evening, but neither lets you believe in green leaves and flowers. I looked for blackbirds and ducks returning in the spring as I listened to the chatter of my year-round friends—the ravens and whiskey jacks.

Today, Carmen had drowned out almost everything. She'd shown up and urged me to ask Martin more questions about ice fishing. But my heart wasn't in it.

The three of us made good time downhill. Once we were past the steepest part, the path was less rock (and mud, it being early May) and more of what we mowed. We called it grass, but it was more wildflowers and weeds of various types mixed with clover and other ground cover.

Chen found a stick and poked at grass tufts all the way down the hill, while Martin made conversation.

Scratch that. Martin asked questions. "So how did you get from Missouri to Canada, anyway? Especially Thunder Bay. Why here?"

"I didn't move to Thunder Bay. I moved to a place I loved. It just happened to be near Thunder Bay."

I let him think for a minute and then relented. "Here's the short version. My mother was born in Port Arthur, now Thunder Bay. Her father built the summer camp just downhill here. I've come up every summer since I was a kid. Finally, when I was no longer young but not yet old, I got smart and moved here. And met my husband. And here I remain."

"Ah."

That was all he said, but I could hear him thinking other things, urban and suburban things, even southern Ontario things. "People do move here on purpose, you know. It's lovely, for one thing."

"Sure." A pause. "You're a ways out of town. Do you go in often?"

"Not every day. I like museums and music, and I go to church. But it takes a lot to get me into town, especially when the days are long and the lake is so beautiful."

"And your husband—William, I think you said? But you didn't take his name?"

I shot him a look. "There was no need."

"Sorry. I assumed."

"Many do. He was William Harrison, widower of Joyce. Their son, David."

"Any family on his side?"

"No. No sisters, no brothers. One of the things we had in common: We were only children of only children." I paused. "Or so we thought, of course."

Martin looked blank.

I went on, "Then you came along, and now I have an uncle and a cousin."

"Right. Two cousins, even!"

I considered asking about his sister, but I decided to leave him in charge of the conversation. The silence lingered.

I cleared my throat. "So have you been to the condo in Florida yourself?"

"Florida?" His forehead puckered. "Yeah, with my father. It's great sometimes, but I like Canada well enough. I don't think I'd use the condo enough to keep it. It doesn't suit my lifestyle." He smiled as if he were proud of himself.

By this time, we'd come to the asphalt circle at the end of the access road. The driveway to the camp branched off it.

I kept up my orientation lecture. If he really was my cousin, he'd need to know some things. "William owned the house and property up to this point. Someday—not today, and I hope not soon—it will go to my stepson." I took a breath to banish thoughts of David gleefully rubbing his hands together at my death. "This circle turnaround went in maybe 30 years ago, but the first dirt road from the highway came down decades earlier, in the 1940s. Before that, my grandfather cleared a path and spread gravel on it. These days, they plow these asphalt access roads all winter, like a neighbourhood in town."

Chen had paused at the edge and looked for cars before running across to the two-track camp driveway. He waited there while we crossed the asphalt, then headed off ahead again.

"Not too far ahead, kiddo," I called. He slowed, still poking at who-knows-what. I said to Martin, "He has to stay where I can see him, in case of bears."

"Bears?" Martin's eyes widened. "Really?"

"Yes, black bears. Usually you can smell them before you see them. They'll avoid us, but we have to be careful with our garbage. They're hungry at this time of year."

His eyes darted left and right, examining the bush at either edge of the path. "Bears, okay. Anything else I should know about?"

"Probably not. The lynx from last winter hasn't been around for a month or so. Some eagles are nesting over there, but you're probably too big for them to carry off."

He looked at me.

"That was a joke. About the eagles. They probably aren't *that* strong. I've seen one flying with a rabbit in its talons, though."

He shook his head. "But everything looks so—civilized. Suburban, almost."

"Yeah, well. Even in the summer, when the population doubles out here, animals are still around. You'll see bear stories on the news all summer. Wildlife isn't all fawns and bunnies, you know."

"I guess not."

"Not part of your lifestyle, huh." I wondered about a guy who ice-fished but didn't think about bears. At last, we were at the camp, with the lake beyond. Chen was already throwing rocks, ka-thunking them to raise a splash.

At the beach, we went through the required ooohs and ahhhs. Even Martin could appreciate the beauty of our secluded bay. To the right, a rocky point sheltered our curving pebbly beach from wind, waves, and too much neighbourliness. William and I had cleared a little in front of the camp proper, but in other places, we'd left most of the undergrowth alone, opening only narrow footpaths through the birch and spruce.

Over to the left—north and east—a cliff towered over the water and stretched back into the bush. The neighbour in that direction owned twenty acres, rocky with boggy patches but a lovely bay at the far end, where he'd built his own home and garden.

Our bay stayed private in both directions. Except for water traffic, which wouldn't appear for another month at least, we could pretend we had the lake to ourselves.

I didn't mind hearing compliments, and Martin's admiration was all I could hope for. I basked in it while Chen tossed a short chunk of driftwood into the water and tried to hit it with rocks.

I decided it was my turn to grill Martin. "Before, you mentioned something about Florida not suiting your lifestyle? What is that, exactly? What do you do for a living?"

He looked out over the lake. "Um. I've done a thing or two, in my day."

Carmen appeared a few metres down the beach, wearing a red floral sundress and sandals. She sat in a folding beach chair, the kind with woven webbed seats, and fanned herself with a straw sun hat, suitable for Florida. "Can't argue with that."

Chen selected rocks with more care and tried to skip them.

Martin crossed his arms across his belly and looked up, as if an answer might float across the pale blue sky. "For a time, I was in advertising."

"False," said my mother.

"A few real estate transactions."

I smiled. "Oh, then you're a broker."

Carmen shouted, "False!"

Martin shook his head. "Nothing formal. I knew a guy that needed a place, and I knew a guy with a place."

"A matchmaker, then." Martin looked doubtful. I added, "A referral service. Matching needs and solutions."

His forehead relaxed. "Yes, that's it exactly. People have needs and I find solutions." He stuck his hands into his pockets.

Hands-in-pockets was supposed to mean he was hiding something. But maybe his hands were just chilly, like mine.

His voice softened. "I sold furniture for a while but more recently I've done a lot of construction jobs. I'm not licensed, but I know my way around basic carpentry. Home repair. I can't do new plumbing but I can replace stuff. Flooring. Tiles. I'm good at landscaping. You design it, I can dig and lay out flagstones. I can do a deck, all of it—foundations, concrete pads, carpentry. Planter beds. Even rough stuff, taking out trees and the stumps. Putting in irrigation systems. Miscellaneous, I'd say."

The surprise in Carmen's voice was obvious. "This is actually true."

Though I could predict his answer, I asked anyway. "Do you

work for a company?"

He hesitated. "No. My buddy's a contractor. I take some of his smaller odd jobs. He has licenses and whatnot and supervises."

"Ah." Sketchy, but not criminal—he had a driver's license, at least.

Chen broke the silence. "What are we doing today, Simka?"

I considered. Though I really wanted to get the shutters off the windows, my hands were chilled enough to make handling small screws difficult. Besides, Chen needed something right this moment, and Martin and I weren't done talking.

"How about raking the beach? Go get that brown rake I used yesterday, and I'll show you."

He headed toward the camp breezeway. *What a good kid.*

Martin said, "I'm sorry. I've imposed enough. I don't want to keep you two from your day. I'll just hike up myself and head out. Thanks so much for showing me around."

He held out his hand and I shook it. "How long will you be in the area?" I felt we still had some unfinished business, though I wasn't sure quite what it could be.

"Oh, another week or so, at least. So I'll see you again, if that's okay." He didn't stop for me to answer. "And now, the house is unlocked? I left my shoes inside."

"Yes, the front door is unlocked." *We just waltz around the countryside with our doors unlocked.* I mean, we did, but Martin didn't need to know that.

"Oh good. I'll just pop in and grab them. See you!" He nodded and headed up the winding driveway, quickly disappearing from view.

Carmen screeched, "You're letting a stranger spend time all alone inside your house? That's okay with you?"

It wasn't, but I couldn't leave Chen alone. I hadn't been kidding about the bears. If Chen had been older, or if I knew him better—if we had more experience together, if I knew he'd be careful, or any of a million other ifs—he'd be fine alone. But I couldn't risk it.

On the other hand, Martin alone in the house? A stranger, if a relative? Free to snoop through my private business? Also a risk.

Gah. No good options.

Chen reappeared with the garden rake. "This one?"

"Yes, that's it. Hey, kiddo, I think I should go back up to the house."

"Aw, we just got here!"

"I know. Listen, can you stay here by yourself for fifteen minutes? Indoors?" I couldn't believe the words I was saying. I glanced at my mother, who pointed toward Martin with increasing urgency. *Wouldn't it be nice if she were useful? Like willing to maybe keep an active eye on Chen, or go check on Martin herself?* No such luck.

Chen's face brightened. "Can I?"

"Promise you won't hurt yourself?"

"Promise!"

"Okay. Come inside. Maybe you can find a book." If nothing else, some books from my childhood would be there. The light coming in the doorway brightened the interior, even with the shutters over windows. In just under a minute, I'd pulled a chair for Chen nearer the door—also, as it happened, near my mother, not that he knew that. She'd left the beach to sit in a chair at this table, which also held her sun hat. Now she moved a chair farther away from him, annoyed at his presence. Chen headed toward the bookshelf in the main room.

I called, "I'll be back soon." Neither responded.

I hustled up the path, trying to catch up to Martin. As I went, I picked up my pace, but I didn't see him ahead on the driveway, and when I got to the asphalt circle, I couldn't see him on the hill, either.

By the time I got to the steepest part, nerves made my breaths quick. My heart pounded. I stopped, hands on hips, to recover until I heard a car door slam and the engine turn over. Heedless of breath, I nearly flew up the rest of the hill. Tires crunched as the car maneuvered in the driveway. I came around the side of the house in time to see Martin's car turn left onto Lakeshore Drive.

Too late. Again.

Panting, I turned back downhill. I wanted to be sure Chen was safe, but running downhill wouldn't have been safe for my own arms and legs. I contented myself with a quick walk, listening for a black bear's growls and the answering screams of a boy.

By the time I got back down the hill, I'd worked myself into a state. My legs shook when I flung open the front door of the camp.

And there sat Chen, right where I'd left him, deep into *The Hound of the Baskervilles*. Relief flooded through me and eased my breathing.

He looked up. "Can I finish this chapter before we do anything else?"

"Sure thing." I sat at the table. *Relax, Simone.*

My mother snickered. "Well done. You had a choice to protect either Chen or your private papers and belongings at the house, or both, or neither, and you picked neither, the only wrong option. Congratulations."

She disappeared, leaving an aura of burned lime. I sat in silence, allowing my heartbeat to slow and my breath to even out.

Chen looked up at me. "Okay, I'm done. Hey, are you crying?"

I threw a tight smile his way as I wiped my cheek. "No, sir. I just worked up a pretty good sweat." I made a show of dabbing at my forehead. "Nothing like running up and down hills to get you warmed up for the day. Ready to get to work?"

While Chen raked beach detritus into piles, I set about disposing of the piles from the previous raking. Again and again, I lifted last year's dead birch leaves into the wheelbarrow and tamped them down, rolling the full wheelbarrow along the path and tipping it onto a brush pile back in the bush. Actual work felt wonderful, physically.

Mentally, I was busy resenting Carmen. None of my options had been good, and I'd done my best. She'd always been generous with "I told you so" but stingy with help.

Stingy with information, too. Like when I noticed something strange about my father. He'd always worked odd hours, and at times he'd be gone for a few days at a time. But around my eighth birthday, he'd been gone for longer than a week and I wondered about it. My mother seemed normal—in bed when I left for school, nursing a drink and a cigarette at the kitchen table when I got home, passing out in front of the TV at my bedtime.

Finally, I had to ask. One autumn afternoon after school, my throat thick with everything I needed to know, I walked straight to the kitchen table, where my mother sat smoking.

My voice croaked. "Where's Daddy?"

"Gone." She stubbed out her cigarette and pushed aside her full ashtray. Elbows on the table, she covered her face in her hands. "Gone. Dead and gone. Probably to hell. You're not to ask about him again." She looked at me then, her eyes red. "Don't you ask me." She pointed at my chest. "And don't you *dare* ask anyone else."

I stood frozen to the spot, the linoleum floor suddenly cold under my feet. Decades later, I could still hear the clatter of my metal lunchbox hitting the floor, followed by a thud from my library book, both lit by the afternoon sunlight slanting in from the kitchen window.

I opened my mouth. She frowned. I closed it. I picked up my book and emptied my lunchbox of its waxed paper and thermos, as on any normal day.

I managed not to ask about him. All the grown-ups at church and around town, even teachers at school, seemed to know something I didn't. They were kind, in a pitying way, and kept their distance. So I found answers to most life questions in dictionaries and encyclopaedias.

Only once did I ask Carmen where our money came from.

She growled in response. One night I watched from the stairs as she slipped a few bills into an envelope sequestered inside the back cover of the phone book, separate from the envelope labeled "Grocery Money" on the counter nearby. After that, when she sent me on non-grocery errands, I took phone book money. The envelope always replenished itself before I'd emptied it completely. We never spoke of it. I learned how to survive on peanut butter sandwiches and canned vegetables. I separated wants (a fancy winter coat) from needs (shoes that fit).

I was so busy surviving that I rarely thought about my father. Dead, gone, it didn't matter. Carmen had said he was dead. He might as well have been.

But that darn Martin had reawakened the curiosity I hadn't indulged since William had become my family. My father must have had parents. I knew nothing about them. Literally nothing, not even their names. Martin could easily be a cousin from a much-younger brother.

I considered it all as I handled leaves: stooping and stretching, tamping down and dumping. The work kneaded the annoyance from my body. With each load, I felt lighter. Eventually, I could focus on good things. Nothing bad had happened to Chen. He'd shown himself to be trustworthy.

In spite of the hassles, the planning and food and "does he need a bath" and "what about brushing those teeth" (and checking the toothbrush to see if it's wet), plus the seemingly endless talking, I liked this kid. He was good at being around adults. And in spite of his losses last January, he'd never shown a sense of injury, even when talk of Job might have made it seem okay. He'd been sad, but I'd never heard him say "why me?" about the accident. I admired that.

I explored a dangerous idea: I'd miss this kid, a little. Maybe he wasn't the exact kid I'd fantasized about, but I wouldn't mind having him around. A little more. Because I liked him. And I think he kind of liked me. I know he liked making me laugh.

When I'd disposed of the leaf piles we'd left on Saturday, I went to throw rocks with Chen. Even though my mother had appeared again at the table, muttering, I felt better all the way around.

MARTIN

Back at his hotel, Martin headed for the so-called Executive Suite, checking the front counter on his way. No Barb.

At the computer, he did a quick search. The obituary for William Matthew Harrison of Thunder Bay listed a surviving son, David, of Toronto. William seemed to have died of natural causes, though, not in that accident Alex talked about. And almost five years ago.

For a moment, Martin stared out the lobby window, where a gull harassed a couple of others.

More searches turned up David Harrison, a financial advisor with only a few social media accounts but many multi-letter certifications trailing his name. Martin saw mentions in articles from newspaper and finance business sections. Martin looked for images to be sure. Yep. There he was.

Well. Mr. Smith was Simone's stepson. Now what?

Martin needed a walk. Without planning it, he found himself at the waterfront. He found a bench looking out to the lake, where a big, serious-looking ship with a black and brick-red hull sat serenely on the calm water. Martin zipped his jacket a little tighter and sat, the metal bench cold beneath him.

David Harrison. Mr. Smith. What did that mean?

First, Mr. Smith didn't want Martin to know who he really was. Why not? The secrecy made no sense. Why didn't Mr. Smith just buy the land from Simone himself? Why send a fake cousin, especially if Simone had a soft spot for family? Stepsons were family. And if Simone didn't want to sell, he could just ask her for an investment. His father probably left something.

Then again, Simone didn't come across as a soft touch, ready to hand out cash. And Simone didn't talk about David—had barely mentioned him, in fact. She hadn't said, "I have a stepson in Toronto."

Something else bugged Martin, something not about them, but about him. Knowing who Mr. Smith really was, without telling either Mr. Smith or Simone, was lying. To both of them.

Unsettling. Martin got up and strolled along the paved paths, hands in pockets.

Lying wasn't healthy. Other people seemed to like gossip or "being in the know." But Martin found secrets dangerous. *You're as sick as your secrets,* Harry would say, a basic from twelve-step meetings.

A few days back, pretending to be Simone's cousin had felt different. Not quite so dishonest. Martin hadn't known Simone. Honestly, he didn't know he *wasn't* her cousin, though no evidence suggested he *was*. (Harry would say, *That's just a technicality, Martin, don't get distracted by it.*)

Also, this was important. Whatever he pretended, he was actually trying to buy something from her. Simone would end up with money. If Mr. Smith were really shady, he'd have leaped on Martin's idea of selling Simone a condo that didn't exist. She'd look vulnerable and he'd take over her property, all of it, no purchase required.

Martin did agree that her property would be a great investment. Mr. Smith could make a killing if he put a new house in on that lakefront place. And it wouldn't be that tough. Hydro poles were already close by, and wells were easy enough to dig.

Why do it this way? Then again, did Martin really need to know? No.

Still, he felt dishonest. Like he should tell Simone he wasn't her cousin. But then he'd have to explain, and he'd tell her stuff she probably didn't want to know about Mr. Smith. David. She'd be embarrassed or cry, or maybe even yell at Martin, even though it was David's fault.

From any direction Martin looked at it, it was better neither of them knew what he knew.

He thought of Harry. What was another way to look at it?

Well, really, he was pretending or even acting, not lying. Nobody went around accusing actors of lying. He could do it a little bit longer, just to get things wrapped up.

Without noticing, he'd wandered to the skatepark. A couple of adults sunned themselves on the concrete bench behind the quarter-ramp. No sign of the Harbour Foods kid. He hoped the kid was okay. Some free sandwiches were really free, but some came with obligations.

Martin could walk up to Harbour Foods, not that he was looking for the kid there, either. He'd get lunch and a book or something. Head back to the hotel.

And find a meeting for tonight. There'd be one somewhere. Martin could always find a meeting.

SIMONE

On the way up to the house, Chen sighed so loudly so many times that even I couldn't ignore it. "What's up, buddy?"

His voice edged near a whine. "Just wondering when you're calling Auntie Sarah."

As it happened, I had forgotten—or hadn't yet remembered—that I was to call Sarah to arrange Chen's pickup, either that night or the next morning. "After supper. Chicken fingers okay with you?"

Shrug. He looked small and tired and, suddenly, quite young.

Wow. When his light went out, it was out. I decided I didn't need to fix it. I was pretty tired, too, and not only from all the uphill and downhill the day had brought.

I sent Chen into the den for screen time and went into the kitchen. I meant to put on the kettle so I could have a cup of tea while I regrouped before making phone calls.

The potted ornamental pepper sat in the sink. I hadn't left it there, had I?

Carmen laughed from her chair at the kitchen table, one finger drawing circles in the air beside her ear. I flushed and dried off the pot before setting it on the table in front of her. She made a face and disappeared.

First, I made the easy phone call. Easier, anyway. I wanted to see how Carole's husband's surgery had gone. She sounded chipper—happy it was over, tired of waiting for news, glad he seemed to be in good spirits.

I was ready to ring off when she said, "So how are you? How's it been with Chen?"

"Fine. He's great company." I left out the nightmares and the endless—endless—talking.

"He's still there? I thought he was leaving today." She laughed. "To tell the truth, I didn't think you'd make it through the weekend. I even let Rev. Phil know that Kelsey and I could handle him along with the surgery, if you called in a panic."

Ouch. I managed to laugh. "Thanks for that vote of confidence. It's been fine."

And then, annoyed and embarrassed and more than a little competitive, I kept talking.

"In fact, if it's okay with his aunt, I'm going to keep him all week."

Carole chuckled but read my silence correctly. "You're serious? But you don't really like—that is, you're—you and William were—you're—."

I bailed her out. "Private, I'm private. That doesn't mean I hate people. Or kids. Of course he'll stay all week. It'll be fun." I hoped.

"Well." Carole sounded impressed. "I guess I owe Rev. Phil twenty bucks."

Carmen appeared at the kitchen table in her red kimono. She drew on her cigarette, which she held in a long, movie-star holder, and blew smoke rings—green, like absinthe.

My voice sounded small, even to me. "You two made a bet? About me?"

Carole joked it away. "A friendly wager. You know Rev. Phil wouldn't bet against you, and neither would I, not really. I'm just surprised. But it's wonderful news! I hope you have a fun week."

I couldn't think of anything to say in the brief pause before launching into all the talk-to-you-soon, hello-to-Kelsey getting-off-the-phone things. After I hung up, I turned back to deal with Carmen and saw Chen standing in the doorway to the den.

"Really, Aunt Simka? Really, I can stay?" His eyes were wide, his face lit again.

Well, I was on the hook now. However exhausted I still was, I'd have to keep my word.

Unless. I cleared my throat. "Only if you want to. I'd understand if you'd rather spend time with your family. You don't have to worry about hurting my feelings."

He was shaking his head. "No, please, pleeeeeease let me stay. I like it here."

I was more pleased than I knew what to do with. "Okay, then. Let's call Sarah now."

Carmen said darkly, "You'll be sorry." Chen was doing some complicated kind of combination martial arts and dance move, though, so I ignored her, and she disappeared.

Sarah was almost abjectly grateful. While I was on a roll making phone calls, I left voicemail for Jessica, so she'd know where Chen was. Presto, that whole loop was closed.

Every time I told someone about keeping Chen, I felt happier about it. Of course I had an ego and liked to feel good in front of other people. And something about saying it aloud made it seem more feasible. Other people did things like this, with kids who were far more difficult than Chen had been so far. So could I.

Plus, I'd lost nothing by having him around. He hadn't driven Carmen away. Both Grandpa and William had made themselves known. Which was selfish, but important to me.

So why not a few more days? That would show Carole and Rev. Phil.

It took all evening to quit wondering if they'd really made bets.

CHEN

Notebook: Monday nite
Martin, Simka's cuzzin. Maybe
Raking the beach: sticks, plastic bobers
Forest = bush
~~Antsy Oatmeal~~ Poor Pluto
Alone in camp
Hound of the Baskervilles = Castle
Sherlock Holmes and contxt
Bible: Jobe

A new guy came today. Martin. He came to the house then walked down to the beach and hung out with us.

I don't know who he is. Aunt says he may be her relative but she's not sure. She said her and me, we aren't really relatives, but she said I was her Chen. That's cool.

So far we have raked and raked.

Simka said, "Raking is better when you decide where you will and won't do it. If you think you have to rake everywhere, you'll feel hopeless."

Then she showed me. "Over here, just rake up the line of sticks. Don't worry about that mess of leaves over there."

I raked lots on the beach. Sticks and some real trash like plastic bags and bobbers from fishing lines, all tangled.

The line of sticks shows where the water came up in the winter, during storms. The water is way low now. Aunt Simka says the snow back in the bush isn't melted yet.

I said, "Where's the bush? There's bushes everywhere."

She laughed but I guess she figured out I wasn't joking. She said, "Oh. That's what people here call the forest. The bush."

I don't know if she's right. If that's what people call it, how come I don't? But she acts like she knows a lot. So maybe she is right. About that.

There is other stuff she doesn't do right. It makes me antsy. She doesn't like to hear about it. She says it is rude to tell her. Like it's rude to show her food when I'm eating, like me and Ry did, and sometimes Daddy too.

Today she was making oatmeal. LIKE SHE DOES EVERY DAY, how can she even stand it? It's so gross.

She didn't measure right, and I told her. I said, "You're making it wrong."

She said, "You use two times the water to oatmeal."

I said, "No, the can says—."

But she interrupted. She said, "Chen, how long do you think I've been making oatmeal?"

"I don't know, every day since forever?"

She laughed, but I wasn't being funny. Not on purpose.

I tried again. "But two times the water isn't always right." I know because I read that cardboard can the oatmeal comes in. It says for one serving, use two-thirds cup of water and one-third cup of oats. Yes, that is two times the water to oatmeal.

But she makes two servings, she said so. And for more servings, you use LESS THAN or < twice the amount. If you don't, you're doing it wrong.

I know because it takes FOREVER for her to cook it EVERY MORNING and I have time to read the whole can. Every day. All the days, Forever days.

I tried to tell her about LESS THAN. But she didn't listen. She said, "What do you care? You don't even eat it."

And okay I don't eat it. But it makes me antsy. She's not following directions. She doesn't even care about doing it right.

I have to think about something else. But not something scary (like how the Greenland ice sheets are melting faster than they thought, and what are we going to do).

Planets. I like planets. Pluto was demoted. Then they found Eris. They say Eris is a planetary body. That's a whole new thing. It changed the rules for planets. It makes them dwarf planets.

Maybe it's silly to feel bad for Pluto because those are just science rules for names, and it's a planet, it doesn't know any better. But Eris also means Pluto isn't all by itself. That helps, if Pluto can't be a planet anymore.

It's like relatives for Pluto even if it isn't in a family with the planets.

I hope Pluto feels better.

...

Aunt Simka left me by myself today. She went up to the house for a minute. I liked being alone in the camp. I was responsible. I looked around just a little bit. Not really snooping. The kitchen has a big stove to burn wood in and the big room has a fireplace. I don't like fires.

I stayed back from the fireplace at first. But then I saw it's made out of rocks from the beach, and I looked at them up close and I made myself touch it. It was cold because no fires have been in there in a long time. Then it wasn't as scary, and I touched it a lot. I just looked at the stove, though.

Across from the stove there's a sink without a faucet. I don't know why you'd need a sink if you don't have any water to run into it.

There's bookshelves in one of the rooms and lots of little books on them, some big ones, too, with hard covers. It was hard to see because the windows still have shudders, mostly. But I could see gold printing on the backs of some of them. One said Dickens and then Great Expectations, and I took it off the shelf. There were lots of old-timey photos inside, not part of the book but just stuck in there. I couldn't see them good. One was an old guy with white hair holding an axe like he's showing it off. He's got a cap on, and he's smiling. His pants are held up with suspenders, like Daddy's when he put on his fancy suit for the party that night of the wreck. I needed to not think about that. So I quit looking at the picture in the back of the book and put that book back. The axe was cool, though.

The different book I got was littler with a paper cover, not so heavy. I sat in the main room to read it. It was a hard book, for grownups not kids. I had to say the words out loud for a while. Some of them I didn't know. Mum tells me to figure it out from context. I might have to look up some of them later. But I kept going. It got easier.

There are rich people in it called Baskervilles, and dogs, and someone dies of being scared. It happened a long time ago and had old stuff in it. It was like a game Daddy and I used to play, with London streets. The game was Castle. It was old timey, like Lord of the Rings, with quests and swords and spells. The hazards had quicksand, plus a moor and a fen.

Daddy made me look up what they are. A fen is like a swamp. A moor is like a field with swampy bits. This book had moors too.

I thought I knew about Sherlock Holmes and he lived in today or in a not-time, like superheroes and people in games live in their own times. But the book was in a real time that wasn't today's time. Holmes smokes. In movies it's a pipe, like the guy at Old Fort William when we went on the field trip. In the book it's cigarettes too. Holmes snoops a lot. Watson too.

I guess Aunt thought I'd be scared alone, but I wasn't because I found the picture of that guy, and I had the book to read. I was glad she came back. I didn't think about things like what would I do if she didn't.

I like having this book.

...

Tonight we looked at an atlas, which is a book of maps, real ones on paper. She showed one of Lake Superior, where we are. Her house is a little bit up on the lake from town. Then Missouri where she's from. Then back to Ontario. We looked for the town where my school friend Joseph said he was from, but it wasn't on the map with that name. I don't know for sure how to spell it.

Then Aunt read Job, a little bit of it, and that's one sad story. Bad stuff happens because the devil bet God that Job didn't really like him, he was just saying he liked God because he was rich. So God made bad stuff happen. Killing his family, which is scary. Job gets pretty mad at all the bad stuff, but there's nothing he can do about it. That's really REALLY not fair. I'd be mad too.

Dr. S. says getting mad is okay. She asked if I was mad at Mum for not taking me on the cruise. I said no because it felt like telling on Mum if I said yes. I got over being mad when I didn't have to stay with grounchy people. And now I get to stay here the whole time, no Auntie Sarah or cousins at all! And maybe I'll see a bear.

Mum's so sad. I hope she feels better seeing a glacier and having Daddy with her. And when she comes back maybe she won't have those really bad stay-in-bed days.

Last night I didn't read anything after Aunt read about Job, but I did look at some comics. A kid and a tiger. And after I went to sleep I didn't wake up. No dreams, not good ones and not bad ones.

Sometimes I think Aunt is tired of me. Lots of times I feel bored of trying to be polite. But if we are tired of each other and in the house, she lets me have screen time in the den. If we're working I can go throw rocks.

Then we both feel better.

It's weird being in someone else's house for a long time. It's like time goes extra slow and everything takes forever. Starting school last September and the accident feel the same farness away, like years ago. Being at Aunt Simka's seems like it's been a long time, too, but it's just been a few days so far. And now more days!

One thing I really like. I like being here, not at Aunt Sarah's, just me, no other kids. I can play whatever I want. I'm the best rock-thrower on the beach. Even Aunt can't always skip stones. I can. Mostly.

I miss Natatorium. But I like the lake. I wish there was animals. Gumpy's farm has animals. Aunt Simka doesn't have any animals, not even a dog. There are squirrels and birds. Simka told Martin about a bear, but she might have been kidding. I wasn't sure.

I really want to see a bear. A lot. If I got to see a bear, even just one little one, from a long ways away, just for a second, I'd be even with Ry.

Maybe Ry would be happy for me if I saw a bear. Like for the laser car tournament, we high-fived after games, no matter who won. If I see a bear, I'll high-five the air and maybe it'll get to him, wherever he is.

MARTIN

After the meeting, Martin introduced himself to the leader, an older guy with a fringe of white hair clinging to his scalp but a firm handshake and hearty manner.

"Hi, Martin. I'm Donald, which I guess you already know. You can call me Donnie. I've seen you before, haven't I? You new?"

"Just here visiting my cousin." The lie came so easily now that Martin almost believed it. *Acting, I'm acting.*

"Well, glad you're here. Hey, on Saturday evenings the meeting's an hour and a half, and we go for coffee after, just up the street. People from several meetings come. It'd be great to see you."

"Sure, see you then." *Nice enough guy,* Martin thought. He caught up to Alex in the hallway and squeezed his shoulder. At Alex's wince, he said, "Whoa, sorry."

Alex gave a small shrug, which made him wince again. "Lost my balance on some stairs. Caught a railing in the ribs, sore shoulder."

Martin saw a warning in his eyes and changed the subject. "So about that guy, Ken?"

"Yeah." Alex said it like a closed door.

Martin didn't know how to ask, "Is Ken really that kid's uncle?" when he obviously wasn't. He settled for, "What's he like?"

"Let's take it outdoors."

Martin led the way out. The still-light evening sky was clear, but it held the feeling of clouds gathering, with rain maybe tomorrow or the next day.

Alex lit a cigarette and turned to Martin. "Don't ask questions about Ken. And watch what you say. Tonight, that shit about your boss isn't who he said he was, and you feel like you're lying? Don't say that. Not where people might tell him."

"That was somebody else. Totally. And *anonymous*."

"Yeah, yeah. You better hope." He winced again and took another drag. "Seriously. It's a small town for a city. People around here talk."

"Got it. Thanks." Martin nodded at Alex and walked away. Even though he'd been talking about David, it sounded like deciding not to do more business with Ken had been a good call.

He picked up his pace as he crossed the street, avoiding the easy left into the casino parking lot.

And back at the hotel, there was Barb, behind the front desk. Finally.

"Hi there," he said.

She looked up, a friendly smile in place, but Martin wondered if it was specifically for him. It didn't look totally sincere. She was also sniffling an awful lot. Maybe she had bad allergies or a cold. He hoped it wasn't anything related to drugs.

Hey, I might be good at this detective stuff. Then he realized he hadn't said anything else.

"Uh, good to see you again." He hoped she'd remember chatting with him before. It had been several days.

"Yeah, you too." Her smile relaxed a little, which Martin chose to see as encouragement.

"How've you been?"

"Oh, you know." She shrugged and sniffed.

Martin noticed black flecks on her cheeks below her eyes, where he was pretty sure it wasn't supposed to be. She'd been crying.

Then she looked up at him and smiled for real. "Sorry. It's just—today's a tough day. It would have been my brother's birthday."

"Oh." Martin heard the "would have been" loud and clear. "Sorry," he offered, hoping it didn't sound too much like a question. He lingered.

She picked up a large tumbler and waved it at him. "I'm just dehydrated." She drank and then sighed, fatigue still showing under her forced good humour. "It's been quite the day. We had a get-together for Shane to put down some tobacco. I didn't feel like eating."

"Oh. So you, your brother, you're...."

Barb eyed him, half-smiling, half-weary. "Indigenous, yes. We grew up on the reserve—Fort William First Nation. Shane and I were close. At the college, he was in mining technology. He had a job, a wife. And then—the accident."

"I'm so sorry. That sounds horrible." Martin fought the urge to tell her a story about Harry. He should just listen.

She dabbed at her eyes, wiped at the flakes. "That damn accident. Did you hear about it?"

"Only a little." First Alex, and today that kid Chen had mentioned it. "Was it on the news?"

"Everywhere, nationally and internationally, for days, before the next catastrophe came along." Barb sounded drained. "I never know, with our guests, what they remember. It was such a big deal to us, but if they're from somewhere else—well. They might have heard something, they might even know it was in Thunder Bay, maybe they said, 'Oh, how sad.' But they don't really know. That wreck touched everybody in this city, I mean *everybody*. That intersection is terrible, trucks coming through fast, can't stop in time. We've all been out driving when maybe we shouldn't, you know? Maybe a few too many. Or even just tired. And in the winter, weather changes fast. Any of us could have been there."

She shook her head. "Regular people. Families. Coming home after eating out or a date or a run to the grocery store. Minding their own business—couples, kids and parents, a grandparent too." Tears trickled down her cheeks.

"Sounds awful."

She dabbed at her eyes and nose with tissue and flashed a polite smile. "Sorry. I'm so sick of crying."

Martin murmured and shook his head. He'd seen plenty of people cry in meetings and learned to let them.

"We had to pretend everything was fine. The guests that weekend, they packed up on Sunday and checked out like normal. They went back to their lives, wherever they were going. But we were still hearing about who died, and what even happened, into Monday and Tuesday of the next week."

"Ouch, that's terrible. I'm sorry," Martin said. "You don't have to tell me about it if you don't want to."

"Thanks." She was quiet for a moment. "But even if we don't talk about it, we can't get away from it. What's saved me is our group text. All of us—people from every family, the driver's family in Nova Scotia, and some from the hospital. When we get down, we can text and know we can talk to someone who gets it."

"Even hospital staff? Wow."

"Yeah. The chaplain they called in, a couple of ICU nurses on duty, a volunteer who stayed with the truck driver overnight until he died. She's close with his family back East now. We'd never have known each other, otherwise. But they get it. Strangers. They're like family. Kind of a miracle, you know?"

"I do know." He thought of Harry, the random guys at random meetings—even Alex, taking time to warn him. He didn't have to. In spite of the Kens of the world, sometimes people could be okay.

She smiled at Martin, a real one. "Sorry to be such a downer. It's just been a day."

Martin waved it away. "Not a downer. Just real life."

"It felt good to talk about it. Thanks." She looked down at her fingers on the keyboard.

Martin took the hint. "Sure, any time. See you." He stepped back but reconsidered. Instead, he peered over the top of the counter and pointed at her wallet, again crammed into the corner. "Just a thought. See that? You might want to make it more secure. It wouldn't be too hard to lift."

Barb reddened and snatched it up. "Gosh, thanks." She put it in a cupboard by her knees and ostentatiously locked it. "Just—thanks."

Martin smiled and lifted his hand, drifting back from the counter to give her space. Instead of going up to his room, he went back out to the parking lot. Nine p.m. and the sun was just setting. Spring in the north, he guessed.

He thought about the accident, wondering if Simone or even Mr. Smith had known people who'd died. He could look it up, read about it a little. It seemed important.

Sometimes watching the sky helped Martin let go of things. Like guilt about lying to Simone (okay, *acting*) and puzzlement about Mr. Smith. Concern for the Harbour Foods kid and wariness about Ken. Even sadness on behalf of other sad people, Barb and Alex and Chen. Missing Harry, and the weird homesickness of being done with one life but not home in the next one.

In every direction, the sky took on shifting shades of orange as the blue above deepened. Under this same sky, people laughed and cried, died and were born. They ate supper or headed off to work, depending on where they were in the big, wide world. Silently, Martin wished them well—everybody, even Mr. Smith and Ken. As he watched, the sky became pink and purple. Soon, it would quiet further to look like a bruise. Like the one on the face of that kid. Except he hoped that one was healing.

TUESDAY

CHEN

<u>Notebook: Tuesday morning</u>
Gramps and Gramm and Grandmother and Gumpy
Ry bein a butt
Target with family on it

Today I woke up early and Aunt Simka hasn't had enough coffee yet. So I'm writing in my notebook. Yesterday I was telling her about Grandmother and Gumpy.

Aunt was confused. She said, "I thought they were Gramps and Gramm. And his name was Joe." Because I told her about Sloppy Joes and Gramps.

I said, "These are different people. Gramps and Gramm are dead, from a long time ago. Grandmother and Gumpy are Daddy's family. Gumpy's the one who's sick now. They used to live out at the farm. Now they live in town and are mad about it, and Auntie Sarah and her family live at the farm. They're not happy because the farm is a lot of work. We still call it Gumpy's farm because he's grounchy all the time about not living there. We all hope he feels better about it soon, but I don't think it's working."

Maybe I shouldn't have said that to Aunt Simka, but it's true. Mum says they are nice people and family, and we love them even if they are different than us.

But one time before the accident, almost at Christmas, Mum didn't know I was listening. She said to Daddy, "Your parents get on my last nerve."

Daddy said, "Join the club, Gorgeous."

They laughed and hugged. That was a good day.

...

Sometimes I forget Aunt Simka is not really my Aunt. I like her lots better than Aunt Sarah. And we aren't even really related.

But now that I'm staying here I want to put her on my target.

I wonder where it even is now. Mum made me draw it one time I was really mad at Ry. We've talked about it a lot.

She got mad when I called it a target. She said, "It's a Circle of Family." She said she read about it in a book.

But it looks like a target, and I kept calling it that and now she does too. We've talked about it more since the accident.

The day she made me draw it was a Sunday afternoon, a while back before Ry started being nicer to me. I was cleaning up the basement so she wouldn't yell after Ry went back to his Mum's. It was never fair. He'd be a butt and do the opposite of what she said. Then he'd go home to his Mum, and I'd get all the yelling for both of us.

I said to Ry, "You don't have to help, but I don't want to get yelled at after you go home. So I'm putting stuff away."

He said, "You're such a suck. What a Mama's boy."

I minded my own business, like Mum and Daddy told me to when Ry bugged me. I picked up some of the crashed paper airplanes lying on the floor. But Ry grabbed up two airplanes before I got them.

I said, "Give me those."

I tried to grab one and he held it. That made it tear even more. I had a little bit, but he had most of the paper. I put down the other airplanes to grab at the ones he had. He was laughing. He took all the airplanes and wouldn't give me them and kept ripping and ripping, making littler and littler pieces, little bitty ones.

He said, "Look, Mama's boy, I'm helping."

He wound up like in baseball and threw a handful of paper bits at me. They went everywhere. Then he turned the TV up so loud I couldn't say anything.

I was mad so I went to my bedroom. On weekends it doesn't feel like my room anymore because Ry is there. I can't say when he's visiting or I get yelled at, because he's not visiting, it's his home too, even though he lives with his Mum most of the time.

It was almost time for Daddy to take him to his Mum's. So I stayed in my room. I put my face in my pillow, and I even had some tears but not a lot. I was still mad but not crying when Mum came to my room and talked.

Mum said, "Our family is hard sometimes. But we love each other. Even when we maybe don't like each other very much. We're still a family."

She said a bunch of other stuff, too. Then she waited. She wanted me to say I wasn't mad at Ry anymore. But I was. So I didn't say anything.

She said, "Chenoweth, I do not need this right now."

Then she left. When Ry was finally gone, Mum started making supper. I came out of my room and put the games back on the shelf and picked up Ry's pop cans and the Twizzler wrappers he left under the sofa cushion and I brought them to the kitchen. It was a start.

After supper I went to finish. I picked up the crayons and put them in the tin where they live, and put away the paper we didn't use for airplanes. Then I tried to pick up those little pieces of paper. It seemed like it would take every minute of every single day all the rest of my life to do it. I tried not to cry but I couldn't help it.

Mum came to see what I was doing. She said, "Chenoweth, come to the table."

She sent Daddy to the basement with the vacuum cleaner. He didn't like it, but she gave him a look and he did it. Then she gave me paper and a pencil.

She said, "Draw a circle."

When I did, she said, "Who is in your family, Chen?"

"You and Daddy and me."

She said, "Draw a picture of us in your circle. It doesn't have to look good. This is a lesson."

So I did sticks for arms and legs. I didn't have room enough for all of us in the middle.

Mum said, "Chen, is that *all* the people in your family?"

I didn't like it, but I knew I had to add Ry.

Then Mum said, "What about Grandmother and Gumpy?"

I turned the paper over and made a bigger circle. I put me and Mum and Daddy and Ry in the middle. Though I put Ry in there just because I knew that was the lesson. And I guess because it made Daddy happy, and maybe Mum too.

Then Mum told me to draw another circle around the middle circle, like a target. I put Grandmother and Gumpy there and Gramps and Gramm. I added Jayme and Maddie, my two cousins in Iowa. Aunt Kimberly is their Mum and she's Mum's sister. I like them a lot. We never hardly ever see them, though.

Daddy came back upstairs with the vacuum and said, "What about your cousins on my side, Aunt Sarah's kids? They're family, too."

I didn't want to add them because I don't like them, and there wasn't room and I didn't want to start over. Anyway it was a lesson and I already knew what he meant. Plus it was a school night and Mum wanted me to start the week with a good night's sleep. So I didn't draw them in.

I got ready for bed. When I was lying there, Mum came to kiss me. She said, "What did you learn?"

"We're all family, and people don't leave the target just because I'm mad at them. And I guess I can love family without liking them."

But I didn't say what I really thought. Nothing was any different. The paper was hard to clean up, even for Daddy with the vacuum. Ry was still a butt. I kind of feel bad now to say it. But he was. Sometimes.

One other thing Mum said when I was drawing people, "It is okay to have dead people in your family, like Gramps and Gramm. You still love them, even though they aren't right here."

Which is good to know now.

I hope that target is still in the basement somewhere. It would be a thousand million times easier to draw if I left off the dead people. But now I don't want to leave off Daddy. Or I guess Ry. He was my brother.

If it is okay with Mum, I would put Aunt Simka on there now because we are sorta family too. Now that I'm her Chen.

MARTIN

On his drive to Simone's about noon on Tuesday, Martin hoped he wasn't imposing, showing up two days in a row. That would be a good thing to say when he got there: "I hope I'm not imposing."

As before, Chen met him at the door and Simone called from the kitchen, "Come on in."

While Martin shed his jacket and shoes, Chen ran and slid on his socks back to the kitchen. "I'm done with lunch," he announced.

Simone's voice held amusement. "No you're not. Look at those carrots lying there sad and lonely on your plate. You sit down. Martin, want some soup? Sandwich?"

Chen sat with a sigh. "I've been looking at them." He picked up a carrot and said to Martin, in warning, "The soup has vegetables in it too."

Simone pointed. "Here, sit, and I'll get you a bowl. I made it myself. Well, some of it. Some parts of it came in cans, but I did open them. And Chen, you can never have too many vegetables."

Martin sat. "Thanks, that'd be great," he said. He could always eat, and food seemed like a way to get on Simone's good side. He looked around and spotted the pepper at the end of the counter.

"Oh good, you found the pepper in the sink. I hope you don't mind. When I was changing shoes yesterday I noticed it looked a little bedraggled after its trip out from town, so I gave it a drink. It didn't have time to drain well, so I left it."

Simone looked at him and turned back to the stove. Martin would swear she looked relieved. What about?

Her voice was muffled. "Thanks for thinking of it."

Chen sighed again and chewed. Simone brought Martin a large bowl of soup, hearty with ground beef and pasta, and topped with shredded cheese.

Simone sat back down. "There's more when you're done with that, or I can make you a sandwich too."

Martin, mouth full, shook his head.

Chen said to Martin, "We've done a lot of work already today." He stretched out his leg and polished the table leg with his sock until Simone caught his eye. He bit another carrot. "She's killing me, in fact." He beamed at Martin, then laughed, covering his mouth and forcing air to bulge in his cheeks before releasing another "phha ha."

Simone said, "I don't know where he heard that, but he finds it hee-lair-ee-us. He's obviously nowhere near dead. If anything, he's wearing *me* out. We have, however, been making great strides in our projects." She named them: raking, lopping, clearing, and other words that Martin knew meant cleaning up outdoors.

Chen asked to be excused and raced off to the den.

When Martin's bowl was empty, he turned to Simone. "I'm sorry. I seem to have been distracted by that soup, which was really good. Did you say what your plans for the afternoon are? I'm sorry to interrupt them." He hesitated, as if he were. Then he took a breath and dove in. "I really enjoyed seeing your property yesterday and learning about it. I wondered if you'd thought about selling it."

She threw him a look that made him feel he was Chen's age and in deep shit. "Lord have mercy, you too?" She took some dishes to the counter and stood with her back to him. "Everybody I know thinks *they* know what I should do." She put a small plate into the bottom rack of the dishwasher with more vigour than absolutely required.

Martin softened his voice. "Oh, I'm sorry. I've obviously touched a nerve. I wouldn't dream of suggesting you can't handle all these responsibilities." He'd practiced that line; it was a good one. "I was just curious about how you handle everything. Even someone who loves winter must get tired of snowblowing. And all that grass, both up here and down near the water. You must have a lot of stamina."

She turned, her blue eyes snapping. "Luckily, I do. I can endure a lot of people telling me a lot of things. Like 'You're getting up there, don't you want to take it easy?' Or 'You could sell one and still have the other.' As if this house and my camp were interchangeable, like pawns on a chessboard." She looked through the kitchen window, arms folded.

Martin shook his head. "They don't know you at all, do they?"

"They do not." Her voice was crisp. And sad? Martin wasn't sure.

He sat back and looked out the big window beside the table. "What a view." *Relax. Keep it easy.* "I'm wondering what to do with my own condo. Like I said yesterday, I don't use it enough. I'd rather have something in Canada. I'd planned to sell it. But even though I don't love it like you love your place, I'd prefer to sell to someone who'd really enjoy it."

Martin looked back at Simone, pleased to see her leaning on the counter, arms uncrossed, her face no longer tense. He laughed. "Hey, you wouldn't want to trade, would you? One of your properties for a condo? It's got a view of the ocean and everything. Let me get my jacket. I brought some paperwork about it, if you want to take a look." He half-stood.

She smiled but said only, "I would not, so don't bother."

Martin sat back down. "Well, it was worth a shot." Maybe she'd reconsider if she was in a better mood, which she usually seemed to be near the lake. "Anyway, can I walk down to the camp again? I enjoyed it so much yesterday."

"Sure. Is there something in particular you're interested in?"

"Not really." Martin cleared his throat. "Though I was wondering—I don't really have a sense of what a five-acre lot compares to up here. Is it big?"

"Yes, by quite a bit. One of my neighbours has more land. But most camp lots are well under an acre." Simone didn't sound proud, just matter-of-fact. "My place wouldn't be easy to develop. Not much value, to an outsider, anyway."

Martin kept his disagreement to himself. "So that camp—is that all your grandfather built? No other buildings?"

"Let's just go down there and you can see for yourself. Chen, shoes!" Simone closed the dishwasher door. Then she put her hands to her lower back and pulled her shoulders back in a stretch. She noticed Martin watching. "From raking. I'm always a little sore, early in the season. Every day gets easier, though."

"Absolutely, it does."

While the three of them were putting shoes on, Martin also slipped the paperwork from the inside pocket of his jacket and left it on the kitchen table.

Simone narrowed an eye at him.

"Just in case you change your mind." He smiled as if it were still a joke. "No pressure."

She harrumphed and opened the door.

On their way down, Martin successfully made small talk—again with the amazing spot, the great view, how on earth did Simone mow this grass all summer long (she stayed uphill from the mower, she said, and changed the subject immediately).

Toward the bottom of the hill, Martin could see the asphalt road up ahead when Simone said, "Let's take the back way this time," and led the way into the bush on a barely visible footpath. "We cleared this earlier today. Chen's getting to be a whiz with the loppers."

Chen followed Simone, looking smug. He turned periodically to talk to Martin.

"Cutting's the fun part. The yucky part is putting the branches in the brush pile. Spruces hurt. They're the prickliest. Even through my sweatshirt. And you have to throw the branches way back in there, onto the top of the pile. Throw cut end first so they go far enough."

Simone said over her shoulder, "There's always more work after the work stops being fun, right Chen?"

"No kidding."

On the new trail, tall evergreens crowded close to them, occasionally interspersed with what looked like slender sticks. Martin guessed that spring would reveal them to be Manitoba maple and alder. The asphalt turn-around circle must be to their right, but Martin couldn't see it. The roots of the evergreens beside them stood up from the forest floor like veins on the back of an old man's hand.

Simone cast a glance backward. "Chen, watch where you're going in here. This isn't easy walking, like the driveway."

On the trail, the birches to their left thinned out occasionally into clearings where Martin could see all the way to the mossy, lichen-encrusted cliff wall. They came out onto the two-track driveway near the camp, at the cleared area big enough to turn a car in. Chen ran ahead, down to the lake.

"Wow, I didn't know where we were at all," Martin said. He looked back. "I can hardly see where we came out, even."

Simone looked almost smug. "It's not a *secret* path, exactly, but we like it natural. Originally, it was a deer track. When William was alive, we opened lots of trails for skiing, some starting up in

216

our backyard."

By the water, they watched Chen successfully skip a rock five times and pump his fist into the air. After a brief dance, he bent over to pick up more rocks.

Watching, Martin couldn't help but smile. He looked at Simone, who seemed to be staring without attention. Martin ventured, "He seems to be having a good time."

Simone blinked and turned to him with a questioning face.

Martin motioned toward the water. "Chen. Is having a good time. He calls you aunt? Does this mean he's my Chen, too?" Martin already knew. That morning, he'd investigated the accident and found all the Robertsons—Andrew and Ryan, survived by Chenoweth and Jessica and grandparents. But he didn't want to admit he'd been researching.

"Not by blood. He's here while his mother's on a brief trip."

"He mentioned an accident? I've been hearing about it in town. Very sad."

"Yes. It touched a lot of people locally. Across the country, too." She folded her lips together.

Martin waited a beat in case she wanted to talk about it. Then he said, "It's nice for Chen to spend time here. Your grandfather sure knew what he was doing when he picked this spot to build. Was the camp always this size?"

"He added rooms through the years. William and I just shored up what's there."

They chatted more about the property. Simone needed only a little encouragement to talk about the woodshed, power tools— anything related to the place.

Martin walked through a natural opening. "I don't want to keep harping on this, but it seems like a lot to keep up, by yourself. William had a son, right? Does he ever come up here?"

Simone's voice was neutral. "He lives in Toronto. To him, it's just real estate. Not an actual place. Same with the house." She didn't meet Martin's eyes. "Still, he'll be glad enough to get them. When the time comes."

Martin knew enough not to ask when that might be. He shifted the topic again. "You don't have extended family? Oh right, only kids of only kids."

Simone laughed, suddenly and short. "Yes, we're it. Sorry, no one else you can sell to. Maybe David." She paused. "Funny how different he is from William. Like my mother. She couldn't wait to get away from here, either. Oh well—parents and kids. Who can predict?"

"Maybe it skipped a generation. My father worked in an office and then sold cars, but I like working outdoors. And you came back here. No chance for David's kids?"

Simone shook her head. "No kids. That we know of, anyway. He's only been serious about his career and wealth." She looked around. "So different. My grandfather focused on tangible things. When something broke, he fixed it, no need to buy a replacement. He wasn't afraid of soldering irons or concrete or construction. William liked figuring out that kind of thing, too. I prefer enjoying it once it's finished." She motioned to the leaf rake, leaning against a birch. "Though I don't mind some light upkeep."

"Your grandfather sounds like the kind of man who knew the value of a good junk pile." At Simone's surprise, he added, "Most people in construction know better than to throw out perfectly good stuff."

Simone looked down and smiled. "I'd guess you're right about that." She blinked a few times. Martin was about to ask if she was okay when she called, "Yo, Chen. What's your skipping record so far?"

"Six. Counting the first one."

Martin wanted to see more of the land. "Mind if I wander around a little?"

Simone headed toward the chair nearer the water. "Knock

yourself out. I'm going to coach the rock-skipping for a bit."

Martin meandered down the beach toward the cliff, the wet sand sliding and crunching under his shoes. He stopped to admire the islands, far out, wondering about Simone and this place. He was surprised everything was so rustic. She'd mentioned a septic system and hand-pumping water from the lake. He wondered if she'd considered a composting toilet. Some had solar power, no need for a hydro line.

Martin turned to examine the camp's roofline. Two chimneys, probably a fireplace and a wood cookstove. No other heat. You'd have to really love it to be here into September, even.

He surveyed the bay. She didn't have a dock, though she'd mentioned rowing. He wondered where the rowboat was. No boathouse.

He wandered away from the water into the bush. Near the cliff, he found some clearings. They got southern sun, so they'd probably be the first places to warm every spring. He'd enlarge this spot, if it were up to him. She could store the parts of a floating dock here. Or put in a garden, a nice one, though she claimed not to garden much.

He lost track of time among trees that had lived twice as long as he had. Occasionally, deadfall blocked his way. He took a couple of photos of the tangles of branches and leaf-covered stumps. Maybe he could ask Simone why she didn't clear it up, and she'd reconsider selling.

But maybe Simone didn't clear up downed trees because she liked leaving things natural. A guy like Mr. Smith—David—wouldn't understand that. He'd think she was weird. So far, to Martin, she still seemed like a relatively normal lady whose stepson was trying, harder than she knew, to pry her out of a place she loved.

But, like it or not, he'd agreed to help with that. His first loyalty lay with Mr. Smith. He could use the money, especially if he wanted to live here or start over somewhere else. Pretty soon he'd have to talk to Simone again, seriously, about buying her place or selling her his condo. He didn't relish the thought.

Circling back, he saw Chen, far off, throwing rocks that sometimes skipped and sometimes didn't in the choppy waves. Simone, meanwhile, sat in one of the beach chairs and seemed to be smiling and nodding at the chair beside her.

Martin walked quietly, though he was pretty sure the waves shushing the sand would drown out his approach.

He paused. As he watched, Simone said something. Her words whipped away on the wind. Then, looking up, she saw Martin and lifted her hand.

Martin smiled, even though she'd just talked to a chair. As he approached, he made a quick decision: no more buying or selling talk today.

"Thanks for the tour. I'll head back to town now. All right if I come back in a couple of days?"

He hardly listened to her response, which seemed positive enough. As he trudged all the way up the path and then beyond it, the steep hill, Martin kept turning over two situations, both of which seemed to be true, and neither of which he liked.

First, Simone absolutely did not want to sell either property. In spite of Martin's hopes, she also did not want a condo in Florida. She seemed stubborn enough that she wouldn't budge from either position, at least not soon.

And second, Simone talked to a chair, and she'd faded in and out several times that day. Was she just weird, or was something wrong?

People. Some things were easy—like he enjoyed chatting with Simone. But what David was up to? Mystifying.

Either way, Martin had done what he could for the day. He'd planted a seed, a condo-shaped one, with Simone. He'd come back in a day or two to see if it had begun to sprout.

SIMONE

I sure didn't mind seeing Martin's back when he walked up the path. I'd at least had the foresight to clear paperwork off my desk, and he didn't seem interested in carting off my furniture, so it didn't matter if he was in the house. But something about him bugged me, even though he was perfectly friendly. Maybe because he was perfectly friendly.

He could be my cousin. But maybe he wasn't. Also, why did he want to wander around in the bush? I mean, I always enjoyed it, but nobody else, except William, ever had.

Grandpa Jackson would have, too. In our recent years together, though, he'd been mostly interested in my near-nonexistent efforts to garden and in my laissez-faire approach to cutting up downed trees. In fact, he'd been hanging around that morning, while Chen and I cleared the back path. William and I had put it in long after my grandfather's death. When Chen and I had quit for the morning, Grandpa applauded, showering us with the scents of vanilla and honey.

Later, when we came back downhill, he waved at us from the path's entrance and, I learned, waited for us in a beach chair. He roared with laughter, slapping his cap on his knee, when Martin made his peculiar comment about junk piles.

After Martin crashed away into the bush behind the camp, my grandfather said, "Does he think there's silver back there? Or a trunk of precious jewels?"

I murmured under the sound of the waves on the beach, "Who knows what Martin's thinking." Yet again, I wished he could hear my thoughts.

He settled back in the chair and rubbed at the white bristles on his chin. "I guess he might find silver. Iron everywhere, of course, but not worth working. Could he claim mineral rights?"

I looked him over. Elbows on the armrests, sepia-toned fingers laced over his transparent belly, he looked right at home. My age, give or take, and fit.

He looked back, raising a bristly eyebrow. "Or, didja think of this? What if he gets it in his head to take this property out from under you? He could make you out to be dotty and boot you off, claiming it was for your own good."

Yeah, for talking to you, I didn't say. I hadn't even considered mineral rights. Great, something else to worry about. I managed a small smile. "Who, Martin? Hardly. And hey, don't feed my paranoia, okay?"

"Suit yourself." Grandpa sat back.

I focused on the sun and scene in front of me. The shifting breeze ruffled the surface of the water one way while the wave action pushed in the opposite direction. Chen struggled to make his rocks skip in the muddle that resulted. I relaxed into the day.

Then I had a thought. "Hey, what do you know about my father?" I turned to my grandfather. Except he'd disappeared.

...

I should have been used to it. The ghosts never took my convenience into account. Even when my William had been alive, he'd not been particularly—what's the word—biddable. He'd always showed up at his own convenience, from the very first time we met.

When I asked William how he came to be standing in the asphalt circle on that afternoon in late September, he was smart enough to say, "I was waiting for you."

Smart but inaccurate. He couldn't have known when I'd arrive. Even I hadn't known. It was September, later in the year than I'd ever been there before. In those days, when I owned the camp but brought Carmen up every summer in spite of her health, I depended on our handyman before Donnie, who was Gordon. In a normal year, I'd call Gordon in June with my estimated arrival date, and he'd clear trees over the driveway and put in the water line.

But Carmen's stroke came in late May. In Missouri, I spent hours by her sometimes-stirring form in the nursing home bed. She died in August, and only then did I realize I hadn't called Gordon at all.

I'd lived away from Carmen for twenty years by then, except for our summer trips, so I thought I'd given up my illusions about mothers and daughters. But with her death, I could no longer pretend that someday, she'd appreciate me and apologize for every horrible thing she'd ever said and done. I also wasn't sure how my beloved spot would feel, now that I was alone. Completely. Forever, for every year to come.

That year, the rest of August melted from under me, obsessed as I was with details of wills and remembrances and cremation. On Labour Day morning, I heeded an impulse and threw some clothes into a suitcase and drove north, without contacting Gordon or any other planning. I wasn't sure what I'd find that September afternoon.

As I approached the asphalt turnaround circle, a person stood beside a red wheelbarrow. It wasn't Gordon, so I aimed an all-purpose nod at the wheelbarrow and turned my little Hyundai down the two-lane path. On its gentle curves, fallen branches might be too big to drive over. To my surprise, I found no hazards.

The open parking area behind the camp looked freshly mowed. First thing out of the car, I walked straight down to the lake, as always. The afternoon sun cast a glow shading to orange on the pebbly beach and the dark-green spruce, and the brisk air gave a sharp edge to the islands out in the bay and the far shore beyond. Whitecaps showed on the mallard-coloured water beyond the point.

Ahh. Home.

After just a few peaceful moments, my business mind clicked in. What was different? A wind-downed tree near the point needed clearing, but not immediately. The lake level seemed lower than usual, but the cheerful bobs of a repurposed bleach bottle marked the end of the water line, ready to deliver water as soon as I raised and lowered the handle on the old blue pump in the breezeway. Everything else seemed the same, too, from the towering, elephantine basalt boulders to the slender birches. Turning, I looked over the ramshackle wood-frame camp—beautiful to me, even though at that time it showed every one of its then-eighty years. The front bedroom corner sagged and the foundations at the back had softened, but much remained sound. Its stone fireplace and wood-burning cookstove would generate enough heat for me to stay a while without worrying about weather.

Before tearing myself away from the shore to get to work, I squatted near the water's edge and dabbled my fingers in its shallows. The lake remained cool in the warm, late-afternoon sun of early autumn.

"Hello." An unfamiliar male voice.

I leaped to my feet—or tried. Instead, I fell sideways and ended up half-sitting, half-lying in the water, which turned out to be much colder than I'd anticipated.

The man laughed, a mixture of friendliness and apology.

I laughed, too, instead of drawing my embarrassment around me.

He held out his hand to help me up, which made me feel demure, and introduced himself to become William. I said, "I'm Simone," and noticed the blue of his eyes.

He had some excuse for being there—did I need a chainsaw or help opening up, did the water line work, did I need more wood. Gordon, taking a rare holiday of his own, had apparently asked William to keep an eye out for me.

William helped me carry in my suitcase and invited me to supper that evening—at his house, as it was then. Unable to resist his crinkle-eyed smile and a ready-made meal, I of course said yes. There, I learned about his son David, working on his business degree, and William's widower-hood.

He confessed to guilty trespasses down my private driveway to see the water—by foot in the fall and muddy season, by skis in winter.

"I hope you don't mind. It's just too beautiful to resist."

"Of course not." What else could I say? I sat at his kitchen table, a plate of roast chicken and mashed potatoes in front of me. Once the phrase had left my mouth, I was surprised that it wasn't a polite lie. If circumstances had been different, I'd have been livid. For example, if we'd met in town and he mentioned enjoying my secluded spot and the beauty of the beach in the fall. Or if he'd been someone else. Yes, the concept of "private property" in the country is fluid at best. We'd always known that curious folks invented reasons to explore our property. Their common pretext was "just to look at the lake." Knowing that they did it didn't mean I had to like it, though.

But I liked William, that afternoon and evening, so much. His thinning dark hair and greying beard. His strong, sun-browned hands. The kindness in his eyes, which widened like a twelve-year-old's as he shared tiny miracles from his year-round life in the place we both considered paradise: the wolf trotting on the thick January ice, the fox dancing with a snowflake. Newborn twin fawns, staggering behind a doe one afternoon in May.

He was perfect, and—most miraculous of all—he thought I was, too.

From there, the days slid into different shades of beautiful, full of platitudinous nonsense—just enough clouds to make us appreciate the sun, enough rain to make us feel young. Et cetera. Fact was, as William said, he and I fit. I never knew, nor needed, another explanation.

That fall, I made several trips south to settle the rest of Carmen's business affairs. I filled out reams of paperwork to immigrate. Meanwhile, William's school year, teaching high school history and geography, had begun in earnest, and I learned that he could be a trifle obsessive about teaching, especially at exam time.

That first Christmas, I'd been nervous about meeting David. He showed no discomfort at all. A small question that loomed large: I wondered whether David and William would hug, and was I supposed to hug David, too. (No and no.)

In retrospect, my presence might have been too soon for David after his mother's death. Joyce must have been a lovely woman to make William so happy. I was sorry not to have met her, but they'd lived in the house only a few years before the quick cancer struck. She was young, in her early fifties, and her death left William devastated. Four years passed while he regained his footing.

Then I arrived, where I felt I'd always belonged. Meeting William was an unexpected bonus. I resolved to make William as happy as possible, and David too. I don't think I succeeded with David. I did with William. No bragging—he said so himself.

But that was partly just William. He found it easy to be happy, and therefore, so did I. We convinced Gordon to retire, mostly. Together, William and I shored up the camp structure, jacking up the corners before settling the frame onto cinderblocks. We tore off roofing paper and laid sheets of particle board before reroofing. A lot of sweat, mostly William's, made the summer camp solid enough to last another century.

We worked well together. And every day began and ended with me in bed next to William watching the sun or moon rise over Lake Superior. How could annoyance and disagreement survive in that world?

Like that, life went along. The days passed, as they do.

When William stopped teaching, I retired from bookkeeping and began my education anew. I read everything he suggested— history, science, literature. We spent long winter hours discussing books, between ski trips around the property. The rest of the year, we worked outdoors, and chores still, always, felt like play.

At last Gordon retired for good, leaving us in Donnie's capable hands, part-time, for what we couldn't do.

We sat on the beach a fair amount of time, and I puttered in my rowboat, too, while William preferred his canoe.

Through the years, lots of people wondered lots of things about us. The reserved, widowed schoolteacher taking up suddenly with a stranger, an American.

Another obvious question: Why did we keep both his house and my summer camp?

It came up again after William died. Why did I stay on, when any normal person would sell the house and move to a condo in town?

Because we were us, and because I was still me. Even without William.

CHEN

Notebook: Tuesday late afternoon
Asia-proprit learning
Look up: dogs. Birds.

After that Martin guy left, we threw rocks a little bit, but Aunt Simka said she was worn out. So we came up and watched a movie about dogs and a cat, *Incredible Journey*. I think Aunt napped during it. She seemed kind of sad when she woke up, but she got out playing cards, real ones, not on a computer.

She said, "Let's play Crazy Eights."

I said, "Okay, but crazy isn't a nice word for people who are sick."

She frowned and shook her head. "You're absolutely right. I'm sorry."

"That's okay." I didn't tell her about the kid at church.

She tapped the cards on the table. "Well. Let's play Go Fish instead."

I beat her twice, and I don't think she let me. She beat me once.

Then I read more in my Sherlock Holmes book. Also I read online about hounds, which are a special kind of dog. I told Simka a lot about them. I've been reading about them and about other animals.

She looked outside. She said, "Hey, it's getting dark. I wish we could throw rocks in the water. Meanwhile, you sound pretty wound up. What if you wrote some, instead of talking?"

She was nice about it, not snappy.

I talked a lot this afternoon again, like a motormouth. Dr. S says I am being anxious. She explained it.

1. I talk too much.
2. Mum calls me motormouth because talk talk talk sounds like a motor. It bugs her.
3. I am not trying to bug Mum, or Aunt Simka either. Sometimes I feel yuck building up, but sometimes I am just anxious about something. Even if I don't know what. Talking too much = anxious.
4. Figure it out. Why am I anxious? Dr. S says to listen to what I am talking about. Or what did I think about just before. Why is it scary?
5. When I know what I am anxious about, I can ask Mum for help with it.

This isn't steps like when Mum and I make cupcakes, but they are anyway things I know about being a motormouth.

So today I am anxious because there is just lots to learn. Too much. Like I didn't even know about hounds before, and now I know there are all different kinds of dogs—different kinds of hounds, even. Same with rocks and birds.

I don't know how to organize myself to learn it all. I want to know everything there is. Mrs. Murray, my teacher, talked about age-appropriate learning. I still don't know what it means. What she meant was, I had to stop asking questions in class. And research the interesting stuff on my own. Like now, Indigenous traditions and the Mayans, and planets.

I want a good job like Daddy. Maybe Mum will be happy again if I learn things. It's okay if I don't go to school, but I still have to do home school right so I don't have to repeat grades. They're boring enough the first time.

I see rocks on the beach and want to know what they are. And I hear birds talking and want to know who they are. Knowing what they're saying is probably too much to wish for.

That's all.

SIMONE

After our card games, I was relieved to be able to make supper in silence, blessed silence, though I felt bad about asking Chen to be quiet. I kept trying to be nice about it, but it still didn't feel good.

I snuck a little zucchini and green peppers into pasta sauce and loaded cheese on top.

Chen speared a spiral pasta on his fork and blew on it to cool it. Then he asked, out of the blue, "Is that Martin guy really your cousin?"

"I'm not sure. Sometimes he seems like it and sometimes he doesn't. What do you think?"

"Mum says cousins can be different from you, but you're still family. My cousins on Daddy's side aren't as sad as I am about the accident. They act like it's all over." He took a bite.

"Well, I guess people are different. It's okay for it to keep being sad for a long time." *Maybe forever*, I didn't say, thinking of William.

"Are you still sad about it? Even if you didn't have relatives die?"

I nodded. "I'm still sad. It's different now. But I still think about all the families." I looked at him. "The driver, too, and his family. I hope that's okay with you."

He shrugged. "Sure. Mum says it wasn't his fault. It was weather. It's kind of hard to be mad at weather. Mum says it's not good to be mad at my cousins, either."

"That's probably hard, too."

He nodded, chewing. Then he said, "I'm just glad I don't have to be at Auntie Sarah's with them."

I smiled. "Me too, kiddo."

After supper, I leafed through the new book of Bible stories while Chen wrote in his notebook and went online. I should have been prepping to read Job aloud.

Instead, I spent some time missing William. He'd have enjoyed Chen's sense of humour. Carmen and Grandpa Jackson had been around, Chen or no Chen. William, not so much. I hoped nothing was wrong. Beyond him being dead, of course. I couldn't help but wonder whether William would come by if I happened to stand by the window as darkness fell.

CHEN

Notebook: Tuesday nite
Martin
Bombships
Birds, basalt
Ice cream

That Martin guy asks a lot of questions. I don't know if Aunt Simka likes it. She sighs a lot.

He is okay I guess. He's old, not old like Aunt but older than Daddy. His hands are kinda brown. There's black under some of the fingernails.

Sometimes when Martin's around Aunt doesn't always make us work. She lets me have screen time while they talk. And she does things in the kitchen, like making coffee or cutting up a cake or stirring something.

At lunch when he showed up, I told Martin, "She's working me so hard she's killing me."

I don't know why that's funny, but it is. It always makes me laugh. He laughed like grownups do when it's not funny but they want you to like them.

Today I threw rocks at a floating log, trying to hit the log then bounce off.

Aunt said, "Where did you learn how to play Bombships? I played that game when I was a little girl just older than you. My father showed me."

I said, "I made it up. I was just throwing and there was a log there. So I aimed at it."

Aunt said, "Well, it's a good game. What do you call it?"

I hadn't named it yet, even in my head. I was just throwing rocks. "Bombships is a good name."

Then I thought about this. Aunt was a little girl? I know she wasn't always old, but it's hard to believe. There's a picture of her and a man on the wall of the living room and she's younger but still a grownup lady, not a baby. I wonder if she has a picture of her as a baby.

Everybody sure loves pictures of babies. I saw lots of them at Grandmother's house after the funeral for Daddy and Ryan. Some were on the table next to Grandmother when she was sitting in that room she calls the parlor. Everybody picked up a picture and said something and put it back down.

Grandmother held up two baby pictures, one of Daddy and one of Ryan. She said, "Oh my goodness! Don't they look alike!"

Then she cried. Mum blew her nose.

Then Mum showed me the pictures. "Look, Chen, doesn't baby Ryan look like Daddy when he was a baby?"

I looked. I guess they did. They looked like babies wearing blue shirts.

I said, "Yes, ma'am."

That was the right thing to say.

...

Part of today's time at the beach Aunt sat in the chair by herself. She looked like she might be talking. She knew I couldn't hear her. Martin wasn't there. So was she maybe just talking, like to herself. Like when she makes those faces, except out loud.

I would worry that she's like that kid at church said, but she seems normal mostly.

Except for oatmeal. And those rocks all over the kitchen. Ry would say, what is up with that. Aunt said the rocks are pretty, and she also said they're nice to have in a pocket. At first I wondered why. It sounded weird.

But she's right. I put a nice gray one in my pocket yesterday. When I put my hand in my pocket, hi, rock, there you are. Then when we were back at the house it went on the dresser in my bedroom, between the picture of me and Mum and Daddy and the one of us in our tournament medals. I got a brown one today.

Today Aunt Simka got kind of mad at Martin, in the kitchen. Not yelling at him but yelling around him. Like Mum used to do during the bad time right after the accident.

Mum would be on the phone. She'd say, "Thank you."

Then she'd hang up and yell, "What kind of idiot do you think I am?"

Or she'd say on the phone, "I'm busy."

And when she hung up, she'd yell about that but then go lie down, not busy. And I had to make a noodle cup in the microwave for lunch and be responsible all on my own.

It's like being polite, how you don't say everything.

Simka was kind of yelling because Martin was like everybody else. I think she hoped he wasn't.

...

235

Mum called. I tried to tell her about all the interesting stuff. But I couldn't figure out how. She's not here, and it's hard to explain it all.

Like the birds. Little ones are everywhere. Aunt showed me a bird book, but it's like one billion years old. Plus it's for all of Canada, not just for this part. When I saw Joseph at the funerals he said our whole grade at school is going to a bird place on the toes of the Sleeping Giant in June. Maybe there's a website and I can look up birds there and learn who they are.

Another thing I don't know about is rocks. On the beach the best ones to skip are black ones. They're flat. They're like a window glass that's broken into big pieces. But black.

Like at that museum Grandmother and Daddy took me and Ry to one time. The Settlers Museum with old farm machines and pails like at Grandmother's farm. One building was a pretend school, and they had a flat black square you held in your hand and wrote on with chalk, like a tablet now. Grandmother said that was slates. Those are the ones Aunt calls basalt.

Aunt also says there's marks in the rocks in the bay around to the left. She says they're like ruts in a muddy road but from a glacier, not a truck. Maybe we can go see it in the rowboat. If it gets warm enough. Aunt Simka says the lake is shoppy a lot at this time of year, and it's more fun when the lake is smooth and the air is warm. She talked a lot about the breeze and the way waves sound against the boat and all the fresh smells.

It sounds like deep water to get there, though. I might be afraid of that. So maybe I won't get to go in the boat before Mum comes home.

I like it when Mum calls. Even if she doesn't know the beach. Or rocks. Or oatmeal.

She talked more at first. Like about the boat she's on. I didn't know it would be like a hotel. I thought it would be more like a school bus, stopping all the time to let people off and on, but I guess you don't sleep on school busses and you do on a cruise. Plus

Mum said it's a ship not a boat. A ship is bigger.

But tonight Bombships was too hard to explain. And anyway, when we talk sometimes my throat closes up around words.

When I get off the phone I feel sad. Aunt got out the atlas and we looked at Alaska. After, Aunt gets us a little bit of ice cream. She says ice cream feels good in throats and smooths out rough edges.

She's pretty smart I think. Not even a little bit crazy. Sick I mean.

SIMONE

After his mother called and we had ice cream, Chen headed to bed. I heard him brushing his teeth without any prompting from me.

It both did and didn't quite feel normal to have someone around all the time. I hadn't experienced someone else's relentless presence since William died. That otherwise normal day, one of the first warm days of June.

To run errands in town, I'd worn sandals for the first time and tossed a light jacket into the back seat instead of wearing it. I waved to William as he trudged behind the lawnmower in the side yard, wisps of grass and flies hanging in the air. He smiled and slowed long enough to wave back, two small white moths chasing each other in a wreath around his hat.

When I got home, I brought the groceries into the house and put everything away. Only then did I lean over the sink to peer out the kitchen window. The lawnmower lay on its side against the trunk of one of the red pines near the steep section of the yard. A lump of fabric lay on the grass nearby. Neither moved.

I knew what that fabric lump was—it was William. Also what it wasn't—it wasn't William. Not anymore. Just the place where he'd been.

The moments after that happened the way everybody always says they do. Time fractured and stopped, stretching into infinity. I ran through the house and around the corner, and I didn't move at all.

Part of me thought that if I got there quickly enough, I could fix it, somehow undo his sudden and apparently painless death. Another part said if I never arrived beside his body, never knelt beside him, ignoring his mottled blue-and-purple face and lips to press my fingers to his neck and listen for breath, his death wouldn't be real.

And even then, he'd still be alive if I just stayed there, without standing up. If I didn't walk indoors, pick up the house phone, say the words aloud, again and again to person after person after official after well-meaning person: "William died."

But I had to do all those things.

I held on the best I could. One evening, I stood watching the Harvest Moon rise over the lake. My eyes told me it was beautiful, but to my head, it marked the end of another dull season. I wondered when I'd feel better.

Then he'd appeared, a warm cloak smelling of woodsmoke and marshmallows. On sunny summer days, mown grass, and fresh work shirts.

That night at the window. Almost every time, at the window. Here. And also not here.

Alive and dead, William knew I wasn't any normal person. He'd been right about Chen—so far, at least.

After acknowledging that much, I went up to say goodnight to Chen. Then I took a book to bed myself, without looking for William.

WEDNESDAY

SIMONE

Wednesday I woke with a shadow hanging over me that even coffee couldn't dispel. As I made oatmeal (Chen wasn't awake yet), I considered the people, dead and alive, casting that shadow.

Martin: It seemed too good to be true. Not him, exactly—he was fine, I guess. My unease was more from the fact of a relative arriving in my life out of nowhere.

Carmen: Aside from the obvious, that she was around at all and still mean, I was thinking about Job. I'd read the story in its easy version to Chen after supper. I'd forgotten to say "donkeys" instead of "asses," so Chen got a good giggle. But I didn't understand why Carmen thought this story would answer Chen's question about capricious gods.

All I'd known about Job was the expression, "the patience of Job." After reading the story, I had no idea why people said it. Job wasn't patient. He cursed the day he was born. His friends lectured him about patience, but that's not the same thing.

I couldn't get over the suspicion that Carmen had sent me on a wild goose chase, and I'd fallen for it while she laughed at me from her perch in the Great Beyond.

Chen: It wasn't his fault he was here—I'd invited him, after all. I thought about Jessica saying she needed a break. I'd understood—or rather, I'd heard her say so, and I knew what all the words meant. But I hadn't *really* understood. Now I did, a little.

Not that Chen was a problem. He was just here, to be planned around and fed. Every day. Three times! And when he wasn't eating, he was breathing. Or talking! Which still got to me. Thank goodness he'd read or write in his notebook when I suggested it. But when he wasn't talking, he was thinking. Which made me think, too, mostly paranoid thoughts. Was he having a good time? Did he like me?

Speaking of always being around for food, Martin had impeccable timing. And voila, we'd come full circle to Martin, the destination when my thoughts were cycling around and around. Martin and family, and now the condo he wanted to swap.

I was feeling, just a little bit, my age. Like I was shuffling many cards, spinning many plates, moving troops on many fronts. However you wanted to express it, life was too busy.

I guess there was a bright spot. I wasn't "sick and tired" anymore.

• • •

After I'd finished my oatmeal, then toast and jam, but before my second cup of coffee, I checked on Chen. He lay in bed, one arm behind his head, reading *The Hound of the Baskervilles*. He waved the book at me.

I leaned against the doorjamb. "It's after 8. You're a little slow moving around this morning."

244

He yawned. "I heard it raining so I didn't think we'd be in a hurry to go anywhere."

"You're right. Get up when you feel like it, and we'll go to town. Pick up a few things."

"Okay. Just a little more to the end of the chapter."

"Great. You'll have time to take a shower before we go."

He sighed but didn't complain audibly. I counted it a win.

With my second cup of coffee, I surveyed my mind map of chores. We'd cleared some overgrown alder and red willow. We'd attacked the endless balsam fingers that poke up in what, according to my grandfather, was once an excellent vegetable garden. With good weather, we'd soon be able to clear the garden plots and turn the soil. I was no gardener, but even I knew it was a full month early to plant anything. Poor Chen would have the work of clearing brush and none of the fun of planting. If we got that far. Rain might have other plans.

As my grandfather said, and my husband agreed, working in the bush makes you feel omnipotent and inconsequential at the same time. They'd both cleared many stands of tag alder and moose maple when they were alive, and they'd felt they'd done something of note. But a year later, that "something of note" would be difficult to see. Creating an absence wasn't as enduring as creating a presence. Even in their own deaths, they weren't as absent as they were present beyond expectation, given their ongoing ghostly selves.

Chen needed the chance to make something, something that would stay after he was gone. He'd learned a lot, and quickly too. Like which blade of the loppers was the sharp one, and where to spray the WD-40, and how to wipe them clean after you use them. The value of long sleeves and work gloves. He had a new appreciation for that most miraculous of inventions, the wheelbarrow.

He'd mentioned gods only once since Sunday. After Martin left Monday, we'd gone back to work, except that Chen couldn't find the place we'd been working. Nothing, NOT ONE THING, looked any different. His brows drew together and I wondered if he'd cry.

I tried to sound encouraging. "Nature is a goddess of fertility. She loves nothing more than growing."

He shook his head. "Aunt Simka, if I were making up the gods, I'd make up a god of *un*fertility."

I laughed till I had to sit down, which pleased him.

My second cup of coffee had become my third and disappeared. I checked on Chen, who was asleep or pretending to be. I poured myself a fourth cup of coffee, though who's counting, really, and headed into the den with Martin's condo paperwork and my notebook. I pondered my notes and almost hoped my mother would show up to ask pointed questions. But she wasn't of a mind to be there.

So I opened a web browser. I typed "James LeMay" in the search box. Then I looked at it for a while, asking myself the same questions: What if I had an uncle? What if I didn't? At last, I pressed Enter.

Results! Too many. I scrolled down the first page—along with the Facebook accounts, I saw several find-a-cemetery-plots and obituaries. One of which could be my uncle. Or none. Did I want to know?

I could search for Martin LeMay. Or even Charles LeMay. Daddy. Instead, I closed the browser and went to roust out Chen. We'd outwit this gloomy, rainy day by running errands.

...

In the car, Chen was quiet for a change. So, I made conversation. "What does your Mom do for work? I'm not sure I know."

"She used to work at the bank but she hasn't since—you know. My Daddy had rent houses and works—worked for Consolidated Business Solutions, in HR."

I let humour show in my voice. "In a jar?"

"HR. Human something."

"Resources. I know. I said 'a jar' because it sounds like HR." A pause, while I kept my eyes on the road but noticed he wasn't laughing. "It was a joke. I was being funny."

He sniffed then and looked at the passenger side window.

"Except apparently it wasn't funny."

A pause. "You mean like you said 'a jar' pretending that's what you'd thought I said?"

"Yes. It's a type of joke."

"Oh! I do that. Mum says I'm being silly. Sometimes, she says that."

He was quiet for another minute. "It's just—it's okay, Simka, I know you meant to be funny. But my Daddy *is* in a jar. Mum gave the big jar to my grandparents to bury. She has some in a box in the closet." He sniffed and finished in a smaller voice. "And I think she has some with her."

I felt worse by the second. "Oh God, Chen, I'm so sorry. I had no idea."

Except that I had known—or at least I should have. Of course there'd be an urn somewhere. Which some might call a jar. But I hadn't followed the thought to its natural conclusion.

I groaned. "Chen, I'm really sorry for making that joke."

"It's okay." His face was still to the window.

"Do you want to talk about your mother having some—some ashes with her? We can or we don't have to. Either way is fine with me."

A shrug.

Okey-doke. I kept my mouth shut the rest of the way to Canadian Tire.

On our way into the store, we passed the hot dog stand. They always smelled so good, though I never ate them. I already knew Chen didn't like them, so I didn't ask.

Inside, I cruised up and down aisles until I found leather work gloves. Chen put on a pair, sized small and probably meant for women. He could have put both hands into one glove, but he grinned so big that we had to get them. Obviously.

Then we stopped by the sporting goods display because I thought he might like to look at the bicycles. Don't kids generally like bikes? Maybe Chen would, too. And yet again, Chen wasn't a general kid but a specific one. He looked briefly while I scanned the cycling gloves on the off chance that something there might fit him better. Fruitlessly, it turned out.

He yawned. "What else do we need, Aunt?"

He looked up at me, such a good sport on a rainy day, with a father in a jar. A tsunami of awfulness washed over me again.

In line at the till, I poked him so he'd stop fingering the packets of gum. In a low voice, I said, "I feel terrible about my joke this morning, and I am in serious need of something to make it go away."

He opened his eyes wide and blinked like Bambi. "When I feel terrible, sometimes I need a treat and then I feel better. Like ice cream."

"Is that so. Have we not been having ice cream this week?"

"Yes, but—but there's a whole store with different kinds of ice cream at the mall. And toppings like candy and sprinkles."

"And you think I'd feel less terrible? Not just the same amount of terrible, with candy and sprinkles on top?"

He smiled at my tone. "Uh-huh. Or—I don't know." He shifted from foot to foot, considering. "Maybe a hot dog. From that guy outside."

"Your mother said you didn't like them."

"I don't, with her. Me and Daddy, and Ryan, we used to come here a lot on weekends, and I always liked getting one with him. That was different."

I didn't really follow, but it didn't matter. "Well, if you want a hot dog, that's an option." I'd have bought him both ice cream and a hot dog, if he'd suggested it. Or a puppy. Maybe a pony.

He considered. "Thanks, but I'd rather have a fancy ice cream."

We paid. On our way out, he eyed the hot dogs but shook his head. As I started the car, I said, "Are you sure, are you absolutely positively sure that fancy ice cream from the mall will make my terrible feeling go away?"

"Yep, for now. But not forever. You might need more ice cream later. But the vanilla at home might be good enough for later."

"I like how you think."

The fancy ice cream was excellent.

CHEN

Notebook: Wednesday afternoon
Polite
Indoors and outdoors
Gloves! For shudders
Condos

It is pretty hard to be here now. So much politeness. I want to be polite, like Mum tells me. It just seems forever. Day after day and more and more. I still like Aunt Simka. I think she is nice. And she is trying her best. But this is a lot of days. And even when she is not doing something wrong, sometimes I just want to be back at my home. I get sad.

Today we did indoor things. I used to like only indoor things, games and movies and books. Now I like outdoor things too. Chores aren't bad I guess. Outdoors has other fun stuff. Like looking at things, rocks and moss and birds. Trees too. I miss being down there by the water, throwing rocks and exploring and waiting for bears.

Being inside means I don't get as dirty and don't have to take baths as much. I took one Saturday night for Sunday. Sunday I stayed pretty clean. Then she made me take one on Monday night. And a shower, too, this morning.

When we went to Canadian Tire, it was rainy and cold outside. Not cold like winter but not warm like summer. It's cold like you wish it wasn't, but it's going to be chilly no matter what. Sweatshirt and warm socks cold.

I got work gloves Simka bought for me. They're size small and too big still but not as big as the old ones I was wearing. And they're not crunchy and yucky.

Aunt says don't try to keep work gloves clean, they're supposed to keep your hands clean. But I like knowing that when there's dirt on them, it's my own dirt. And just my hands have been inside. Nobody else's.

At the bookstore at the mall, I got a graphic novel of the same Sherlock Holmes story, the Baskskervilles one with the dogs.

See, this is how it's hard being polite. I think it's funny to say Baskskervilles or even Baskskskskerskervilles. It's a fun word to say, and I think it's funny to say it just a little bit wrong. It makes me laugh.

Ry would say, "That's not funny. That's just stupid baby talk."

It's not baby talk. It just makes me laugh. When I said it today in the bookstore, Aunt Simka looked at me like maybe I didn't know they were really just Baskervilles.

I guess I am the only one who thinks it's funny. So I am trying not to say it out loud.

When we got home, I wanted some screen time. Aunt said first could I help her on the computer a little bit, to look up that condo Martin told her about. I showed her how Daddy looks up things online, if a property sold lately and how much. He'd let me sit on his lap or sometimes stand between him and the desk while he worked. Sometimes I got to drive the mouse.

Aunt was surprised when she found a complex like the one on the paper Martin gave her. I guess she thought they were maybe fake? Maybe for not a real place, like Neverneverland isn't really real. But one unit in there sold with lots of zeroes (that's how Daddy always says it) (or he used to).

She said, "Well, I'll be."

I said, "What. What'll you be?"

She laughed. "Surprised. Martin is being honest about some of this."

She didn't want to explain more, though. She let me look up kinds of birds. And she asked if she could have more quiet time. She was pretty nice about it. Not snappy. So I tried to remember, but she had to tell me another time to be quiet.

Not very many days left. But so much politeness.

MARTIN

The rain made Martin's determination to be outdoors a challenge. Then again, he didn't mind a challenge about rain. Easier to handle than a people challenge.

At the waterfront, he'd found a pavilion sheltering four picnic tables. He sat near the edge. Three other guys, maybe living rough or maybe just rained out of the day's work, chatted at one of the other tables. One had a fast-food coffee cup, but from the slurring of his words, Martin guessed whatever coffee it held was doctored with something. They ignored him.

Even in the rain, Martin liked being in a new place. The downside to traveling, though, was not knowing people. Even at the meetings, he knew only Alex and that Donnie guy. He'd nodded at a few others, but that was it so far. Harry would say, *It takes time.* Which Martin knew. He just wished it didn't take so much time.

He found himself missing Harry all over again. It meant a lot to him that one of Harry's buddies had recommended him to that guy at the food truck. Connections reaching that far back felt good.

Come to think of it, he did know other people here. Simone and Chen, though it wasn't Martin, exactly, but Martin-as-possible-cousin that they knew. And Barb, though she knew him only as a hotel guest. Thanks to her, and even Alex and the rest of them, he'd looked up that accident. It helped him understand a little more about the people here, and it gave him the beginning of community feeling. Maybe.

He opened the paperback book he'd chosen from the meagre selection at Harbour Foods. White cover, black lettering, red blood drops. He didn't read much, but he felt pretty sure that if he really were Simone's cousin, he might, so having a book was a good prop.

And while he hadn't seen Ken himself at Harbour Foods, a different morose black-clad person kept watch at the door. Where the kid wasn't, either.

In fact, Martin hadn't caught up to the kid yet. After almost freezing to death on his walk to Harbour Foods that morning— just looking for something interesting for breakfast, he'd told himself—he'd found a Value Village. He bought a heavyweight hoodie, like hunters wear, and a compact umbrella.

Part of him wondered why he was so hell-bent on being outdoors. But hanging around in his hotel room or sightseeing in the rain weren't appealing. He'd always enjoyed being outdoors, so by God he was going to spend time outdoors. For no other reason. It had nothing to do with anybody else, nobody to protect or watch out for, the way he might have wished someone had cared about him, years ago.

Whatever you need to tell yourself, Harry would say.

He'd driven to the parking lot at the waterfront, but he couldn't see anything from the car. Between downpours, the rain swirled and slacked off, sometimes to nothing, and Martin had taken advantage of one of those breaks to find this pavilion, with an empty table.

He read a few pages and looked to see if anyone had showed up at the skate park. Not yet. He tried a few more pages. Wash, rinse, repeat. It was hard to keep his mind on the story.

The sky lightened—not for long, by the looks of the scudding clouds, but long enough for a change of scene. The other guys in the pavilion got up and drifted toward a pedestrian bridge that led to fast-food restaurants.

At last, some privacy. No chance of being overheard, not by Barb or some other random hotel guest, or one of these other guys in the pavilion. It was show time. Martin reviewed his opening lines and the information he was trying to get. *Acting isn't the same as lying,* he reminded himself. Then he pulled his phone from his pocket.

Mr. Smith answered on the first ring. "Why are you calling? Has she agreed to sell?"

"Working on it. But listen. I have an idea. This Simone lady has quite the nice setup, that house, good stuff in it. Valuable. And she's all alone." Martin pushed some bite into his voice. "I've met some guys. They could break into her house. Maybe rough her up a bit, enough for the hospital. Once there, she'd be easier to talk into selling. Vulnerable, you know."

Silence.

Martin wasn't sure Mr. Smith had heard. "You there?"

"I'm thinking." More silence. "No. Not necessary. What's taking you so long, anyway? It's not hard. You're looking out for your beloved cousin's best interests. Shit." He sounded wound up.

"She's old but no pushover. And you said it might take a couple of weeks."

"It's *been* a couple of weeks. You should be talking contracts with her." A pause. "Don't try this other shit."

The phone went dead. Martin scowled. Mr. Smith—David— had not only listened to Martin's ridiculous idea, he'd actually thought about it before warning him off. Martin didn't like that at all.

...

The rain let up, mostly, but still the afternoon dragged. He was about to give up and head back to his car when a group of kids crossed into the skate park.

Martin got up and stretched, glad to see the group, happy they seemed okay.

Then two other guys, one of them the older bald guy from the weekend, strolled up to the kids, and Martin sat back down.

They went through the same routine—claps on the back, pokes in the rib, more laughter, but Martin thought the kid's laughter had become nervous. The older guy caught the kid in a headlock and punched him in the ribs, hard, before releasing him with a laugh and a push.

Martin stood again, but stopped himself. He had to stay out of it.

The kid stayed doubled over while his friends backed away. One older guy followed in a swagger, and they backed up further. The other older guy bent over, his hand on the kid's back, and said a few things into his ear. The kid straightened up. The guy patted his back and strolled away with his buddy. The kid's friends gathered around him and herded him to a bench.

Martin covered much of the distance between them as casually as he could. From twenty feet away, he said, "Hey. Hey, are you okay?"

The kid and his friends turned frowns toward him, but the whine of a souped-up car engine diverted their attention.

Martin looked, too. A cop car pulled up to park illegally at the edge of the lot. No lights or sirens, but two uniformed officers got out in a hurry, heading toward the skate park. Martin altered course, drifting toward the parking lot.

A third officer too-casually intercepted him. "Excuse me. Sir? Did you see an incident here?"

"An incident?"

"Maybe a fight?"

Martin edged toward his car. "Oh, I don't know." He waved in the direction of the kids, now talking to the other officers. "The people there were laughing. Then some of them left. I don't know why." He paused. "That one kid looks hurt, maybe."

She flashed a glance toward the kid. "Ah." She turned back to him, watchful. "Is he a friend of yours?"

"Not really. I've seen him around." He all but shrugged. "They seem like good kids."

She nodded. "I hear you." Then she flashed an interested smile. "So what's your business down here? It's rainy—not a nice day to hang around."

Martin wasn't fooled. He smiled, his eyes wide and unthreatening. "It feels good to be outdoors, even in the rain. Winter gets long."

The cop looked him up and down. "Well, enjoy it. Listen, if you see something you want to tell me about, call the anonymous tip line. And stay dry. Looks like more rain's on the way."

"Yeah, sure will." Taking a step backward, Martin resisted waving. He sauntered to his car, just someone who hadn't seen anything.

Once in the car, he made no move to leave.

He didn't feel good about himself anymore. That whole conversation with Mr. Smith, whether it was pretending or acting or downright lying, had come easily to Martin. Too easily. And then Mr. Smith had paused too long for Martin's comfort. What if Mr. Smith changed his mind and decided roughing up Simone was a good idea?

And Martin really needed to let go of this kid. The kid didn't want help from him, no matter how sorry Martin was for spying on him. The envelope Ken had given him, holding five twenty-dollar bills, was zipped into his portfolio, back in the hotel. For no good reason, Martin didn't want it. But giving it back to Ken felt ridiculous. So there it sat.

Martin groaned. Everything today felt wrong. Work like this took him several hundred steps backward, back to the kind of life he really wanted to put behind him.

He thought about the old guy under the pavilion with the boozed-up coffee. How far away, really, was that world?

Pretending, acting, lying. They felt all the same. Like they'd risk his sobriety.

He had to figure out something to do the envelope and resolve things with Simone and Mr. Smith. Tomorrow. Then he'd be free.

CHEN

We had more quiet time in the afternoon. I was thinking about something she said about the accident. I hadn't thought about it before.

The man who drove the truck that slid in the accident, he died too, but not till the day after, not right away like Daddy and Ry and Ry's Mum. He was far away from his home in Nova Scotia, no family with him in the hospital. Maybe a nurse or a doctor, and maybe they were nice, but they didn't know him, not his wife or son or grandson or anybody.

Aunt said, "I couldn't do anything about it then and I can't fix it now, though I think about it from time to time. It's just a sad fact of life. Not like in Job, where the devil is being mean and

259

God's letting him, not stopping it."

She thought a little bit and then said, "I think I need to read that story again because I don't understand it."

I didn't know that about the truck driver in the accident. And I didn't tell her the thing about the accident that I don't like to think about, that Mum and Dr. Samuelson say I am not supposed to think about.

...

Mum called tonight. I didn't tell her about Simka telling me to please be quiet, yesterday or today. Or that Eights card game. Those are hard to talk about on the phone.

Tonight at supper Simka said I could talk again. It had been a while. I told her about learning and jobs, what I thought about yesterday, and what to be when I grow up.

Aunt said, "There's plenty of time for jobs. You're learning a lot this week. Things you learn from working outdoors are good to know in the future."

I said, "But Daddy went to an office, not outdoors, and he didn't rake there. He never talked about raking. And I don't want a job like raking when I grow up."

Aunt laughed. She said, "You are smart and will be able to learn lots of things that nobody even knows about yet. But if you end up raking, that's okay. It's good work."

Then she said, "Write down what you are learning. You can tell your Mum. And maybe you know more about things than you think. Maybe you know enough to pass a test."

I said, "Only if they ask me about raking and lopping."

She laughed again. Which is good. That's why I said it.

...

I didn't say I feel bad about growing up, but I do sometimes. Ryan doesn't get to. It feels like it's my fault. Like I cheated.

One time I even thought, what if I don't get to grow up? Ryan didn't get to, and he didn't know he wouldn't. I hope I get to. I want to be as old as Daddy someday. Maybe even as old as Gumpy or that man with the ax in the picture in the camp.

So here's what I learned. So far.

Raking. Make a circle in your head.

Lopping. It's more fun than the piling part.

Piles 2 GIANT steps. When you make a pile of branches and leaves, you have to take at least two steps off the path. Throw them in far, branches go stick end first not the fluffy end.

Garden, where. Where it's been before.

Paths. Where the deer already go is good.

Tripping. Watch your feet so roots don't trip you up.

Life isn't fair. She hasn't said it as much lately. But it's not—grownups are in charge. And even then, there are accidents.

There's always more work after the work stops being fun.

...

Yesterday we were down at the lake and I had to pee. I didn't want to go all the way up to the house. But Mum never liked it when we peed outdoors. Ry did sometimes in our backyard and made fun of me for going inside.

But Mum always said, "That's gross. We are civilized."

When we were going fishing that time everybody else saw the bear and I didn't, Mum made me go in the outhouse and boy it stank. Ryan snuck away and peed outdoors.

Anyway, today I really really had to pee. So I asked Aunt if I could pee outdoors.

She said, "Okay. Do you know how?"

I said, "I know how to pee."

She laughed and said, "Well, that part's important."

But then she told me some other stuff.

First you go away from where people are or where they walk with bare feet. Nobody walks anywhere with bare feet now because it's cold but I knew what she meant. Then you go behind something for privacy and stand uphill from your target tree and face downhill.

I said, "How come?"

"You'll see."

She was right. I didn't have to try it, even. "To keep your socks dry."

I like making her laugh.

When I was done, she said, "I understand why your mother doesn't like it. It's different in a city backyard. In general, I find that peeing outdoors is okay when you're considerate of other people."

She meant like not peeing where people walk. I went back near the cliff.

And Aunt Simka wasn't embarrassed to tell me about how to be considerate. I wonder what Mum will think.

•••

I really think Aunt Simka doesn't read this. I think she is not nosy. I know Mum read my notebooks. She said she didn't, but she did. Maybe Aunt doesn't read them because she doesn't care. She seems to like me, though.

I wonder if Daddy would like her. He might talk bad about her because she's old. He talked bad about Gramm and Gramps even though they were dead. He said we didn't need their old stuff, who cared.

Mum got mad. She said, "They loved me and anyway your family's not full of angels."

He didn't talk bad about Gramm and Gramps after that.

Lots of angels in the family now.

I guess it doesn't matter anymore if Daddy likes Aunt Simka. That makes me sad to think about, so I won't.

SIMONE

After Chen went to bed, I looked around for a book to escape into. There was his *Hound of the Baskervilles*, the source of his chatter about hounds lately, which had led me to asking for more quiet time.

I winced. I'd told this thoughtful, imaginative nine-year-old to stop talking to me. More than once, even! I was a horrible, mean person. I was an apple falling not far from a tree.

Instead of reading, I looked out into the evening. In spite of the clouds, I knew where the stars glimmered and the lake lay. I painted them in mentally.

I waited. Nothing.

The past few days had shown me a lot about myself. However late and reluctant my offer to keep Chen had been, I'd meant it. And I thought we'd had some fun. Everything had gone reasonably well.

But my shortened fuse sobered me. I didn't want to yell at him. Would I be able to make it till Saturday? Part of me thought, "Just a few more days," and another part shouted, "*more* days?"

Maybe this is what parents felt like.

At last. Amusement, the first inkling I had of William's presence. Not laughter, exactly, nothing I could hear. Just an unexpected shimmer in the evening, like the peek-a-boo moon.

William had taught me all I'd ever understood about the mystery of parental hopes and dreams. One Christmas that David was with us, he had spent the better part of a night on the phone, struggling with an Asian investment gone wrong. David blamed the problem on miscommunication and cultural differences.

William had been so proud: *My son does international business deals with Japanese companies.* William's own parents had emigrated from farms in Scandinavia, with hit-or-miss educations and childhoods full of hunger and backbreaking labour. William's university degree and teaching career left them in awe. They could never have imagined their grandson's life, the amounts of money he handled.

At the time, I'd made polite "hmmm" noises, not mentioning David's tenacity, what some might call stubbornness, which he'd inherited from William. And of course William had known David longer. The young boy opening birthday presents, heading off to school with a brand-new loose tooth, graduating Grade 8. William must have been able to see those versions of David in the grown-up man with a hard exterior and know, or remember, that David was soft inside.

Fortunately, William had been clear-eyed about investing. He never put money into David's deals. We never discussed that David lost money as well as making it.

Now, clouds shrouding the moon, I felt William's amusement fade. A shadow fell, something not quite right between us. He was gone.

I let it be. He'd come back. Chen hadn't driven him away. I'd been busy, but I still had room in my life for these moments. And so, apparently, did he.

THURSDAY

CHEN

<u>Notebook: Thursday morning</u>
Rain = 4 + EVER
Snow = rain but pretty. Fog = mist-sterious. Haha.
Baskskskervilles books. Dog = scarry.
Is a bear scarry I HOPE I FIND OUT

It's been raining a lot. Like a LOT a lot, all night and all day so far. Here are some things I know about rain.

> 1. Rainy days = I want to stay indoors. Sometimes.
> 2. Sometimes I'm mad because I want to go outdoors.
> 3. Wet from rain = bad. It feels prickly on my skin. Itchy like bug bites after you itch them a little bit,

but all over. And cold.

4. Dry off. With a towel. After you go outside in the rain you don't ever feel dry and warm again unless you get naked and dry off with a towel like you just had a bath.

5. You need dry clothes. Separate from drying off. One time we got wet in rain and Mum tumbled my shirt and socks in the dryer, but they never felt all the way dry. I put on different ones. Maybe the first ones were okay dry. But sometimes you just need to know you have dry clothes on.

6. Snow = rain but pretty. Grownups get grounchy about snow, but they still say it's pretty. Till January or February maybe. Then they complain. Nobody hardly ever says rain is pretty. Maybe in that movie *Bambi*.

7. Fog = rain but also not. Some grownups think fog is mysterious. Like in the *Hound of the Baskervilles*. Lots of fog in that book.

Mum said one time her brain was foggy. It was after the accident and she forgot things. A lot of things. And had to stay in bed some days. And I had to be responsible.

It felt cozy sometimes. I did my school even if she wasn't in the room to make me. Mostly reading. When she feels good, Mum sometimes sits with me, and she always makes me look up stuff for myself even when she knows the answer. Sometimes on her tablet but sometimes in the print encyclopaedias. They're hard, almost like the Baskskervilles book.

Aunt Simka and I talked about my book some. About what the story means. I kind of don't see why the dog is so scary. Yeah it howls. I guess it's big. And its teeth glow in the dark. Okay maybe that would be scary in real life.

Aunt said, "Don't forget—they didn't have the kind of movies you do. They didn't have any special effects. They had to imagine everything."

So maybe in imagination it would be bigger and scarier.

I still don't think I'd be scared if I saw a bear. I am running out of days to find out.

Aunt said the weather is iffy today, but we're going out anyway. I want to read but I want to look for bears too. I don't really like being in the rain but a chance of bears might make it okay.

SIMONE

Thursday the sky threatened rain without delivering, an in-between state that left me equally unsettled.

I dithered. We'd survived one lazy day, but Chen had brand-new work gloves that needed to get dirty. Neither the threat nor the promise of rain was actual rain.

I said to Chen, "Let's go outside. Maybe then the weather will make up its mind." He didn't leap up. "Who knows, maybe there will be a bear."

His face brightened. "Can I throw rocks first?"

"Of course."

The walk down was uneventful. While he warmed up his arm, I found the coffee can for the screws and planned our attack. First, we'd take shutters off the windows along the front, so he could watch how I did it. Then the bedrooms, where the shutters were smaller, held by just a couple of screws near the bottom. By that time, Chen would probably want to use the battery-powered drill.

We finished the shutters on the front and back. Then we went to the side. Chen extracted exactly two screws before the rain became uncomfortable. I sent him into the camp while I finished that one and stowed it with the others by the woodshed, back where Martin had headed into the bush in search of junk piles. By that time, the rain had stopped again. But only temporarily, by the looks of the sky. We sat indoors for a while, waiting for the sky to make up its mind.

Chen poked around on the bookshelves, making just enough noise to jangle my nerves. I gritted my teeth as I stood at the front window, newly un-shuttered. At least that was done. I forced my attention from Chen's restlessness to focus on the lake. I watched patterns on the waves scud left to right while the water moved right to left. Yet the overcast skies didn't change.

At the table, Carmen said, "Boy, do you know how to show a kid a good time." She wore camp clothes again, a different sweatshirt and slacks. Red lipstick, though.

I looked pointedly through the window, where rain dripped from bare branches and fog swirled. I then sat in one of the big wicker chairs, uncomfortable though they are without cushions. Well. It was an uncomfortable day.

Carmen shook her head at me. "The weather? An excuse. You're full of them, when there's work to be done."

"Hey Simka, can I play with this?" Chen, at the bookshelf, turned toward me, holding a dark box. "I think it's Dominos?"

"Sure. Take them to the table." Carmen shot me a dirty look and moved down a chair. I suppressed my smile. "After I collect my thoughts, maybe we can play a game."

He settled in, absorbed in laying out lines for what seemed to be a small house and corral.

Carmen said, "He hates this, you know. Whatever he tells you. You can't trust what he says, and you can't trust him. You obviously don't know little kids."

As if you did, I couldn't say. Infuriating.

She drummed her fingers soundlessly on the table. "That Martin, too. You can't trust him. You need to be more suspicious. Gifts from the sky usually are too good to be true."

For a moment, I agreed. Then I remembered William. He'd landed, unasked-for, in my life, and made it better than I'd imagined. Carmen was wrong, again. I shook my head at her and then froze—Chen, though, had most of his back to me and was absorbed in his structure.

Pretending to ignore Carmen, I closed my eyes.

Immediately, I was back in Missouri, nearly twelve, on an autumn afternoon. We sixth-graders had just finished lunch and waited in single file to troop indoors for the last two hours of the school day. The Missouri hillsides gleamed red and orange, yellow and rusty brown.

Ahead of me in line, Linda, the principal's daughter, whispered something to two other girls, and all three giggled.

I ignored them. Everybody whispered, and they'd whispered more since my father died.

The class played a spelling game to review for a quiz the next day. When I correctly spelled "typhoid," a word from the eighth-grade graduation exam, Mrs. Franklin gave me a look I couldn't read.

She caught me on my way out of class. "Simone, dear. Linda just told me about your parents."

"What about them?"

She lowered her voice. "Their *divorce*. You've been doing so well at school. I hope you can keep it up."

I tightened my fingers on my notebook and stared at the bridge of her nose. "They're not divorced. He's dead. My mother said so. That's what's true." I turned on my heel.

She never brought it up again. Nobody else ever tried to talk to me about it.

For a while, I wondered, "divorce" hissing in my ears. I couldn't ask Carmen, obviously. Asking someone else would be embarrassing, and hell itself if Carmen found out. So I forced myself to stop wondering.

When I was in late high school, a parade of young men from our town served and died in Vietnam. Then I did become suspicious. Carmen and I had never gone to a funeral, and we never visited a gravestone. We didn't mark important dates—"gone one year," that kind of thing.

When Carmen said my father was dead, had he actually ceased breathing on this earth? Or did she just wish he had? It probably didn't matter. He was dead to her, which amounted to the same thing. And dead or not, Daddy was gone.

Later I learned that never asking anyone about anything had cost me my Jackson grandparents, Carmen's parents. They might have seen me as an infant or toddler, but I didn't remember. When my grandfather's ghost appeared, I caught glimmers of something: vanilla ice cream, in a gleaming minaret rising from a cone, held by a man's hand. Nothing clearer.

At 17, I took a part-time job as a file clerk to pay for a bookkeeping certification. Later, I chose to live in Taos because it was a very long day's drive away from Carmen. For years I lived like a monk, working and saving money so I could buy the camp someday, phoning Carmen occasionally, dealing with her every summer for our time at the lake.

In all those years, Carmen never once talked about her parents. When I finally moved here, I learned that they'd been alive until I was nearly twenty. If they left her anything in their wills, she drank it away.

As William and I built our life together, pieces from my childhood fell into place. During the summers when I was young, we hadn't gone to church. Only when I was in my mid-twenties and brought her up every summer did we slip into the pews on Sundays—my grandparents would have been gone by then. After the service, our conversations with other churchgoers were ten-minute pleasantries over coffee, just time enough for them to be kind, but not for questions that approached trickier territory.

My grandparents, my father. Blank outlines where people should be.

William had to listen to me think aloud about it for a few years. I'd go around a loop: My father might be alive. But in all the years since, why hadn't he looked for me? Same with my grandparents. Even if they didn't want to see Carmen, they'd known I existed. So why hadn't they tried to find me?

As William pointed out, they might have tried. Carmen might have ignored them. She might also have used me as a pawn, taunting them by keeping us apart. I'd never know.

I'd indulged my hurt feelings and never checked. After all, I had William. What did I need probably-dead relatives for? I finally stepped off the "what if" merry-go-round.

Family. I'd always made a mess of it, and I'd ended up alone in the world.

Alone with my ghosts.

Unless I believed Martin. Which I wanted to. Suspicious or not.

MARTIN

Thursday morning, Martin felt hopeful. By the end of the day, he'd be out of every single mess he'd gotten into. And whatever came next, at least he'd be telling the truth.

First, he looked up the anonymous tip line that the cop had mentioned. From his burner, he left a message with Ken's name and number, saying that Ken claimed to be the boy's uncle but didn't seem to have his best interests at heart. Then he hung up. Done.

Next task. He drove the route he'd planned the evening before. The Harbour Foods kid wasn't at the skatepark yet. A couple of slow circuits of the parking areas at the waterfront yielded no sightings, either. So Martin went to Harbour Foods itself, and bingo, the kid stood beside the door, hands in hoodie pockets. Martin parked and took a deep breath before getting out and walking over.

The kid squinted up at him, face unfriendly.

Martin handed him Ken's white envelope, the crisp bills still inside. He wanted to say something important. He managed, "Take care of yourself."

He didn't look toward the kid before leaving the parking lot.

And that's that. A good start. He wound through town to the highway that led to Simone's house. Just beyond the city limits, fog lay across the trees to his right, shrouding the lake beyond.

His burner phone rang. Martin ignored it, but a beep a minute or two later alerted him to voicemail. He pulled over to check. Mist swirled, making spots on his windshield.

"New plan," Mr. Smith's message said, by way of greeting. "Something you said yesterday made me wonder. Is she really healthy? Is she competent to make decisions? Things like that. We may need to adjust our strategy."

"Oh my God." Martin said aloud.

"Good news for you. With this information, I'll pay you double."

Martin groaned. Money again. But this money would be tainted, even more than the cash in the envelope he'd just ditched.

Mr. Smith went on, so smoothly that Martin could almost imagine him smiling. "Look carefully. Is everything falling apart? Does she say weird things? I need to know if she's failing, decrepit, making bad decisions. Get back to me today." Beeps indicated the end of the message.

Martin sat in the unmoving car, unhappy. Mr. Smith wanted Simone to be incompetent.

Worse, Mr. Smith thought of it because of Martin's test yesterday. Lying got Martin in trouble every single time. He groaned again.

He'd had it all worked out, picture-perfect. He'd park in his usual spot in front of Simone's house. He'd knock and be welcomed into the house, which would smell like a mouth-watering late breakfast. Then he'd ask to speak to Simone alone. Chen would love to go off and play on the computer.

He'd say, "Look, I'm not your cousin, but I think you should sell your place." He'd probably have to backtrack at that point, explain the independent operator for a numbered company. But he wouldn't mention David or even Mr. Smith unless he had to. He'd even own the idea that maybe she'd sell more readily to a long-lost cousin. And of course he'd have to confess to the condo he didn't have.

After that, the details were hazy. Who said what, whether there was yelling, how often Martin had to apologize, whether they had a chance to calm down together. A lot depended on Simone's response, and Martin couldn't control that. Or predict it, either.

But telling her in that way could bring the best of all possible outcomes. No more lying. Mr. Smith would get the property, and Martin would get the remaining payment.

Even Simone would benefit. For one thing, she'd be out from under all the seasonal work she had to do. Hell, Martin was some fifteen years younger than Simone and loved landscaping, and even he got tired of caring for sod and plants some days. She must, too. The money part would be great for Simone. Of course, nothing could compensate Simone for her love of that little shack by the lake.

Martin winced. How do you put a dollar amount on love?

Selling her lake property wouldn't make her leave the area. She'd still live in the house, where she'd have a front-row seat to all the changes. The teardown, the bulldozing, the trucks and powerlines, the digging for septic tanks and wells, all the destruction and mud. That would be hard to take, but probably not enough to drive her away.

Someday, everything would fall apart. Sooner or later, she'd figure out that the person behind the numbered company was David.

That would hurt, too.

The whole thing might not work. She might refuse to sell the property. Martin wouldn't get the rest of his money. And the devious and disappointed Mr. Smith would be furious.

And what if Simone got mad enough to call the cops like he'd worried about, back at the beginning of this whole adventure? Then Martin could be in trouble with the law *and* Mr. Smith *and* Simone.

Martin sat in the car on the side of the road. No good options.

The rain began. Not much. Just enough to remind Martin how absolutely sick he was of rain.

He flicked on his wipers. Left, then right, they carved and maintained a clear spot in the windshield. Left, then right.

At last, he looked at something he'd been ignoring. Maybe Mr. Smith was right. Or at least not wrong.

Maybe Simone wasn't okay. She blanked sometimes, almost like she heard things Martin didn't or she lived in a world he couldn't see. Maybe she only seemed organized because she was abrupt and kind of prickly. Maybe just below that surface, she was barely holding on, or even making big mistakes. Was it safe for her to live alone anymore? And right now, Chen was with her. Was he safe?

Martin sighed. That put a different light on things. Maybe he didn't have to tell the truth, not yet.

Okay, new plan, but not Mr. Smith's. For now, the responsible thing to do was really watch her. See if she was okay, and if Chen was.

As Martin drove, the rain eased, becoming thick mist before petering out. The fog banks swirled over the road.

SIMONE

Crashing dominoes startled me. Chen looked sheepish. "Sorry, Simka."

Had I been asleep? Carmen sighed audibly, arms folded on the table, and dropped her head to rest on them.

I went to the window again to survey the sky. I needed to get outdoors. So I made an executive decision to do something else. And had an idea.

It sounded genius. A bonfire on the beach. Moving the stones for the ring would be satisfying to Chen right away. Maybe we'd even cook hot dogs for lunch there today or tomorrow, if that arrangement met Chen's somewhat complicated rules about when he did or didn't like hot dogs.

And I decided to keep it a secret. While we got our gloves back on, Chen pestered me: "What's the job? What are we doing? What if I don't like it?"

The more he asked, the more determined I was not to tell him. He went to throw rocks to calm down, and he couldn't get a rock to skip right away.

He was annoyed with me and most of the rest of the world. And perhaps vice versa.

"But *why* do we have to move *boulders*?" His voice climbed into audible-only-to-dog territory.

"Rocks, not boulders." I pretended not to notice incipient tears while I gauged distances. Where the beach's pebbles gave way to sand, with the heel of my rain boot, I drew a large circle eight or so feet across.

"Around here." At the moment, the ring sat closer to the tree line than the water, but snowmelt would bring the lake up. This spot would be halfway between, and thus perfect.

"Under a layer of sand, we should find some larger rocks. Got your gloves?"

Shock sent his voice high again. "I dig with my *hands*?"

"More like sweeping than digging, to see the tops of the rocks. After that, we'll shovel."

On his knees, he moved sand out of the way. I poked around, too. In about five minutes, we'd found three chunks of granite smaller than soccer balls but larger than softballs.

"Great! We'll set these on the line I marked and find more. They have to touch all the way around the circle. If they're too heavy, roll them."

I glanced at him and stopped. He stood still, arms at his sides, clenching and unclenching his gloved hands. His face paled and his breath came quickly.

"This is—this is—it's for a fire!" His voice held anguish.

I wasn't pleased that he'd guessed. "Yes, a beach fire."

He started to shake.

"What's wrong?"

He stared over the water, his voice a sob. "Fire." Tears fell down his cheeks.

And then I remembered. Of course.

The accident. Fire.

He ran away from the water past the camp, the yellow of its walls a beacon in the wisping mist, and around the corner out of my sight. I followed, but he was fast.

A skunk-like tang in the air made me slow and look around.

I rounded the corner where I'd last seen Chen. He wasn't there, but a large black form disappeared into the bush near the woodshed.

Oh God, a bear. A bear got Chen.

Crackling and rustling noises came from the bush behind the woodshed. The bear was still close.

I looked around wildly. At last I spotted Chen. He huddled in a tight ball against the far wall of the camp. I ran to him.

"Are you hurt?" I couldn't see blood, but he shook.

More rustlings. We weren't safe.

"Chen, kiddo." I forced my voice low and as normal as possible. "I know you're scared. We need to go into the camp. In there, we'll be safe. C'mon, stand up."

He shook his head. I looked around—nothing. No more noises. The scent had faded a little. This bear was probably heading away from us as fast as it could. But fifteen minutes indoors was the best idea.

I encircled his shoulders in a loose hug and spoke softly. "I need you to do this. We'll be safe inside."

He tried, he really did. He stood up but stayed frozen.

I took his upper arm and pulled him back the way we'd come. He tried to shake me off.

"We're not going to the beach, just into the camp. We're really close." I murmured it. "We're nearly there, that's good, almost there."

He ran to the front door of the camp and pulled at it, but it stuck. I caught up and wrenched the door open. He went straight to a chair, pulled up his knees and hid his face in them, his arms over his head.

I wished I could, too. Instead, I squeezed his shoulder. "You did great, Chen. You're really brave."

Energy buzzed through me, alarm flickering through my forearms. A bear. Wild. Even after seeing dozens over the years, I never got used to it.

I brushed past Carmen at the kitchen table to look out the front window. Nothing moved on the beach. I looked out the back window in the main room, where I could see a wide swath of bush, all the way from the woodshed to the two-track driveway. Nothing.

Finally, I could tend to Chen, whose shoulders shook with sobs. I pulled the old rocking chair over at an angle and sat.

Carmen yelled over Chen's sobs. "Your bear's not the half of it. He was already freaked out by your brilliant beach fire idea."

"Stop it!" I bit the words. "Just, for once, shut up, would you?" She smirked, and I wiped at my face with my hands.

Chen sat quite still in a ball in the chair.

Patting his shoulder, I took a breath and calmed myself, making my voice low and gentle. "Hey, buddy. You okay?" He sniffed hard and moved one elbow in a sort of shrug. "Look, you're safe. How about sitting up straight in the chair and taking some deep breaths?"

He kept his face averted and his knees up, but he raised his head. Two spots in his cheeks burned red. I handed him tissues, and he wiped his face and nose before burying his head again.

I checked out the windows—still no bear. I debated: Stay here or walk up to the house?

Chen lifted his head again and a second later, I heard it too— whistling. I looked over to the kitchen table, but Carmen had disappeared. Through the side windows, I saw someone in a brown hoodie walk around the camp and pause at the corner, looking down to the beach.

Martin wasn't a bad whistler, though his choice was odd: "The Wreck of the Edmund Fitzgerald." I *really* didn't feel like handling him. However. With a sigh, I stood up.

"Aunt," Chen almost whispered.

I paused. "Yeah, buddy?"

"I—I peed my pants."

I rested my hand on his shoulder, still looking at Martin. "I know. Don't worry about it. Just sit tight. I'll be right back." I put on my game face and went out.

Martin heard me. "Oh hello, Simone. I hoped I'd find you here."

I walked along the beach, drawing him away from the house and Chen. "We'd hunkered down indoors. A bear was here just now." He looked at me, eyes wide, and I couldn't quench a smile. "Didn't you smell it? An adult. Probably gone by now, heading back that way." I waved a hand vaguely toward the woodshed.

"I was just back there! Gosh, I wonder how close I came." Hands in his pockets, he looked up and down the beach. "Had it come to the water, maybe? Wow. I don't know if it's luckier to see a bear or miss it." He sounded oh-so-hearty and cheerful, which would get on my nerves at the best of times.

Then he looked at me again. Like he was counting something, or figuring something. As if I might have mistaken the sound of his approach and a shadow for a bear. Or made up the bear entirely.

Which I had not. So I lightened my own tone. "Well, Chen and I have to go back up to the house. It's—oh, it's time to get going on lunch. In about an hour, you're welcome to come up for some fresh cornbread and soup. But take your time."

When I was back indoors, I peeked out at Martin. He walked along the beach, peering right and left. Looking for the bear, perhaps.

Indoors, Chen sat where I'd left him, his face crumpled and freshly wet.

I touched his shoulder. "Do you want a towel? Or you could just walk up as you are. Once we're at the house, you can take a shower and change clothes, and I'll make lunch and do laundry, and then we'll start this horrible day all over again."

He rubbed his face with the sleeves of his jacket. "Let's just go."

It was the longest walk of his visit. He stayed just a foot or two in front of me, walking in the other track of the driveway, silent, head down.

My head was full of my own reproaches. *How could I have forgotten about Chen and fire?* But I hadn't forgotten, exactly. I just hadn't paid attention. The information hadn't registered. I'd been more committed to my fantasies than his reality.

I felt terrible again, an exponentially larger version of the daddy-in-a-jar feeling. This time I resisted apologies. I might be oblivious to nuance and generally bad with people, but even I could tell that Chen's fear that morning was nothing an "I'm so sorry" and fancy ice cream could fix.

CHEN

Time
Bein scared and polite
Mad

Down at camp, Aunt said, "We can start this day over again."

I don't think time works like that.

After a shower and clean clothes I still felt bad. I was dry and warm and didn't smell bad. But I had lots of yuck, and I don't know how it will go away. I read some in my book, but it feels like everybody everywhere is scared. In the book they are. Down at the camp, Aunt maybe even was. She kept talking about being safe and I don't know why.

I was scared. Because of fire.

Ry would say I was being a baby. He would say, *There's no fire, it was just talk about a fire some day. Why were you scared?*

I don't know why.

Plus I was mad at Aunt. We didn't get to start on shutters again. She was so stupid and mysterious about what we were doing on the beach. I didn't get to play or throw rocks enough. I had to do what she said, and I didn't know what it was, and it wasn't funny when she was making me. Like she was teasing or being a butt like Ry. And it turned out to be something terrible.

And then I was crying, and she yelled at me to shut up. That really really wasn't fair.

I'm still mad at her. Madder than mad. It's all her fault, all of it. It's all her fault I got scared and peed my pants and cried. If I had that target and I'd put her name on it, I'd line through her name a bunch of times so nobody could read it any more.

I want to talk to Mum. Not to tell her what happened. Just to say I love you, and she'd say it back and hug me.

It's just been a hard day. And no bears. Again.

Simka says lunch is in five minutes. I guess I'll have to go. And still be polite. Which isn't fair when she told me to shut up.

It all stopped bein' fun a long time ago.

SIMONE

I made and served lunch, like any normal day in this string of not-normal days. Soup. Cornbread, which my mother called johnnycake, which was a topic of conversation once Martin showed up.

The conversation struggled after that. Carmen seemed to be waiting for something to happen. We all felt it, I think.

And then, as I was gathering dishes, it did. Darn that Martin.

He used his hearty voice, so I knew he was talking to Chen. "What was the bear like?"

Chen sat up straight. "What bear? There was a bear?" He shot me an accusing glare that made my insides wilt. My mother cackled.

Martin looked at me, too.

I kept my voice light and bent to hide my face in the dishwasher for a moment. "I saw it from the side of the camp. That's why we went inside." I straightened to reach for another bowl.

"But I didn't—oh." Chen flushed.

Turning to Martin, I added extra faux cheer to my own voice.

"That's wildlife for you—there one minute, gone the next. Blink and you'll miss it, like Chen did. But that bear wants to avoid people. You're perfectly safe and more than welcome to go back down to the water. We have a few things to finish up here before we head back down."

He and Chen got up from the table at the same time. Chen frowned and escaped into the den. Martin left, whistling.

My mother laughed again, a short ugly sound. "You always were terrible with kids. Grownups, too."

As I wiped the counters, I blinked back tears. She was right.

Martin

Martin scuffed his way down the hill in the grey weather. The bear didn't worry him. There hadn't been a bear, Martin was sure. Pretty sure.

To help him not think about bears, Martin looked more closely at the birches and poplars. They seemed to be greening, just a little. But when he looked right at a tree, he couldn't see it, after all. Maybe it was his imagination.

He wondered what it would be like to camp like Simone did, indoors. He was used to tents. Sometimes he'd save rent money and camp for a few weeks at a time near one of the sites where he was working. One August, his tent was far away from streetlights, and he saw a lot of that meteor shower, the Perseids. Even on a really dark night, stars were hard to see when you looked right at them, but out of the corner of your eye, you could do okay. Like with the trees.

And even people. Like, something was wrong between Simone and Chen. How could Chen have missed a bear? He wanted to see a bear so bad, he was more likely to imagine one that *wasn't* there.

Martin crossed the asphalt circle. Mist fingers writhed up the two-track driveway toward him.

He looked around for the place the secret little path went off. He tried two spots, but within a few steps, balsam fir branches blocked his way in every direction. Finally, he crashed back to the asphalt and walked on the regular driveway.

Maybe that secret path was magic and opened only when Simone was around. Which wouldn't actually surprise Martin at all.

The mist deeper in the trees wound amid the evergreens and birches, creating a backdrop for those that lined the driveway. Martin slowed and looked at them closely.

Again, maybe it was his imagination, but when he got here a couple of weeks ago, didn't the balsams and spruce still have that black-green look from the winter? He loved winter scenes, especially when you couldn't tell if a photo was black-and-white or in colour.

He also loved spring, though waiting for it was a killer. At last, the first week into May, Martin could almost believe it was coming.

The mist became fog. He could see only a few feet in front of him, just his feet on a path going who-knows-where. Finally, the brilliant yellow of the camp's walls cut through the murk.

His day had started so good, ditching that envelope. Even after Mr. Smith's message, he'd figured out what he needed to do.

He didn't like watching Simone. And there'd been a bear. Maybe.

Martin sighed. First he'd talk to Chen, who was the most vulnerable, and then Simone. Then he'd decide if he had anything to report to Mr. Smith. David.

Just do the next thing.

At the beach, the fog had thinned. He wiped the seat of one of Simone's chairs with a tissue from his jacket pocket and sat. It was still damp, but the view, even on a foggy day, more than made up for it.

Martin leaned back. For a moment, just one, he wanted to sit and enjoy it all—the lake, leisure time, being outdoors without having to work, the scenery. If he wasn't Simone's pretend-cousin by the end of the day, he'd be free to find something else.

What would his next move be? Well, what would Harry do?

Or perhaps Martin should phrase it differently: What would Harry tell him to do? Because maybe what Harry did himself wasn't the best example. Harry's solution to whatever problem he'd had, on a hot August night, was to get killed in the subway. He'd even been to his regular meeting beforehand. Nobody knew for sure what happened. Camera evidence was inconclusive. Maybe he jumped, maybe he fell. He wasn't pushed, anyway. Jumping or falling, though—that would make a difference.

Martin hadn't been around. He'd gone to a different meeting in a different church basement closer to his job, a half-hour away. He didn't have a cell then, so he saw Harry only at meetings, and hadn't even known to wonder about Harry until Tuesday, when Harry missed their weekly half-hour check-in. By then, Martin could ask all the questions he wanted—had Harry seemed down or different, couldn't somebody have stopped him, why hadn't somebody noticed—but his only answer, ever, was to wonder.

A year ago, this coming August. In the months since, Martin hadn't looked for another sponsor. At first, he was too pissed off at Harry. First for dying, and second for not asking Martin for help before he did whatever he'd decided to do. Unless it had been an accident.

Besides, Martin didn't really need a new sponsor, what with Harry in his ear, nagging and cajoling and generally calling Martin on his BS. It might be kind of nice to have one now, though. Or if not a sponsor, at least someone who could toss ideas around with him. Someone not afraid to tell him an idea was stupid but still might let him make his own mistakes. Someone he could talk to about Harry, about how Harry died, even. A friend.

Someone who was actually alive.

(Harry: *Someone like Simone?*)

Martin sat up straight in the chair, his mouth open. Yes. Like Simone. Who, suddenly, he really sincerely wished was his cousin, even with a few personality quirks and imaginary bears.

Coolness washed through him, tingling in his face, his hands. (Harry: *Name the feeling, Martin.*) Not quite regret, not sadness, but close. An ache. Wistful, maybe? Wishing things could be different?

Yes. That. A whole lot of that.

SIMONE

After lunch, Chen called his mother again. Voicemail again. "I miss you. Can you call me tonight? Love you." He punched the red button and, without meeting my eyes, turned back toward the den and computer.

I addressed his back. "She's probably out of cell range. She'll call soon."

He pulled the chair close to the desk, thereby showing me more of his back, and wiped his face with his sleeve. I really wanted him to blow his nose but resisted reminding him.

While I finished the dishes, I faced several unfortunate realities. Eventually, Chen and I would have to talk. He'd been scared beyond anything I'd seen before. I didn't know what to do for him. He obviously really wanted, and maybe needed, his mother.

It was all my fault.

I'd felt terrible several times in this past week. I thought I'd plumbed the depths of feeling terrible, but new facets of terrible kept opening up. Guilt, embarrassment, rudeness, meanness.

"Bingo." Carmen waved her hand in the air as if she'd just won. I narrowed my eyes at her on my way to the dryer, and she smiled sweetly. The scent of fresh-squeezed lime wafted my way as she raised her full glass in a mock toast.

With that, I realized the other part I'd temporarily forgotten. I'd yelled at my mother in front of Chen. My mother, whom I saw and heard plainly even though she wasn't there. So maybe the bear had been a ghost, too. Or maybe I'd made up the bear completely. Maybe I really was becoming dotty.

My mother's drunken laugh. Not of amusement, but of triumph, and at my expense. Confirming she'd been right about me all along.

So familiar. I let the dryer door slam closed and twisted the knob to give it twenty minutes. I looked for Chen and found him on the living room couch, clutching one of its smaller pillows to his chest. He seemed deeply asleep.

I needed a moment. Just one. All to myself. Upstairs, I retreated into the little bathroom off my bedroom, away from the living—and, even more, from the dead.

And I cried for one of the first times since William's death. My mother's scorn had again penetrated all the layers of armour I'd built to hold her away. Decades' worth. In fact, since the December I was fourteen, bursting out of my clothing and bumping into everything. She'd mouthed off to a customer and been fired, which meant an early kickoff to her holiday drinking. I studied for semester tests while monitoring her wellbeing and hiding her car keys.

One midnight I put her to bed, as usual, trying not to sound tired or impatient.

"Here's your bucket. Your water's on the nightstand." In a clear plastic cup. It took only one broken glass for me to learn.

She lay on top of the lemon-pale comforter, the back of her hand on her forehead like a movie star, eyes closed. "Go away."

I stopped in the doorway to turn out the light. "Good night,

Mom." I didn't mean to. It just came out.

That word, Mom, seemed to flip a switch in her head. She raised up on one elbow, shouting and pointing at me. "Are you being sarcastic? What do you mean, calling me that? You're a terrible daughter. I hope I live long enough to see the terrible mother you become."

Fifty-five years later, I grimaced. *Well, Carmen—Mom—somehow you've managed it.*

Chen's visit had been a gift, unforeseen and precious, and I'd let it slip through my fingers. If keeping him safe and un-traumatized for a few days was beyond my skill, maybe I deserved to be surrounded by stupid ghosts.

Damn Carmen, anyway. I indulged a small flare of self-pity. Why could she never help me?

I washed my face and rubbed some life back into my face with the hand towel. Tired and empty inside, I leaned on the counter to rest my eyes on something beautiful.

As usual, the lake delivered.

Some days, the sunshine glinted off waves that bustled along the broad surface of Lake Superior. Today, swirls of fog and mist covered the water's surface and crept onto the shore. The house sat above the fog, and I watched it crawl toward us. The peninsula across the bay showed a mottle of taupe and chartreuse, a flush of spring after the recent rainy days.

This place, this landscape I loved. My safe place. With ghosts, some of whom made me happy. Whose company I'd chosen instead of reaching out to family or making friends.

But it was time to change that, because I had to fix problems with the living, breathing people in front of me. Starting with an apology to Chen. Together, we'd figure out what came next.

When I got downstairs, the dryer still whirled, with several minutes left on the timer. I'd cried in that bathroom for ten minutes—fifteen, tops.

But Chen was no longer on the living room couch. I quickly checked the den, and then the whole house. He was gone.

CHEN

Notebook: More Thursday
Bored bored boreder bored
Bear

After lunch, I left a message for Mum. I didn't say anything about Simka yelling.

I looked up stuff on the computer. What Daddy calls noodling. In the past he did.

I got bored.

I lay on the couch with a pillow. I tried to nap. I didn't want to talk to Simka yet. She walked around doing stuff.

I kept thinking about that bear, the one Aunt saw. It's probably still down there.

I know how to be responsible. I have been responsible the whole time with Aunt, and polite! And a good sport. Especially about chores.

And anyway I've come down here a million times. This morning it was foggy but I wasn't afraid of the fog. I don't have to be afraid now.

On the hilly part before the asphalt, there's a hole. Aunt said she thought maybe a bunny or squirrel lives in there, and she is careful when she mows. At the bottom, by the asphalt circle, there's a ditch where some water sits, like a moat to jump across.

The fog makes everything look really cool. The moss growing on tree stumps and stuff is greeny superhero green, and then greyish-white fog comes over the top like a finger pointing at something. It makes me shiver like I'm chilly, but I'm not. Where the fog finger points, there's a drippy spiderweb and some birchbark all curled up.

It makes me think of the Baskskervilles because they're all scared of fog. I guess fog does make a good hiding place.

I wonder if the bear would be scared of me and hide in that fog.

MARTIN

Martin heard scrabbling and thuds. He craned his neck to look back toward the camp, about thirty feet away. Thin wisps of fog swirled around it, blocking any view of the driveway behind.

Nothing appeared.

A sudden chatter in one of the tall evergreens behind him made him start. Another squirrel, down the beach, scolded back. Martin raised an eyebrow. Maybe the squirrels were yelling about a bear. Or maybe just him.

Another thud, still near the camp but closer to the beach. He stood and stretched, hoping to look relaxed to a person, or maybe a bear. Something disappeared into the trees. Something that in no way resembled a bear, but in many ways resembled Chen.

Martin strolled to the water's edge and picked up a couple of flat rocks. The rocks and the water reminded him how to make a stone dance along the water's surface. Every kid learned to skip stones. Every boy kid, anyway. He hadn't known any girls who could, till Simone.

After he threw a few more, a second rock skipped across the water in front of him. He gasped. Chen stood at the other end of the beach, a proud smile lighting up his face.

"Hey there." Martin waved a little.

Chen waved before turning to pick up more rocks. Martin waited until Chen stood and then he threw another one, this time back toward Chen. Chen launched one that skipped twice across the path of Martin's four-skip. Then Chen threw one, a five-skip, and Martin tried a cross-throw, but the angle was hard and he was hasty, and his throw hit once and went straight into the air before crashing through the surface with a loud splash.

"Sorry." Martin meandered up the beach toward Chen. Chen threw another three-skip and then a four.

"You're getting good," Martin said.

"I've been practicing in between work."

"Your aunt, or whatever, she works you pretty hard, looks like." A pause. "Where is she?"

"At the house. Hey, did you see the bear? Or smell it maybe?"

"Nope. You?"

"I maybe smelled it. I know what skunk smells like because they get smashed on roads and you can't keep it out of your nose. What I smelled wasn't strong like that. But it had that thing that makes your eyes water. Maybe it wasn't, though. Maybe just wet leaves."

Martin watched while Chen foraged for rocks, wishing he didn't have to ask. "This morning. Was there really a bear?"

Chen looked up at him. "Aunt Simka said she saw one. Why would she lie?"

Martin looked out over the water. Fog swirled, sometimes thinning to reveal the islands a half-mile offshore before thickening again.

"Maybe she didn't lie, but maybe she was wrong."

"Like maybe she saw a deer or something, or even you walking around back there, and her eyes played a trick on her?"

"Yeah, like that. Or maybe she didn't see anything at all." He paused. "*You* didn't see it."

"Yeah." Face flushed, Chen bent over to scavenge rocks, then stood and hurled a few into the water, not even trying to skip them.

Martin tried another angle. "How do you like staying with Simone?"

"Okay."

"She let you come down here by yourself?"

Chen shrugged.

"She doesn't know you're here?"

Another shrug.

"Whoa, she's gonna be mad at you."

Chen's voice was soft. "She already is."

He sounded sad, not sullen. Martin matched Chen's tone. "What happened?"

"She told me to quit crying, and then she said to shut up."

With horror, Martin saw tears on Chen's cheeks. Grownups crying at meetings was one thing. Crying kids were something else again. "Harsh. I'm surprised."

"Me too. She never said it before, when I was talking too much and she needed quiet time. And she never yells." He wiped his cheeks with the sleeves of his hoodie. "But today was going pretty bad."

Martin paused to regroup. "What were you up to?"

Chen bent and grabbed a fistful of pebbles and threw them, hard, at the water.

Martin watched the ripples expand. Aha. Something was there. All he had to do was follow up on it. And then, the harder job: decide what to do with what he learned.

SIMONE

I could say my highly developed sense of ethics kept me from reading Chen's notebook for clues to his whereabouts. But honestly, I didn't think of his notebook until later.

And I didn't need to wonder. He'd gone to find the bear.

In the house, while I called his name and went from room to room, my mother laughed from the kitchen table. When I circled back to the kitchen, her "tut tut" and wagging finger sent me over the edge.

I shouted at her. "You're right, I'm a horrible person who shouldn't be trusted with kids. Just like you! I'm not one bit sorry for leaving you alone in your old-lady bitterness. And if you're never going to help me, then to hell with you! You're not even real!"

She disappeared without leaving even a hint of lime, and I felt I'd won something, equal parts stupid and good.

Until I focused on the counter behind her and saw Martin's pepper plant. Martin. He was also down at camp. Where Chen was going.

I threw on a jacket and headed around the side of the house

and downhill. Along the way, I wondered if my shouting scared Carmen away for good. Maybe she'd be back to gloat over my next mistake.

Chen had asked the right question that very first afternoon: if you're making up gods, why a trickster? Or someone mean, like my mother? Easy enough to understand why I wanted William around. Even Grandpa Jackson. But why Carmen? Why did I summon a ghost who was at best unpleasant and usually downright hateful? Was I lonely enough to settle for her maddening presence, just for company?

With every step downhill, the fog increased.

MARTIN

Chen picked up a rock as big as his fist and hurled it into the water.

"Hey, what's this?" Martin motioned at the scuffed sand between the water and the treeline. "Were you guys digging?"

Chen shuddered. "Yeah. Aunt Simka wouldn't say what for. She talked about lots of things we'd do if the weather was good. Like go out in a boat or have lunch down here. But it rained." He looked around, sniffing the air.

"The bear?" Martin looked around too.

"I wish," Chen said. "I really want to see one. Ryan always talks—talked—about the time he saw a bear. A lot, like all the time. And if I saw one, I'd be ahead."

"Who's Ryan?"

"My brother." Chen made lines in the sand with his foot. "He's dead." He turned his face away.

"Oh. I'm sorry," Martin said.

"S'okay." Chen wiped his face with the sleeve of his hoodie.

Martin felt bad for him—dead brother, dead father, and being stuck here with Simone while his mom was off somewhere.

"So you think Simone really saw that bear. Is she kind of weird? Huh. She's my cousin and you're a stranger, but you know her better. You've spent more time with her than I have."

Chen threw a rock. He scowled at the water. "She does some stuff wrong."

"Like what?"

"Well, she makes oatmeal wrong. Plus she's got rocks everywhere. That's weird."

Martin thought about it. "I guess. But does she drive okay? Like when you go to town, does she ever get lost?"

"I don't think so. Nobody honks, and she doesn't yell at other cars, like Mum does sometimes." Chen threw another rock.

Martin smiled but kept asking. "Do you think it would be easy to trick her online? Like send an email asking for money or something?"

"Nah. She's pretty suspicious. She doesn't play games or anything. When we go online to look up something, she lets me be in charge. I know lots more than she does. Daddy knew about real estate, and we've been looking stuff up."

Martin caught a sideways look from Chen and wondered if they'd researched the condo information he'd left behind. "Like what?"

Chen turned toward him, ready to say something, but his eyes got wide and he pointed behind Martin toward the rocks.

Martin turned.

Emerging from the trees and undergrowth onto the beach, a large black bear swung its head from side to side and sniffed the air.

Chen whispered, "Whoa. It's giant!"

SIMONE

On my way downhill, I fretted about Martin. Chen and I checked on his stupid condo, but I'd never checked Martin himself. Was it safe for Chen to be with him, unsupervised? *Fine time to consider that, Simone.*

My brain sorted and circled. Martin's car had been up at the house, so he hadn't taken Chen anywhere. And for all Martin knew, Chen was still with me.

I had to be careful. If Martin were a criminal and I called for Chen, Martin would know that Chen was vulnerable. If I called for either Martin or Chen, and Chen was mad and avoiding me, he could get lost in the fog, or pretend to be. We had plenty of property for both of them to wander around in and get scared. Chen had handled a big scare already. And if my ghost-talking had also scared him, getting lost would total three times. *Geez, Simone.*

Not to mention the day's wildcard, also out there in the fog somewhere: the bear. *Which I know I saw.*

Yet again, I worked myself into a state. I checked my watch—

not an hour since we sat together at the table. Plenty of time for bad things to happen, though.

At the asphalt turnaround, the fog had stopped roiling to lie thick and full, so thick that I could barely make out the other edge of the road, a few metres away. The fingers of bare birch branches seemed not to grow from trunks but to emerge, head-high, from nowhere.

I stopped to listen. Nothing—no high-pitched background hum from cars, no high-pitched chatter of squirrels, no birds.

Had something scared them off?

Hurrying down the driveway, I became aware of someone in the other track. I looked at my grandfather and raised my eyebrows.

Without breaking stride, he said, "The kid will be okay—that Martin's not a bad guy. It's the bear you need to worry about."

I sighed. "I'm in the weird position of hoping there *was* a bear."

He laughed—kind laughter—and walked into the ether.

And of course I'd seen a bear. *I know what I saw. It was a real, live bear. Oh wait, just like this man I was talking to who wasn't real, never mind.*

MARTIN

Martin stood immobile, mouth open.

A cub trotted out of the bush past the big bear, heading toward the lake beyond the rocks where Martin had stood a few minutes earlier.

Martin tried to think. He felt a grip on his arm and stifled a squeal.

Behind him, Chen said, "Aunt told me if we ever saw a bear to not take your eyes off it and go into the camp. Back up. Walk, not run."

With Chen holding on to his jacket, Martin kept his eyes on both bears and shuffled backward, toward the path up to the camp. When they moved, the larger bear looked toward them and took a step or two closer to the cub. Martin inhaled sharply and shuffled faster.

Once inside, Martin latched the screen and closed the wooden door firmly.

Chen danced into the living room, peering through different

windows to find the best view. Any glimpse they might have had through trees was obscured by fog.

"A bear! And a baby, too! Aunt says this is why she doesn't lock the camp at this time of year, because you might need to get inside from a bear. And we did!" He laughed. "We saw a bear! Two of them!"

Martin crossed the main room to sit, trembling, in the rocking chair. Wacko kid.

Chen's face shone with excitement and happiness. "You're not scared, are you?"

Martin said it without thinking. "Of course I am. That thing is a wild animal."

"I know." Chen turned back to the window. "But I'm not scared. I'm cautious. Aunt said they're different. We're safe in here. I've been reading about animals, all different kinds, ever since I came. That bear knows we're here and there aren't food smells. That's a mama with a baby. They'll probably stay away."

"It's that 'probably' I'm afraid of."

"But." Chen sounded perplexed. "They can't get in here."

Martin bristled. "Okay, boy genius, but we can't get out, either." Feeling stupid, he stomped to the front window. "I mean, sure we *can* get out, like, we can turn the handle and pull the door open, but we can't *leave* because we don't know where those damn *bears* are or where they're going."

Chen pushed beyond the kitchen table to stand as far away from Martin as possible while staying indoors and near a window.

Martin stared out at the swirling fog between them and the beach, holding different colors of gray, silver, and mercury. Another day, he might find it pretty, but today, the fog made him feel off-balance, like this whole place held unknown terrors.

He breathed deeply. He needed to think straight. One question, for sure, had an answer. There was definitely a bear, so Simone was probably okay. And if he got over being annoyed, he could confirm that with Chen. *Calm thoughts*, he told himself.

He peeked into the kitchen. Chen's face was blank, as if he'd never been happy in his whole life.

"Sorry for yelling. I know you're excited about this bear." Saying it aloud made it real all over again. Martin shook his head. A bear. What were the odds? "This day. None of it has gone like I thought it would."

From the kitchen, Chen said, "Me neither. Mine started off really bad. But then I saw two bears! That makes it an awesome day."

"You were brave. And smart. You knew what to do."

"I was brave, wasn't I? It's easier to be brave if you know what's coming."

"Think so, eh." Martin was pretty sure he disagreed.

"Yeah. Like earlier? The bad part? I wasn't brave at all. But I didn't know what was coming, so I didn't have a chance to get ready."

Maybe he had a point. "Okay, but you can spend a lot of time thinking about things that scare you and getting ready, and then they never happen. And you've wasted all that time dreading them."

Chen wandered back into the living room. He ran his hand along the mantel of the stone fireplace, fingering the edges.

"Yeah, I do that sometimes. Sometimes thinking about all the things that can go wrong makes me anxious and I talk a lot." He fidgeted his fingers around and around the fireplace rocks. "Hey, do you know about Job?"

Martin did not.

"Me neither, when I came to stay with Aunt Simka. He's a guy in the Bible. A bunch of bad stuff happens to him. His whole family dies, and he loses all his money. His friends tell him he deserved it, and he has to figure out what he did wrong so he can say sorry to God."

"Some friends. So what happens?"

"He finally gets mad at God and asks how come he's so mean. God says you're just a man, what do you know? Then Job says yeah, okay, you're right, and God gives him another family and everything he lost, and more. Aunt and I read it together."

"Seems like a weird choice."

"Aunt brought up Job when I first came here. We were talking about trickster gods, how they get blamed for making bad stuff happen. In Job all the bad stuff happened because of a bet between Satan and God, and Job's the one whose life sucks. It's not fair."

Martin shook his head. "Nope, it's not fair. People tell themselves all kinds of stupid stories when they make bets. And bad shi— stuff happens all the time to people who are just minding their own business."

"So why would bears happen? Except to be awesome and make me awesome, too, because I've seen TWO BEARS."

Martin let him dance a little before asking again. "So earlier today, when you were scared? What about?"

Chen stopped dancing and stared out the window.

"I lied a little bit before. Aunt Simka said the rocks were a ring to put a fire in. And cook. I'm afraid of fire. The accident made Daddy die in one. My brother too." He shivered and tears welled up in his eyes. He wiped them on the cuffs of his hoodie.

Martin wasn't sure what to say. "Sorry." That made approximately one thousand times he'd said it that day. Meant it, too.

Chen turned back to the window. "I wish Daddy was here." He sighed. "And sometimes even Ryan. Dr. Samuelson, I write in a notebook for her and she helped me with nightmares, she says I can still tell them things, even though they're—not here anymore." He sniffed.

"Huh. Well, she'd know." He paused, thinking of Barb at the hotel, still crying. "I guess that accident was hard on a lot of people. I heard about it in town."

"Yeah. Aunt Simka didn't even know anybody in it, and she says she thinks about it a lot. She's really sad about the driver because he didn't have family around. And she wishes she had more family, too. Like you being her cousin, she likes it."

"Did she tell you that?"

"Yeah, sorta." He considered. "I guess maybe she didn't. But who doesn't want family?"

Martin thought of Mr. Smith's alternate identity. Or David's, rather. "If you don't get along with them, maybe you don't. Like your brother, I bet you fought."

Chen nodded. "Yeah, we did. Not all the time. Sometimes he was okay. But Mum and Daddy kept saying we were family, and we'd understand someday. It's harder with cousins. I have some I like and some I don't. You can be sort of strangers but have to be family too."

"Yeah, and sometimes cousins like me come out of the blue. Strangers but family." Martin cast about for something cheerful to say. "So are you going to be staying with her for long? Like all summer? Beach fires can be fun, in the evening after a hot day."

Chen breathed on the window glass and traced a square in the damp with his finger. "It doesn't sound like fun to me."

"It is, though, with friends. My best friend, the closest thing I had to a brother, died last August."

Another sniff. "Was it an accident?"

The million dollar question. Martin made a split-second decision. "Yeah. Yeah, it was." He blinked, surprised to feel teary. He coughed the tears away.

Chen sniffed again. "Do you still talk to him?"

"Sometimes." Although technically, Harry did most of the talking. "We used to work together, building houses." Martin smiled, remembering. "One summer we tamed a chipmunk."

Chen turned his full attention on Martin. "How'd you do that?"

"Our job site backed up to Crown land and green space, and the lot we were working on was pretty far from the rest of the development. To save on commute time, I camped near the lot." Not strictly legally, but whatever. "The chipmunks were curious.

I guess some of the other crews had been feeding them, too. They stayed away during the day, mostly. But mornings and evenings, they'd come up to me and see what I had to offer."

"What did you feed them?"

"What I had. But they liked me better once I got sunflower seeds. Lordy, chipmunks are smart. One little guy figured out I had a big bag of seeds. He'd sit and chirrup, and I'd put a few seeds a few metres away and sit real still, and he'd come. I moved the seeds closer and closer. I put a couple onto my arm, even. Before long I got him to eat out of my hand." Harry had shown him how.

"That's cool."

"Yeah. It'd gnaw the shell off and put the seed into its cheek, working those front paws like little hands."

Sitting in his chair, Martin could almost remember the feather-light weight of the chipmunk on his forearm.

"Did you ever catch it? Like in a cage?"

"Nah." Martin thought about what to say. Some other guys on the crew had threatened to trap it, mostly to be mean. Harry had told Martin to cool it. Martin tried ignoring the chipmunk for a day or two, but that was hard. So Martin dumped his remaining seeds a couple of lots over and moved his campsite. "It seemed like the wrong thing to do. If you make a wild thing dependent on you, or if you or trap it, you have to be responsible and take care of it. Like, feed it all the time."

As he said it, he recognized the feeling. Of course he and Chen were trapped inside by the bear, he hoped temporarily. But he also felt a weight on his shoulders, a duty. He had to question Simone about taking care of Chen. Then he had to tell her things about her family. He didn't want to do either one.

Chen wiped his nose. "Yeah, wild things should live in the wild. Aunt says so, too. She said people like to feed deer, and she thinks that's wrong. It's dangerous for the deer. I guess it wasn't dangerous for the chipmunk, though."

"I hope not. Hope he just had a lot of food stored away that year. Anyway, it was fun for a while."

Chen glanced through the window hopefully. "I see how stuff like that would be fun. But I still don't know about a beach fire." He paused. "I'm not afraid of bears, though."

"I know, you're cautious. Well, I'm still afraid." Martin didn't mind saying it to Chen.

"Then I guess you have to live here forever and ever and the rest of your life." Chen laughed. "That's a joke. No way Aunt Simka would let you live here. Besides, there's no water in here right now, and it gets cold at night."

Martin smiled. "Staying in here is easier than facing down the bear *or* Simone, either one. Ha, that was my joke. I guess we'd better go up to the house. Even if she yells at you and me both." He stood up. "I don't suppose she gave you instructions for walking in bear-filled woods."

"Course she did. You carry a saucepan and bang on the bottom with a spoon."

Martin stared, open-mouthed. "You're shitting—sorry—kidding me."

Chen shook his head. "Nope. That's what her grandfather told her mother, and her mother told her, and she's had to do it before. A long time ago, she said. I'll go see where a saucepan is."

Martin laughed. "Well, I guess this isn't the stupidest thing I've ever done."

SIMONE

I knew Martin was real. Assuming the bear was, too, fog made its presence extra-dangerous. Fog changes sounds, muffling some, magnifying others. Would I hear the bear—or would it hear me—in time to stay away? I didn't have anything to make noise with, no keys. Not even Chen to talk to.

Feeling the fool for the millionth time in two weeks, I sang, a tune my mother hummed often. "Every tear will be a memory, so wait and pray each night for me." By the time I got through "Till we meet again," I heard something percussive. A sort of lopsided beat with a tinny sound. Two tinny sounds.

And a high-pitched voice sing-songing, "Oh bear, we're coming through. Don't mind us."

Chen. He was safe. He'd listened to my lecture about bears. I wanted to sit right down in the middle of the road and cry with relief.

What a great kid. I blinked back tears, and though I don't really pray, I clasped my hands at my heart and sent up a quick "thank you" for this miraculous boy, and the fog's beauty, and the hope of spring, and all good things.

When they emerged from the fog, I was almost—almost—happy to see Martin walking alongside Chen.

"Hey there, kiddo," I said to Chen, standing between him and Martin. "I guess you saw a bear."

Luckily, beating on his saucepan made him miss the narrowed eye I trained on Martin.

Martin stepped farther away from Chen, palms up, an old frying pan in one and a rusty fork in the other. He said, "Chen saved the day. He knew all about unlocked doors and going in the camp, and making noise outside."

Our return parade up to the house was led by Chen, who kept beating on a saucepan with his spoon, because "You never know." I walked just behind him with Martin off to my side.

When my breathing calmed down, I hissed at Martin, "I don't know if I can trust you around him."

He didn't seem to take offense. "You can. Can I trust *you*? There's a question."

I scowled at him, but he had a point. Miserable, I focused on Chen's back. Carmen's laugh rang in my ears. Every beat of Chen's spoon on the pan throbbed in my forehead, but I didn't stop him. He'd been such a good sport. He was also right.

...

Even up at the house, the fog swirled in interesting patterns. Inside, I confiscated their instruments. I motioned Martin into a chair at the kitchen table and put on water for tea. It was what one did.

Chen exulted. "A mum AND a baby, I saw TWO bears. TWO! BEARS!" Then he did his martial-arts-style dance with a bizarre chortle. It had been cute the first ten times I'd seen it that week.

While he danced, I dropped bags into the teapot. "Say, how

about some time online in the den? We'll talk later." He scampered off.

I set out two mugs and poured tea. Eventually I needed to both apologize to and yell at Chen, but Martin came first.

Martin apparently felt so, too. He watched Chen retreat before setting his tea on the table.

I couldn't stop myself. "Got something to say?" It sounded more abrupt than I'd intended, but I let it be.

"Yeah, I do. And I don't even know where to start."

"Why you don't think you can trust me with Chen?"

His voice was sharp. "Because he was upset about the fire ring and you told him to shut up."

"I didn't! I was talking to—myself. Not him!" I covered my face with my hands. *Oh God, Chen did hear me yell at Carmen, and he thought I'd meant him. This is the worst.*

"He said you tell him that a lot, to be quiet." Martin's tone changed from accusatory to reflective. "I guess I get that. You wouldn't be used to having him around. And he does talk."

I looked at him. "He does. However, we're getting used to each other. Managing."

"Managing?" Martin shook his head. "Is that what you call letting him run around the countryside alone when there's a bear around?"

He had me there. I closed my eyes. "I had no idea he'd run off. He'd never done anything like that before. I thought—I don't know what I thought. That he understood how dangerous bears are, for one thing. I'd better fix that."

Martin sat in silence for a moment. "You were lucky."

"I know. I was. I am. He's a great kid." *Get a grip, Simone.*

I drank some tea to buy myself some time. I hardened my voice. "We were lucky that you're a good guy, too."

Martin nodded. "Yeah, you are." Then he blushed. "Uh, yeah."

Carmen popped in, red kimono sleeves billowing. "I'm not

sure who's the dimmer bulb in this conversation, him or you. Bad guys don't go around confessing, you know. Of course he's going to say he's a good guy." She played with a silver cigarette lighter, turning it over and over on the table. I pulled my eyes away from it to focus on Martin again.

He cleared his throat. "So, about that. Me. I am a good guy. But I have to tell you something you won't like."

I half-rose from the chair. "What? Did you hurt Chen?"

"God, no. Sorry, sorry. I'm doing this all wrong. Please sit." He waited until I sat. When he spoke, his voice was calm and measured. "I get that you don't know me. And this isn't going to help you trust me." In the split second before he spoke, I knew what he'd say.

"Simone, I'm not your cousin. I'm real, real sorry I pretended to be."

He was right, I didn't like it. I'd grown pleased at the idea of cousins in general—even Martin in particular. He didn't need to know that, though. I kept my mouth shut.

"I pretended to be your cousin for this job I got. I was supposed to buy your lakefront property, and, uh, the person who sent me said you had a soft spot for family. And selling to me would mean it would stay in the family. Which would be important to you."

"It would be. Or could have been. Maybe."

Carmen raised her eyebrows. "Interesting." She took a drag on her cigarette and exhaled a mixture of grapefruit and lime.

He obviously had more to tell me, and I didn't interrupt.

"I gotta say, I really do think selling that property would be a smart move. You'd come out ahead and could do whatever you want."

"Ha, like buy a condo in Florida? Which I guess you don't have?" I was almost amused, and Carmen laughed outright.

He cringed a little. "Yeah, you're right. Never had a condo. And our fathers weren't brothers. My father was a mechanic, but mostly a drunk. He never worked in Ottawa or at a dealership."

"And no sister."

He shook his head. "Nope. No family. An only child of an only child, in fact." He smiled, a little tentatively, and I nodded back.

"Yeah, welcome to the club. Martin—is that your real name?" He nodded. "Okay. Let's do business first. Who wants to buy, and why my place? Or am I just one of many brand-new cousins you've been trying to finagle out of their camps?"

"No, just yours." His eyes flicked to the window and back. "It's a great place."

"Yes, it is. But if I sold to you, it'd be bulldozed for a big fancy house."

He hemmed and hawed, so I rescued him. "You still think I should sell it."

"It makes a lot of sense. They're offering a fair price. And selling would give you lots of options."

Carmen had been watching Martin with interest. She tilted her head. "He's right. You could do whatever you wanted."

I tried to ignore her, speaking directly to Martin. "I don't want any other options. I'm not selling. Not to anyone, cousin or not."

"I'm not surprised. It's a great place. I know you like it rustic and don't want a hydro line. But solar could be pretty easy. It would make some things there nicer. Hot water. A flush toilet."

Solar power wasn't a bad idea, but I didn't want to talk about my camp. "You've never said who you work for."

He looked at his hands and mumbled. "Numbered company. Real estate investments."

Carmen blew a large smoke ring followed by a smaller one.

I put all the kind firmness I could muster into my voice. "Martin."

This. I could feel it in my stomach. This was the part I was going to like the least.

At last, it came out in a rush. "It's a numbered company, but there's family involved, and it's a mess."

Of course. It explained that shadow between William and me. "You mean David."

"Yeah. You knew?"

"No. But on the list of people who want something from me, David's at the top." I sighed. "So, let's hear it."

Martin told a semi-involved story about a Mr. Smith, and an assignment from a friend of a friend, one of whom was apparently dead and the other had something to do with a food truck. And his hope to find better work, which seemed to involve greenhouses and furniture somehow before the drinking, with construction and landscaping since.

"Told you that was true," Carmen gloated.

I interrupted Martin's story. "Wait. David told you I'd be more likely to sell to family? And then he sent you, a fake cousin? Instead of asking himself?"

Carmen cackled. "Shows David's opinion of you."

Martin shook his head. "Gotta say, I didn't get that part, either."

"And the condo?"

"Oh, that was my idea." He seemed proud. "I thought it'd be easier to sell you something than talk you into selling to me. But after I met you, I guessed I'd never be able to talk you into anything you didn't want to do."

"Well, you almost talked me into believing you were my cousin." I didn't want to let him off the hook. "That's nothing to be proud of, you know. Being a good liar."

He looked down. "I know. It always brings trouble."

Once again, I'd crossed a line from "being direct" to "being rude," and I didn't like it. I cleared my throat. "Not that you're a terrible person. But you're not who you said you were, and it's going to take time for me to get over that." He started to say something else and I held up my hand. "Just—give me a minute, okay?"

He sat back.

I tried to think clearly about David, but all I could hear was him saying "batshit crazy Simone." Humiliation flooded me.

Carmen said quietly, "'How sharper than a serpent's tooth it is to have a thankless child.' A lot of people think that comes from the Bible, but it's Shakespeare. Lear says that to Goneril, and she dismisses him as old and dotty." She snapped her lighter open and shut. "That's gratitude for you."

I took a couple of deep breaths to regain my composure. Martin, meanwhile, stared out the window.

MARTIN

Not for the first time, Martin wished that telling the truth felt good while he was doing it. It usually felt good eventually. And Simone had been great, so far, even though he wasn't sure she'd ever be friendly again. Especially if he ended up telling her about David's call that morning.

So he wouldn't. He'd done enough truth-telling. It was a natural ending. Aside from no payment from Mr. Smith. He'd have to find a job, hopefully not for someone like Ken.

A small voice piped, "Aunt?" Chen, almost tiptoeing, left the den.

Simone smiled broadly at him. "Hey there, kiddo."

He stood beside her. "Is there anything besides tea? Like that corny-cakey-something stuff?" He beamed hopefully.

She teased, "Aren't you dancey of feet and fidgety of fingers? Let me guess, you saw a bear?" She got up.

"Not just A bear, TWO bears. TWO. BEARS."

Martin stood. "Look, I should go."

"Nonsense, stay for johnnycake. And I'll make more tea." Martin sat, and Simone opened a container sitting on the counter. To Chen, she added, "I'm glad I've made something you like."

"Ha but you'll never get me to eat oatmeal, not ever." He added, to Martin, "Because she does it wrong." Martin flashed him a smile.

Chen said to Simone, "He didn't know about the saucepan and spoon."

"So wasn't it a good thing *you* knew what to do." She sounded almost smug. Martin couldn't blame her.

Watching them together, Martin knew Simone was fine. And she'd be even more watchful of Chen. Though she was right; she'd been lucky.

We all were lucky about that bear, Martin thought. Then he tuned into Chen's chatter.

"I'm gonna add stuff to my notebook about bears. Like for one thing, keep doors unlocked in bear times. Two, back up into the camp. Three, the pan and spoon." To Martin, he said, "I'm writing down everything I'm learning about, like raking."

"Sounds like a good idea."

"Yup. Mum will like to see it." He hopped and tilted his head from side to side to accompany his singsong. "Saw TWO bears, saw TWO bears."

His dance took him jittering around the kitchen and eventually to the windowsill. He picked up each rock and put it down. "Hey Martin, don't you think this is kind of weird? All these rocks?"

Martin looked over. "That's a lot of rocks, all right."

"And they all deserve to be looked at. Right, Aunt Simka?"

"That's right, kiddo." Simone lifted plates from the cupboard.

The golden scent of warming johnnycake filled the kitchen. It made Martin feel okay, like whatever other mistakes he might make that day, telling Simone too much or not enough about David, he was doing the right thing.

Maybe she'd even forgive him. Someday.

SIMONE

I got out butter and corn syrup and cutlery. I settled Chen at the table with his plate, trying not to think about his giggle-fits after sweet things. I served Martin and took a piece myself. To Chen, I said, "Maybe your Mum will call tonight."

Chen chewed and swallowed. "It'll be fun to tell her about the TWO BEARS." He lit up all over again, and I couldn't help but smile. I set aside my worry about explaining everything to his mother—not just about Martin but about Chen's basic safety. That could come later.

At the table, I willed myself to relax. Utensils clinked against dishes. A moment of quiet, not tense silence or eerie calm. Peace.

I caught the scent of vanilla. My grandfather sat in the other chair at the table, by Martin. I listened, smiling, while he talked softly and fiddled with his tweed cap.

"Simone, really, this guy isn't bad. He's a worker, not a foreman. Give him a project and he'll do fine. He could help with those propane leaks and new gutters to divert water from the foundation.

Maybe even that boathouse you want."

He stopped listing projects, which I appreciated, since I had a substantial list of my own, thank you very much. Inside the camp: the uneven floors and peeling paint. Outside, those large trees, nearing the end of their lifespans, all leaned in worrisome directions. Et and cetera.

Grandpa tapped his cap on the table. "Think about it. This guy could help." He put his cap back on and gave me a nod and smile before fading.

I blinked. I returned my attention to my own plate and those in the room with me.

When we'd finished eating, I said to Chen, "Hey, buddy, could you give Martin and me a few more minutes alone? You can have more screen time."

He looked at Martin and back at me, still pleased about the bears but apprehensive underneath. He said to Martin, "Are you gonna get yelled at?"

Martin laughed. "Probably, but it'll be okay." Chen looked relieved.

I added, "Later I'll get you to help me with some research."

"Okay." He scuffed his socks on the linoleum.

I listened for the desk chair to squeak as he sat. "Martin, I have some advice for you."

Martin toyed with his fork, not meeting my eyes. "What."

I tried to be both direct and gentle. "This kind of thing, the lying and secrets—it doesn't suit you. You're not cut out for the shady side of anything. You should do things that make you feel good, not bad. Maybe you need better friends. Certainly better business associates than David."

He looked at me then, a mixture of curiosity and sadness. "I hope you know I'd never hurt Chen."

"I believe you," I said carefully. "But I also know how lucky I was that you're a good guy, and that Chen was safe from the bear."

"*He* kept *me* safe. For real, I was afraid to move." He shook his head.

"It's understandable." I sighed. "So, about David. I probably owe you an explanation." I sketched a version of David's life, brief and general—an ambitious man, looking for an angle.

I ended by saying, "He's not evil. My—William, my husband—he died without a will. Everything came to me. I've tried to pass along what I could to David." I shrugged. "I guess I've lived too long and moved too slowly. I want to stay out here, near the camp, as long as possible. I'm not surprised he's impatient." I didn't *like* it, though.

Martin, who'd been staring at his hand on his mug, looked up at me. "You're gonna talk to him about all this, I assume." At my nod, he said, "Okay, then. Here's something else. As I got to know you, I didn't feel so good about lying. So I pretended I knew some guys and asked if he wanted me to get them to break in and hurt you."

"What?" I sputtered. "You what?"

"It was a test. And Simone, listen, he passed. David said no." He paused, then said it again. "He said no." He seemed to be holding his breath.

"Well, I'm glad of that." Martin nodded, but I knew something was wrong. "That's not all, is it? Let me guess—he called me 'batshit crazy Simone' or something."

He seemed shocked. "No." Then he winced. "Well, kinda. He suggested you were, uh, impaired, maybe. Vulnerable?"

I blinked to keep tears from starting. "Not surprising."

"I'm sorry." Martin paused. "Your family is kind of complicated, huh."

"Aren't most? Under the surface, anyway."

Carmen appeared at the end of the table. Her eyes crinkled into half-moons as she smiled and took another drag on her cigarette.

I could see Martin wondering if he should say the next thing, so I helped him. "Out with it."

"Simone, I'm sorry to say this again, but David's got a point. Most ladies of your age, men too, are looking to get out from under upkeep on a house or cottage or camp. And you've got two. You can do all the work *now*. But for how much longer?"

"It's the work itself that keeps me young. The more I do, the better it is for me." I swallowed. *Why not ask?*

"Funny you should mention it, though. What if you helped me out? As a handyman-type person. If you're looking for work."

"Wow." Martin's surprise came through, loud and clear. "I— that's really nice of you, Simone, considering how we started out, you know."

I cleared my throat to let the humility out more easily. "Well, some things, like roofs, have always been beyond me. I couldn't hire you full-time, but I know a guy who might have other work to send your way. I could introduce you."

He said it again: "Wow." He seemed completely unable to think of something else to say.

Or completely uninterested. What if he didn't like me well enough to accept? "If you have a better offer, of course, that's fine, too."

He shook his head. "No, not at all."

"Okay." I mentally reviewed my calendar. "Come over Sunday afternoon for an early supper. I have Chen through Saturday, and I need time to figure out a few things." I pointed at him. "And don't contact David. Just disappear."

"I get it. Absolutely."

We sipped tea in silence.

He cleared his throat. "I'm sorry I pretended to be your cousin."

"That's okay. I'm kind of sorry you're not." I didn't mind admitting it after all.

"Me too." He looked down at his empty plate. "Well, now I really should go."

He sat to put on his shoes. "Oh, before I forget. That accident?

Chen said you feel bad about the driver. Well, I met a gal in town, her brother was killed. She says a group of them is still tight. The driver's family, too. I guess the volunteers who stayed with him till the end, they're now friends with his family. She said everybody still stays in touch." He shrugged. "I guess it makes sense, family being the people who step up for you when you need them."

It was my turn to be incoherent. "Oh, my." So the driver hadn't died alone. I felt something in my neck soften as I let go of the loneliness I'd held for that poor man. And that Martin had told me, that was unexpected. People can surprise you.

I cleared my throat. "Thank you. It's good to know." I thought of something. "So you're not Martin LeMay. What's your real last name?"

He stood at the door, ready to open it. "Bailey. Martin Bailey."

I held out my hand. "Nice to meet you, Martin. I'll confirm about Sunday night. At the phone number you gave me?"

He shook his head. "Better lose that one." He wrote a number on a piece of paper.

As he left, I again stood at the window and waved. And as before, he lifted his hand and smiled.

So maybe he wasn't my cousin. But I liked what he'd said about family. Maybe we could work out a way to be familiar, if not family. Given that the best families seem to be made, not born.

Family. Blech. I'd have to deal with David at some point. But not today. I still had Chen and what had happened this morning to deal with. Some apologizing, and some listening. I hoped I could get over not having cousins, and forget the ghosts I'd created.

Though Carmen, who smirked at the kitchen table, didn't make it easy.

MARTIN

As he turned the key in the ignition, Martin caught Simone's wave. He raised his hand. It was what people did—when someone waves, you wave. He laughed a little, about her, himself, the ridiculous situation.

He liked her. And he liked himself today, too. He'd told the right people the right things.

Harry would have been proud.

He still had stuff ahead. Lose the burner he'd bought for Mr. Smith and maybe find a cheaper motel. He could ask Barb. He'd like a reason to keep talking to her.

Giving the Harbour Foods kid Ken's envelope had closed that whole episode. Thanks to Simone, he wouldn't have to do crap jobs for people like Ken anymore.

And until Sunday, he could just poke around. See more of the area. And generally stay out of trouble.

He shook his head again. That Simone. A surprise.

If something worked out with Simone or her friend, he'd be

able to stay in northwestern Ontario for a while. Maybe always. He could get a regular job, like sales at a home reno store. Maybe rent a house someday, with a garden for squash and tomatoes. Flowers, too. He might even meet someone who trusted him and get married, a new person with a new person.

On the road to town, the fog eddied. It thinned, deepened, and faded again as the highway climbed and dipped and wound around rock outcrops. He watched for deer through the curves and rises.

As a younger man, he'd walked beside fields. He'd seen how messy plants could suddenly reveal themselves to have been arrayed in tidy rows all along.

He wasn't sure, but in the trees along the road, he thought he caught a glimpse of a white pine. A good omen?

CHEN

BEARS! TWO BEARS TWO! BEARS!!!
Momma and baby
Writing notes
Oatmeal choc chip
Lived to tell the tale, bears tailes
Telling Mum and haha Ry, I saw TWO BEARS

This is the day I saw TWO BEARS. That's one more than Ryan, haha!

And also, high-five in heaven, Ry!

One was big, a momma. And one was little. The big one came out of the forest and swung its head. Then a little one came out behind it. Like the big one was scoping the situation. Then the little one got a drink from the lake and the big one was the lookout.

Martin was afraid but I wasn't. We went into the camp. And

later we beat on the saucepan with spoons when we walked home. Like Aunt told me to.

Aunt Simka and I talked a lot just now. Like when Mum and Daddy and I had family meetings. Before Simka and I talked, I felt a little yuck in my stomach because Martin said she'd be mad and yell at me.

She talked first. Not yelling.

She said, "I'm sorry about the fire ring."

I know she didn't do it to be mean. I said, "It scared me. A lot."

She got all red in the face and I thought she might cry. I was kind of afraid she was getting ready to yell at me.

But then she said, "If I'd just told you, you could have told me in words, and we could have avoided all the bad things."

I thought about it. "Maybe. I might have been too scared to talk about it, though."

We didn't say anything for a while.

Then she took a big breath. She said, "Chen, when I said to shut up, I wasn't talking to you. And I wasn't mad because you were crying. I was mad at myself."

I was kind of embarrassed to think about when she did it because I'd peed. "But I was the only person there besides you."

She said, "Not really. I was there, too. And I was yelling at myself."

I said, "Like when you make those faces because you're not saying things out loud? Only you said it accidentally?"

"Yes. Exactly. That's exactly right. And I'm sorry."

"That's okay," I said. "It was a big mixed-up time."

I was waiting, but she has never said anything about how I peed my pants. I don't know if doing it was a bad thing or just a thing that happened. I guess maybe it's over and done now.

Then she said, "I know we're just getting to know each other, even after all these days, but I hope you can tell me things that are important to you. Is there anything else you're scared of? I won't ask why if you don't want me to."

"You know about my bad dreams," I said. "Well, they're about Ry and Daddy being on fire and I can't get to Daddy."

She looked like I'd hurt her, but her voice sounded okay. "Yes, I remember them now that you've reminded me. I'm sorry you have them."

"Me too. But that's pretty much all I'm afraid of now. Maybe snakes. Movies sometimes. If we are ever out in a boat, maybe deep water. But I don't know yet."

She said, "If we get to go in the boat, we'll be sure to stay in shallow water. And you'll wear a life preserver. We'll take it slow and easy. Okay?"

"Okay." Lots of the yuck went away then. Martin said she would be really mad. But Aunt wasn't. Or not anymore. Mum used to do that. She'd be all mad at me and we both had a time out from each other, and then she wasn't mad anymore.

Aunt said she was scared about not knowing where I was. And the fog made her scared worse. And the bear. And being just me alone with Martin because we don't know him hardly. She didn't say it but it was stranger danger stuff.

I said, "Martin's okay."

Then she said that from now on every time I go somewhere if I don't tell her to her face I have to leave a note on the kitchen table. She showed me pens and papers I could write on.

She said, "It probably won't come up because we'll be together till your Mum gets back."

I got sad missing Mum. And also, more days to be polite.

Then Aunt said, "Chen, one more thing. Maybe looking for a bear isn't a good idea. Maybe there are enough bears looking for you."

I said, "I really wanted to see a bear, though."

"I know, and you got to see two of them. But I don't mean just bears."

And all of a sudden I know what she meant. "You mean things

that are dangerous like bears. They happen to people when they are minding their own business. Like in Job."

"Chen, you are one smart cookie."

I said, "I hope I'm oatmeal chocolate chip because they're the best."

She laughed at my joke. The real kind of laugh.

Then we talked about cookies some. I didn't say anything about the accident, but I was thinking about it. Then I had to stop so I didn't think about the things I'm not supposed to think about.

Instead, I said, "What a good day. I got to see TWO BEARS."

She said something funny. "You lived to tell the tale." She meant tale like story but it was funny because of the bears' tails.

She said she was scared when she couldn't find me. I thought grownups got mad, not scared. But she was scared, and Martin got scared. And the fire ring scared me.

She didn't do the fire ring to be mean, and I didn't scare her to be mean. They are just things that happened. And we won't do them again.

I want to tell Mum about TWO BEARS. TWO. BEARS.

I know Ry can't hear me. I like to say TWO BEARS. Just in case he can.

I guess the big one was a momma not a daddy and the little one was a baby bear not a kid, but I still thought of Daddy and Ry. How the Momma stood between the baby and us like Daddy is maybe protecting Ry wherever they are now. We did the right thing by backing away and leaving them alone.

I can't wait to tell Mum I saw TWO BEARS.

FRIDAY

SIMONE

Friday. It wasn't until Chen and I headed down to the beach together that I realized I was again missing coffee with church folks. No matter. I had no desire, none, to be anywhere else.

After our talk about the bear and the fire ring, I thought Chen might be self-conscious, but he didn't seem to be built that way. For him, Thursday was over, except for the bears, and when Friday dawned, there was new stuff to do. He could still talk about bears—*that* wasn't over.

I was glad that prepping the rowboat soothed my awkward feelings. It got us closer to the time when camp was 90 percent playing and only 10 percent chores, instead of spring's vice versa.

If I made a list about Chen, the first item would be this: conversations with Chen are about him, not me. He cared nothing about the trees that came down the previous autumn, that I had to sharpen the chainsaw partway through clearing them out, or that later, one of the fattest pieces of spruce had made the splitter hang.

Maybe that's how parents feel. What they do is invisible, mostly.

William and I had always talked together about our days. Beyond the chores and plans, we talked about books, and he told me about the stock market and commodities futures. He could never make me care about all of it, but he still liked to talk and hear what I thought. Since he died, no one else has cared that way, not one whit. Maybe no one ever will. And I might just have to get used to that.

Item number two on the list about Chen: I couldn't predict what Chen would care about. Martin's chipmunk story made Chen want to tame one. But he was unimpressed when I tried to tell him about ducks, how in the rowboat, you wait in unmoving silence to see if the female merganser and her ducklings continue sunning themselves. Maybe he had to see it for himself.

Doing things together made being together easier. I wish I'd learned that with Carmen. Or—an awful thought—David.

I'd decided to wait to deal with David until Chen went home. Meanwhile, since I could have no more illusions about "cousin" Martin, I spent some time wondering how fair I'd been to David. What *did* David enjoy? I'd never considered that before. Since William's death, being mad at him had always been a whole lot easier. Still was.

But if I wanted some interaction other than a yelling match, I had until Sunday after church to get my thoughts in order. And then I'd phone, and hope for a conversation that went somewhere good.

CHEN

Dolly
Cleaned roboat and looked for leeks
How do wetsuits work

The main thing so far today is the rowboat. On the way down earlier, I carried the life preservers and seat cushions.

Now I know some kind of funny things about the boat. In winter, Aunt leaves it sideways in the camp breezeway, like somebody's floating from the kitchen to the bathroom on their side. We lifted one end and put a little board-on-wheels under it. She said it was a dolly. Then we could roll it out. We took the dolly out from under it, and let it down *gently* (Aunt said it loud a lot) so the boat was flat, like somebody was sailing on the grass but away from the water. The inside was yucky with spiders and even leafs that blow in the breezeway. So we washed it out.

That's funny. A boat goes in the water so you would never

343

think it was dirty. Like if you had a pet duck that lives in the water would you give it a bath? I don't think so.

We pulled it down to the beach, back end first. She held handles on the back and I held on the front. It was heavy, but we were going downhill and she was in control. And we took breaks. I wore my new gloves.

At the beach, she showed me a ring at the back where you lift up and pull out a plug and water can get in and out. She put the plug in her pocket. For safekeeping, she said.

I poured water inside the boat with an old bucket, and I had a sponge and she had a brush and we got some dirt off the inside. We washed out the dirt and sand, and the water ran out the hole in the end. Then she put the plug back in and we pulled the boat into the water. She rinsed the outside and we looked for leaks. There weren't any.

But it was too shoppy to go out in it in the morning. So we pulled it up on the beach again, real high. Off the beach, really, onto where the grassy stuff grows.

It was sunny but not warm so we wore boots not bare feet. I wore rubber boots she had in her hall closet. I got water in them, but it warmed up in there with my feet. She said that's like a wetsuit. That's on my list to look up how they work.

We took off the last of the shudders too, and I got to use the drill some more.

It's been a good day so far. Even though zero bears. Bummer. Mum doesn't know about the bears yet!

It feels funny to know things that Mum doesn't. There's so much to tell. It feels like forever since we talked. Fog and bears and that fire ring and Aunt Simka and me having a serious talk.

Today being with Aunt hasn't been so hard, being polite. It's almost like being regular.

SIMONE

After a sandwich for lunch, we headed back downhill. And he sniffed the air the whole way, as usual.

I tried not to smile where he could see it. "No bear?"

"Nope." He tried not to show disappointment.

The wind had shifted, and the lake had calmed a little during lunch. If we stayed in our sheltered little bay, we'd be safe enough.

I sent him to bring the oars, one at a time, from their rack along the back wall of the camp. "Don't touch the metal, or you'll get black and greasy hands," I warned him. He did, of course. I let him wipe his hands on his jeans. Let that be Jessica's problem in a day or two.

Meanwhile, I pulled the boat down to the beach, its stern in the water. I showed him how the oars sat in the locks and went into the sockets. While we talked about boat safety, he put on his life jacket over his hoodie—the day was bright but chilly. He also wore a baseball cap leftover from William's working days. Cinched up tight, he could almost keep it on without thinking about it.

We stood on either side of the boat, then. With me bearing most of the weight, I was pretty sure he'd be strong enough to help lift the boat and move it into the water, a few inches at a time. I hadn't anticipated his grin, though.

Then he held the bow still while I tossed in the cushions. We traded and I held the bow still while he walked down the centre line and sat in the stern.

Still holding the bow, I waded a couple of feet out, the water chilly even through boots. With one foot in the boat, I kicked the other backward like a donkey against the sand-and-rock lake bottom. As we floated free, I settled my weight onto the middle seat. Not my most elegant or graceful move, but Chen had the kindness not to laugh.

I adored these tasks—their quiet progression, the way they all made sense. And they were finite. Once the boat had been readied for the season, you could be out in it quickly.

For a long time, the novelty of floating was enough to keep Chen occupied. While I rowed us around in our bay, he squinted through the sunlight at the cliffs, the trees, the rocks, astonished at how different everything looked from "out here" instead of "in there."

He learned to row the same way I had, when I sat with Carmen on the centre seat and took just one oar. He found it awkward but of course wanted to try both oars while I sat in the stern. Predictably, he became frustrated when the boat went in circles instead of in a straight line.

I knew how he felt. "You're doing fine. You're just pulling harder with one arm than the other. And remember to catch the water with both oars at the same time."

He squinted up at a gull. "I guess birds do that too. With the air."

Always surprising, that kid. "You're right. I'd never thought of that."

He managed to move us twenty or thirty feet in one direction before asking to switch again so we could "go faster."

Too soon, the sun showed the passing of the afternoon. After stowing the oars and cushions, we pulled the boat up high, a good two feet beyond the high-water mark, and rolled her over. I wished briefly for a boathouse or a safe way to moor her in the bay.

I dawdled a bit in a beach chair, while Chen waded. But at last, we really had to go.

Chen gave a big sniff and cast one last hopeful look around the big rocks.

We walked most of the way in silence before he said it. "How come bears aren't there when you want them?"

"They're wild, not pets. The only sure place to see a bear is a video. Hey, what did you think of rowing?"

"It's weird. In the Olympics there was kayaking and canoeing, and they face forward so you know where you're going. But rowing, you're backward and everything you do is opposite."

"It takes practice. Remember when you were learning to ride your bike? How it felt so tippy and awkward but one day it just didn't, and you didn't have to think anymore?"

"Yeah. But you're facing forward on a bike. And if you go right, you go right. Not like with oars. Why don't you like kayaks? They have them at Canadian Tire. Daddy and I looked at them one time."

I shrugged. "I enjoy the rowboat. It feels like it's part of me. A kayak seems like a toy or a prize, just one more thing to take care of." I wondered if David kayaked. Maybe after I got done yelling at him tomorrow, I should invite him up this summer. Perhaps if I had a kayak, he'd enjoy himself.

Chen narrowed his eyes at me, appraising. "You like the rowboat bestest of all, don't you? Because of the going-backwards part."

"Yep. I like the metaphor of it." He looked puzzled. "A metaphor is a thing that stands for something else. The rowboat stands for life."

"Like when you talk about bears. They're bears but you really mean trouble."

"You're smart." Then I stayed quiet.

He thought for a minute. "Okay. How is a rowboat like life."

What a good kid. "Lots of ways. In both a rowboat and real life, you can't see into the future—you can see only where you are, and where you've been. You can have a goal, but you can't watch it get bigger while you row. You can only sneak a peek. Rowing takes skill, and some things in life are worth working for. Sometimes you have to do what feels like the opposite of what you want—be uncomfortable for a while to get more comfortable. Stuff like that."

"That's a lot to get from a boat. You should talk at church." He said it without judgment.

"I've been told I make things too complicated." We walked in silence. Then I sighed. "It's been a fun day, but I have to make a phone call when we get back."

"Do you ever like talking on the phone?"

I laughed. "Good question. Not so far." Then I did it—a little, tiny risk. "Maybe after you go home tomorrow, I'll call you sometimes. And you and your mother could come out here to have fun."

"Sure." He sounded nonchalant, but he grinned and danced ahead, up the path.

I felt like grinning too.

Once indoors, I marched myself straight to the phone and called Donnie. He was surprised—we hadn't socialized over the years—but I told him I knew a good worker, and that was all it took to make Donnie one happy man, with the prospect of a meal even better. Then I left a message for Martin. Sunday night's supper was a go. All I'd do was introduce them. They'd have to take it from there.

I was sitting at the table, thinking about food for Sunday, when Chen slid into the kitchen on his socks. "Can I come out now?"

"Sure. What were you up to?"

He stood by the table, jiggling and dancing. "I was researching Martin. But I didn't find anything about him, not even with Bailey as his last name. Too many people."

I considered. "Would you be interested in a bigger project?"

"More things to look up?"

"Yes. I think I should know more about my father's family. And my mother's. I bet you can find a lot of things I don't know about. Do you want to do that?"

"Sure. Hey, who's the old guy in the suspenders and cap? Is he your family?"

"What old guy? Did you see—?" I forced myself to stop talking.

"It was down at the camp. A man with a cap and an axe. He was smiling."

I stared at him, open-mouthed. Had he seen my grandfather?

His eyebrows drew together. "It was a picture stuck in the back of a book. On the shelf down there. I just looked at it a little bit." He hung his head.

"Oh." A picture. "It's perfectly okay you looked at it. I'm glad, in fact. Tell me about it."

"It's black and white. In a fancy book, one of the heavy ones. There were papers and maybe some other pictures but the shutters were still up and I couldn't see them good."

I'd never poked around on the shelves to see what my grandparents had left. I hadn't wanted to—I'd preferred to nurse my hurt feelings. Well, time to grow up.

I cleared my throat. "That's pretty cool. You can show me which book sometime. And yes, that sounds like my grandfather."

Suppertime. I was so sick of planning, fixing, and cleaning up meals, and here I'd just committed to having guests for Sunday night. What the hell had happened to my life?

When I stopped complaining, it was almost fun to think about.

But I needed a break. So we got a hamburger at the little restaurant on what used to be the Trans-Canada highway, right by a convenience store and gas station. It was a relief to let other people bring us food. After supper, I sent Chen to his notebook and thought about what he and I would do tomorrow while waiting for his mother.

Finally, his last day.

I'd been looking forward to it for what seemed like eons, years, months. Okay, a week. But now that it was here, my heart hurt, just a little.

I wondered about Jessica. Maybe I could be someone she could ask about the unmapped territory of widowhood, whatever that would look like to her. Presumably, it wouldn't have ghosts. I'd have to be a bit vulnerable, though. Take a risk.

Well. I could probably do that. We'd go slowly, Jessica and Chen and I. All that remained was her return.

Then I had another thought about Jessica. I gave Chen a piece of plain paper. "Sunday is Mother's Day. Want to make a card? You could draw some things we did and then write 'Happy Mother's Day' on it."

He grinned, eyes wide. "Like two bears!"

"Yes, and maybe a leaf and a rake. Ice cream. Work gloves."

He folded the paper in half and set to work. Besides two large bears, his final product included a shack (no chimney, I noticed), a boat, and two stick people by wavy water.

He pointed at them. "We're skipping rocks."

I felt proud. We put it in the big envelope I'd found.

Chen insisted we not seal it yet. "I might see more bears."

I laughed. And the project kept me from thinking about William. Almost.

CHEN

Notebook: Friday nite
Zero 0 bear day
Rowwing!!
Water: clear, tan, turkwoise COLD!
Rocks: slimy underwater
Wading. Fell on my bum

This is my last night here because Mum is coming tomorrow to get me. Today was a really good day. Even though zero bears.

After lunch we finally got to go in the boat. I wore a baseball cap she found and those boots. Her front closet is like the bag in Mary Poppins, there's one of everything. We went around the bay for a while. The lake was flat, not shoppy at all!

I thought water was blue, but it's not! It's clear! The sandy bottom showed tan where the water was shallow and then where it was deeper it got dark green like turquoise. I saw the sun winking in it.

Aunt doesn't like it when I move around a lot in the boat. So

I sat still in the exact middle of the stern seat and held on to the edge behind me. My life preserver zips up the front and sticks way out all around me like I'm fat with no neck. When we went fishing before at the river, Mum and Dad and me and Ry, that preserver did too.

The rocks by the cliffs feel friendly. Maybe because they are still connected to land. Part of them is underwater and slimy but part is dry and black with orange lichens. There's a bigger rock in the bay and it looms up out of nowhere and that makes it scary.

I got to row. It's hard work, but it's fun to be in charge of where we go.

Then it got shoppy out by the point, which is where the land sticks out into the water. We landed the boat by the camp, and I was hot and I waded. Aunt sat on the beach in a chair.

I said, "Aunt, aren't you coming wading?"

She said, "No thank you. I do appreciate the invitation, though."

She's funny sometimes, not always like haha. It was way warmer than on the first day I came and she waded that day.

I rolled my jeans up and went out where the rocks are slick. I fell on my bum. Aunt laughed but it was a nice laugh. I got just a little bit wet.

She said loud so I could hear, "The first time every year is the hardest."

She has said sorry again about the fire. She said maybe Mum and me would come back this summer and we could cook marshmallows if it didn't scare me. She said she likes to cook hot dogs on a fire too, they are easy. They don't taste like at Canadian Tire but almost.

It feels like I have rowed a lot, but it was just today. I know lots more about boats and water and even rocks. Everything looks different from the boat.

•••

Last night Aunt and I talked about Job a little bit. How he got everything back here on earth, not in heaven. Aunt says she believes in heaven on this earth, and for her, that's her camp.

I don't know if I believe in heaven. If I did I would make it not scary, but not like a birthday party either. Maybe it's someplace you do what you want, like you can play all day. Ry might be getting really good at games. Maybe he's got somebody to have tournaments with. I hope he has something good where he is because he's missing out on bears and boats here.

Sometimes I worry about bad things, but like Aunt says about bears—they're just bears being bears. It's just life and you learn how to deal with it. Like she told me to go into the camp when a bear came and I did and I was safe. Martin too.

I guess I can deal with bad things.

I don't like believing it's gods making bets and sending good things or bad things, like in Job. Aunt says what she learned about Job is that bad things happen and we don't always get to understand. And she looked up about tricksters. They show us what life really feels like, not what we wish it did. That's like their job.

She's pretty smart.

. . .

Today at lunch we were eating potato chips. I told Aunt the thing about the accident that I'm not supposed to think about any more. Dr. S. told me I should replace it with calm, positive thoughts and not feel bad about it. But sometimes I think about it, and when we were talking it kind of just came out.

I said, "Me and Mum were supposed to drive Daddy home from the party that night. It was a fancy party for a wedding and everybody in the family was there, cousins and everybody. But I got sick on the cake, plus the cousins were being mean and made me cry, so Mum brought me home early. Daddy had to catch a ride to our house with Ry and his Mum. And that's when they were in the wreck. If I didn't get sick nobody would have been there and they'd all be alive. And it makes me feel bad sometimes to think about it."

Aunt stood up and grabbed me and hugged me. "Chen, that is not your fault." It looked like maybe she was going to cry. "It was nobody's fault. It was an accident."

I said, "I know, I guess. But I still wish it didn't happen. I wish we didn't go to the stupid wedding party and I didn't get sick. I wish everything had turned out different.

She let me go and sat back down. "I know that feeling. But this is how things are, and we can't change them no matter how much we want to. And anyway, I'm glad you and your Mum are safe."

She didn't talk for a little bit. She didn't make any faces but she was maybe thinking.

Then she said, "Make a list of what you want to do this summer. I can't promise any more bears, but I'll see what I can do about rowing. And maybe you can invite your school friend."

That would be fun, to see Joseph again.

Aunt is interesting. I'm glad she's on my target now. I'm sorry I ever wanted to take her off.

•••

What I want to do this summer with Aunt and Mum and Joseph:

1. *see a baby deer.* Aunt says they are spotty and cute as pictures
2. *catch a chimpmunk.* Martin did it. I bet I can.
3. *cook hot dogs.* I know this is something Aunt wants to do. Maybe when summer is really here I'll be okay with it.

4. *boats.* She said she wanted Martin to help build her a boathouse.

5. *garden.* Help plant it. Is she growing food?

6. *more bears.* The real kind not trouble. Maybe if I get to see them, I could look at them for both me and Ry. Maybe he'd even like that.

SATURDAY

SIMONE

His last morning, we got up early and headed down to camp before breakfast. As I'd hoped, the water was calm. Chen said deep water was maybe okay, so we rowed out into the main bay, where deep water lay along the cliffs. Chen had learned to sit mostly still, even when he was excited and wanted to point at things. Back in our bay, he rowed again. He was learning.

After the rowing, hanging around the camp all morning dragged a bit, even after breakfast. Chen had been a really good sport for ten days, and I'd done my darndest to be patient. But between us, we'd used up all our best behaviour.

He talked a mile a minute. I knew he was just excited. It annoyed me nonetheless.

He tried to skip stones, but he couldn't settle in. He rushed his throws and didn't choose well to begin with. Frustrated, he threw in a handful of pebbles, willy-nilly.

I took myself down the beach to deprive him of an audience, and to wonder, a little, where my grandfather was. Looking around, I noticed that the birch branches seemed green near the ends. The morning sun, reflecting off water, warmed me, inside and out. Spring was on its way.

Slowly but surely, being on the beach calmed Chen, too. He threw several four-skips and even a six, which made him happy.

Luckily, I had a surprise for him, which I was proud of. And I had the sense not to pull it out the moment Chen became restless. Partly, I was shy—what if he thought it was stupid? But mostly, I wanted to let him work through his frustration. Maybe I was learning about being around kids. Or Chen, anyway.

When he lost interest in skipping his rocks, I produced my surprise from under my jacket. "Guess what this is!"

"A plastic bag!" He added his "aren't I cute?" smile.

"Yes! With rocks in it."

"Oh! From your kitchen?"

"Yep. I decided it's time to set them free."

He looked up at me, doubt written in his forehead. "How can a rock not be free?"

"You tell me—you're the one who said rocks should be outside."

"Yeah. I like having them inside to look at, though."

"Me, too. But you were right, there were a lot. These aren't even all of them." I picked one out of the bag and launched it into the water. "Be free, little granite one."

He laughed and picked out a perfect square of basalt. "Be free, basalt."

One after the other, we threw rocks into the water until the bag was empty, and I wasn't sure whether I wanted to laugh more or cry a little.

After that, we were both really ready for Jessica, so it was about 11 when we headed up to the house.

On the way, he pulled a rock out of his pocket. "I'm putting this in Mum's envelope."

It was reddish and smooth. "I bet she likes it."

He grinned. And when we got to the house, Jessica was there, waiting for us.

Chen ran toward her. "Mum! You look different!"

She did, a little. She'd lost that overtired look. I bet I'd find it in the mirror, if I'd chosen to look.

Their reunion was like a Saturday afternoon movie, lots of hugging and "I missed you" and "Did you have fun?" and "Two bears."

I asked her in. She said she knew she was early and hoped it was okay that she'd stopped to get some soup, a kind she knew Chen liked, and some buns.

Lunch, planned and provided by someone else, was heaven. Afterwards, while Chen was packing, she wanted to know more about Martin. I told her what I knew, and she seemed reassured.

I seized the chance to say, "Was your trip all you wanted it to be?"

At that, she smiled. "Yes. And no. But mostly yes. I am *so* glad I went, and so grateful." She talked about the glacier, and the chance to decide what to tell other people about herself. She didn't mention the ashes, so I didn't, either.

As Chen dragged his bag downstairs, I hemmed and hawed around a speech I'd practiced. "I've thoroughly enjoyed having Chen here." Then I got stuck and stopped talking.

She said something polite. We both turned to help Chen with the bag.

I said to him, "Do you have your envelope?"

He nodded, eyes big with his surprise.

And that was that. Neither she nor Chen offered a hug, so I didn't either. I stood at the window, waving, while they backed up and turned up the driveway. I stayed at the window a full five minutes after their car turned onto Lakeshore Drive.

Twenty minutes after that, I was back down at the camp and out in the boat. Because that's where I go when I need to be sure things will be okay, and where I go when I'm pretty sure they already are, even if I can't quite understand how just yet.

CHEN

Feelin weird at first
OK to have fun
Normal now

After waiting so long for Mum to come back, it was weird when I was in the car and we were going home. I felt shy a little bit. I'm glad to have a card to give her tomorrow.

She said, "I have lots of pictures to show you from Alaska. It was a really good trip, and someday we'll go back. I think you'd like seeing a glacier."

"I do want to see a glacier." I wanted to ask if she missed me, but I didn't.

"Did you have a good time with Simka?"

"Yeah, especially the bears. And rowing. And I have work gloves, but I left them with my rock collection at Simka's in my room."

But then I wasn't sure I was supposed to have fun. What if I

363

was supposed to have a terrible time with Simka so Mum knew I missed her?

But Mum made it all okay. She said, "I'm glad you had a good time. I did, too. But mostly I'm glad to be home. I missed being at home. I wanted to tell you things."

I almost had tears. I said, "I missed you, too, Mum, lots. I wish you could see a bear."

She laughed. "It's okay with me if I never see a bear."

I had so many things to say. I started with Aunt Simka's story about beating on the pan with a spoon and how I got to do it. Everything felt better again.

HOW IT ENDED, OR DIDN'T

Simone

Sunday, I zipped into town for the church service. I spared a moment to feel gratitude for Chen and hopeful for the future. With him, at least. It felt too pretentious to pray for grace for that afternoon's uncomfortable task.

Though I didn't stay afterwards at church for coffee, I also didn't go straight home.

Instead, I stopped at the cemetery. I forced myself to walk from the car to the far section, where the stately granite headstone bore William's name, and Joyce's.

A large bouquet, an assortment of yellow roses with baby's breath, sat near the stone. It didn't have a card. I looked around. Maybe it had been mis-delivered. A bouquet wouldn't last long, even in this unseasonably warm weather. I decided I didn't need to figure it out.

Instead, I willed myself to look at the stone and the names. *William lies here. He's not alive. I know he's not alive.*

Nothing. Hope made me stay several minutes, but no warm glimmer of summer grass, no circling moths, no fresh kiss on my cheek. Nothing I could construe as either "hello" or "goodbye."

I pulled a piece of white quartz from my sweater pocket and set it on top of the tall granite block. I didn't know what to say. Amen? Thank you? I sighed and moved on.

On my way back to the car, I stopped by the gravestones for my Jackson grandparents, and the smaller one for Carmen. "Doris Marie Jackson LeMay," it read.

Yes. My mother, Doris, had changed her name to Carmen. I'd learned that only as an adult, when my mother and I came to church up here. One of the ladies from her high school class called her Dorie, and she was Doris to the others. I knew better than to ask about it. My father, to my recollection, had called her Carmen. Maybe he'd been the one to re-christen her.

I'd considered putting Carmen on her headstone, but using her real name had been my effort to get the last word. Which hadn't worked. Though, come to think of it, she'd been notably absent since Thursday.

I missed her. Almost. "Happy Mother's Day, Carmen." Nothing. What I'd expected.

Back in my car, I phoned Carole. After wishing her a Happy Mother's Day and asking about her husband, I said, "I'm at the cemetery. Do you know anything about this flower arrangement at William's headstone?"

"No. You didn't do it? There was a big arrangement last year, too. See, that's why I thought you'd changed your mind about Graveside Gardens. The cut flowers don't last well at this time of year."

"Well, it's a mystery to me. But sure, let's add that grave to my list." After a little more chat about chrysanthemums and other deer-proof flowers, we hung up.

Wondering about the bouquets at least distracted me from sadness. Home at last, I listened to two messages on the house phone. One was a hangup. The other was Jessica, thanking me for helping Chen with her Mother's Day card. *He remembered.* I glowed inside.

Then, I ate a sandwich. I pulled out the frozen hamburger for that evening's chili. I stalled and dithered and eventually stood at the window, minding my own business and looking out at the afternoon sun on the lake. Then I dialed.

When David picked up the phone, he had the grace to sound surprised to hear from me. "Simone! At last!"

I decided not to waste time, his or mine. "Listen, what's with sending Martin up here pretending to be my cousin?"

Which, on reflection, wasn't the best opening if I wanted to have a conversation instead of a yelling match. To my surprise, David was calmer.

"Aha. So he's told you. I wondered. He disappeared from the face of the earth."

"Yes, he told me. And I'm the one who told him to stop contacting you. *He* felt bad about the lying. Unlike you, perhaps?"

Carmen appeared at the end of the kitchen table, dressed for an opera in a red-sequined evening dress. She looked at me through a lorgnette studded with pearls. I raised an eyebrow at her—why had she chosen to appear at this moment? She widened her eyes in anticipation. Oh, right. Drama.

As I expected, David sounded defensive. "I can explain."

I was not in the mood. "Can you? First you decide to buy my most precious place out from under me. As if I'd sell it to anyone, just like that."

Carmen snapped her fingers once.

I didn't slow down. "Then you send someone else so I won't figure out it's really you writing the cheque."

Another snap of Carmen's fingers. I felt tears gathering.

"And, the pinnacle of this ridiculous idea, you pay him to pretend to be my cousin." I fought to keep humiliation from my voice. "Sure, I'd love to hear you explain."

I inhaled deeply and exhaled. Carmen applauded, puffs of white, lime-scented smoke appearing every time her palms met.

David had waited. When at last he spoke, he sounded different than I'd ever heard him. Softer.

"You're right. The whole plan was ridiculous. And I don't really have an explanation. Maybe an excuse? I want to buy your camp, and I knew you wouldn't sell to me. Do you know how much it's worth?"

"It doesn't matter. I'm not interested in selling. Not now, not ever."

"It's worth a lot."

"It must be, if you paid Martin to try to buy it. How much money did that cost you?"

He made a dismissive noise. "A few thousand. Nothing I can't spare."

I met Carmen's gaze and rolled my eyes. There was the David I'd known. She laughed.

"I don't know why you bothered. You can't afford what it's worth to me."

David said carefully, "I know you think that. But—look, I'm not trying to be mean. You're getting older. I know I am, or I feel it more. I'm looking for a way that you can live how you want and I can get what I want."

I heard something unsaid. "Wait a sec. You feel older? Are you sick?"

"No, nothing like that." He sounded almost embarrassed. "You know that accident, back in January? Well, I knew a guy who was killed, Michael. Mike. I'd lost touch with him, but his name—it hit home. It could have been me."

"I understand. I'm sorry." I felt guilty for assuming David's stony heart extended beyond me to everyone.

"We weren't best friends or anything, just in French Club and lab partners in chemistry. He and his husband were both killed. They owned a restaurant south of town and were going to open one in Intercity somewhere."

I sat down at the kitchen table, trying to take it all in. "I'm surprised that his life here sounds appealing. When you left, you left."

"Yeah. But I kept thinking about Mike, how he worked so hard to build his business and family. Geez, it sounds so corny, but I wondered what I'd leave behind."

I tried to keep the suspicion from my voice. "So after all these years, what you really wanted was to come home? Like in a Christmas movie?"

He laughed. "Not like that. But maybe?" He told me that his company had a branch in Thunder Bay. They wanted to expand, and he could start as branch manager. Maybe, eventually, a partner, or a better job in a bigger city.

I listened, thinking of William, how proud he'd be. "Well, I can see why this would appeal to you."

"Oh yeah, I for sure wouldn't come back if it weren't a good move for me."

He paused and I smiled. He might have changed a little. But not completely.

"And—oh hell, I'll just say it. I didn't want to move back if things were, um, weird between us."

"Really? And your way to dispel weirdness is to send Martin up here to pretend to be my cousin?" I had to laugh. I couldn't help myself.

His voice radiated frustration. "Well, I wouldn't have if you'd just pick up the damn phone when I call."

Carmen threw silver and red confetti into the air.

That made me laugh harder. Eventually, he laughed too.

I pulled myself together. "Sorry for laughing. If it's any consolation, I don't have caller ID. So it's not just your calls I don't answer."

"Thanks, I guess?" He sounded half-exasperated, half-amused.

I wiped my eyes. "I have some questions." I started with the easiest. "What did you think of Martin?"

"Oh Lordy. I met him just once, and I was nervous the whole time. I didn't want him to ask too many questions, so I tried to scare him. But geez, he's no salesman."

"I think he got sidetracked early on. He really seemed to like this place—both the house and the camp."

"You mean he's sentimental, like you? Not into fixing up the place or buying a jet ski?" He laughed to soften any scorn his words carried.

I said mildly, "You might call it sentimental. Regardless, Martin sees that your ideas might be different from mine."

"Well, when I met him, my main impression was that he was broke and needed work. I didn't want to know any more. But about the middle of the week, I got nervous. He seemed too chummy with criminals."

"He wasn't. Actually, he said he was testing you and you passed."

"Good. Of course I didn't want you to get hurt. I was worried that someone really could take advantage of you. But by that time, I couldn't explain that to him."

I wanted to believe his concern was real. But I'd also wanted to believe Martin was my cousin. And, as Carmen's presence at the table demonstrated, I'd invented ghosts, which David didn't even know about.

I said it lightly. "I can take care of myself."

He laughed. "So I see. Anyway, it was stupid, Martin and the rest. I'm sorry. I went about this all wrong. I was trying to think through moving there, the logistics. My salary will go a lot farther up there. I thought maybe I'd live in town but buy the house from you, and you could live there until you're ready for a condo in town yourself. Or if you'd sell your camp, I could build down there."

As he talked about salaries and details, I got up from the table and paced around the kitchen while Carmen frowned. I knew David was just throwing out ideas, and none of them required an immediate decision from me, but still, I needed him to stop.

When he got to my camp, I interrupted. "Whoa. Not my camp." I swallowed. "I'm sorry, it's all just too much. A few days ago, I had two cousins and hadn't spoken to you in years, and now I'm back to zero cousins and you're moving to town. I need a minute."

What he said next surprised me. "Yeah, I get it. I know after Dad died, we didn't part on the best terms. I was furious. Not at you, really. I was mad at Dad because he didn't have a will, like he didn't care about me. We were just supposed to figure out everything, never mind how hard it was he'd just died. So sudden."

I conceded his point. "It was. Like that accident." I sighed. "About the will—we hadn't gotten around to it. We should have. It wasn't fair to you. I'm sorry."

"Well, it didn't justify me calling you crazy."

I tried to sound amused. "I believe it was 'batshit crazy,' not that I've been dwelling on it for five years."

He sighed. "Really, I am sorry. I don't think you're crazy."

"Good. I'm not. And as a new young friend has pointed out to me recently, 'crazy' isn't a respectful term. So let's put that behind us, okay?" I looked at the clock on the wall. "However. I have people coming for supper." I felt proud to say it. "I should get going, but I'll email you in a day or two, when I've had some time to think."

He seemed okay with that, and we hung up.

Hands shaking, I sat down again, unsure whether I wanted to laugh or cry.

After a few moments, I said to Carmen, "Aren't you going to gloat? This whole episode wouldn't have happened if I'd answered the phone in the first place."

She raised an eyebrow but didn't say anything.

I looked out over the lake. "Then again, I guess I wouldn't have met Martin, huh. And that could turn out to be a good thing for everybody. The camp, too."

I looked back toward Carmen, but she'd disappeared.

...

Martin arrived a few hours later, just as the chili was settling in for its final simmer. He wore a hat with his tan jacket and khaki slacks, and he looked more like a unique person than when we'd first met. Maybe my eyes were all that had changed, though.

I took his hat and set it on the buffet beside the stack of mail. "Very nice—it suits you, somehow. It's responsible, yet jaunty. Like Indiana Jones, maybe." He looked pleased. "So, I talked to David. You're released from doing any more work for him, no problems."

He sat on the bench to take off his shoes. "Good. I mean, sorry. I still feel bad about it all."

"You met him, I take it, in Toronto?" Martin nodded. "How did he look?"

Martin paused, shoe in hand. "Nervous?" He thought some more. "I mean, he's not sick, if that's what you're asking. High-strung. Focused, for sure. Not much interested in me, if that makes sense."

Donnie's car turned down the driveway then, so I said only, "It does, thanks. He's not as bad as you worried about. I'll tell you the whole story someday soon."

When Donnie got out of the car, Martin laughed and shook his head. "That's Donnie? I've met him. At—a meeting, at church, the other night. How about that."

Donnie seemed surprised to see Martin, too, but happy. They talked a little about their recent experience—Donnie wiring a camp with solar panels, Martin putting in solar sprinkler systems. As we sat at the table with our bowls, they discussed logistics for Martin to start doing jobs for Donnie: an old truck, a place to stay with a friend of a friend.

They didn't need me, and I was only half-listening by that time. I'd caught sight of the ornamental pepper plant, brightening the kitchen counter.

As I waved goodbye, I felt proud. And hopeful. I'd solved my "Donnie is retiring" problem and found Martin an opportunity in the process. Eventually, I might even get that boathouse I'd been dreaming about.

...

Over the next few days, I recuperated. I did a grocery run. I napped. A lot.

And I addressed unfinished business.

I decided to tell people—living people—about some things, like talking with David and even what he'd sent Martin to do. I didn't look forward to conquering my love of privacy, but I set up a lunch date with Carole for the following week and left a message for Rev. Phil. I actually liked them both.

Maybe it wasn't too late for me to make friends. Why had it taken me this long?

On Monday, I emailed David.

> *Thanks for our conversation yesterday. We can keep talking about possibilities related to your move, but remember how little I enjoy change. And my camp is off the table.*

> *A question: Out at the cemetery last Sunday, there were flowers at your parents' headstone. My friend*

Carole said there were some there last year, too. Do you know anything about it? They were very pretty.

He answered Tuesday.

I've been sending flowers for Mother's Day since Dad died. The florist is supposed to pick them up Monday and take them to a nursing home, but last year there was a snafu and they sat out there for several days. If this year's bunch is still there, you're welcome to take them home.

Here's a possibility: My high school reunion is in June, just before Canada Day. I've never been interested before, but this year's different. Go figure. I plan to stay a week or so. Could we get together during that time? To talk about the house, maybe. Or not. To have lunch, even?

Well. Could I look forward to this? Cautiously, of course. I could invite him to stay here, at least part of the time. I'd get a better sense of who he was. Someday, I'd ask him about the photo he'd given Martin, ostensibly of my father and uncle, but not yet. Maybe I'd be ready by June.

Which reminded me, I'd asked Chen to help research that. I still liked the idea. In theory.

Instead of doing anything about either idea, I made an appointment for a checkup with my family doctor. It had been years, and I knew I needed one. I suspected that preoccupation and basic selfish inattention, to say nothing of the presence of ghosts, had made me forget Chen's nightmares and fear of fire. But checking never hurt.

I did have some fun, though. Every day, I went down the hill to the camp. Along the way, I admired the grass as it greened underfoot. I watched the spruce and balsam fir ready themselves for their new, bright-green fingers.

And I went out in the boat, far enough that I could see the full sweep of the land behind the camp rising to the house, and then the next range of hills farther inland. Each ridge carried a new flush of spring green on aspen and birches. Gulls cried their plaintive "hey! hey!" overhead, and the oars in the locks set up an echo until I put a stop to it with WD-40. As I rowed, the lake splatted against the boat's aluminum hull.

While changing Chen's sheets, I saw his work gloves and rocks on the dresser. I found a bowl for his rocks and then wrote his name inside the gloves, at the wrists, in permanent marker.

Wednesday morning, I stood by the phone, debating.

Carmen appeared at the table, this time in her red kimono. She made clucking noises and even said "Chicken," in case I'd missed her point.

I ignored her.

Her tone was anything but sympathetic. "Poor you. If you call, you're opening up a giant can of worms. Responsibilities. Obligations. Never-ending demands. Hopes and wishes you can't fulfill, no matter how hard you try." She took a puff from her cigarette and blew a smoke ring. "But if you don't, you live lonely and die alone, misunderstood for eternity." She paused. "It's heartbreak either way, really."

I looked at her. "You didn't die alone. I was there."

She shrugged. "So why am I *here*?"

"You tell me."

She smiled, then, a smile that looked almost real, and nodded toward the phone.

I half-turned from her. I picked up the phone and dialed.

When Jessica answered, I skimped on the preliminary "hi-how-are-you" stuff. "Look, I miss Chen. Would you both like to come out this Saturday morning to spend the day? Weather permitting, we could have a late breakfast down at the camp. Maybe go for a row. Chen probably wants to show you what he got to do."

Her silence made me worry for a moment, but when she spoke, she sounded enthusiastic. "That's really nice. We'd like it a lot. I have to tell you, he has talked nonstop about bears."

We both laughed, and settled it, then, for nine on Saturday.

I looked at my mother, who sat up straight in her chair. Her eyes met mine, and she was no longer a bitter, unhappy woman. Instead, I saw a young woman in a dark skirt and royal blue sweater set, red-lipped and bright-faced. She couldn't wait to elope with the man who might or might not have been her advanced business math teacher but was absolutely the man she loved, she hoped forever, who became my father. This young woman had felt hemmed in, somehow, by Doris and became Carmen. She stood, radiating joy and hope, and smiled at me. With a citrus-infused swish of her skirt, she sashayed toward the lake, disappearing on the way.

"Bye, Mom." My voice echoed. Unless that was my imagination.

I wondered what I could learn about that younger woman. I was glad to know she'd existed.

...

At Friday morning's coffee hour, I bragged a little to Rev. Phil about having Chen and Jessica out the next day. He was pleased with me and also, I thought, with himself. Maybe the way I felt about putting Donnie and Martin together.

I worked to clear Grandpa's old garden at camp almost all afternoon Friday, between boat excursions. I enjoyed pummelling the soil until my muscles protested. Then I'd sit in the boat in my bay, letting the breezes blow me around and refresh my warm face.

Considering how tired I was Friday evening, waking at four a.m. Saturday was an unwelcome surprise. After waiting a half hour for sleep to return, I pulled on sweatpants and a sweatshirt. With a cup of tea, I sat at the kitchen table and faced some facts I'd successfully ignored for several days.

I hadn't seen William since Chen went missing, more than a week. William, in all his forms, might be gone forever. A ridiculous thought, almost five years into widowhood. Of course William was gone forever. He had been ever since the June day I'd found him lying crumpled on the grass.

That first year, I mowed with tears streaming down my face. It was hard work. Not the physical labour; that was easy. The hard part was trying not to hate. I hated the grass for growing. I hated spring and summer for their sunny beauty. I hated the whole wide world for going on without William in it. I boiled with rage at William for dying.

I worked through it, raking in the fall, blowing snow from the driveway in the winter, cleaning in spring. But that next summer, I was still sad. So I'd conjured him to comfort me. I'd grown used to him in this new form, just being around, keeping me company, still loving me.

Even now, I couldn't believe how much I missed him. Sunday's stop at his grave was the first since David and I had left his ashes. I wondered how many visits, how many rocks I'd need to choose especially for William and leave at his headstone, before his death felt real.

I was awake. Maybe we could have another conversation, if he was willing.

I stood at the window, feeling foolish and looking out over the lake. In another six weeks, the sky would be light green at 4:20 in the morning, but that morning, the stars still showed. Then the warm blanket of his presence wrapped me. I hugged myself.

"Hello, Love. I missed you. Can you help me with David? I don't know if I can trust him."

Silence in the warmth.

I sighed. "Okay. You're right. I haven't even given him a chance since you—died."

William seemed amused. "Sorry about that."

I smiled at the stars. "Not as sorry as I am." A pause. "But what about David?"

"People change. You've changed. You and David have time."

I thought about the accident that had hurt so many and made even David reconsider his life. "Or maybe not."

"Yes. Maybe not. So what are you going to do?"

What he always urged me, alive or dead. "Be the bigger person. If I can." The scent of a clean cotton shirt, green-cut grass. Hope.

"That's a good start."

I thought of Jessica and Chen. David. Even Martin. I tried not to whine. "Everything ahead of me involves people."

"Yes. Some of whom are family, or may someday feel like it." I felt regret seep into his amusement.

Over another wave of sadness, I said it aloud, to be sure. "I won't find you here, at this window, anymore. Or anywhere else, either. Not like this."

"No. But you'll be busy. With living people."

"Yes." I promised him, and myself.

He hugged me, deep and rich, like velvet. When he let go, I sobbed, the air as hard as hate and every breath a gasp of burning dust. Hot rain, waves of it, turned the dust to mud and pulled me into myself.

I wanted to curl into a ball and give up. But I'd promised William I wouldn't. So I opened my arms wide to the sky. I let the storm beat my chest and face. I couldn't think or breathe.

Still it came, and I held on.

At last, it stopped. And I was still there.

...

I woke up, surprised for a moment to find myself on the couch instead of in bed. I looked at the portraits on the wall. David and his proud parents. The smaller photo of William and me.

William. Gone. I felt it all over again, a grey and unpromising world. I pulled one of the couch pillows to my face, wanting to cry. Instead, I remembered Chen sleeping on this couch after he'd been so afraid of the fire.

The doorbell double-rang in a way that hinted at previous rings.

Of course: Chen and Jessica. Wiping my face on my way to the door, I invented an apology for my slowness.

Chen yelled "Aunt Simka!" and nearly tackled me in a hug.

No apology needed, then. I put my arms around him and enjoyed it.

Jessica held out a small flat of pansies. "These were at the Farmer's Market, and I thought you might like them. I know it's too soon to put them outdoors, but I couldn't resist."

Surprise made me babble. "Thank you so much, I adore pansies! I'll put them in the kitchen window till it warms up."

"Can we go straight down to the camp so I can show Mum how to skip rocks?"

"Of course! I'll bring breakfast in a half hour. Watch for bears, Chen."

He grinned at me. "You know it."

Less than an hour later, Chen stood on the beach in his life jacket, taking bites from a scone and waiting patiently to show his mother how to row. Inside, at the table where I used to see my mother, Jessica and I sat with coffee and scones of our own, talking over summer plans.

ACKNOWLEDGMENTS

Thank you, readers. Stories are meant to be shared, and I'm grateful you chose to read this one.

This novel is a work of fiction. I want to make that clear because I've written nonfiction, including personal essays, about my mother and our relationship. But just as I am not Simone, my mother was not at all like Carmen.

In fact, no character in this book is based on a specific person in northwestern Ontario, Missouri, Oklahoma (where I grew up), or anywhere else. My husband, Roy Blomstrom, resembles William in some ways, except he's not a ghost. My stepchildren, Bill and Karen, are nothing like David. The horrible traffic accident didn't happen, although since I began writing this novel, several vehicle accidents have caused great hurt in communities across Canada. Chen is, at the same time, no specific child and all of them I've known and been. Northside United Church and Rev. Phil don't exist, although my beloved friends from Trinity United Church, who have been so accepting and to whom I owe great thanks, might find their names borrowed for characters. Similarly, Rev. Randy Boyd might recognize an iPad and a sermon style. And the grandchildren of Peter Hardisty first showed the perfection of "Gumpy" as their name for their grandfather.

It's all fiction except for the landscape, which is directly based on the Lake Superior shoreline in Shuniah, a township just north of Thunder Bay, Ontario, in Robinson-Superior Treaty Territory. Thank you to the Anishinaabe and Metis peoples, especially the Fort William First Nation, for their deep and caring relationship with this place I've grown to love and where I am a grateful guest.

I am as attached to this place as Simone is to hers. However, hers is different: I've flipped its orientation, adjusted the relationship between the house and camp, completely eliminated the old railroad tracks, moved it a little closer to town, and in general tried to simplify the setting.

As writers walk the line between making things up and writing what we know, we need colleagues. I've been working on this novel for a long time, and I'm grateful to the writers who helped me figure out long fiction. Elizabeth Ruth and Gary Barwin led workshops some ten years apart, both sponsored by the Northwestern Ontario Writers Workshop, that kicked off and helped finish the novel.

I'm grateful to Jacqueline Baker at the 2018 Sage Hill Summer Writing course, especially for the exercise in writing cemetery scenes. My fellow fiction writers—Susi Lovell, Liisa Kovala, Larry Gasper, Carol Tulpar, and David Burtt—helped create a welcoming, positive space for deepening characters.

Through a nonfiction mentorship with Susan Olding, I learned the creative satisfaction of revising work. It was fun to apply those skills to fiction. Thank you, Susan.

At a local workshop sponsored by the Laughing Foxes, Angie Abdou provided feedback on the first pages; at a later Laughing Fox writing retreat, I found the time and space to plan and commit to a "final" revision. Kerry Clare's input in the last push was invaluable.

Generous writing friends read early, very weedy drafts of this novel, and I can't thank them enough. Susan Goldberg, Jean E. Pendziwol, Rebekah Skochinski, and Cathi Winslow all helped me both develop and focus the story I wanted to tell. Our discussions helped me learn and persevere, as did supportive chats with Marianne Jones and Maureen Nadin at Calico Coffeehouse over coffee and scones.

Regional writing groups, such as the Northwestern Ontario Writers Workshop, create many opportunities for writers through workshops, readings, and contests. They rely on volunteers to function—volunteers who set aside their own writing time to provide these opportunities. I'm grateful to everyone who has volunteered time and energy to NOWW through the years.

The same is true for national writing organizations, such as The Creative Nonfiction Collective and the Writer's Union of Canada. Their programming has helped me continue to learn and grow as a writer.

Thank you to Heather Campbell, the publisher at Latitude 46, for her devotion to publishing stories from Northern Ontario, to Mitchell Gauvin for his editorial eye, and Lindsay Mayhew for her attention to detail; thanks also to the rest of the Latitude 46 team.

Special thanks to Erin Stewart, of C and F Paper Creations, for the cover image. I treasure it.

Many individuals and groups mentioned above receive funding from federal and provincial cultural organizations, such as the Ontario Arts Council. The OAC also directly supported this novel with a Literary Creation grant. The OAC makes it possible for stories of all kinds, in many forms, to make their way into the world.

Thank you to my family. To my late parents, Jeanne Starrett LeCaine Agnew, who first loved our camp, and Theodore Lee Agnew, Jr., who understood and supported her love. In different ways, they encouraged my fascination with the everyday lives of regular people. To the Agnews with whom I grew up, who also felt the enchantment of this place, and to my brothers' extended families, who understand how cool rocks can be. To my sister, Sue Agnew, who listens to me blather about writing and protects me from mice. To my friend Tricia McConnell, who firmly believes

I can do anything and almost makes me believe it, too. To my stepfamily—Bill and Marcio; Karen; and the "g-kids" Jacob, Isaac, and Daniel—and to those who love them, including Matthew and Julie, Glenn, and their families.

Most of all, I'm grateful to Roy, who is my home and who makes everything possible.